Clare Connelly was raised in small-town Australia among a family of avid readers. She spent much of her childhood up a tree, Mills & Boon book in hand. Clare is married to her own real-life hero, and they live in a bungalow near the sea with their two children. She is frequently found staring into space—a surefire sign that she's in the world of her characters. She has a penchant for French food and ice-cold champagne, and Mills & Boon novels continue to be her favourite ever books. Writing for Modern is a long-held dream. Clare can be contacted via clareconnelly.com or at her Facebook page.

Joss Wood loves books and travelling—especially to the wild places of Southern Africa and, well… anywhere! She's a wife, mum to two teenagers, and slave to two cats. After a career in local economic development she now writes full-time. Joss is a member of Romance Writers of America and Romance Writers of South Africa.

PREGNANT PRINCESS IN MANHATTAN

CLARE CONNELLY

THE TWIN SECRET SHE MUST REVEAL

JOSS WOOD

MILLS & BOON

www.harpercollins.co.uk

HarperCollins*Publishers*
1st Floor, Watermarque Building,
Ringsend Road, Dublin 4, Ireland

Pregnant Princess in Manhattan © 2022 Clare Connelly

The Twin Secret She Must Reveal © 2022 Joss Wood

ISBN: 978-0-263-30108-3

11/22

MIX
Paper | Supporting
responsible forestry
FSC™ C007454

This book is produced from independently certified FSC™ paper
to ensure responsible forest management.
For more information visit: www.harpercollins.co.uk/green.

Printed and Bound in Spain using 100% Renewable Electricity
at CPI Black Print, Barcelona

PREGNANT PRINCESS IN MANHATTAN

CLARE CONNELLY

MILLS & BOON

PROLOGUE

'LOOK AT THIS, *caro mio*.'

Rocco Santinova, only nine but tall for his age, with inquisitive eyes and a serious face, moved closer to his mother, craning to see in the department-store window, past the small crowd of well-dressed shoppers. A Christmas scene was on display: tall, craggy, snow-capped mountains were painted as the backdrop, and in the foreground there were small fir trees, models of children ice skating and Alpine homes with their trademark A-frame roofs.

'It's just like where I grew up,' she murmured, but in a strange, faraway manner, as though she wasn't really talking to him at all. 'Isn't it beautiful?' She asked the question in her native Italian and Rocco nodded.

'*Si*, Mama.'

When she turned to face him, tears moistened her eyes. 'I want to take you there one day. We'll go skiing down a hill, just like that one.'

Rocco's heart kicked up a notch. The hill she pointed to was a sheer mountain face. Adrenaline was a spike in his blood. He looked at the hill and saw a challenge: he wanted to conquer it.

'One day, we'll go home.'

The words were bold but there was ambivalence in the

sentiment, an ambivalence Rocco didn't properly understand. His mother spoke of 'home' often. Rocco didn't
know how to tell her that New York had become home
to him. It felt like a betrayal, and so he'd said nothing.
But the truth was, these metallic skyscrapers were his
version of those craggy mountains, they were his challenge—one day, he'd own one. He swore it.

'In my village, there's a restaurant, right in the centre,
that makes the best food you could imagine. I used to go
there every Sunday, after church.'

His mother's smile was wistful and despite being
young—too young to understand the emotion that made
his tummy ache—he knew he didn't like it. He didn't
like seeing his mother sad.

He looked up at her; she was staring at the village
scene so intently, her eyes misted over, so he asked,
'What else will we do?'

It seemed to rouse her. She looked down at Rocco,
a strange smile on her lips. 'There are the most beautiful carol singers in the village each night. We'll buy hot
chocolate and sit and listen to them for hours. Just like I
did when I was a girl.'

She took his hand in hers, the calluses in her palm
from the grip of her mop making young Rocco's heart
twist painfully. He was powerless to address his mother's
worries, powerless to fix them. Powerless to do anything
but listen and nod.

She began to walk them away from the department
store, towards the subway. But all the way she spoke of
her village, describing it in great detail for Rocco, so that
by the time they boarded the dingy train to their tiny
Brooklyn apartment, he had sworn that he would take
his mother home one day. She was the only family he

had, it was the two of them against the world, and, the nine-year-old believed, it always would be.

He couldn't have known that only ten years later he'd be utterly alone, unloved and deserted, and that the life he'd sworn to deliver to his mother would be within his grasp too late to make a difference to Allegra Santinova.

CHAPTER ONE

PRINCESS CHARLOTTE ROTHSBURG's heart had not stopped racing for almost an hour. Not since giving her guards the slip—most unfairly—towards the end of the event she'd been attending. It had been reckless, spontaneous, utterly thoughtless, and wonderfully fun.

Charlotte had been a good girl almost all her life, and she stood now on the brink of the monumental event of having her engagement to the Sheikh of Abu Hemel announced, the arranged marriage one she'd agreed to simply because she was aware, as she always had been, that it was her fate. More than that, it was the purpose of her being: to provide an heir. Bitterness curdled in her gut.

Her job was to secure the royal lineage. To grant her kingdom the baby her brother was unable to provide.

She'd been raised to understand what was expected of her, but that didn't mean she had to like it, and it didn't mean she had to willingly walk into the future without a tiny hint of rebellion first—a last taste of freedom before she subjugated herself to that destiny.

She deliberately pushed from her mind the one other time she'd stepped out of line, refusing to think about that now. Yes, the consequences had been excruciating, but then, she'd been only a girl, and now Charlotte was a woman, and this act of rebellion was different anyway. There could be no consequences to this little thrill-seeking mission. She was just trying to absorb a little of New York's famed nightlife without her ever-present security guards. They'd never have let her come somewhere like this.

A thrill made her pulse twist as she wove through the packed bar, inhaling deeply and tasting expensive perfume, the hint of cigar smoke, the heavy spice of alcohol, and polished brass. The noise was a din—the background sound of chatter and laughing, and, when she paused and focused, the muted strains of classical guitar songs being piped through speakers overhead.

At the bar she looked around, casting more than a cursory glance at the people gathered together. Women and men, corporate types mostly, dressed in suits—expensive, tailored suits—and finely cut dresses with kitten heels and pearls, and she had no doubt the outfits were owing to the bar's proximity to Wall Street.

This was madness.

Her security guards would probably get fired.

She should *not* have run away.

But the idea of flying into New York to attend a single event, *again*, to smile and nod for three hours straight and then be bundled back to her hotel room, surrounded by security and handlers, had seemed abhorrent to Charlotte. It hadn't been premediated, but when the opportunity for escape had presented itself she'd slipped out of a back access point, past the caterers' vans, and onto a busy, vibrant street.

A man laughed and she turned towards him instinctively, a smile curving her lips as she studied his relaxed pose, and the way the woman he was talking to leaned closer to him, her smile natural, her body language clearly flirtatious.

Awareness pulsed low in her abdomen now as she studied their interaction, the chemistry between them, and allowed herself to wonder if she and the Sheikh would share that same desire?

It was impossible to know—she'd only met the man a handful of times, and, as handsome as he was, she hadn't left fantasising about him. Did that matter?

A small sigh touched her lips as her gaze carried onwards and landed with a resounding thud on the face of a man at the bar who left her utterly breathless.

His face was symmetrical and determined, his features almost too harsh and angular, giving him a ruthless quality that sent a tingle running down her spine. He was big and tall, broad-shouldered, strong-looking, like a wild animal that had been caged too long. Her mouth went dry as she took in the breadth of his shoulders, the muscular strength of his arms. Her eyes went from his hand-stitched shoes to a pair of black jeans that fitted his body like a second skin, then higher to a shirt untucked at the waist on one side, and rolled up at the sleeves, so he had a look of devil-may-care that set her pulse going for a whole other reason entirely. He was over six feet, his chin covered in several days of stubble, his eyes were oval-shaped and a dark brown, rimmed by thick, curling lashes that almost gave the effect of eyeliner, and his hair was thick and dark, with a slight curl.

Something hot and urgent spread through her body, starting in the pit of her stomach and moving to the tips of her fingers and all the way to her toes before pooling between her legs.

Her lips parted, her heart in overdrive, as he lifted his drink in the air with a single cocked brow. The question was obvious: *join me*. On knees that shook, she propelled herself across the room, briefly wondering if this was a form of stupidity as she made her way towards him, her heart hammering against her ribs, her body completely thrown off course by the man's appearance.

She should turn back. Leave him, leave the bar, go and find her security guards and apologise for disappearing. But the thought of that had her chin lifting in a defiant tilt.

Not *once* had she questioned her life.

Not once had she shown her anger to her parents, the resentment and hurt she'd felt ever since learning that she'd been born for the sole purpose of providing the heir her older brother could not. Not once had she argued with them about their choice of school for Charlotte, about their choice of groom, about their natural supposition that she would be happy to fall in with their plans, predetermined before birth. She'd nodded along with all of it, dutiful and agreeable, just as she'd been raised to be, but tonight freedom had lit a fire in her belly and she wanted to fuel it, to allow the flames to spread, before stepping back into the gilded cage that was her life.

'Can I buy you a drink?' he asked when she was close enough to hear him, his voice deep and slightly accented. Italian? Greek?

She knew she should say 'no'. The thrill of having eluded her security detail was fading in the face of other feelings that were more complex and somehow required more consideration. And yet she angled her face to his, slowly, the air immediately fizzing out of her lungs as she looked at him again and his perfection hit her like a punch in the solar plexus.

Her lips parted, and words were almost impossible to find, so she nodded and forced her legs to carry her the rest of the distance to the single empty bar stool. He didn't move backwards, so when she sat down they were only inches apart, and his woody, masculine aroma teased her nostrils, intensifying the beating of a drum low down in her abdomen. 'Thank you.'

He was drop-dead gorgeous, but also undoubtedly self-assured. He was the only man in here not wearing a suit; clearly he didn't need to impress anybody. 'What would you like?'

She tilted her head, scanning the bar. 'What are you having?'

'Whisky.'

She wrinkled her nose. 'Too strong for me. I rarely drink.'

'Champagne?'

She nodded. 'Just a little.'

Another cynical twist of his lips as he lifted a hand and a bartender immediately appeared. He ordered a specific champagne she knew to be exceptionally good, and a moment later an ice-cold glass was placed in front of her. Charlotte's eyes rested on the bubbles for a moment—they were matched by the frantic humming of her pulse—and then she lifted the glass towards him in a silent salute.

Only their eyes clashed and all the air in Charlotte's lungs evacuated her body in one big whoosh; she was powerless to look away, and the hand that held the champagne flute aloft began to shake slightly. She drew it back towards herself quickly, trying to cover the tell-tale gesture, but she was not swift enough. Speculation darkened his eyes and her stomach swirled in response. She took a quick sip of the champagne then pushed it away. If she wasn't careful she'd swallow it all, just to soothe her suddenly frazzled nerves.

'You don't like it?' He moved closer, to be heard above the background noise of the bar, but all that did was make her strange nervousness more pronounced. Up close, he threw her senses into disarray. His fragrance was more intoxicating, combined at this distance with the spice of his whisky, and his eyes were more complex than she'd first appreciated: not simply dark brown, but flecked with grey and silver, and across his nose, beneath his swarthy tan, there was a clutch of freckles. There was also a hint of dark hair curling at the top of his shirt that her fingers ached to reach for, to curl in. Her reaction was terrifying. She couldn't remember *ever* feeling like this: such a visceral, animalistic need, with no sense or reason.

Her pale blue eyes widened, locked to his as though he were some kind of magnet. 'Don't like what?' She frowned, belatedly catching his question.

His eyes flicked to the drink, then back to her face.

'I don't drink often,' she said again.

'Would you prefer something else?'

She let out a small breath of relief. 'Actually, a mineral water would be perfect.'

Again, he summoned the bartender with incredible ease, given the Friday-night crowd, and ordered a mineral water. They waited in silence while it was poured, and then, when the barman left, he eased back, just enough to allow her to soothe her dry throat with the cool drink, and replace it on the counter.

'Where are you from?' His question was direct and rang with confidence. She liked that. Most people she spoke to were in awe of her title and reacted with deference. It was a novelty to be treated as an equal, without any sort of marked respect or awe, and to know her handlers hadn't provided him with a list of talking points to cover.

She instinctively shied away from answering his question, wanting to protect the secret of her identity. Anonymity and freedom went hand in hand. 'What makes you think I'm not from here?'

'Besides your accent?'

'You have an accent too,' she pointed out. She took another sip of her mineral water, appraising him with unashamed curiosity.

'I was born in Italy,' he said after a beat.

'Ah. I thought so.'

'Did you?' He leaned closer. 'What else did you think?'

Her eyes widened, the sensation of being flirted with also completely unfamiliar. Her pulse kicked up a gear and she crossed one leg over the other, her insides trembling with an irrepressible excitement.

'I…'

His smile was teasing and sent a quiver of arrows down her spine. She straightened her back, narrowing her eyes as she tried—and failed—to get a grip on her rioting emotions. Desire was swirling through her, tempting her, tantalising her, for the first time in her twenty-four years.

'You…?' he prompted.

'I…was just going to say that New York fascinates me.'

'Why?'

She was grateful he allowed the conversation change.

'It's so fast-paced, and despite the fact there are millions of people in Manhattan I feel so anonymous.'

'And you like that feeling?'

'Oh, I really like that feeling.' She grimaced, thinking of her very controlled life, imagining for a moment that she was free to stay in Manhattan for a time, to really enjoy it. 'Here, it's as though I can do anything I want.'

'That's a novelty?'

She was startled, aware she'd revealed too much. She blinked away, frowning. 'What line of work are you in?' she asked a moment later, when she was able to regain her composure.

'Finance.'

She wrinkled her nose. 'That's a broad church. What exactly do you do?'

'Invest.'

She laughed. 'Are you being deliberately secretive?'

'No. It's just not particularly interesting.'

'I see.' She nodded sagely, reaching for her water and taking a sip. 'Then why don't you tell me something that *is* interesting about you?'

'What else would you like to know?'

She tilted her head, considering that. 'Whereabouts in Italy are you from?'

'The north.'

Vague. She recognised the technique—she was also adept at giving half-answers.

'Do you miss it?'

'No.' He paused again, and she wondered if he was going to expand. After a moment, he said with a tilt of his head, 'I travel there frequently.'

'Why did you come to America?'

'My mother wanted to.'

She skimmed his face, wondering if she was imagining the tight set of his features, reading too much into the unwitting expression. 'For work?'

'No.'

'What about your father?'

'He wasn't in the picture.' He paused. 'My mother did an excellent job of being both parents to me.'

'Are you close to her?'

'She passed away.'

'Oh, I'm so sorry.'

'It was years ago,' he dismissed, reaching for his Scotch and cradling it. 'Is that interesting enough?'

She frowned. 'I didn't mean to pry. I was just curious.'

'Curiosity isn't a crime.'

'I suspect it's a trait we share.'

'What makes you say that?'

Good question. 'It's just a feeling.'

'Are you good at reading people?'

'You tell me. Am I wrong?'

'No.'

A smile tilted her lips and her tummy popped as though it were filled with champagne bubbles.

'Did you go to school in the city?'

'No. My turn. What brings you to New York?'

Careful, Charlotte. 'Work,' she said with a lift of her slender shoulders. 'That's boring as well.'

His eyes narrowed, though, his perceptiveness obvious. 'How long are you in town?'

'I fly out tomorrow.'

'That doesn't leave much time.'

'What for?' she asked breathlessly.

His smile was the last word in sensual seduction. 'Exploring.'

She looked away, embarrassed by her interest in this man. 'No. There's never time for that.'

'Do you travel often for work?'

'Yes, most weeks I'm away for some of the time.'

'Do you like it?'

'It depends where I'm going and what I'm doing.'

'What's your favourite place?'

'Actually, I adore Italy,' she said with a sigh. 'I love everything about it. The food, the culture, the history, the scenery. But most of all, I love…' She broke off, half embarrassed by the admission.

'The men?' he prompted, wiggling his brows so she laughed, the joke unexpected from someone so serious-seeming.

'Ah, you got me.' She grinned, sipping her drink. 'No, I love their approach to family life, actually. The idea of big, multi-generation families getting together regularly to cook and eat, to laugh and drink wine in the sun. I'm sure it's idealised and yet, when I'm there and I pass restaurants, that's what I see.' She sighed. 'It's probably one of those "grass is always greener" things.'

'You don't have this in your family?' he ventured, and, although Charlotte *never* shared details of her personal life with *anyone*—she'd learned that lesson the hard way in high school when her trust had been betrayed in a manner that was impossible to forget—she found herself relaxing into this experience. After all, he had no idea who she was, and after this interlude she'd go back to her hotel and resume the mantle of Princess Charlotte.

'No. We're not close,' she said slowly, still choosing her words with care. Confiding was one thing, blowing her cover completely another. 'My mother and father were older when they had me. My brother was a teenager.'

'You were an accident?' he probed.

'No.' She shook her head. Her conception had been master-planned. 'I was planned, but that doesn't change anything.'

'Doesn't it? I would have thought that made you more valued.'

'That's simplifying things,' she said with a shake of her head. 'Lots of children are conceived without being planned and they're still desperately wanted and loved.

And then there are children like me, conceived to fill a gap in someone's life, or as an insurance policy. In these instances, it's less about the child than their role within the family.'

'And what is your role?'

'Insurance,' she said with a tight grimace.

'Against what?'

'My brother fell ill when he was eleven.'

'Seriously ill?'

'They thought he was going to die.'

She dipped her head forward without going into the further issues. He was the only heir to the throne. If he had died, it would have caused a constitutional crisis.

'I would have thought, going through something like that, your parents would have been extra-close to you?'

Perhaps in a normal family, but they weren't normal, and her parents were bound by the requirements of their position. She didn't answer the question.

'It's more than just parents,' she said, after a beat. 'I wanted the whole box and dice. Grandparents, cousins, noise, cheer, laughing.' She shook her head. 'Siblings galore.'

'Instead, you were lonely.'

She was startled, eyes wide, at his intuition. 'Yes.'

'I understand that.'

'Did you wish you had a bigger family?'

'I'm not one for wishing,' he said with a small smile. 'There were certain things I wanted to change, to improve, but—'

'Like what?' she interrupted without realising it, fascinated by him.

He finished his drink, replacing the glass on the bar. 'My mother worked very hard. She wanted me to have the best in life and did all that she could to accomplish that. I often wished I could make things easier for her. She died before I could help.'

She shook her head sadly. 'I'm sure just knowing how you felt meant the world to her.'

Their eyes held, and her breath began to burn inside her chest, so she stood abruptly, overpowered by the strength of her desire for him. 'I should go.' This was getting way, way out of hand.

His eyes roamed her face a moment and then he nodded once. 'I'll walk you out.'

'You don't have to—'

'I was leaving anyway.'

He put a hand in the small of her back and her knees knocked together, the simple, innocent contact spearing her with a rush of need.

She jerked her gaze to his and then away again, cheeks pink.

The air around them seemed to beat like a percussion instrument; he could feel it in the depths of his soul. His hand on the base of her spine throbbed with warmth and needing, aching to move lower, to run over the curve of her bottom, or higher, to strum the flesh between her shoulder blades. He wanted to breathe her in, to taste her, to hear her voice soft and breathy as she called his name—hell, they hadn't swapped names. But the truth was, their rapid-fire exchange had set a part of him on fire, a dangerous part of him that he usually worked very hard to keep in check, for the simple reason that Rocco liked to be in control.

When they stepped out of the bar, a frigidly cold blast of air whooshed past them and she shivered, despite the warmth of her wool coat. His eyes caught the gesture, or perhaps it was that he was aware of her on a strange, tantalisingly intimate level.

'Let me get you a cab,' he offered, even when it was the last thing he wanted. It was as though he was testing himself.

She nodded, and disappointment seared him. He looked towards the kerb, but before he could make a move towards it she stared up into the sky. 'It feels cold enough to snow.'

'It's forecast.' He didn't move.

She looked around, and he understood the emotion on her face: reluctance. Something like triumph soared inside his chest.

'My place is around the corner,' he said after a beat, the invitation smooth even when his gut was tightening. 'Would you like to come and see the view?' He threw down the gauntlet and he waited, wondering why he was suddenly, uncharacteristically, on tenterhooks.

'I...' Words failed her; her mouth was dry. She was torn between what she really, really wanted and what she knew she ought to do. But returning to her hotel, and her security detail, brought her just three short steps from marriage, and suddenly the idea of making that commitment without ever having lived—truly lived—was anathema to Princess Charlotte. 'To see the view,' she repeated, looking up and down the street.

'It's the best in the city.'

Why shouldn't she go and do something truly fun and wonderful and spontaneous? One only lived once, but the truth was, Charlotte hadn't lived at all yet, and at twenty-four years of age she had the power to change that, right here, right now.

'Yes,' she agreed on a rush. Everything inside of her

was inflamed. Heat was burning her alive, but she didn't back away. Instead she tilted her face towards his, a challenge in the depths of her crystal-clear eyes, boldness flooding her in that moment. 'Let's go now.'

CHARLOTTE DIDN'T KNOW what she'd expected. Her mind and body had been too frazzled to put any logical assessment into his offer, but as the doors of the lift slid open into his Fifth Avenue penthouse she realised that, whoever this man was, he was seriously loaded.

Places like this went for tens of millions—hundreds of millions?—of American dollars. He seemed completely normal, not like the sort of men she knew who had this kind of wealth at their disposal. 'The view.' His deep voice curled around her, pushing everything from her mind except the strange, thudding awareness of him, drawing her to him as though a string were tied around her waist.

The air between them crackled with the kind of physical connection she'd only ever read about in books, but it was more than that. She was *fascinated* by him. His mind, his voice, his insight. She'd loved *talking* to him. For Charlotte, that sort of quick conversation was a novelty, and she was hungry for more.

'Let me take your coat,' he offered, from behind her. She unbuttoned it with fingers that weren't quite steady and turned to hand it to him. Their eyes met, something assessing in the depths of his, before they slid downwards, to the vee of her tailored shirt, and lower, to her slender waist and the slight flare of her hips, all the way to her shoes, and then back up, where they lingered for a moment too long on her breasts, so she felt as though she were some kind of supermodel and not a modestly proportioned normal woman.

He stalked away from her, draping her coat over the back of a chair then turning to face her from a much safer distance. Unfortunately, that did nothing to steady the frantic racing of her heart.

'Would you like a drink?'

She shook her head. Another sip of champagne and she might say or do something she'd regret. It was a far better idea to keep her wits about her.

'Tell me about the city,' she invited.

He moved towards her and with every step she felt like a piece of prey in a lion's path, and yet still she didn't move. When he was right in front of her and they stood toe-to-toe with only an inch or so between them, he stopped moving, his nostrils flaring as he looked down at her.

'Do you know, you have a habit of giving orders rather than asking questions?'

She sucked in a sharp breath, again, shocked by his perceptiveness but also appalled by how close she'd come to revealing the truth of her identity.

'Do you have a problem with that?' she volleyed back.

'Actually, I find it incredibly attractive.' His grin made her toes curl. 'What would you like to know?'

She couldn't think straight. 'The buildings…' She waved a hand through the air then brought it back to her side, only it connected with his hips and she didn't immediately pull away, because the contact felt so good. Her eyes lifted to his, a frown on her face, a pucker between her brows.

This was getting out of control. She should leave. Make an excuse and get out of here.

But even when she knew that was the sensible option, she would never do it. Not when she felt alive for the first time in for ever. Her feet were glued to the floor, her existence completely bound up in being here, with this man, in this moment.

He reached around and put a hand in the small of her back, as he had at the bar, turning her slightly. Her reaction was exactly the same: fireworks in her veins. 'There's the Empire State Building.' He pointed to the left a little, and she recognised the famous shape, but she was no longer looking at the view, nor particularly interested in the city. Everything inside her was focused on the man at her side, and the way his hand was touching her back, his fingers splayed wide, his thumb moving slightly up and down, so she was tantalisingly aware of feelings she'd never known before, that made her want to learn more about herself and her femininity, to understand the ancient impulses that ran through her yet had lain dormant all her life. It was a moment of awakening and she sucked in an uneven breath.

'When we first moved here, I was fascinated by it,' he admitted, almost against his will.

'Did you spend weekends going to the top?' she teased.

'We could never afford the admission,' he said. 'I still haven't been up, in fact.'

'You're kidding?'

'Is that amusing?'

'No, it's surprising, I suppose.' She turned to face him then wished she hadn't, because in profile there was such raw masculinity and power that her gut twisted like a kite in a hurricane.

'I'd never be able to sleep if this was my view,' she

admitted, quickly turning away from him lest he misinterpret her words.

'You get used to it.' The cynicism in his voice sparked curiosity within her.

'Do you…?' She frowned. 'I don't even know your name.' A thrill of pleasure ran through her at that. It made this all the more illicit. When she'd woken up this morning, she could never have guessed her day would turn out like this.

He turned to face her, lifting a thick, dark brow as though he didn't believe her. 'Rocco Sa—'

She lifted a finger then, pressing it to his lips, silencing him even as a storm of awareness whipped through her. 'Let's not do last names,' she said, eager to keep her own name to herself. It was obvious he hadn't recognised her, but there was no way he wouldn't place her surname.

Her family was one of the oldest reigning monarchies in Europe, and despite the fact Hemmenway was a geographically small country it existed on a natural store of oil and diamonds, and its location meant it was a vital part of many trade routes, so had enjoyed political power for centuries, and continued to be prosperous. Her family was well known, and she'd prefer not to admit to being a Rothsburg. She wanted freedom from that title tonight.

'Charlotte,' she said softly, eyes blinking at him, relieved when no recognition flickered in their depths.

'That suits you,' he said against her finger, so she dropped her hand away quickly, as though burned, because his warm breath immediately fanned flames inside of her that demanded indulgence.

Pleasure ran over her skin—and a hint of guilt, too, because her security agents were probably being berated right now for having lost her. None the less, this was her life, and she deserved to live it, even if just for this very small window of time. She hadn't asked to be Princess of Hemmenway. She hadn't asked to have an older brother who couldn't have children. She hadn't asked to have the expectations of her parents tightly around her neck all her life, and yet she'd done everything that was expected of her, believing that one day her contrition would earn her their love. At twenty-four, she'd given up on that, but the habits of a lifetime were hard to break.

Her lips parted and she swayed forward unconsciously. Her lack of experience with men meant she had no skills in conquering temptation, nor in hiding what she was feeling. Someone like Rocco, who she suspected was every bit as experienced as she was inexperienced, must be able to read her like a book.

'And you? Do you like living in the city?' she asked, barely able to hear her own voice over the rushing of her blood.

'At times.'

'That's very cryptic.'

He almost smiled but instead it was like a smirk. 'I'm a man of mystery, what can I tell you?'

'Like James Bond?'

'Isn't it Austin Powers?'

She laughed softly at the absurdity of that, for this man was all that was suave and confident—he couldn't be further from the bumbling satirical spy. 'I don't think so.'

He moved closer by degrees—or did she?—so they were touching, their bodies brushing, and it was like a thousand fireworks exploding just beneath her skin. Pins and needles pricked her from the inside, and the warm heat between her legs warred with the sensation of her nipples tingling against the fabric of her bra. She lifted her eyes to his, her breath rough now, emerging as small gasps, as if she'd run a marathon.

He lifted a hand, rubbing his thumb slowly across her cheek, so she sighed, savouring the contact. 'You have beautiful eyes.'

She blinked them at him, his compliment combining with his touch to make her feel as if her body was made of melted butter. She was soft and gooey all over. 'I was just thinking the same thing about you,' she said huskily. 'In fact, I've been trying to work out if they're more brown or silver or gold.'

'And what did you decide?' His head dropped lower, closer, ostensibly to grant her better access to consider that.

'I couldn't,' she murmured, her hips brushing against his waist. 'What do you think?'

'I can't say I've ever given it any thought.'

'No.' She nodded, and somehow the action lifted her face closer to his. Her heart was running at a million miles an hour. Could desire actually lead to a heart attack? She lifted a slightly shaking finger to his cheekbone, pointing towards one eye. 'The outside is dark, like the trunks of forest trees, but towards the centre it's like sunshine.'

'Sunshine?' His gruff voice was rich with scepticism, and she smiled in response to that, nodding slowly.

'And then there are these little flecks of starlight, trapped in the forest. You have to look closely. They're quite mesmerising.'

'You have a vivid imagination.'

'I'm simply describing what I see.'

'And what do you feel?'

Her breath hitched in her throat, and her lips parted to form a perfect circle. 'Confused,' she responded honestly, after a beat.

He grinned, such a sensual smile that her tummy flipped and flopped.

His hands moved to her waist, holding her steady so

his body formed a sort of cage around her. 'Is there anything I can do to clear up your confusion?'

She swallowed, trying to think, but her brain had turned to mush, her mind a cataclysm of misfiring neurons. 'I… One-night stands aren't in my repertoire.'

He made a low, throaty noise. 'And yet?'

'I'd be lying if I said I'm not fascinated by you.' She bit down on her lower lip, her heart like a butterfly in her chest. 'This is crazy. I should go.'

'Do you want to leave?'

Her stomach squeezed and she shook her head slowly. 'Hence the confusion.'

'I can think of one way to help you make up your mind.'

'A list of the pros and cons?'

'Or something even more evaluative,' he responded, moving then so fast she barely had time to realise his intention before his lips brushed hers, lightly, and yet it was as though her spine was being whipped. She startled, jerking towards him, hands lifting to cling to the fabric of his shirt, and she made a husky noise of surrender in the base of her throat.

'Oh,' she said when he pulled away, just enough to scan her face.

'Any help?'

Her tongue ran over her lower lip, which tingled from the brief sensation of his kiss.

She angled her head to the side. 'I think I need a larger sample size to be certain.'

'That can be arranged.'

She tasted like strawberries and summer, despite the frigidly cold night. When he kissed her for a second time, something ignited in his bloodstream, turning him into volcano man, so he couldn't go softly and gently as he'd intended. His mouth claimed hers with desperate passion, his lips parting hers, his hands on her hips holding her hard against him, then shifting her sideways so her back was against a wall and his body pressed against her, so he could feel all her soft curves, all her sweet undulations, and his body stirred to life, his arousal immediate. She gasped as she felt it, then rolled her hips, silently inviting him for more.

A drum beat with urgency, and he listened to it, letting it propel him, his hands untucking her shirt from her trousers and connecting with her bare flesh, which was even softer than he'd imagined her hair might feel. She shivered as he touched her, so he pulled away for a microsecond.

'Cold?'

'No.'

He kissed her again, smiling against her mouth as his hands worked the buttons of her shirt, undoing them quickly, his fingertips acting on muscle memory until the shirt separated and he could push it down her body. Her skin lifted in goose-pimples and he pulled back to see her properly, his arousal straining against the fabric of his trousers.

She was stunning.

Her skin flawless and golden, the cream colour of her bra perfect to offset her complexion, her stomach flat, her waist narrow, her breasts generous and curved, so he couldn't resist moving his hands upwards, stroking the underside of her bra.

'I've never done this before,' she reiterated, so he felt a rush of excitement, because the fact she didn't do one-night stands but was prepared to with him was a heady aphrodisiac. She was different; that explained why he found her so hypnotically mesmerising.

'I won't hold that against you,' he promised with a droll expression, reaching behind her for the clasp of her bra. A sharp intake of breath sounded in his ear as he undid the clips and pulled the elasticised material away to reveal her naked torso to his hungry gaze. He was staring at her body so didn't see the way her whole face flooded with pale pink, nor the way she bit down on her lower lip.

He dropped his head to one breast so he could draw a nipple into his mouth, flicking it with his tongue, revelling in the way her body reacted to his, her quivering so sensual and natural that he felt a rush of need for her, as though he was an inexperienced teenager rather than someone who'd had a hell of a lot of practice taking women to bed.

But there was something different about this woman. He couldn't put his finger on it but nothing about this night felt like a normal date. Perhaps it was the unexpectedness of it, the swiftness with which their connection had formed. Impatience cracked against him and then he lifted her, no longer able to simply kiss and touch, but needing to feel all of her with all of himself. He carried her towards his bedroom, staring at her flushed face as if to read her as he went, shouldering in the door, enjoying the feel of her in his arms, the taste of her on his mouth. At his bed he placed her down, so her body slid against his and her arms naturally stayed hooked around his neck, her naked breasts pressed to his chest.

'Wow,' she murmured, eyes shifting to the view from his bedroom window—Manhattan, sparkling like a jewelry box beneath them.

'That is precisely what I was thinking.'

Her eyes slid back to his, desire turning her pupils into huge black pits of need. 'I—'

He dropped his head and kissed her, swallowing the words, needing more.

She made a groaning noise then her hands were performing their own exploration of his body, pushing, trying to liberate him from his clothes, needing skin-to-skin contact, wanting to run her palms across his chest, feeling the sparse covering of hair there, to feel his nipples under her hands.

She ripped at his shirt finally, pushing it away like an inconvenience, a noise of exultation flying from her lips before she pressed kisses along his collarbone, licking the centre before running her mouth lower, to his chest, teasing his pectoral muscles then flicking his nipples with her tongue, the pleasure so unexpectedly sharp and strong that his breath hissed between his teeth and he caught her waist, digging his fingers into her soft flesh in a knee-jerk reaction. Her eyes lifted to his, her lips quirking in a smile that was laced with feminine knowledge. She understood exactly what she was doing to him.

Hell. He felt more out of control than he'd been in a long time and he did not like the sensation. Rocco Santinova was all about control. It was how he'd dug himself out of poverty, how he'd risen to the top of New York's finance industry, how he'd become one of the richest men in the world. He didn't give in to impulses, and he didn't let passion dictate his actions. He was the exact opposite of his father in that sense: he made choices with his head, not other parts of his anatomy, not his heart.

Yet control was slipping through his fingertips now and it felt so damned good, he was inclined to allow it, just this once.

She reached for his trousers, her fingers uneven and clumsy as she tried to push down the zip, but everything felt all wonky and strange inside of her, as if she wasn't just riding a roller coaster but somehow flying across one. Her body was divorced from her mind and her feelings; nothing was holding her together any more. Being near him was intoxicating; kissing him was a drug without which she feared she might die. He became her life blood, just in that fraction of time and place, where nothing else seemed to exist. There was no crown, no impending engagement, no obligations beyond this.

He was warm and smooth beneath her touch, his muscled abdomen making her feel safe, as though some sort of ancient instinct had kicked in where sheer physical strength was a desirable attribute. She tasted his chest, making a noise of relief when his trousers finally gave way and he stepped out of them as she pushed him down, revealing the force of his desire to her, concealed only by a pair of black boxer briefs. Her heart missed a beat as the enormity of what she was about to do landed in her throat, making it hard to breathe. But then he lifted her under the arms, bringing her back to his mouth, kissing her as he tumbled her backwards, onto the bed, their limbs intertwined, his powerful arousal striking at the core of her being so that heat exploded through the layers of her clothes, and his. She tilted her head and he dragged a stubbled kiss across the flesh there, leaving a trail of red; signs of passion and need.

Her heart twisted as he removed her trousers with far more ease than she'd found disposing of his, sliding them down her legs, his hands then caressing her thighs, her calves, sending goose-pimples all over her, making her startle a little at the unfamiliar intimacies of his touch. But sensations overrode everything else. She was conscious then only of how right this seemed, of how great it was to be held by him, touched by him, of how she felt like a woman for the first time in her life. It was as though something inside of her suddenly flicked into existence, and she hadn't even realised it had been missing.

His hands moved higher, to her inner thighs, then out to her hips, holding her still as he propped himself up to look at her, his expression impossible to read. 'You take my breath away.'

She ignored the compliment. Words were neither here nor there when bodies could sing like this.

'Show me,' she demanded, every inch the princess and he her sex slave.

'Gladly.' He reached out and opened his bedside drawer, retrieving a foil square and lifting it. He stood, eyes on hers, and with distance between them the spell was momentarily broken, so she pushed up onto her elbows, her heart racing not just with desire now but with a hint of panic, because this felt like a decision she should have put more consideration into, and yet, when he brought his body back to hers, instincts kicked into life and she was absolutely certain she wanted this and needed him.

He separated her legs, his hand confident, his body strong and dominant, so ultra-masculine and in command. He was a natural born leader, that was obvious in everything about him. From the sureness of his movements to the confidence in his voice when he spoke: he was a man it was impossible not to pay attention to.

'The second you walked into the bar, I wanted you,' he murmured in her ear, his accent more pronounced, his voice deeper and huskier, so shivers ran the length of her spine, and then he drove into her, hard and fast, with no preamble, and the sensations of pleasure were quickly usurped by pain as an invisible barrier was broken, his body invading hers, possessing her, and she cried out, squeezing her eyes shut. He grew still, and when she opened her eyes he was staring at her, his features contorted first into a mask of confusion and then one of angry disbelief.

'Charlotte?'

But the pain and shock were receding and the waves of desire returning, so she dug her fingernails into his shoulders, her lips compressed. 'Don't stop.'

He swore softly under his breath, his mouth a tight white line. 'What the hell?' He shook his head once, his eyes focused on her forehead, disbelief in his features. But pleasure was threatening to shift, to fade away, and she couldn't bear the thought of that.

'Please don't stop,' she implored him.

His eyes flickered to hers and she felt the battle being fought inside of him, she saw it play out in his eyes, but thank God, decency prevailed because he began to move once more, slower this time, treating her with kid gloves as she lifted up her legs and wrapped them around his waist.

'I want all of you,' she demanded. 'Don't treat me as though I'm going to break.'

'I haven't slept with a virgin in a long time,' he responded tightly, but he kissed her, a kiss that resonated with a dark emotion, anger evident in the lines of his face.

She kissed him back, her own emotions fraught, impossible to discern. 'I'm not a virgin any more.'

He didn't respond to that, but he moved harder now, possessing her as she wanted and he needed, making her his in a way that rocked her to her core. Pleasure was a thousand spirals inside of her, making her wild and out of control. Her nails scratched down his back, her hips moved of their own accord, their wild, frantic rhythm beyond Charlotte's control. She dug her heels into the mattress, pushing up, and he was so deep inside of her, so completely a part of her, that she had no idea where he began and she ended. The waves of pleasure built faster and with more urgency, changing her, reshaping her, making her feel as though she was moving into the stratosphere, and then everything was spinning wildly out of control, heat blinding her, body quivering uncontrollably, a low moaning sound escaping from her mouth without Charlotte's awareness. Her breathing was rough, frantic, her lungs impossible to inflate, but even as the wave was crashing down around her he was showing no mercy, building her pleasure anew, stoking those fires until whatever receding she'd enjoyed was back stronger than before, and she was close to the edge again.

This time Rocco was with her, his own release accompanied by a low, guttural cry as he shuddered, his body pausing as the effects of his own release travelled through both of them, and she exploded beneath him, so much more intensely the second time, because her body knew what to expect and somehow defied those expectations. She made a shuddering sound and closed her eyes, feeling every single inch of her release, the pleasure like seafoam breaking over her in the shallows.

It was impossible to talk or form words at first. All Charlotte could think was that rebellion had never, ever, not for a single moment, felt so damned good.

CHAPTER THREE

'WHAT THE HELL?'

'You said that already,' she murmured, the smile on her lips beyond her control. She lay there, feeling the weight of his body, his breathing, his fragrance, and a small sigh escaped her.

'You should have told me.'

'I *did* tell you.' Her huge eyes softened slightly as she frowned.

He matched her expression, lips tugged downwards at the corners. 'I thought you meant you didn't do one-night stands.'

'That too,' she said, the bubble of her happiness shifting slightly in the face of what was obviously his disbelief. And anger? Disappointment? She pulled away, wriggling beneath him, but it was Rocco who moved, giving way so she could stand up. 'I'm sorry if you didn't expect—'

'How could I expect this?' he interrupted, lying on the bed, eyes on her with such intensity it felt as if her skin were catching fire. 'You're not a teenager, but a grown woman.' His face paled. 'Right?'

'I'm twenty-four.'

'Thank God.' He dipped his head for a moment, and when he lifted his face to look at her anew he was completely in control again, all-powerful and determined to understand. 'So how in the world were you a virgin?'

She hadn't expected such a direct question. It unnerved her, and Charlotte had no idea how to answer.

'Are you a nun? Amish? Did you escape a cult?'

'No, no and not really,' she said with a small lift of her lips. Her heart though was stammering, and her tummy felt as though it were falling out of her body.

'This isn't funny.' He moved to standing, his magnificence breathtaking. She could only stare at his naked form, which belonged in a gallery, his sculpted body like something carved from stone. 'I don't appreciate being lied to.'

'I didn't lie,' she said firmly, glad her voice sounded calm even when inside she was trembling. 'I told you I'd never done this before. I didn't realise you'd misunderstood until it was too late.'

His lips were grim. 'Okay. But how…why were you a virgin?'

She angled her face away from his, unable to answer. How could she explain to a man like this what her life had been like? How could she tell him without giving away the truth of her identity? 'That's not really any of your business.'

'It just became my business,' he corrected sharply, and she turned her face to his, studying him again. Whatever he did, he was obviously in charge of a great many people. He spoke with such natural authority, and an unquestioned faith in his right to demand information, that it was immediately apparent he was used to being obeyed.

'No.'

His eyes drew together at the single word, spoken directly and clearly.

'We had sex; that doesn't give you a free pass to know anything about me.'

His eyes flexed with surprise before he could tamp down on the emotion, returning his expression to a mask of arrogant disdain. 'Then answer this—and surely I have a right to know—why me?'

Her lips parted to form an 'oh'. 'I don't know.' For a moment, her cool façade slipped, and the words were husky, shaken by uncertainty. 'It just felt right.'

'And until tonight, no one else has ever felt right?'

She shook her head. 'There hasn't been the opportunity.'

'That makes no sense,' he ground out. 'Who are you?'

She flinched, the idea of revealing that to him anathema. This had been *her* night. Not *Princess Charlotte's*. She bit down on her lower lip, emotions rolling through her. 'Someone who walked into a bar and saw a man she couldn't resist.' She attempted to lighten the mood, but her voice trembled, earning a sharp look from Rocco.

He swore softly, then turned his back, his shoulders moving with the force of his breaths. 'I wouldn't have brought you here if I'd known. I thought—'

'That I was like you,' she whispered, strangely pleased by that, even though he was angry now. She liked to think she'd seemed like a confident, independent woman, completely in charge of her life and destiny, just for a night.

'That you had experience,' he muttered, turning back to her, his expression stern and commanding. 'You shouldn't have come here.'

She visibly flinched now. 'Are you saying you regret what just happened?'

'Yes.'

It was the certainty of his response that hurt the most, though the sentiment was also damaging. 'Wow.' Now

Charlotte turned away from him, so she didn't see the look of frustration that crossed his features as she bent down and grabbed for her clothes.

She had to get out. God, please let her not cry in front of him.

He expelled a rough breath. 'I don't want to be the first man you slept with.'

'Why not? Someone had to be.'

He eyed her steadily. 'I don't want you to think I can offer you more.'

She tilted her face. 'Like what? Marriage? Love?' She rolled her eyes. 'This is the twenty-first century. A woman deciding to sleep with someone doesn't mean she's desperate for them to go down on one knee and propose.'

'Your first time should be with someone you've known for more than an hour.'

'Says who?'

He narrowed his eyes.

'I'm serious. Is there some rule book regarding sex I don't know about?'

He lifted a hand to the back of his neck, rubbing the muscles there. 'I have no interest in arguing with you.'

He was dismissing this—and her—and damn it, Charlotte had too much pride to try to argue with him anyway. Besides, what was the point? Her real life was just outside this luxurious penthouse, waiting for her. Shaking a little, she pulled on her underwear, and her trousers, without looking at him, then sucked in a deep, fortifying breath before stalking from his room.

She was disorientated. He'd carried her into the bedroom and she hadn't been paying attention, but she moved down the hallway, the only logical way she could go, and found her shirt and bra, where they'd been thrown in the passion of the moment.

She felt him in the room even without turning to look at him, but a quick glance in the mirror showed his strong body, tall and confident, and half dressed in trousers. When her buttons were done up she turned to face him, back straight, shoulders squared, inwardly channelling Princess Charlotte.

'I'm sorry you were caught off guard. That wasn't my intention.' Her tone was haughty. She lifted her jacket, sliding her hands through the sleeves. 'And I'm also sorry that you'll regret tonight. I won't.'

His expression gave nothing away. He watched her walk towards the door, then belatedly moved after her, a frown on his handsome face as he got there first and pressed the button for the lift.

'You are beautiful,' he growled, as though with disapproval. 'But I don't do complicated. Or relationships.'

Her lips twisted as she blinked up at him. 'And I *am* complicated.' The words were wistful, the duty that was before her heavy on her shoulders. Her future had been mapped out for a long time. Tonight had been both an aberration and a gift, but now it was time to get back to reality. 'Don't worry, you won't hear from me again, Rocco.'

A muscle jerked in his jaw as he nodded once, and then, almost as though he couldn't help himself, as though he tried to hold himself back, he kissed her. A slow, drugging kiss that robbed her of breath and sense and made her fingers and toes tingle, so she swayed forward and his hands came around her back, holding her tight, and they both surrendered to the passion that had been momentarily quelled but not silenced, not satisfied. It stampeded through her like a team of wild horses, and she was powerless in the face of this desire, but Rocco wasn't. He was in command and before she could do something truly stupid and beg him to make love to her once more he pulled away, staring at her for several moments before taking a step backwards.

The lift doors pinged open and she looked from the lift to him.

'Okay,' she said with a nod, lifting her fingers to her lips and touching them as sensations rioted through her. 'Goodbye.'

He dipped his head once in farewell, and she stepped into the lift, her heart pounding with the surreal nature of what she'd just done.

When the doors closed he waited a moment then pressed his back against them, closing his eyes on a wave of bitterness and shock.

What the hell had just happened?

He felt as though a grenade had been thrown into his life.

But hell. A virgin? He was *so* careful. It was his personal code of honour, something that mattered to him as much as anything ever had, not to lead women on. He was always diligent about that.

He spelled everything out, always. He usually took his dates for dinner first, got to know them a little. If he'd done that with Charlotte, he would have seen what she was. Her innocence, now that he looked back, was obvious. From the way her fingers had shaken when they'd first met to the little tells when they'd been making love.

She hadn't been with a man before.

And, instead of saving that experience for someone who meant something to her, she'd used him to get rid of her virginity, regardless of the fact he didn't want to be that to her. And he always would be. Despite the fact they were nothing to one another, he would always be her first.

He ground his teeth together as distaste flavoured his mouth with metal.

But he'd lied to her too. Even though he was angry with himself, he didn't regret what they'd shared. He couldn't. When he remembered the way they'd made love, he wanted to do it all over again, to hell with her innocence and the expectations she might start to harbour.

He let out a groan, moving through the apartment and pushing the sliding glass doors open.

It was icy cold and he was barely dressed, but he didn't care. He stepped onto the terrace, glad of the bracing wind, glad of the ice in the sky. He braced his palms on the railing, staring down at the street just as a yellow cab pulled over. He was too high up to see clearly but he could tell from the way she moved that it was Charlotte. He watched, mouth dry, pulse racing, as she opened the back door of the cab and slipped in, without an upwards or backwards glance.

That, then, was that.

The second she looked at her phone she felt a tsunami of regret. Not over Rocco, but over her whole mad escape. Forty-seven missed calls and twenty text messages. From her brother, her parents, the palace chief of operations, and her security agents.

She grimaced as she triaged them, writing back to her parents first.

I'm fine. I'll explain when I see you.

She had no idea what form that explanation would take but at least it bought her time. Her brother got a similar text. For a moment she allowed herself to imagine that their worry had been about *her*, and her safety, rather than the threat her disappearance would bring to the lineage, but such indulgence left her cold. She pushed those silly, childish wants aside.

Concentrating on her phone gave her a moment's reprieve, but when the text messages were dealt with and she put the device away again, to stare out of the windows, a lump formed in the back of her throat. She couldn't dislodge it, no matter how many times she tried, so she gave up and allowed a tear to fall softly from her eyes, and then another, before she lifted her fingers and dashed them away.

This was ridiculous.

She should feel happy. Relieved. She'd done something incredible. Something that was all hers, a secret that would sustain her, she suspected, for the rest of her life. She might be planning to slip right back into the role of Princess Charlotte of Hemmenway but she'd pulled off a little escape first, and she'd called the shots for the first time ever. She refused to let anything, or anyone, take the shine off that.

She'd never see Rocco again but she'd always be grateful to him for what they'd shared.

Three days later, Rocco awoke in the same foul mood he'd been in since Charlotte Whatever-her-name-was had left, with a raging hard-on.

He cursed as he hit the pillow beside him, angry that his dreams had, yet again, been filled with her. Those sweet, drugging noises as he'd moved inside her, the look of awakening in her eyes, the way her body had responded to his. The way her muscles had squeezed him, so tight and responsive. He pushed out of bed, stalking to the shower and flicking on the cold tap, despite the snow that was still blanketing the city.

He stepped into the stream, not even flinching as ice water deluged his back.

Three nights of torturously haunting dreams. Of wanting her in a way that made his cock throb in his sleep, aching to bury himself in her.

But it wasn't just that.

He couldn't forget their conversation in the bar. The way she'd effortlessly drawn admissions from him, her questions sparking something in him he hadn't known for a long time. He'd opened up to her, and it had been strange, because Rocco was not the kind of man to confide easily, and yet…it hadn't felt wrong. It had felt, if anything, good. Intriguing and powerful. Perhaps the conversation had been a powerful form of foreplay. It was as much a part of what he craved, when he thought of her, as her body's delightful, addictive responses to his.

He pressed his forehead to the shower tiles, eyes blinking down at the floor.

This would pass. There'd never been a woman who'd stayed under his skin for long; he was determined that Charlotte would be no different.

'Charlotte? Are you even listening to me?' Charlotte blinked across at her mother, inwardly cursing the direction of her thoughts. A week after returning to New York, she felt as though her feet weren't anywhere close to the earth.

'I'm sorry. What did you say?'

'Damn it, this is important. Is it too much to ask for a little focus?'

Charlotte pressed her lips together. She'd long ago given up on sharing any true intimacy with her mother, but she didn't particularly appreciate being berated before she'd even had her first coffee. Nor did she relish how distracted she'd been this past week. Any time she had a moment to herself, he was there. Rocco Sa— filling her thoughts, making her body tremble, her nipples tingle, her insides clench with remembered pleasure, so at night, when she was alone, her hand moved between her legs, trying, desperately needing, to recreate the blessed euphoria he'd shown her.

But it was nothing compared to what he'd made her feel.

'The Sheikh will fly in late next month. There'll be a state dinner hosted by your brother, following which the announcement will be made.'

Every cell in Charlotte's body screamed in reaction to that. She wanted to tell her mother '*No*'. To say she couldn't go through with it after all. And how would the Queen react?

'Are you...?' But the words died on her lips, at the look of disapproval that was glaring back at her.

'Yes?'

'It's just, I hardly know him,' she said after a beat. 'Perhaps I should...' Go and meet him? The idea left Charlotte cold. The only place she wanted to go was New York.

The Queen stood, regarding her daughter for several beats. 'You're twenty-four, and we require at least two children, although three would be better. You cannot put this off again.'

Charlotte dug her nails into her palms. 'I'm not trying to put anything off,' she said, frowning, unsure of exactly what she wanted.

She stood, moving to the window, looking out at the stunning palace gardens. When she blinked, she saw him.

That intense, mocking, assessing look, his magical eyes, his arrogant, confident, sexy body. She almost groaned, so fierce was the longing overtaking her.

'What was it like when you met Dad?' Charlotte asked, without turning back.

'What do you mean?'

'I mean,' Charlotte turned to face her mother, 'was it love at first sight?'

The Queen pursed her lips. 'What a childish question. Love at first sight? Of course not. Our marriage was like yours: arranged. The point is, we respected one another. It was a sensible match, just as yours will be.'

Rebellion fired through Charlotte, only there was no back entrance she could escape out of now. She was trapped, by her royal life, the expectations on her to produce an heir, and by the fact her marriage was rushing towards her like a freight train.

'Are you happy?'

'Happiness is for other people. We have been born into a different kind of life. Responsibility is a part of being royal.'

Charlotte closed her eyes at that truly chilling admission.

'Your marriage will make me happy,' her mother said after a beat. 'And when you tell me you've conceived the Sheikh's baby, I will know peace and relief for the first time in decades,' she added, so Charlotte's heart broke a little for her mother, cold though she may be, and Charlotte couldn't help but pity her.

Yes, she was beautiful, and intelligent, and successful, but Rocco had never been more bored in his life. He stared across at his date, watching as she seductively sipped her wine, and drummed his fingers against his thigh.

He looked around the bar, to the chairs he and Charlotte had occupied, and felt the same spear of need that had been driving through him for weeks now. Any time he thought of her, it was the same. He'd lost count of how many cold showers he'd had, how many mornings he'd woken and given himself the relief he'd wanted to take in her body. She'd possessed him. If she hadn't been a virgin, the solution would have been simple: he'd have asked her out again.

A repeat performance, to get her out of his bloodstream once and for all. But her innocence complicated everything.

That and the fact they hadn't swapped numbers or last names. He knew nothing about her, except that she wasn't American.

Finding her again would be like looking for a needle in a haystack. Besides…even as he wanted to see her again, and he did, there was something in that idea he instinctively shied away from.

A danger he couldn't quite comprehend, given that he'd never had a relationship he couldn't control. But with Charlotte, he suspected things might not be so easy. Their night together had been beyond his experience. He was better to let it go; forget about it. Move on.

He focused his attention back on the brunette opposite, his gut twisting at the idea of making love to her.

It would be better than another night alone in his bed. Or would it?

At least in his bed, he had the memories of Charlotte.

Lifting his hand to gain the waiter's attention, it had the simultaneous effect of silencing the woman opposite.

'Is something wrong?'

'I have to go,' he said unapologetically, throwing cash down on the tabletop and gesturing to a waiter to let him know it was there. 'Goodnight.'

'Rocco? Shall I call you tomorrow? Rocco?'

He stalked out of the bar without responding, already itching to be alone with his memories of that one god-forsaken night.

A month after returning from New York, Charlotte was officially in hell. As arrangements were firmed up for her marriage, all she could think about was Rocco. It was terrifying and exciting, but ultimately futile. She couldn't see him again. Even if she could contrive a way to get to New York, he'd made his feelings perfectly clear when he'd seen her to the door.

He didn't want the complications of her inexperience. And that was without knowing anything about her background!

'You can't seriously be telling me I have to get a full medical exam before he'll announce the engagement?' she muttered.

'It's not him,' her most trusted aide, Iris, said with a sympathetic shake of her head. 'It's his "people".'

'His "people" sound like monsters,' Charlotte responded archly. 'I hope I don't need to have too much to do with them when we're married.' Her heart gave a strange pang and the words were heavy with uncertainty. 'What do they think, anyway?' she muttered, nodding to Iris to allow the doctor to enter her apartment. 'That I'm half-mutant, perhaps?'

'I think it's more to do with your ability to have children,' Iris explained gently. 'I understand His Highness is in need of an heir rather quickly as well.'

Charlotte stared at her aide with a familiar sense in

her chest, and that rock lodged in her throat once more. It made breathing almost impossible; stars formed at her eyelids. 'I see.'

Children. An heir. Sex. With her *husband*. She reached behind her, curling her fingers around the back of a chair for support. Of *course* she'd have to sleep with her husband. Only the idea of another man touching her, kissing her, making love to her, filled her veins with acid.

She breathed deeply, doing everything she could to quell the panic, and years of training meant that the doctor didn't even notice anything was amiss. She came, took Charlotte's blood and temperature and asked her a host of general questions, then smiled and said she'd be in touch the next day.

Charlotte nodded, and didn't say another word.

'Oh, Doctor, hello.' Charlotte looked up from the papers she was reading—regarding a charitable endowment for one of Hemmenway's smaller universities. Charlotte had given it a lot of focus this year, and in addition to the new library facilities, she'd also pledged enough to modernise their two lecture theatres. 'Did we forget something this morning?'

Iris followed in the doctor's wake, shrugging her shoulders.

'Not exactly.' The doctor looked from Iris to Charlotte. 'May I have a moment of your time?'

Charlotte gestured to the seat opposite. 'You've already had a moment of it, but you are welcome to several more.'

The doctor didn't smile. She was nervous.

Charlotte sobered. 'Is something the matter?'

'Well, you see, Your Highness…'

Charlotte waited, watching the doctor with enormous blue eyes.

'Yes?'

'I have received the test results back early. The lab put a rush on them.'

'And?' Charlotte prompted.

'This is a little delicate.' The doctor cast a glance over her shoulder. 'Would you prefer us to speak privately?'

Iris was the only other person in the room. Charlotte shook her head. 'It's fine, please, go ahead.'

The doctor gave the full force of her attention to Charlotte. 'Everything was okay,' the doctor said firmly, slipping into the persona of medical professional. 'Your iron levels are good, your Vitamin D is good, but your HcG is elevated.'

'What's HcG and is it a bad thing to have too much of it?'

'Not if you're pregnant,' the doctor responded with a tilt of her head.

Charlotte froze, her jaw dropping, her heart leaping into her throat. It took a full minute before she was able to speak again. 'What did you say?'

The doctor grimaced apologetically. 'I take it this is a surprise.'

Charlotte's mouth formed a circle, and Iris took over, moving towards the desk. 'There must be a mistake.'

'I had the lab retest Your Highness's blood,' the doctor said with a shake of her head. 'There is no mistake.'

Charlotte stood uneasily, walking across her office and staring at one of the ancient tapestries that adorned the walls, this one of the flowers that were native to the riverbanks in Hemmenway. 'I can't believe it.'

Iris and the doctor remained silent. Charlotte lifted a

hand to her lips, closing her eyes as she tried to process this bombshell.

Pregnant.

She groaned, dropping her head forward in disbelief. This could *not* be happening. Not to *her*. Charlotte's life had been master-planned from before her conception. That one night of freedom she'd had had been a wonderful, wild aberration but it couldn't be allowed to dictate her future.

Except… She curved a hand over her stomach and her heart gave a hard, urgent thump. *Love.* She felt love. The second the baby was mentioned, she'd fallen in love with him or her and nothing else mattered now. Nothing and no one was as important to Charlotte as her child. Every decision she made from that moment forward would be in their best interests. She was a *mother,* and she'd be a *real* mother to this baby. She'd love him or her with all her heart. This wasn't about duty and lineage. There was no way on earth she'd let this child feel, for even a moment, the same aching sense of rejection she'd grown up with. Her baby would be a person first, a prince or princess second.

She turned to the doctor. 'What do I need to do now?'

'I can't advise you on that.'

'I mean medically,' Charlotte clarified. 'Do I need more tests? A scan?'

The doctor shook her head. 'Everything looks good. Your HcG levels suggest you're about four or five weeks along, so it's still early. I will bring some pregnancy vitamins to you this evening.'

Charlotte nodded, numb.

'When you're closer to twelve weeks, we'll organise for more tests and a scan. Between now and then, you should simply eat well, enjoy moderate exercise, rest whenever you're tired, and try to relax.'

Charlotte's lips twisted into a sardonic smile. That was easy for her to say!

As soon as the doctor left her office, she felt the questions from Iris buzzing through the air. Naturally her aide and friend had questions, but Charlotte couldn't answer them yet. She had questions of her own.

'Iris, I'm going to give you an address and a first name, and I need you to find out whatever you can about the man in question.' Her expression turned pleading. 'And naturally, I would appreciate your discretion.'

'You know you don't even have to say that, Your Highness,' Iris murmured, moving closer to Charlotte. 'Are you okay?'

'Of course,' she lied, shocked and terrified in equal measure, moving to her desk and pulling out a piece of paper.

She wrote down 'Rocco S' and all that she could remember about his apartment building on the Upper East Side. 'It's not much to go on,' she apologised, handing the page over.

'I'll find him.'

Iris's confidence was exactly what Charlotte needed. She nodded her thanks, maintaining as calm an air as possible until Iris had left and Charlotte was all alone. Then she sank into her desk chair and put her head in her hands, with absolutely no bloody idea of what she was going to do next.

CHAPTER FOUR

IT HADN'T BEEN easy to organise another trip to New York, but every time Charlotte thought about telling Rocco about the baby over the phone, she'd balked. This was not the kind of news she wanted to break with the Atlantic Ocean between them.

She stared at his phone number until the digits blurred together, and finally forced herself to dial. The first night they'd met, she'd been operating under her own steam. She was emphatically aware of how different this time was.

'Rocco Santinova.'

His voice sent a thousand shards of desire through her body, like lava, fast-flowing and urgent, so it was almost impossible to speak.

'Hello?'

She squeezed her eyes closed, looking across at Iris for courage. 'Hi. It's… Charlotte.'

Silence stretched between them and her tummy did a thousand somersaults. Not quite silence, she realised. Behind Rocco there was a gentle hum of noise, people talking, Christmas carols playing, laughter.

He wasn't alone.

Jealousy speared her, unexpected and fierce, and it

wasn't just jealousy of any other woman he might be with, but jealousy of his freedom as well.

'Where are you?' The words breathed out of her.

'That's a strange question, given we haven't spoken in five weeks.'

She nodded awkwardly.

'Come to think of it, how did you get my number?'

'It wasn't difficult.'

'It's unlisted.'

It probably wasn't the time to tell him about the Hemmenwegian Secret Service.

'That's not important right now.'

'So? What is?'

'Are you free?'

'In what context?'

'Can you meet?'

'When?'

'Now, if possible.'

'I'm in the bar.'

Her heart turned over. She closed her eyes and imagined him there. She'd intended to meet him at his apartment, or to invite him here, but she made a snap decision that his plan was better. Having this conversation surrounded by people offered a level of protection. It would ensure they kept things civilised. And out of the bedroom. Yes, she wanted to rip his clothes from his body but that would complicate matters even more.

The bar would be perfect.

'I'll be right there.'

In the end, it took Charlotte half an hour to wrangle agreement from her security detail—a compromise was reached. Iris and three guards would accompany her, and keep a distance from the entrance. She changed quickly, into a pair of dark jeans and a simple blouse, slipping her feet into ballet flats. It was snowing, and she bundled herself into a thick jacket, pausing to survey her appearance in the mirror and wishing her eyes weren't shimmering with excitement.

He'd take one look at her and know how happy she was to see him again, and that definitely wasn't the point of this visit.

There was no quick cab ride this time. Instead, a black armoured SUV collected her at the kerb, taking her to the bar. Outside, she sucked in a breath, aware that her life was about to change beyond all recognition.

'Ma'am?' Iris queried gently.

'I'm okay.' And she would be. One of her guards entered first, pushing in the door, scoping out the room before allowing Charlotte to enter.

Her heart was in her throat as she scanned the crowd and saw him within seconds. He'd taken a booth against the wall. More private than she'd anticipated. And he'd ordered a bottle of wine.

Her pulse kicked up a gear as she wove through the revellers, unable to take her eyes off him. Rocco, however, observed Charlotte quickly, standing as she approached, before flicking a glance behind her, to the two burly men and Iris, then back to Charlotte, so her blood sizzled.

'Hi.' She stood at the edge of the booth, staring at him, awkward, uncertain, wanting to reach up and kiss his cheek, but self-conscious in the face of their audience.

'I didn't expect to hear from you.'

'As you pointed out, we didn't swap numbers,' she said, taking the seat opposite his then startling when their knees brushed beneath the table. 'Besides, you made no bones of the fact you wouldn't welcome a repeat performance.'

His expression didn't change, but something in his eyes sparked with hers. 'And yet, here we are.'

Adrenaline pumped through her. 'I need to talk to you.'

He poured two glasses of wine then settled back, watching her. It answered the question of whether or not he had any clue why she'd called.

'There's something I have to tell you.'

'So I gather.'

She bit down on her lower lip. 'We didn't exchange last names, by agreement.'

'And yet you found me.'

'Do you wish I hadn't?' she asked, tilting her face to the side.

'I didn't say that.' Heat flared between them, and the drugging temptation to abandon herself to this desire again almost overwhelmed her.

She had to get this over with, before she lost herself to the quicksand of her need for this man.

'I wasn't honest with you that night.'

He went very still. 'Oh?' Suspicion underscored that small question. 'About what?'

She knew what she had to tell him but, sitting across from him, she would have done *anything* to be normal.

'Are you married?'

'No. Not yet,' she said, pressing her fingertips to her brow.

'Not yet?' he responded, his mouth tightening.

'I'm—'

'Your Highness?' She was approached by a woman in, Charlotte guessed, her forties, speaking English but with a heavy accent. When Charlotte turned to face her, the woman switched to Hemmenwegian, but she only got four words out before a security guard was there, putting himself ostentatiously between the tourist and Charlotte.

'It's okay,' Charlotte murmured, dismissing her guard, refocusing her attention on the woman.

'I thought it was you! My goodness. I'm starstruck.'

Charlotte winced, but went through the motions of the responses she was expected to give, all the while conscious of the Rocco's eyes on her, of his assessing look, piecing things together.

'Is it possible for me to take a photograph?'

Consternation flared inside Charlotte but she nodded and stood, moving to stand beside the woman and smiling obligingly for the selfie.

'Would you mind not sharing that on social media for an hour? It's a question of security,' she said with an apologetic smile.

'Of course, Your Highness. What an honour this has been.'

Charlotte waited until the woman had left then folded herself back into the bench seat opposite Rocco.

'It seems you weren't honest with me at all,' he said after a beat. 'So why don't you start at the beginning?'

She dropped her gaze to the table between them. 'Beginning, middle, end, it doesn't particularly matter. I'm a princess.'

'Of?'

'Hemmenway.'

His eyes narrowed. 'Charlotte Rothsburg,' he murmured. Her insides squeezed, hearing him say her full name.

'Yes.'

'And you didn't tell me.'

'I wanted to escape for a night.'

'To live like a commoner?'

She pulled her lips to the side. 'Nothing quite so pre-meditated,' she said with a shake of her head. 'I just…saw an opportunity to get away and took it. It's very hard to explain what my life is like to an outsider, but suffice it to say, places like this are a total novelty to me.'

His eyes splintered when they locked to hers. 'And this deception has been eating at your conscience ever since? Or are you worried I'm going to sell the sordid details to a tabloid?'

He couldn't have known how close the latter sugges-tion hit to her previous experience.

'No.' Her brow furrowed as she attempted to slow her breathing. 'In fact, that's not really important. It's just… a part of what I needed to tell you.'

'Why?'

'So you'd understand…the delicacy of our situation.'

'Our situation was a one-night stand,' he said, and she leaned forward, lifting a finger to her lips.

'Please, remember there are people everywhere.'

His eyes flared with hers, silently arguing, then he dropped his head once in silent acknowledgement.

'Are one-night stands forbidden to princesses?' he asked softly, and she bristled, because she hadn't ex-pected the slightly mocking tone from him. She tilted her face sideways, regaining her composure. 'Is that why you were so inexperienced, Charlotte?'

She liked that even now he didn't use her title. 'My experience is irrelevant.'

'Not to me.'

'To this conversation.'

'What conversation, exactly?'

'I'm trying to explain—'

'But you're not. Why did you call me?'

She focused on a point beyond his shoulder. 'That

night…' she said softly, forcing her eyes back to his. 'Despite the fact we…' She paused again, the intimate conversation almost impossible to broach.

His nostrils flared as he expelled a rapid breath, his impatience obvious.

'I'm pregnant.' Her voice shook only the slightest bit. 'And you're the father.'

It was as though every single person in the room became still and silent, and yet, at the same time, the room seemed to turn into some kind of roller coaster, tipping and tilting wildly. The sole noise she was conscious of was the hissing of air between his teeth.

'What did you say?' He could only stare at her as those words unfurled inside of him—the last thing he'd expected. Foolishly, he supposed, given the timing. But pregnancy! It was impossible. He'd actually thought she'd called to suggest a repeat of the other night, and he hadn't been able to think straight since. The idea of taking her to bed was nirvana to him after five weeks of craving her, of reliving every moment of their time together.

'I'm pregnant,' she murmured, *sotto voce,* so he leaned closer, eyes staring at her lips, wondering if there was some disconnect between her brain and mouth.

Suddenly he was a young boy again, hiding behind a door, eavesdropping on a conversation that he shouldn't have been privy to.

'I already have a family. That child is not mine.'

'He is your son, whether you choose to acknowledge him or not. He's your responsibility.'

'No, the responsibility was yours. You told me you'd taken care of it,' the man snapped.

'I couldn't do it.' His mother's voice had been shaking. *'I couldn't have an abortion. And if you met him—'*

'No. I will never meet him, and if you tell another living soul that I'm his father I will destroy you. Do you understand?'

'But you can't be,' Rocco said with a small shift of his head. 'I used protection.' It was a weak, feeble response. Obviously condoms weren't fool-proof.

'I'm pregnant,' she said for the third time, her expression showing concern.

'And I'm the father.'

'It's physically impossible for it to be anyone else.'

'You said you were engaged. What about him?'

'No. It's not that kind of relationship.' He filed that claim away for later. 'There's been no one but you.'

Despite the panic that was curdling his blood, her admission triggered an unexpected cascade of masculine pride. Despite his protestations on the night they'd made love, the idea of being her first and only was a heady aphrodisiac.

'I can see how you feel about this,' she muttered, eyes flicking towards the door. He followed the direction of her gaze, looking at the security agents and the woman who stood stationed there, hardly blending in. 'Don't worry, I'm not here to ruin your life.'

He turned his attention back to Charlotte.

'I don't need anything from you. I just came because I thought you should know.'

'I wish he'd never been born. I wish I'd never met you.'

'If only you knew what a wonderful young man he is. Your son, so strong and smart, and so like you in many ways. Except, thank God, he doesn't have your ice-cold heart.'

Rocco had sworn to himself, and on his mother's grave, that he would never be like his father. The void in his life had been bad enough, but as he'd grown older, and come to understand the depths of his father's hatred of him, Rocco had built a hatred of his own. Of his father, and of the way he lived his life. Yet history seemed to be repeating itself with the unexpected pregnancy, just as Rocco's conception had been for his mother, unplanned, perhaps initially unwanted.

His father had failed Rocco in every way, and Rocco swore, in that moment, he would do the exact opposite.

'And now what?' he prompted silkily, his mind made up, so that he could observe her carefully, understand this woman's thinking.

'I don't know,' she answered, honestly. 'I haven't told my parents or brother yet, but I must. They'll be furious,' she murmured, closing her eyes, sucking in a steadying breath. 'The engagement will be cancelled. Constitutional lawyers will be consulted.' She was evidently thinking aloud. 'None of that is your problem though.'

'Isn't it? From my perspective, the baby is our equal responsibility.'

She startled, obviously surprised by that.

'You don't understand.' She frowned. 'I'm telling you that you don't have to do anything. You're off the hook.'

Anger sparked in his gut. 'That's quite an assumption to make.'

'An assumption? Not at all. I'm remembering the way you reacted after we…' She leaned closer, remembering they were in a public place. 'You made it pretty obvious that you weren't interested in commitment of any type.'

'You can't see that this changes things?'

'It doesn't have to,' she said firmly. 'I have everything I need to raise this baby.'

For a moment he admired her bravado and courage, but only for a moment, and then anger expanded through him.

'And what about the baby? Do you think you have any right to unilaterally choose to excise me from his or her life?'

Her lips parted, not expecting that.

'You have no idea what you're suggesting.'

He sat back, watching her, interested to see where this went.

'I'm not—this isn't a normal baby,' she said after a beat, focusing on the tabletop. 'Do you remember I told you about my brother?'

He nodded. 'That he was ill?'

'Yes. He had cancer. The treatment he received was experimental, and quite remarkable. It cured his cancer, but left him infertile. When my parents found out, they conceived me.'

'An insurance policy,' he murmured, remembering the way she'd described herself that night.

'Right. I have known, all my life, that the job of providing a royal heir would fall to me. You can't imagine what that's like,' she whispered, running a finger around the rim of the wine glass that sat, still full, in front of her. 'No one ever asked me how I felt about it. If I wanted children. Marriage to some foreign prince. These were not decisions I got to make. I was born for this purpose, so naturally it was expected I'd fall in.'

'And you did?'

'Yes,' she muttered, bitterly. 'I did. Always. Almost always.' Her brows knitted together, a darkness on her features. 'This baby is a diversion from their plans; they're going to kill me,' she said with a tight smile, but her words lacked any humour.

He straightened his spine. The situation wasn't the same as for his father, but it sure as hell felt like it—a powerful, wealthy man refusing to acknowledge him, because he was the illegitimate son of a cleaning lady. Or his grandparents, who'd thrown his mother out when she'd fallen pregnant. It was all so familiar. There was no way he could toss Charlotte, or their baby, to the wolves.

'What will they want you to do?'

'To do? I have no idea.' She shook her head, her eyes meeting his with spirit and defiance. 'But I'll likely never hear the end of it.'

'Will they welcome this child?'

She paled. 'I don't know.' Her eyes were hollow, panic obvious.

'Will they love him or her?'

She shook her head, eyes misty. 'I don't know,' she repeated.

His heart dropped to his gut. He suspected she *did* know. It wasn't a difficult question for someone to answer, but her family was obviously far from ordinary. He sympathised with that.

'Listen, Charlotte,' he leaned closer, 'I have a solution.'

'I can't do what you're suggesting,' she said after a beat. 'I'm having this baby.'

'Yes, I can see that. But you're what, five weeks along?'

She nodded once.

'You're not visibly pregnant.'

'It's too early.'

'Which gives us a few weeks.'

'For what?'

'To get married.'

She froze, her skin paling, so he knew for sure the idea hadn't occurred to her before this.

'What?' It was her turn to stare blankly across the table.

'You're pregnant with my baby. The solution is obvious.'

'It's far from obvious,' she murmured. 'We can't get married.'

'Why not?'

'We hardly know each other, for one thing.'

'How well do you know the man you were intended to marry?'

She blinked. 'Not at all,' came the grudging acknowledgement.

'And at least you know we have chemistry,' he pointed out, revelling in the way her cheeks flushed pink. His groin hardened, straining against his trousers, reminding him that he was sitting opposite the object of his fantasies for the past month and a bit.

'You don't understand. He is a sheikh…his life is like mine. You have no idea what it would be like to become a crown prince. You'd hate it.'

'Perhaps.'

'No, not *perhaps*, absolutely. All these freedoms would be gone, like that.' She clicked her fingers.

'It is the lesser of two evils,' he said, after a pause. 'From the moment you conceived this baby, our fate was sealed. We have to do this.'

She gaped at him. 'Absolutely not. It's crazy.'

'You're objecting for the sake of it.'

Her tongue darted out, licking her lower lip, and he stared at the gesture before reaching over and putting his hand over hers, but she pulled away quickly.

'People could be watching.'

'So?'

'This is my point. You have no idea what my life is like.'

'Miserable, by the sound of it.'

She looked away from him. 'Let's say, for a moment, that I was to agree—which I'm not, but just playing devil's advocate—you do understand that would mean you'd have to move to Hemmenway?'

'Is that where you intend to raise our baby?'

She nodded.

'Then I'll move there anyway.'

Her jaw dropped.

'I can work from anywhere. I have no family here, no ties to Manhattan. It doesn't matter to me.' He was surprised to find the words were true.

'You're mad,' she said softly. 'Why in the world would you even suggest this?'

He hesitated a moment, not used to baring his soul to anyone, but this was different. Charlotte deserved to know the truth. More than that, by sharing the truth, he might help her understand that his offer was genuine. 'Because my father didn't want me,' he said, voice blanked of emotion. 'I was an accident. Unwanted. Unacknowledged. There is no way in hell I'll ever let my child know what that feels like.'

Sympathy softened her eyes; he didn't want it. 'Marry me, Princess. You know it's the right thing to do.'

He could see she was weakening and, more than that, feeling sorry for him, which he hated. To prove that point, he sat up straighter, squared his shoulders, stared across at her unapologetically.

'I need to think about it. I can call you in a few days...'

'No.'

'You can't just...say no,' she said with a shake of her head.

'Think about it here, now, with me. You have questions? Let me answer them.'

'You might not have the answers.'

'Try me.'

'Well,' she hesitated, 'is there anything in your past

that would embarrass the palace?' She winced. 'I'm sorry. If we had the luxury of time, I'd find a way to be more diplomatic.'

His eyes latched on to hers. 'What kind of thing do you imagine?'

'I don't know. Another love child? Anything in your business life? Jilted ex-lover? Sex tape? Anything that could become a problem?'

'No.'

'No?' She lifted a brow. 'I beg your pardon, but I find that almost impossible to believe.'

'Why?'

'You obviously sleep around. How can you be so sure there's not a scorned lover waiting for a chance to embarrass you?'

'I choose my partners wisely.'

She tilted her head to the side.

'Okay, but then, you hardly sound like the marrying kind. Are you sure you can deprive yourself of your... lifestyle?'

'It's not about what I want. You're pregnant, case closed.'

Her eyes dropped to the table, her breath burning in her chest. She moved on quickly, unable to focus on his words, or to reflect on why they were so hurtful to her.

'We'd need to get married *soon*,' she said. 'I'll be showing within another six weeks, probably.'

'Yes.'

'Yes what?'

'We'll get married soon.'

She shook her head softly. 'I appreciate the offer, Rocco, but we *both* need to think about this. What you're suggesting will throw a grenade into your life. You need to take tonight, at least, to consider it, see how you feel in the morning. Then we'll talk.'

His eyes glittered when they met hers. Her ambivalence was infuriating. Didn't she understand? He wouldn't allow this baby to be raised away from him.

'I'm not being clear,' he said slowly. 'Marriage is my first option, but there are others.'

'Such as?' she asked, leaning closer.

'We share custody.'

Her eyes flared to his, fear in their depths. 'That would never work. The heir to the throne of Hemmenway couldn't be shuttled from continent to continent, between two parents.'

'Then I'll raise him or her,' he said, regarding her without blinking.

She sucked in a sharp breath. 'Absolutely not.'

'Why? It solves all your problems. Just lay low for the duration of your pregnancy, avoid getting photographed, and you can smuggle the baby to me in eight months' time. I'll never bother you again.'

'How dare you?' she demanded hotly, and to his chagrin he saw a sparkle on her eyelashes, tears unmistakable. But it was a point he needed to make.

'How dare *you*?' he volleyed back. 'How is my suggestion any different to yours?'

Her lips formed a perfect circle.

'Why should either of us give up our baby?'

'You don't want children. I'm sure of it,' she returned, but tremulously.

'I never planned for them,' he agreed. 'But that horse has bolted, and I'm telling you, I want to be in *this* child's life. I want my child to know I fought for them, from the very first.'

'And if I don't agree?' she whispered, asking him to repeat his threat, perhaps needing to hear it clearly.

'I'll sue for custody,' he confirmed, crossing his arms over his chest.

She bit down on her lip, her nostrils flaring as she tried to bring her emotions under control.

'How can I say no?' she said with a shake of her head. 'Under those conditions, of course I'll marry you.'

It was a victory, but Rocco didn't feel a hint of triumph at her acquiescence. He couldn't; not when a single tear rolled down her cheek and she surreptitiously dashed it away.

CHAPTER FIVE

SHE COULD BARELY SLEEP. The agreement they'd made sat inside of her like a butterfly, beating its wings all night long. A secret engagement. A baby. This wasn't love, but it was her life, and decisions she'd made. Somehow, that one night of defiance had morphed into something bigger, something much more permanent, and adrenaline and excitement kept her awake. She paced the carpet of her room, imagining how she'd break the news to her parents, her brother, and deciding it would all be worth it.

She was having a baby—the one thing they all desperately wanted.

They'd forgive her the circumstances, purely for the heir she was adding to the family tree.

But none of that mattered to Charlotte.

All she could think about was Rocco. His face, his body, his voice, his honourable offer to marry her, his heartbreaking confession about his own father, and the way that had sculpted his immediate response to her news.

How could she have said no?

And why hadn't she wanted to?

Anticipation built inside of her, so she lay back down in her bed, hands roaming her body, and with her eyes closed she imagined it was Rocco, and moaned softly into the night air. Desire was a tsunami, drowning her, swallowing her. She had accepted his proposal because it made sense but there was nothing rational about the feelings besieging her now.

When Charlotte awoke the next morning, it was to a veritable flurry of activity on her mobile phone. She had several missed calls and texts. Still bleary-eyed, she swiped open her phone and began to scroll through her messages, until she saw one from her brother, Nicholas.

Are you actually engaged? To an American? I've been in meetings with the Sheikh's team all week. You need to call me and explain this. Immediately.

She squawked, pushing her feet out of the bed and onto the plush carpet of her bedroom suite. Beyond her window, Central Park was a stunning green oasis. With shaking fingers, she loaded up one of the social-media tags, which pointed to a news article.

> *Reports have it that rumours about the Princess of Hemmenway's engagement were wrong—at least as to her choice of groom! Reports from the States overnight are now suggesting the Princess will marry billionaire financier Rocco Santinova. More details to come.*

She groaned, pushing a hand through her hair. 'Great,' she muttered, fingers trembling. She should call her parents, but instead she dialled Rocco's number.

He answered on the second ring, his tone of voice relaxed and frustratingly sensual, so she ground her teeth together with barely concealed annoyance. He had no right to sound so damned gorgeous when she was having an emotional breakdown.

'Did you leak this to the press?'

'And good morning to you too, Princess.'

'I'm not messing around here.'

Silence met her tart response but she was in no mood to apologise.

'Why is news of our private arrangement all over the internet?'

'I suppose your engagement is newsworthy.'

'Yes, which is why the palace would have made an official announcement later today.'

'And now the news is already out there.'

A suspicion began to form. 'You did this on purpose, didn't you? You wanted to make sure I'd agree to this.'

'I'm flattered you'd think me so Machiavellian, but I had nothing to do with it.'

'Then how—?'

'Our conversation took place in a bar. It's possible someone overheard.'

'But what about the pregnancy?' she pushed back. 'Surely that would be just as newsworthy.'

'Perhaps they guessed when they saw us together, or maybe they heard some of our conversation but not all,' he said impatiently. 'Does it matter? It's out there now, as we both agreed, given your position, it would need to be.'

'How are you not more bothered by this?'

'Because it doesn't change anything.'

'No,' she murmured, pressing her head to the glass window. 'Still, it's far from ideal.'

'True, but it can't be helped.'

'I wanted to tell my parents in person.' She wasn't

close to them, but they were still her parents and they deserved at least the courtesy of an explanation.

'You can confirm it to them in person; we'll do it together.'

Something warm expanded through her belly. The idea of facing them with Rocco at her side was strangely reassuring. He wasn't exactly an ally, and yet he was the closest thing.

'Text me your address. I'll come to you now.'

'What for?'

'We agreed this needs to happen as soon as possible?'

She made a noise in the affirmative.

'So why prevaricate? I'll be at yours in an hour, and from there we can leave for Hemmenway.'

Her head was swimming with the matter-of-fact nature of his statement, but her heart was thundering through her chest like a wild horse. 'You realise you're talking about moving to my country *today*.'

'I will continue to have apartments in cities all over the world. I'm not moving to Hemmenway so much as travelling there with you.'

'But you don't have to,' she said with a shake of her head. 'You can take some time, come in a few days, if you'd like.' She felt bad enough for how she'd disrupted his life.

'You're carrying my baby. If you think I intend to let you out of my sight—particularly overseas—then you are crazy. Text me your address.' He disconnected the call before she could respond, and perhaps that was a good thing, because his words set off a domino effect of sadness and loneliness that she'd prefer to keep shielded from him.

Charlotte's only value, all her life, had been for the heir she would provide, and now she'd found herself in a situation, engaged to a man who was marrying her purely for the baby inside her. Her wonderful little escape now seemed like the compounding of her life's greatest sadness.

He arrived fifty-five minutes later, dressed in jeans and a black sweater against skin the colour of burned butter, and despite the fact she'd seen him the night before she'd somehow forgotten the effect he had on her, so her pulse began to roll like a tidal wave, leaving her light-headed and tingly all over.

Perhaps because her security agents stood just inside the door, hovering with uncertainty, he moved towards her, eyes slightly mocking as he got closer, and closer, until he stood just a foot away and then he brushed his lips against hers. A chaste kiss of greeting, nothing more, but her heart leapt into her throat and she almost jumped out of her skin.

'Good morning.' His sensual voice ran down her spine like treacle. He was playing a part, she knew that, but her reactions weren't fake. Her whole body shook as though she was a fault line come to life.

'Rocco.' Her voice was breathy, and inwardly she winced. It would be easy to convince the country that this was a whirlwind love affair—she just had to remember it was all make-believe.

She turned towards her guards. 'Thank you.' She nodded curtly. 'We'll be fine now.'

They nodded deferentially and then turned, leaving the elegant suite.

'Nice guys,' he said with a lift of his brow.

'They're not charming,' she agreed. 'But they could break your neck with their little fingers.'

'I doubt that,' he said with quiet confidence, and again

she shivered, because he was right. No one could hurt Rocco Santinova. She was as sure of that as she was of the nose on her face. He was strong and virile, an ancient god brought to life. It was the last thing she should be focusing on. His virility was not in question; her sanity was.

He strode towards her, holding out a black velvet box. She took it, the weight pleasing in the palm of her hand, until she considered what might be contained within and her stomach dropped to her toes. Sure enough, when she cracked the lid there was a ring in the centre. A large green stone surrounded by a circlet of diamonds. It was old-fashioned and beautiful—the last sort of ring she'd expect he would choose for her.

'It's lovely,' she said quietly, her heart in her throat. 'How did you find the time to organise this?'

His eyes probed hers as he lifted the ring from the box, then slid it onto her ring finger. They both stared at it. 'The jewellers opened for me this morning.'

Of course they did. He was Rocco Santinova. Her eyes lifted to his and her pulse throbbed, desire washing through her so she took a step back, desperately needing to gain control of this situation.

She cleared her throat, gesturing across the room. 'Have a seat.'

He made no effort to move, so she did, stepping away from him with more effort than she could admit, walking slowly across the room towards the deep sofas. Rather than sitting in one, she moved behind it and braced her hands. 'I've arranged for a photographer to come and take a formal picture,' she said crisply. 'Given someone saw fit to expedite our announcement, an official statement will have to be released sooner rather than later.'

He said nothing and nerves zipped through her. She

was unused to the feeling, but he managed to unsettle her easily, and always there was the sense that he was laughing at her. She bristled, squaring her shoulders.

'Once we get to Hemmenway, you'll have to meet my family—my parents and brother first, then the extended family in due course. You'll be assigned a protocol officer to get you up to speed on how things work. I'm sorry, there's a lot to cover, and it's very boring, but it's also important.'

'We'll see,' he said with a shrug.

She paused. 'What's that supposed to mean?'

'Only that I don't have much patience for meaningless protocols.'

Oh, hell. What was she doing? 'None the less, Hemmenway has one of the oldest reigning monarchies in the world. Our lives are steeped in tradition. It might seem foolish to you but that's just the way it is.'

'Forse.'

She narrowed her eyes, studying his face. 'You're trying to bait me.'

His smile was just a flash in his face. 'Then what?'

It took her a moment to refocus her energy on their conversation. 'Then,' she shrugged, 'you'll be a free man. I've spoken to Iris about arranging an apartment for you—near mine, of course, but you'll have your own space, so you don't need to worry about privacy. It's very spacious—you'll have your own bedroom, bathroom, lounge and kitchen.'

'An office?'

She hesitated a moment. 'It's not usual for members of the royal family to work outside of our public duties.'

His nostrils flared. 'And yet, I'll be working.'

This was an argument that would wait for another time. 'There's already an office available to you,' she said after a moment. 'Though it's more for the work you'll carry out in your role as my husband. Interviews, representing charities, that sort of thing—'

At this point he lifted his palm into the air, silencing her with a gesture first, and then by a word. 'No.'

She bit down on her lip. 'Excuse me?'

'I'm marrying you for the sake of our baby. There is no alternative. But I have no interest in becoming some kind of ceremonial object. I have my own business, my own life. While I'm happy to move that to Hemmenway, I will not allow it to be overtaken completely, whether you are a princess or not.'

She should have felt infuriated by Rocco's demanding insistence that his life not be disturbed, but his strength and power were unbelievably attractive.

'We'll see,' she simpered, passing his own lack of commitment back to him.

'You'll learn that I'm not an easy man to live with, *cara*.' The term of endearment slid through her like melted gold. 'The best thing for you would be to accept that now. Choose your battles wisely.'

'Is that a threat?'

He laughed, a short, gruff noise that turned her blood to lava. 'It's a foretelling. I'm thirty-two years old and have been single all my life. That's no accident. If you leave me alone, I will leave you alone, and everything will be just perfect.'

He wasn't joking.

From her side of the plane, she caught the look of exasperation on the protocol officer's face and could only grimace in silent apology. Rocco was recalcitrant and stubborn. And she liked that. Her lips tugged to the side in a half-smile as she sipped her herbal tea, eyes focusing on the fluffy clouds just outside the window, while her body—every single cell of it—was aware of him across the aisle. She couldn't hear what he was saying, but the tone of his voice left her in little doubt: he wasn't having a bar of the suggestions.

It was a spirit of defiance she'd struggled to find. Even that night in New York had been about hiding from her life, not facing it front on and living in the face of it. She'd been a coward for too long.

Her hand crept to her stomach, curving over the flatness there, and out of nowhere tears misted her eyes. For the first time since discovering she was pregnant, it started to feel *real*. She blinked rapidly, embarrassed by the show of emotion, but she wasn't quick enough. From several feet away Rocco's eyes landed on her face, and without missing a beat he cut off the palace staffer.

'That's enough for now.'

'Sir, we still have several matters to discuss.'

Reluctantly, Rocco drew the full force of his dark brown eyes to the man's face. 'It will keep. My fiancée and I would like some privacy now.'

Without waiting for a response, he unclipped his seatbelt and stood. Whether it was because he was engaged to Charlotte, or because he was Rocco Santinova, the staffer quickly cleared the cabin, taking two other staff members with him. Charlotte had evidently not realised; her face stayed angled away from his, a single tear rolling down her cheek.

With an unfamiliar sensation in the middle of his chest, he crossed the aisle, moving into the seat beside hers. She startled—he felt her jump beside him—turning to him with obvious reluctance.

'Finished already?' She pushed an overbright smile to her lips. 'That was quick.'

'We covered the essentials.'

'Meaning you weren't interested in hearing him out?' She sighed, lifting a hand and wiping at her cheek, just as she had the night before. His gut twisted now, as it had then.

'You don't think I can handle this?' he prompted, a cynical look on his features.

She hesitated and then shook her head slowly. 'Actually,' her frown showed confusion, 'I think you're the one man who can handle it all perfectly. I'm not worried.'

'Good.' He crossed his legs at the ankles, assuming a relaxed pose. 'Besides, I would rather hear about palace life from you.'

'Why?'

'You're better to look at, for one thing.'

'Charming.' She rolled her eyes, but her cheeks flushed with pink, the effect spellbinding.

'Tell me about the man you were supposed to marry.'

'Why?'

'So I know what your parents would have wished,' he said, even when he wasn't sure what had prompted him to ask the question. 'You said he was a sheikh. Was that the prerequisite for your hand in marriage? A royal match?'

Her nod was hesitant.

'What about your feelings?'

Her arched brow showed rehearsed cynicism. 'Love doesn't come into it; it never has.'

'That's never bothered you?'

'Actually, yes. But my parents' marriage was arranged. They saw no problem with this.'

He considered that.

'It's just as well I wasn't set on falling madly in love with a man of my choosing—given that I've ended up marrying you.'

'True.' He leaned closer to her then, watching her skin lift with goose-pimples as his warm breath fanned her throat. Her responsiveness fascinated him, intrigued him, pulled on him. 'But that's not to say our relationship is without all feeling.'

Her eyes flew wide. 'What does that mean?'

Desire flared inside Rocco, as hot as lava. 'That our wedding night can't come soon enough.'

Her eyes flew open, and her lips parted on a quick breath. 'Rocco...' His name was a strangled plea. 'That's not... Remember what this is.'

'And what's that?' Closer he moved, and his voice was more sensual, more teasing, so she made a garbled moaning sound.

'An accident,' she responded, but her voice lacked conviction. 'If I hadn't fallen pregnant, we'd never have seen one another again, right?'

'No,' he agreed, wondering if he'd imagined the look of hurt in her eyes, then deciding he must have. 'But let's not deal in hypotheticals.' He moved even closer, brushing his lips over her shoulder first. 'You are pregnant. The baby is mine.' He wondered if the possessive note in his voice was as recognisable to her as it was to him. He felt it deep in his soul. *His* baby. Hers and his. Theirs. 'And as soon as is humanly possible, you'll be my wife. I see no reason to deny us both something we know we'll enjoy.'

Her lips parted as she racked her brain for something to say, some demurral, but, sensing his opportunity, Rocco dispensed with a verbal campaign of persuasion and instead moved quickly to claim her mouth, his lips meeting hers, separating them, his tongue darting inside, duelling with hers, teasing her, dominating her, making her admit what she wanted to fight, making her face the reality of this.

Her brain was shouting at her to put space between them, to wrest back control, but her body, which had been craving him every minute of the last five weeks, was powerless to resist. She moaned low in her throat, his kiss overwriting all her senses until she was kissing him back, her tongue flicking with as much urgency, her hands lifting to curl in his hair, her body pushing forward, desperate to be closer to his, to be as close as humanly possible. She had to fight this—they couldn't start their marriage like this—but her brain refused to comply with common sense. She whimpered low in her throat, swamped by desire and need, her nerves white-hot in the face of his onslaught. She trembled against him, lifting a hand to his shoulder, all the while a little voice warning her to pull away, to stay calm, to keep a level head. But what fun was there in that?

Just like the first night they'd met, the spirit of rebellion stirred inside of her. She kissed him back with total abandon, and when he lifted his head to look down at her Charlotte had to swallow a groan of disappointment. The kiss hadn't been enough. She wanted more.

Where Charlotte felt as though her brain was going to explode, as though her body were on fire, Rocco looked every inch the calm and in control billionaire financier. If anything, a hint of amusement lightened those spectacular eyes to the colour of fresh honey.

Charlotte was uncharacteristically lost for words, but her brain was desperate for her to beg him not to stop. She tilted her face towards his, an invitation in her pose, but he stayed resolutely where he was.

'Your first time was a mistake.'

The words pelted against her like stones. She blinked, unable to keep the hurt from her eyes.

'I didn't know you were inexperienced, or it would have been different.'

Finally, she found her tongue. 'It wouldn't have happened at all.'

His smile was wry. 'No.'

Her eyes sparked with his. 'Why not? Is there something terribly wrong with virgins?'

'Generally, being someone's first comes with expectations. I prefer not to disappoint the women I sleep with by promising more than I can give.'

'That's…' She searched for the right word, then shook her head in frustration. 'I didn't sleep with you because I wanted a relationship. I just wanted to have sex.'

'With me,' he prompted gently.

'Well, yes.' Her eyes held a challenge. 'I was attracted to you. But also, I didn't want to be a virgin any more. And there you were, so irresistible…'

'You used me,' he said quietly.

She frowned. How could she answer that? She had planned their sexual relationship, but it hadn't occurred to her that her inexperience would be a problem.

'You wished to get rid of your virginity and so you came home with me. You must have known I had no idea.'

'I didn't think anything about it.' She cleared her throat softly. 'I lost the ability to think clearly the minute we met,' she said with a frustrated shake of her head, because those same eddies of confusion were swamping her now. 'And you're obviously as clear-headed as ever.'

'It's not worth discussing now,' he confirmed with a crisp nod. 'We can't change it; it's done. But your first time should not have been like that.'

Her breath grew forced. 'It's fine.' She waved a hand through the air, searching for a distraction. 'You're over-thinking it. Besides, like you said, we can't change it.'

'No.' He considered. 'But that was not sex, Charlotte.'

'Then my pregnancy is a real miracle.'

His smile was a quick lift of his lips—a brief conces-sion to amusement before he returned to a half-scowl. 'I mean to say, there is so much more to sex than what we did. You deserve to enjoy all aspects of that.' He leaned closer, his lips close to her ear. 'And I intended to teach you, night by night by night.'

She knew she had to fight what he was suggesting, just for the sake of her sanity. Only she was so tempted, so unbelievably turned on. 'I think that would be a mistake.'

'Do you?' He was teasing her now, as aware as she was of how much she desired him. 'Why?'

She floundered, common sense deserting her. 'This marriage would be easier if we maintain a distance…'

He made a throaty sound of agreement. 'I will stay out of your life,' he promised, leaning closer, lifting a hand to her starched shirt and wobbling a button between his fingertips until it parted from its hole. 'And you will stay out of my life.' He moved lower, to the next one. 'Ex-cept at night, when you will no longer be a princess, but a woman, and I, your husband,' the word was coated in mockery, as though he derided the institution of marriage, 'will teach you the true meaning of pleasure.' He slid his hand beneath the fabric of her shirt, cupping one of her breasts, so all her breath whooshed out of her. 'Deal?'

She tilted her head back on a moan, and somewhere between her euphoric noises of pleasure she was sure she agreed to his terms, to deal with the devil, her hus-band-to-be.

CHAPTER SIX

CHARLOTTE FELT NERVES yet rarely revealed them, but as she stood on the threshold of the main court room, the marble stretching for what felt like miles before her Charlotte's stomach was tangled into a bundle of knots. Even the Christmas decorations adorning every window, the large fir wreaths and delicate little carved ornaments, couldn't ease her panic.

'Breathe,' Rocco murmured.

'Easy for you to say. You haven't met them.'

A moment later the chief of her father's staff appeared with a deferential bow to Charlotte and barely a look at Rocco.

'Their Highnesses are ready for you, ma'am.'

'Thank you, Davisson.' She turned to Rocco, ignoring the chief of staff's presence. 'It's not too late to back out.'

His eyes dropped meaningfully lower, to her neat waist. 'Isn't it?'

She was both reassured and despairing. A real marriage had never been on the cards for Charlotte, but for the briefest moment she felt a sharp blade of resentment for the circumstances of *this* marriage, that they were to become husband and wife *only* because of the child they'd conceived.

Her fingers shifted at her side, forgetting, for a moment, all of the deportment coaching she'd received, the lessons that had prepared her so well for this royal life.

'What's bothering you so much?'

She lifted her eyes to his, and almost laughed at the absurdity of the question. 'Well, let's see. Could it be arriving here pregnant and engaged to someone they definitely won't approve of? Or the fact they're going to have to cancel the marriage negotiations with a man they selected for me more than five years ago? Or the fact…?'

'Yes?' he prompted when she didn't continue. His eyes were on her, burning her with their inspection, seeing way too much.

'Nothing,' she muttered, closing her eyes and sucking in a deep breath. The air was spiced with the slightest hint of his fragrance and her body felt like somersaulting as awareness kicked up a gear. 'Let's just get this over with.'

She opened her eyes and went to take a step inside the court but his hand curved around her wrist, and sparks flew through her whole body. 'Listen to me, Princess. I don't care that they won't approve of me. That is nothing new. But I will not have this baby treated as an outcast because of these circumstances. Tell me now if our child is to pay for the price for our choices, and I will take you away with me.' He stared down at her, intense determination in his eyes. 'I will take you far away from here, and provide everything you and our child could ever need. If you want to run away, to really run away, tell me and I will make it happen.'

She sucked in another breath, overawed by him, absolutely certain that he was the one man on earth who could do as he'd said, who could remove her from the life she'd always found so cloying and help her build a new one. But a lifetime of training, of expectations, were now a part of Charlotte's soul, woven into her DNA.

'I can't leave,' she said with a small shake of her head.

'Is this the best decision for our baby? The best life? Think of what I can provide for you both. The comfort, the security, the wealth and privacy...'

She couldn't lie. It was tempting. Imagining what he was offering made her feel jumpy with possibilities, and that same sense of rebellion and freedom she'd felt the first night they'd met was waving itself in front of her eyes, so for a split second, she wanted to tell him 'yes', they should simply run away.

Duty, though, reasserted itself. 'I will love this child so much that it doesn't matter how anyone else feels,' she said firmly. 'I will make life here wonderful for him or her. I promise you that. But if you are having doubts about remaining...'

The fire died down in his eyes, the intensity ebbing for a moment. 'Doubts are irrelevant. My place now is with you. If this is where you choose to be—'

'It's not a choice,' she said, needing him to understand. 'What you describe is...' *wonderful, amazing, tempting* '...very generous, but it would never work. I can't turn my back on my life here, my duties, even if I want to. It's not who I am.'

Something else sharpened in his features, something that warmed her and made her chest puff out, because it looked, for a moment, like respect.

'Then let's get this over with.'

He knew wealth and privilege like the back of his hand, and yet Charlotte's family were something else. There was a part of him that had believed she might have been exaggerating, but from the moment they stepped into the formal sitting room he was struck by the tremendous coldness and formality of the moment. Here was their daughter, returned with her fiancé, apparently joyously happy and in love, and they stayed seated when she entered the room, a look on their faces of icy disdain.

It wasn't that Charlotte meant anything to him, but she was pregnant with his baby, and that brought out his protective qualities. How could it not? Given what he'd seen his mother go through, the difficulties and challenges she'd faced, every single day. Naturally he wanted to spare Charlotte from that pain. Not because she was Charlotte, but because the situation was his responsibility, and unlike his father he had no intention of ignoring that. He moved closer to her, close enough for his warmth to reassure her, close enough to hear her gentle exhalation.

'Mother, Father,' she murmured, then nodded at her brother. 'Nicholas.'

They nodded, a greeting that was as impersonal as any he'd seen.

'I'd like to present Rocco Santinova. My fiancé.'

He stood firm as three pairs of eyes turned to face him, each regarding him with a measure of scepticism and displeasure, both of which he was amply familiar with. Boarding school had prepared him well.

'This will never do.' The Queen turned back to Charlotte. 'We have reached the final stage of negotiations.'

'The story's in all the papers. We can't undo it now,' Nicholas muttered. 'They'll have to marry.'

'Papers make mistakes. Our PR team could work out something.'

'No.' Rocco's voice broke into the room, his patience already at breaking point. He felt Charlotte's eyes on him, silently pleading with him to be quiet, but Rocco understood what she did not: they held all the cards. 'This marriage will go ahead, as planned.'

The Queen's lips parted, shock evident.

'I beg your pardon?'

'I've proposed to Charlotte. She's accepted. Our marriage will take place as soon as it can be arranged.'

'But—you—don't understand.'

He reached down for Charlotte's hand, squeezing it to reassure her. It trembled within his own.

'I think I understand perfectly. We're sorry your plans are ruined, but it can't be helped. Charlotte will be marrying me.'

'The negotiations have been ongoing—'

'Who is this man?' Charlotte's father cut over her mother. 'What do we know of him? Nothing, except he's worth a fortune. Money isn't enough, Charlotte. You're supposed to marry someone royal, to beget a true royal heir.'

Rocco felt Charlotte tremble and wanted to punch something. This was completely absurd. How could anyone think they had a right to control another person to this degree?

'Let me be clear.' Rocco spoke again. 'Charlotte and I will marry. Unless you intend to imprison us, the marriage will take place in the next week or so. We will happily relocate to Europe, or America, and raise our family there, if that's more palatable?'

Silence.

'Or…' he softened his voice, aware he was calling their bluff and that they'd fold like a cheap suit '…if you can find it in yourselves to be supportive of your daughter's choice, and to respect the boundaries of our marriage, we'll stay here. But only for so long as this works for us. Is that clear?'

Charlotte could only stare at him as they left the parlour, her eyes huge in her face.

'Oh, my God,' she whispered, trembling. 'You're…'

'Yes?' He looked down at her, his eyes sparking with hers.

Her tummy rolled. 'I can't believe it. *No one* has ever spoken to them like that. The things you said—'

'Don't tell me I went too far,' he said, lips grim. 'Not after the way they treated you.'

Warmth spread through her. 'No, I think you were wonderful,' she corrected, reaching out and squeezing his arm. 'It never occurred to me to threaten to leave, but of course, they don't want that.' Her eyes dropped. Not because of her. Not because they loved her and wanted to be with her, but because she was necessary to them.

Bitterness spread through her but only for a brief flash. It was impossible to indulge that negative emotion for long when a moment of such triumph had just been enjoyed.

'How can you let them treat you that way?'

Charlotte sighed. 'It's just the way they are. I'm used to it.'

He stopped walking, his features rigid in his handsome face. 'It's a wonder you have any self-esteem at all.'

Her eyes lifted to his, and her heart stammered, because she felt so exposed to him, so incredibly seen.

'They're products of their upbringing and experiences.'

'That's true of everyone. But at some point, we all learn to treat other people with civility.'

'Is it true of you?'

His nostrils flared. 'Of course. I'd be stupid to think my mother's treatment didn't shape me into the man I am today.'

She hesitated, then reached out, putting her hand

lightly on his arm. Sparks travelled through her and she blinked at him, lost in a vortex of swirling desire.

'Your parents don't deserve you to make excuses for them.'

'They're not wholly bad.'

'Really?'

She let out a soft laugh. 'Do you know, my brother, Nicholas, once told me that before he got sick they were totally different.' Her hand dropped lower and then fell away to the space between them. 'I'd made a misstep at school,' she said unevenly, preferring not to think of that time. 'It was bad. They were furious. He was the only one who sought to comfort me. He tried to explain them to me. He told me what I'm telling you—life made them this way. Their fear of losing him, of being without an heir. It cracked something in them, and nothing can put it back together. It's not making excuses,' she said after a beat. 'It's…sympathy. I feel sorry for them, and I understand them.'

His eyes held hers for a second too long and then he lifted his hand, cupping her cheek. 'You are nothing like them.'

She startled, blinking up at him, curving her face into his touch instinctively.

'I do not think any tragedy on earth could make you treat our child that way.'

Fierce maternal instincts whipped at her spine. 'Never,' she promised, loudly enough for the tiny little life inside of her to hear.

His look of satisfaction made her tummy twist. She stood there, trapped by the power of the moment, the sweet warmth of his connection. 'Why don't you show me to my room?'

She gasped softly, the question burning through her,

so she nodded, not wanting to dislodge his touch, but desperately wanting to be somewhere more private with him.

'The family suites are in the east wing. Upstairs.'

'Show me.'

Anticipation fired a thousand arrows beneath her skin and she turned at the same time he dropped his hand. It was a long walk, and each step of the way she was aware of his frame, his strength, his power, as he strode. Every time his hand brushed hers an electrical current sparked through her body, so it was both a relief and torture when they reached the door to his suite.

'My apartment is just there.' She gestured down the corridor, to two wide doors, then pushed in the doors to his room. Security was light in this part of the palace—only two guards stood sentry at the top of the stairs. She relaxed as they moved into his suite, in complete privacy.

Rocco stood, hands on hips as he surveyed what he could see from this vantage point—an entranceway, a lounge area, a small kitchen, mainly for making tea and coffee—and then he moved deeper, poking his head into the bedroom, another room—a larger sitting room—then through the French doors that led to a balcony.

'I'll convert that into an office.'

She wasn't about to argue. Not after he'd just defended her so spectacularly. Not when her body was alight with desire and need.

'Just let your staff know if there's anything you require.'

His lips quirked as he turned to face her.

'How do you feel?'

'What do you mean?'

His eyes dropped lower, to her stomach, and her heart squeezed at the reminder of the baby that joined them.

'Fine. I get a little tired, but that's the only symptom I have so far.'

He nodded his approval, then moved to her, putting his hands on her hips, eyes intense. 'When will you tell your parents?'

'After the wedding,' she said quickly. 'I know it would get them off our case, to some extent, but,' she searched for the right words, 'I'm not ready yet. At this moment, the baby is just ours. Once it's public the world will know and the publicity, the press…'

'You're not ready.'

'I'm not ready to share it,' she said, meaning both the baby and whatever was burgeoning between her and Rocco.

'We should discuss the wedding,' he said, moving closer, his body taunting hers, so she gasped when his frame connected with hers, all the ridges of his hard strength pressing against her.

'What would you like to discuss?' she asked unevenly.

'When? Where? How many people?'

'Lots of people,' she responded. 'Palace staff will take care of that. Just give your staff a guest list of anyone you want invited,' she prompted. Then, with a frown, 'Who will you invite?'

'No one.'

She lifted a brow. 'No one?'

He shook his head slowly. 'No.'

'No friends?'

'Is it necessary that I ask my friends to come?'

'No, but…it's normal.'

'This isn't a normal wedding,' he pointed out. 'We're marrying for this baby. I don't need friends to witness that.'

'Oh.' Her heart dropped for a moment at the stark,

honest reminder of their situation. It made her feel foolish and confused for forgetting, for letting herself get
carried away in desire, and by the way he'd defended her.

'That upsets you?'

'No,' she lied, forcing her face into a mask of composure. 'It doesn't bother me at all, one way or the other.'

'Good. I'd hate to bother you,' he said, voice low and
teasing, so desire spread through her.

She sucked in a shuddering breath. 'As for when,' she
said, trying to concentrate, 'you said within a week and
I think that makes sense. The timing of the baby means
that fewer questions will be asked...'

'Yes,' he agreed, dropping his face so his mouth was
only inches from hers. 'It also means we only have to
wait a few nights, at the most.'

She blinked up at him. 'For what?'

His smile was a flash on his face and then he was kissing her, his hands on her hips digging in, holding her hard
against him, so she trembled, the feeling of his arousal
stirring her to fever-pitch. 'I can't wait,' she said honestly.

He laughed softly, drawing his mouth down her throat,
teasing the flesh there, flicking her with his tongue. 'Yes,
you can,' he promised, lifting her up, carrying her towards the doors. Only instead of taking her through them,
he put her feet down and pressed her back against them.
She stared up at him, lost and confused and awash with
a need that was making her body sing.

'Has any man ever touched you here?' he asked, slowly
drawing his hand up her thigh, beneath her skirt, to the
lace edge of her knickers.

She shook her head, biting hard into her lip at the totally intimate touch.

'Not like this?' he asked as he brushed a part of her

that made Charlotte feel as though she could launch into space.

'No.' The word trembled out of her, uneven and desperate.

'No? You want me to stop?'

'Don't you dare,' she bit out. 'I meant no one has ever touched me there, and you know that,' she panted as he moved his fingers faster, eyes watching her with a scrutiny that made her ache, and made her feel vulnerable, all at once.

'Ah, I see.' Faster, until she couldn't keep her eyes open a moment longer, until she was trembling with the force of what he was doing to her, heat exploding through her. He drove a finger into her then and she bucked against him and might have fallen if his other arm hadn't clamped around her for support. She was a rag doll in his arms, riding the eddies of pleasure and satisfaction he'd given her.

'You are so wet,' he murmured in her ear, his voice light and warm, so she turned her face and captured his lips, kissing him with all the passion that was moving through her. 'I cannot wait to make you mine again.'

'Then don't wait,' she begged. 'I want you now.'

'I know.' He pulled away, moving his hand from her, straightening her skirt, though he kept one hand wrapped around her elbow, just in case her wobbling knees gave way completely. 'Organise our wedding for as soon as it can be arranged.'

She wanted to weep with frustration. His touch had been fabulous, but it was a foreshadowing of more, not a conclusion. Not enough on its own. 'This isn't fair,' she said, pouting softly. 'What difference does it make whether we're married or not? You don't strike me as the old-fashioned type.'

'I'm not,' he agreed, kissing the tip of her nose. 'But you are. And Charlotte?'

She blinked, her heart strangely full, given his reasoning.

'Would you ascertain that rigorous physical activity doesn't pose a risk to the pregnancy?'

Heat bloomed in her cheeks at the promise in those words, at the imminence of their wedding. 'Consider it done.'

A week after their return to Hemmenway came the morning of their wedding. Charlotte had barely seen Rocco. Not since the meeting with her parents, for any real stretch of time. She gathered, from Iris, that he worked during the days, and she hadn't dared ask about his nights. Not because she doubted his fidelity, but because imagining him at night led to all sorts of issues, namely with the strength and regularity of her heartbeat, and she wasn't sure she could manage it. It had seemed wiser to give him a wide berth. She wasn't sure she trusted herself to be near him and not throw herself at his feet and beg him to finish what he'd started the other day.

Every now and again she'd caught a glimpse of him, walking through a corridor, or through an open door, and her pulse had gone haywire, her body trembling as though convulsed by electricity.

It was a strange torment. She'd existed all her life without him, but suddenly, knowing he was here, in this very building, that they were about to become man and wife, had been a form of torture, even more so than the weeks after that first night together.

The wedding morning stretched interminably. Attendants helped her into the stunning cream gown, and a team of stylists completed a sophisticated updo, alongside elegant, understated make-up. She wore a ceremonial crown—heavy and sharp where it dug into her head—so she wanted the wedding to be over with for many reasons. Butterflies assaulted her belly. She walked with her father—who had been giving her the silent treatment—out into the sunlit courtyard of the palace, waving at the assembled crowds, who cheered loudly at their first sight of her. She smiled but her heart was doing somersaults.

Her life had begun to spin wildly out of control.

They were marrying for the sake of their baby, and yet the baby was the furthest thing from her mind as she slid into the open-top carriage, taking a seat beside her father. The crowd cheered loudly as he waved, and then the horses moved off, guiding them away from the ancient palace and towards the Royal Abbey with its stunning views over Halønner Valley.

People lined the streets the entire way there, held back by security cordons that were surely unnecessary. Their faces beamed with well wishes and happiness. Charlotte waved, pretending her tummy wasn't flip-flopping all over the place, until the carriage came to a stop at the historic abbey, a dusting of snow over the eaves.

She was marrying Rocco because it made sense. It was the right thing to do. They both felt that. And yet pleasurable anticipation zipped through Charlotte and the heat rushing in her veins had nothing to do with pragmatism and everything to do with raw desire. The same insatiable need that had overtaken her that night in New York pounded her body now so she was impatient with the fanfare of a royal wedding. She only wanted this over and done with, so the rest of their lives could begin—starting with tonight.

Twelve children had been arranged as flower girls and pageboys. Charlotte waited as they made their way

down the aisle, a smile pinned to her face that didn't
falter even when her nerves were pulling harder than a
tightrope. Finally the music changed, and with her hand
in the crook of her father's arm she began to walk the
long aisle of the abbey. Invited guests sat on either side
of the aisle. She barely registered them. From the moment her high-heeled shoes hit the carpet of the aisle, all
she could do was stare at Rocco. It was as though their
eye contact formed a vacuum, and the rest of the world
ceased to exist.

The air around them hummed and it was his gaze
drawing her forward, his cynical expression that was setting fire to her heart, making her cheeks heat and her fingers spark. She kept a smile on her face, the same smile
she'd employed for years, regardless of what she was feeling inside, but her eyes spoke to Rocco's showing exactly
what she was thinking, and what she wanted. Desire was
overtaking her, overriding sanity and sense. By the time
she reached him she was a live wire, so that the slightest
touch would likely set off a full-blown electrical storm.

Perhaps he knew, because he made no attempt at physical contact. Not for the entire ceremony. That much was
protocol and yet she'd expected—hoped—that Rocco's
penchant for doing his own thing might lead him to take
her hand, or reach across and press a kiss to her forehead.

Sexual chemistry was one thing, so too the decision
to marry for a baby, but to expect him to offer comfort
or reassurance was expecting too much. The way he'd
defended her to her parents had made her heart swell, but
she couldn't start relying on him for that, or for anything.
If she didn't want to be disappointed she had to keep reality locked firmly in her mind, and that reality was one
of convenience and necessity, nothing more.

The out-of-body sensation persisted, all through the

vows until the very end, when the bishop concluded the ceremony and issued the famous line, 'You may now kiss the bride.'

The audience erupted into cheers and their clapping popped in Charlotte's ears, amongst the humming and washing of her fast-moving pulse. Rocco's eyes held hers, probing them, something teasing and merciless in their depths, a promise that had her breath bursting through her body as she swayed forward. His arm clamped around her waist, drawing her the rest of the way to him, and she bit down on her lip, trying to remember where they were, and the fact they were being watched by hundreds of people, not to mention the hundreds of thousands across the country viewing the wedding on television.

His lips pressed to hers, and a thousand blades of lightning sliced through her, electrifying her, welding her to the spot, so she lifted a hand and curved her fingers around his arm, not for the need of physical contact so much as for support. Understanding that, he tightened his arm around her waist as he deepened the kiss, just enough to melt her bones, and then he pulled away, eyes flashing to hers with warning and promise. Her heart soared.

Neither spoke. They simply stared at each other, and for Charlotte it was as if she was trying to make a piece of the puzzle fit, or to massage her brain into working order. The world had ceased to make sense, but she wasn't sure she minded.

The kiss was an oasis in the midst of a long day of polite socialising. Far from her being able to get close to Rocco, it was as though the entire roster of guests was conspiring to keep them separated. She watched him from afar, trying to focus on the conversation swirling around her, even as her brain hurt from the reality of what she'd just done. No, not of what she'd done but of what stretched before her.

They were married.

Excitement trilled in her veins and, even though circumstances had forced them into this, she felt a rush of pleasure at having subverted the life that had been carefully planned for her. It wasn't as though she'd co-ordinated this, but at least it was more a future of her choosing than anyone else's.

Finally, after what felt like days, the formal proceedings came to an end, and tradition allowed the couple to depart. Her insides squirmed with the now familiar sensation of anticipation. Iris had mentioned something about a honeymoon, but Charlotte hadn't been paying attention; everything she was had been focused squarely on the wedding itself. As they left the palace via a side gate, it was to see a black four-wheel drive with darkly tinted windows. There was no crowd, no fanfare, just a single driver waiting with the door open.

Charlotte slid into the back of the seat, a thousand emotions rioting through her.

Rocco took the seat beside her and reached across Charlotte, drawing the seatbelt across her body, clicking it into place before lifting his eyes to hers, impossible to read and ever-assessing. A faint noise indicated the blackened screen was lifting, to give privacy from the driver, and a thrill of excitement rushed through Charlotte at the idea of being closeted away with her husband for the first time as a married couple.

'Mrs Santinova,' he said quietly, as though testing the words in his mouth, with no idea of the effect they had on her. Charlotte's heart slammed to a stop.

'Your Highness,' Charlotte responded, because their wedding had conferred titles on Rocco. He was now

Crown Prince of Hemmenway, as well as Count of Al-
amorrën.

Cynicism touched his face. 'I think, for me, we will
stick to Rocco.'

She angled her face sideways, studying him as the
car pulled away from the palace, onto the dark streets of
Hemmenway. Christmas lights were strung from pole
to pole, creating a magical effect that Charlotte always
loved, but tonight she paid it no heed. 'You aren't someone who aspires to this lifestyle, are you?'

'Does anyone?' he volleyed back, shifting so he could
see her better, his body unconsciously forming a frame
around her.

'I think a lot of people probably do.'

'There's a level of fantasy about it, true. But you've
lived it. Would you wish this on your worst enemy?'

The coldness of his voice surprised her, so too his
conviction. 'It's not so bad.'

'Really?'

She turned her face slightly, but his hand lifted, catching her chin and guiding her back to him, so their faces
were separated by only an inch.

'You are monitored everywhere you go. You have no
personal freedom, no ability to live the life you would
choose for yourself. You are a captive of your kingdom,
Princess. I don't find the idea of that appealing.'

'You do realise we just got married?' she responded
breathlessly, unable to think straight for how close they
were. 'This is your life now too.'

'We'll see.' His rejoinder was now familiar to her, and
something like worry unfurled in her belly.

'Rocco, please…' But what could she say? 'You knew
what you were getting into when you proposed this,
right?' Anxiety pummelled her.

'Sure.'

'And you're going to behave—'

'Like a good little crown prince?'

She almost rolled her eyes, but they were so close, and her pulse was doing funny things, so instead she just nodded, once, her throat thick with unspoken words.

He moved closer, his lips teasing the flesh beneath her ear. 'Even when being bad is so much more fun?'

Her heart started somersaulting through her body. 'Rocco...' But her hand lifted and curled in the fabric of his shirt, so she couldn't have said what she was thinking, nor what she wanted. Pleasure exploded through her, desire thick in her veins.

Whatever she'd been about to say was swallowed up by his kiss, the brush of his lips against hers making speech and thought impossible. She groaned low in her throat, knowing she should fight this, that she had to retain control, but that was an almost impossible feat in the midst of the assault her body was waging on her mind.

He moved his mouth lower, to the flesh at her neck, and when his tongue lashed the pulse point there she felt as though her soul was divorced from her body, shooting into the heavens. 'In answer to your question, no, I do not particularly respect any royal institution.' His words were at odds with the delicious feelings that were spreading through her. 'I despise the idea, in fact.'

'And yet you married me.'

'You are carrying my baby. What choice did either of us have?' His mouth moved lower still, teasing the fabric at the top of her wedding dress, before his hand pushed down the strap, and then, lifting his eyes to hers with a cynical expression, he pushed it even lower, challenging her all the while to say something.

Everything shifted. Danger felt so close and so too

did release. She wasn't under any illusions, she knew why they'd married, but hearing him distil everything they were down to one pragmatic sentence made her ache inside.

'Our baby is going to be a prince or princess one day.'

He released one of her breasts, holding it in his hand a moment before dropping his mouth to it and taking her nipple in his mouth so she exclaimed loudly, bucking her hips forward. Thoughts scattered like marbles thrown across the floor; stars lit in her eyes.

'That cannot be helped.' His words no longer made sense. She couldn't keep hold of their conversation. Her mind was in total disarray. She knew there was something important there, something she should probe, but how could she marshal her thoughts when he was doing such wonderful things to her body?

His sucked on her nipple until she couldn't bear it and she moved in her seat, trying desperately to be closer to him, but there were too many impediments—from the close confines of the car to the seatbelt she wore, to his suit and her voluminous wedding dress, but all of a sudden the flicker of desire she'd been feeling since they arrived in Hemmenway, the sleepless nights spent wanting him, craving him, exploded into a bonfire of savage need.

'I want… This isn't…' She searched for the right words, desperate to express how she was feeling. His hand moved between her legs, fighting to find a path through the heavy skirts she wore until finally his fingertips brushed her bare thigh and she jolted at the contact.

'What you need is for me to make love to you,' he said gruffly, moving his mouth back to hers, kissing the words into her soul. 'But I'm going to make you wait just a little while longer.'

Her heart stammered and disappointment lurched through her.

'Why?'

His fingers crept higher. 'There are many things that come before sex, Princess.' He brushed aside the satin of her underpants, finding the heart of her sex and pressing against it so she cried out, the sound involuntary.

He dragged his mouth down her front again, to her other breast, biting down on her nipple through the structured fabric of her dress so the pressure was just right. More stars burst through her field of vision and she shifted a little, trying to give his hand better access to her sex. He made a throaty sound—a laugh?—but he did what she desperately needed and pressed a finger inside of her, so her muscles squeezed around him in gratitude and her heart sped up as his mouth shifted to her other breast, and he rolled his tongue over her exposed nipple. 'I am going to make you beg for me, *cara*. I am going to make you want me more than you have ever known you could want anything in your life. I am going to make you mad with longing. *That* is desire.'

'You almost make it sound like a punishment,' she said quietly, uncaring, though, as she tilted her head back to give him better access to all of her.

He stilled, the finger buried inside of her stopping its circling, so she ground her hips, inviting him, begging him, for more.

'There is so much you have to learn,' he said gruffly.

'I'm a quick learner.'

'I hope not. I intend this to take a long, long time.' The car pulled to a stop, jolting her out of the sensual web he'd spun through the air. She looked around, aware the driver usually appeared at the door within seconds. Rocco moved with laconic efficiency, removing himself and straightening her skirt, before lifting a hand to her dress and repositioning it so she looked almost as she had when she'd entered the car. Only a flush on her cheeks provided any indication how they'd spent the drive.

His promise ran through her head—'*I intend this to take a long, long time...*'—so her legs weren't at all steady as she stepped out of the car and found them at the royal airport, a gleaming plane right in front of them.

Rather than the official jet for the royal family, which was run by the armed guards, this bore a gold R and S along the side, so it took her only a moment to realise this was his plane. He put an arm around her waist, drawing her to his side as they moved towards the steps, the driver following with their luggage. Charlotte had been so focused on the wedding, she knew nothing of the details of the honeymoon. In fact, she'd presumed they'd spend a night at another palace, and then return to their lives as they'd been before. The idea of going away with Rocco flooded her with excitement, but that was nothing to how she felt when he leaned closer and whispered in her ear, 'Lesson number one, Charlotte. You're going to see what it's like to lose your mind at thirty-one thousand feet.'

She couldn't get on board the aircraft quickly enough.

CHAPTER SEVEN

IT WAS FAR more luxurious than the royal jet, which, for the sake of appearances, had to walk a fine line between being suitable for the country's perception of the royal family, but not be too ostentatious. The furnishings were minimal and in keeping with an ordinary aircraft, whereas aboard Rocco's jet everything was the last word in extravagance.

A single, wide armchair sat on either side of the aisle, though they could be swivelled to face backwards, to enable conversation. Behind the armchairs was a room with a sofa and large-screen television and, behind that, a boardroom. They moved beyond it to two bedrooms, one after the other, and every bit as beautifully appointed as a five-star hotel.

Charlotte eyed the beds with a growing sense of need, heat flushing through her at his promise.

'Come and sit down, for take-off,' he said, drawing her back through the plane towards the armchairs. He gestured to one, standing over her as she sat down, arranging her wedding dress over her knees primly, so his smile was mocking.

'Don't bother. I'm going to get rid of that as soon as we're up in the air.'

This version of Rocco was setting her pulse on fire.

He was being so direct, so sensual, blowing any expectations she'd had of their marriage out of the water.

He took the seat in front of her but pulled a lever and swivelled it, so that they were facing each other, too far apart to touch, their eyes locked so her pulse went haywire regardless, because looking at Rocco and not being able to reach for him was its own form of torture. Or perhaps that was pleasure? She knew only that her nerves were stretched tight, and her pulse was quivering.

'You must have had fantasies,' he said quietly, so she had to strain to catch the question.

Her heart stammered and heat pooled between her legs. 'I'm sorry?' She wasn't about to reveal the thoughts that had kept her up every night this week. Not to Rocco!

His eyes probed hers. 'Every person has sexual fantasies.'

Her lips formed a perfect circle. Not only did she have no real experience with sex, but talking about it also felt wrong. She hated that prudish side to her nature, she hated that even with this man, who drove her wild, she didn't feel as though she could own this side of herself. 'Not really,' she responded with a shrug.

His laugh teased her, so embarrassment formed a rock in the pit of her stomach. 'Don't laugh at me,' she said with quiet strength. 'I might not have your experience, but that doesn't mean you can treat me with disrespect.'

He sobered immediately. 'That wasn't my intention.'

She looked away from him, swirling with uncertainty, as the jet's engines fired to life, powerful and raw. The plane reverberated and she gripped the armrests, staring out of the window as it began to taxi.

'Look at me.' His words were low and raspy, a command that she wanted to ignore, but couldn't. Slowly, she pivoted to give him the full force of her attention and her heart exploded. 'Tell me what you want.'

'I can't,' she whispered, not pretending to misunderstand. 'I'm rubbish at this. I'm not like you. I don't have any idea what I want, because I have no experience, no vernacular around sex. I only know that when you touch me, I feel as though I'm about to incinerate. I know I like that.'

Triumph flared in his eyes, but he concealed it quickly. 'That's a good start.'

The plane picked up speed, taxiing quickly down the runway before lifting up, tilting at an angle. She held the armrests more tightly, not because she was afraid of flying, but because of the sensations that were rioting through her, the strength of desire that was strangling her, making her feel as though everything in her life depended on being in this man's arms, on feeling his possession of her once more.

'What are your fantasies?' she pushed back at him, as the plane climbed higher into the sky.

'I'm looking at one.'

She furrowed her brow. 'That's cheating.'

'Why?'

'Well, I could have said that.'

'Is it true?'

She hesitated a moment. 'What do you think?'

His smile showed slow, sensual approval. 'You never thought about escaping from the palace, Rapunzel-style, and living a little?'

'Not until that night.'

'Tell me about it,' he invited, his pose relaxed, in direct contradiction to the way her own nerves were misfiring.

The plane began to level off and her heart pounded, his promise ringing in her ears. She was nervous, and talking was both a blessing and a curse. In a sense, it soothed her nerves, but it also prolonged her wait, and all she wanted was to be close to him now.

'What would you like to know?' The question emerged breathy, and his smile was knowing. He clearly understood what effect he was having on her.

'You went to school in England.'

She frowned. 'How do you know?'

'Your brother mentioned it.'

'Oh.' Her brow furrowed; she vaguely recalled her brother having made a comment during their first meeting. 'You've been speaking to Nicholas?'

'Briefly. He wanted to speak to me about some opportunities. Given my background, he thought I might be interested in being the head of the finance committee.'

Her jaw dropped. 'What did you tell him?'

'That I'm happy to advise.'

Her heart stammered but something a bit like jealousy moved through her. Charlotte had been given frothy roles within the palace, but never once had she been looked to for anything beyond breeding.

'He said you were sent away at eleven.'

She flinched. 'Did he?'

Rocco's eyes held hers, studying her. Charlotte nodded slowly.

'Yes, I attended Halforth.'

'Halforth is co-educational. You must have met boys there?'

'Sure.'

'No one you liked though?'

'Not particularly.' She plaited her fingers together in her lap, fidgeting in that moment as she remembered past hurts, pains that had, at the time, felt as though they would never lift. 'Not enough to jump into bed with them.'

'Heaven forbid.'

'Okay, Mr Cynic, what about you?' she asked, frustration chafing her. 'You're acting like my virginity is some kind of crime against humanity. How old were you?'

He regarded her thoughtfully and for a moment she thought he wasn't going to answer. 'Sixteen.'

Her eyes widened. Now she really did feel as though she'd been left behind. 'To whom?'

He hesitated, eyes probing hers for several beats.

'What is it?' she asked, leaning forward. 'Cat got your tongue?'

'There are some things I prefer not to discuss.'

Curiosity brimmed. 'We're married. Doesn't that mean we're not supposed to have secrets?'

'I don't think there's a hard and fast rule.'

'Fine, indulge me anyway.'

He lifted his shoulders slowly in a nonchalant gesture of unconcern that didn't quite ring true. 'She was the mother of a boy who went to my school. Someone in my grade.'

Her lips parted. 'A friend of yours?'

His mouth tightened into something that was neither grimace nor smile. 'No.'

She blinked, confused. 'How old was she?'

The only sign that he was bothered by her question was the tightening of his hand on his knee, so his knuckles turned white. 'Old enough to know better. She would have been in her late thirties.'

'You were just a child,' Charlotte said angrily.

'I knew what I was doing.'

'You were *sixteen*.'

'Yes. And I regret my actions on that day, but I was angry, and she was there.'

Charlotte's heart was thumping for a different reason entirely now. 'That's amoral.'

'It was sex and I was a hormonal teenager.'

'I mean of *her*,' Charlotte spluttered. 'You should report her.'

'I seduced her, *cara*. I made it happen.'

'She should have said no.'

'Perhaps.'

'Why did you seduce her?' Charlotte pushed, absolutely certain there was more to it than a case of misfiring hormones.

But when she asked the question he looked away, his face in profile stern and unresponsive.

'Did you think you were in love with her or something?'

He made a sharp noise, a sound something like a bark. 'Love? No, Charlotte. I was as little interested in love then as I am now. I've always been a realist. I saw her as a means to an end.'

The hairs on the back of Charlotte's neck stood up. 'To lose your virginity?'

He slid his gaze back to hers, the look in his eyes now completely unapologetic. 'To hurt her son.'

Charlotte gasped. 'You're kidding me.'

A muscle throbbed in Rocco's jaw. 'I wouldn't make that decision today, but at the time I was furious. It seemed fitting.'

'And you got to have sex, so you were really killing two birds with one stone, right?'

'You're angry about this.'

She made a sound of surprise. 'I'm—not angry, no. I'm…'

'Disgusted?'

'Using someone for revenge is pretty disgusting behaviour, isn't it?'

His features tightened, his eyes showing a dark emotion she didn't understand. 'Yes.' He hesitated a moment in an uncharacteristic gesture of uncertainty. 'As I said, I wouldn't make that choice now.'

'But you were only sixteen,' she murmured, her tone softening as she made allowances for his age, and remembered how he'd defended her to his parents. He deserved the benefit of the doubt, particularly over something that had happened more than a decade earlier. 'And angry.' She leaned forward, reaching for a bottle of mineral water that had been stashed in the pocket beside her seat. 'What about?'

'Nothing important.'

She frowned, digesting that. 'It was important enough to seduce his mother.'

'It seemed important at the time. I can barely remember now, however.'

Charlotte turned her face towards the window as she considered what he'd said. She was almost positive that he was lying. Even as a teenager, Rocco Santinova struck her as someone who would have a non-negotiable moral compass, meaning that if he'd been angry enough to take such drastic action, his anger must have run deep—and been serious. And yet she was asking him to reveal personal information about himself when she had done little of that herself. She hesitated a moment.

'I did meet a guy once,' she said quietly, already regretting her honesty.

He made a noise of enquiry, urging her to continue.

'Well, I met him online,' she said softly. 'I was fifteen, and away at school. I was...' She hesitated, because exposing the truth of her adolescence was something she'd avoided for a long time. 'I was not having a particularly good time. I didn't have many friends, and believe it or not I missed home tremendously. It's not like our family's close, but at least at the palace I was left alone. I could read in my room all day and no one would care. Whereas at school…' She paused, hesitating.

'Yes?'

'I didn't fit in.' She shrugged. 'I was awkward and shy, and a late bloomer,' she said, focusing on her hands. 'Whereas most of the girls in my year had started to fill out, I was still flat-chested and had zero interest in boys, which earned me a lot of mocking from both the males and females in my form.'

When he said nothing, she risked a glance at him. His features were locked in a mask of concentration, his eyes focused intently on her face.

'I started going online more and more, losing myself in games. I did so under an alias, because it's been programmed into me from a very young age to be careful about what I share. I thought I was safe.'

'But?'

'They knew who I was,' she whispered, then cleared her throat, reminding herself this had happened almost a decade earlier. 'I wasn't chatting to one young man, but a team of frauds.'

'You were catfished.'

She nodded awkwardly at his pronouncement. 'It went on for months. I truly thought he cared for me, so when he asked me…' She paused, sucking in a deep breath then taking a sip of her mineral water to compose her fraying nerves. 'When he asked me for a topless photo, I sent it. I felt stupid—it wasn't like I was well-endowed—but I *trusted* him.'

'And?'

'They sent the photograph to my father, with a request for one million American dollars or they'd share it.'

'I can imagine how he reacted.'

'He was furious.'

Rocco's hand formed a fist and his eyes narrowed. 'You were the victim.'

'No one saw it that way.'

He swore softly. 'Did your father pay the ransom?'

'No.' She dropped her eyes to the floor between them. 'Interpol got involved. Technically, it was child pornography, and they were able to act swiftly to find the perpetrators. I was lucky.'

'Bastards'

'Yes.' Her lips formed a grimace. 'I learned a valuable lesson that day. Trust no one. It could have been so much worse.'

He nodded slowly. 'And so you locked yourself away from the world, avoiding relationships, avoiding sex, because you couldn't trust that your partner wouldn't have an ulterior motive.'

'Pretty much.' Her eyes met his. 'And then, that night, when I met you, everything felt different. I'd run away from Princess Charlotte. I was in New York, just a single woman finally taking a few hours to live my life, before I returned to Hemmenway and the marriage I'd been destined for. It was like I'd pressed pause on my usual responsibilities, on all the doubts and concerns I held, and I could finally live. When I slept with you I wasn't thinking about consequences or trust, because I wasn't expecting anything from you beyond that night. It was very liberating. Even the fact that you didn't know who I was made me free from the oppressive strictures of my normal life.'

'And then, ironically, you ended up trapped in this marriage to me.'

It was on the tip of her tongue to deny that. After all, that wasn't how she felt at all—if anything, this marriage had liberated her properly—but it was obvious he felt that way, so how could she contradict him? 'I think we're both trapped,' she muttered eventually, with a dip of her head, so he couldn't read the hurt in her eyes. It wouldn't do either of them any good to wonder why his description had cut her to the quick.

'And yet, there are some silver linings,' he murmured, unbuckling his seatbelt and standing, staring down at her for several beats, so her breath grew fast and raspy. A moment later, he held his hand out to her, and she put hers in it, standing until their bodies met and her heart thumped so hard she was sure he'd feel it.

Nothing had changed, really, and yet something within Charlotte was different, and when he kissed her it was as though bubbles were bursting all through her core, and she surrendered to him completely—even as the constant beating of a drum served as a portent for danger.

It was not a long flight into the north of Italy and it seemed to go far too quickly, given how they spent the time. The plane touched down before they realised it had commenced its descent, and Rocco had barely two minutes to find something for Charlotte to wear—Charlotte, who was trembling from the pleasure he'd given her, again and again, using only his mouth, so his own nerves were stretched tight, his arousal a deep pain now for how desperate he was to bury himself in her. But he'd promised himself he'd take his time. Charlotte deserved a proper sexual awakening—everyone did. If he'd known she was a virgin, he'd have avoided her with a ten-foot bargepole, but if under any circumstance he'd ever been convinced to become her first he would have stretched it out over days, building her to such a frenzy that the inevitable coming together was the icing on the cake rather than the whole event.

The cockpit doors opened, and the pilot stepped out, approaching Rocco as usual.

'Thanks, Ashton,' Rocco said with a nod. His pilot was ex US Air Force and he was built like it.

Ashton nodded. 'The car is waiting, sir, and the cabin is ready.'

'Cabin?' Charlotte appeared at his side, and now she looked every bit the regal Princess, her silky blonde hair secured in a low ponytail, her tailoring impeccable. Only a hint of his stubble rash on the side of her neck gave any clue how they'd spent the last forty minutes. He ached to pull her close, to kiss her again, to mark her some more so she could be in no doubt that she was his, and that temptation was all the more reason for him to keep his distance.

'Where we'll be staying for our honeymoon,' Rocco said carelessly, intentionally downplaying the significance of such an event.

'Where exactly are we?' Charlotte took his lead, and her voice remained level, her body carefully distant from his.

'The Aosta Valley.' He was careful to conceal the importance of this region to him. 'I have a place here.' He didn't tell her why he'd bought it, the grudges that had defined his life and actions for so long. None of that was relevant.

'Is this where you're from?'

He put a hand at her back, propelling her forward without answering.

'Where are my security guards?' she asked, frowning.

'I've made arrangements for your safety.' Hard-fought arrangements. Given the disdain with which her family treated Charlotte, they went to great lengths to protect her. The reason set his teeth on edge.

They valued her uterus, not her.

She was a commodity to them, born solely for the purpose of providing the heir Nicholas couldn't. Only Nicholas spoke of her like a human being, with her own wants and feelings and values. The similarities between his mother's treatment and Charlotte's had further underscored, all week, how right he'd been to pursue this marriage.

'Arrangements?' Her lips parted. 'I can't believe you were allowed to do that.'

'I can be very persuasive.'

'Meaning you bullied them into this?'

'I gave them my word you'd be safe, and I meant it.'

She nodded, but there was a look in her eyes he didn't understand, a look of hurt and sadness, so he wondered if he'd said or done something wrong, but then she was moving, stepping down and out of the aeroplane, her back straight and body language confident.

She was a mystery to him, more so than any other woman he'd ever met. Just when he thought he'd started to understand her, she morphed into something else, or closed a part of herself to him. He knew one thing for sure: she deserved a hell of a lot better than the life she'd been living.

He wasn't a knight in shining armour, but he'd been given an opportunity he hadn't known he'd needed. He could help Charlotte. He could give her a better life, make her happy, and, in doing for her what no one had *ever* done for his mother, he'd make sure their baby never felt as Rocco had. The impotence of seeing your mother's grief and rejection was a feeling their child would never know.

A moment later they were on the tarmac, where a black four-wheel drive with dark windows was waiting. Rocco held open the passenger door for her, then came around to the driver's side, jumping in and starting the engine.

'You're driving?'

'Why not?'

He caught the hint of a blush in her cheeks and found it hard to conceal his amusement. She preferred it when they were chauffeured, leaving him free to entertain her? Good to know.

'My cabin isn't far from here. Be patient, Princess. The night is young.'

CHAPTER EIGHT

NOTHING ABOUT ROCCO SANTINOVA had been run-of-the-mill. In every way since they'd met he'd defied her expectations, and this was no different. The cabin he led her into was rustic and charming, with none of the sleek elegance of his Manhattan penthouse. This was a proper, comfortable home, with a low-set sofa pointed towards enormous windows that she imagined would provide a lovely view in the morning. For now, all she could see was the milky moonlight and the silhouette of Alpine trees against an inky sky. The stars sparkled like diamond dust, and for a moment it was easy to forget any of her worries and simply exist—in the safety of the knowledge that the universe was ancient and expansive and she just a tiny, tiny part of it for a relatively infinitesimal time.

But then he spoke, and she was drawn back to the here and now—their wedding night—and her nerve endings frayed with anticipation and need. Despite how they'd spent the flight into Italy, desire was exploding through her, demanding indulgence.

'I'll give you a tour.' His voice was gruff but there was something to the words that had her pausing. He seemed hesitant. Nervous? Or apprehensive? Neither made any sense. She didn't know Rocco that well but on some basic level she understood that he wasn't someone who was nervous in any circumstance. He had the world at his feet and was more than happy commanding it.

As for Charlotte, her stomach was in knots, but the good kind. Pleasurable anticipation had settled low in her belly and all she could do was surrender to it. 'That sounds nice. I'd like to see it.'

He lowered his head in acknowledgement, gesturing around the room. 'This is the lounge.'

She tilted her head to the side. 'So I see.'

'Kitchen.' He moved closer, brushing past her as he headed towards a large, open-plan kitchen with a big wraparound bench and an island set up with bar stools. Despite its enormous size, the timber finishings made it feel homely.

'It looks so comfortable, so…lived-in.'

'I'm here quite often.' The response was cryptic. It sounded as though he was answering her question but actually it gave very little away.

'How often?'

'Whenever I can be.'

She frowned, because his life of being able to come and go at will was about to be curtailed. Did he understand the restrictions he'd face as a senior royal? She pressed her hand against her stomach and bit back the question. She didn't want to draw attention to how much he might hate his new married life, but deep down she suspected this was going to be a tough adjustment for someone like Rocco.

'You must love it.'

He frowned. So that wasn't it, then. Curiosity expanded inside of her, filling all the crevices. He told her he'd been born in Italy, but raised in New York, and suddenly the dearth of what she knew about the man she'd

married—the man who was to be the father of her baby—
hit her like a sledgehammer.

'Are you hungry?'

She shook her head. She hadn't eaten much at their
wedding reception but all her senses were occupied by
Rocco and her desire for him. Food was the last thing
on her mind.

'The kitchen's fully stocked. If you need anything,
help yourself. Or if that's not something princesses know
how to do, let me know and I'll fix you something.'

Her heart stammered, because he was right—she
didn't generally wade into kitchens and prepare her own
meals, but she was pretty sure she could work it out. 'I've
seen it done on TV,' she responded archly.

Her reward was Rocco's grin, sensual enough to set
her soul on fire. She sucked in a deep breath, needing
more air in her body. 'Then you're practically a chef.'

Her own lips twitched with a small smile, and then
Rocco was moving once more, to the back of the kitchen,
where there was a door with a glass circle halfway up.
'The boot room. Skis, coats, that sort of thing.'

'Skis?' Her pulse picked up a notch.

'Sure.'

'You ski here?'

'We are in the northernmost point of Italy. Yes, the
skiing is excellent.'

She loved skiing. It was one of the few sports at which
she excelled, and as a teenager, when things had been
particularly difficult for her at school, she'd lost herself
on the hardest courses in Hemmenway, loving the sensation of being almost in free fall. It had been invigorating
and strangely reassuring.

He moved back through the kitchen but this time, as
he passed, he took her hand, holding it in his, so electric

shocks seemed to travel the length of her arm. She tried to conceal the response but failed.

Beyond the lounge room, there was an office space, sparsely furnished with enormous windows behind the desk, and then timber stairs that led to a landing with a big skylight overhead. For the moment, it showed only snow, so she smiled, imagining how beautiful the outlook would be in the morning.

Upstairs was…intimate. There was no other way to describe it. One bedroom with an enormous, four-poster timber bed, a bathroom, and a small sitting room with a lovely fabric-covered sofa.

'It's like something out of a picture book,' she said softly, her voice quivering a little as she contemplated the bedroom. It was their honeymoon, but somehow she'd imagined they'd continue to have a degree of separation. This cabin promised a whole lot of proximity, and the idea made her blood flow warm. 'It's definitely not the kind of place I'd imagine you owning.'

'No?'

She shook her head, trying to ignore the bed in the middle of the room.

'What did you imagine?'

'Something uber-masculine and modern, like your place in New York.'

'You don't find all this…' he banged the timber side table '…masculine?'

Her heart lifted into her throat and she didn't say what she was thinking—that Rocco could make a doll's house look masculine. 'I like it,' she said, simply. 'It suits you.'

'The furniture came with the place. I saw no reason to change it.'

'When did you buy the cabin?'

His expression hardened for a moment and then he

smiled, but it didn't change the emotion in his eyes. She felt wariness there and shivered. 'A few years ago.'

Another evasive answer.

'Is this where you're from?' She repeated the question she'd asked earlier, the question he'd simply not answered.

His eyes probed hers, darkly intent, as he began to walk towards her. 'You're full of questions tonight.' Again, he evaded. She took note, filing that away, to resolve another time.

'I suppose I am,' she agreed.

'And is talking what you really want to be doing?'

Her breath caught in her throat, because he was so close now, and his question such an obviously leading one that her heart pummelled her and she felt pulled in a thousand directions. On the one hand, she wanted to understand the man she'd married better than she currently did. On the other, her body was alive with desperate longing and all she could think of was how he was capable of making her feel. He was using her sexual appetite to curtail her questioning, but she was full enough of raging desire not to mind.

Nerves made her fingertips tremble. It wasn't her first time, and in fact she'd been naked with him on the plane, but she was nervous now, because it was their first night as a married couple and he'd brought her to this incredibly beautiful and *real* place, somewhere that seemed important to him. It was way more than she'd expected, and it added an extra layer of meaning to what they were about to do. She tried to stop herself from reading into it, but her heart was flooding with warmth regardless.

She lifted a hand to his chest, feeling the beating of his heart. She was fighting a losing battle and yet she knew she needed to say something to show him how grateful she was. He'd taken their practical marriage of convenience, something neither of them wanted, and was finding a way to make it work. 'Thank you for bringing me here.' Her eyes locked to his. 'I really like it.'

His square jaw remained locked, his eyes probing hers. 'In the morning, you will like it even better. The view in New York is nothing compared to this.'

'I can't wait,' she whispered, but all thoughts of the morning, the view, and conversation fled her mind when he kissed her, and she lost herself to him completely. He was her husband, and for that night they were not a prince and princess but just two people completely at the mercy of their bodies' desires…and it was wonderful.

He'd promised her the view would be lovely, but she hadn't expected anything quite so breathtaking as this.

'I've woken up in a postcard,' she said with a shake of her head, pushing her blonde hair over one shoulder and out of her eyes so she could see better.

'Who's looking at the trees, though?' he responded drily, and a quick glance in his direction showed that Rocco's attention was focused squarely on her negligee-clad body. Heat flooded her cheeks as memories of their night came back to her—the way he'd pleasured her with his hands, his mouth, teasing her, driving her to the edge of sanity before pulling back and kissing her, so she was pleading with him, over and over, to make her his. It was a delicious torment—the elongating of desire, the extension of their pleasure, so that finally, when he did enter her in one hard thrust, she'd almost fallen apart at the seams, the satisfaction of finally feeling him inside her again like nothing she could describe.

And despite the fact she'd already been at breaking point, and tipped over the edge almost immediately, Rocco's control was incredible. He waited for her to come back to earth and then began to move, again showing his mastery by bringing her to the brink of explosion and this time tipping over it with her, so their cries mingled and limbs entangled, and they fell asleep in one another's arms, covered in perspiration and satiated by passion.

At some point in the small hours of the morning they'd made love again, more urgently this time, with far less restraint, as though they'd woken a primal, hungry beast and it demanded feeding. He'd taken her as if his life depended on it, and she knew in that moment that hers did, too. Every breath she took was for the purpose of this satisfaction. She had started to exist purely for the pleasure of being with him, and that knowledge sat inside her like a warm, glowing beacon.

After twenty-four years of being told how to live her life, there was an illicit charm in having this real, passionate relationship, something that was all hers. No one in her family, no one from the palace staff, had any say in her marriage. This was all Charlotte's doing. And their baby's.

And just like that, the pleasure and warmth disappeared for a moment, as she forced herself to remember that passion was only a product of necessity. It was the silver lining he'd found to their marriage, but, given the choice, he wouldn't be here with her. This was all because she'd fallen pregnant.

Charlotte was excited about the baby; she couldn't wait to meet him or her, but for a moment she wished, with all her heart, that they'd had a chance to be a couple just for the sake of it.

It would never have happened though. He'd also made that clear to her. Rocco Santinova was not a man looking for love. He didn't want a real relationship, and this was simply sex. Because she was there. Available. His by marriage, and now, in many other ways, too.

A danger siren she'd become familiar with blared, as she told herself she needed to keep that perspective, to remember that this was just a marriage of convenience, just as her marriage to the Sheikh would have been.

She pushed her feet out of bed, intending escape, only her stomach lurched and a wave of nausea assaulted her. Charlotte closed her eyes a moment, until it had passed, and, though it was only the work of an instant, Rocco saw and moved quickly, a hand on her back solicitous.

'Princess?'

She blinked across at him. 'I'm okay.' Her smile was weak. After all, this marriage was starting to feel like a double-edged sword, but she couldn't think about that.

'You're ill?'

'Just a little nauseous. It's normal.'

He frowned, eyes probing hers. 'Are you certain?'

His concern made her laugh, and it caused her heart to stir, too, so she stepped out of bed to prove her point. 'The doctor told me to expect it.'

His face was a mask of concern. 'You must let me know if I'm tiring you. Last night…'

She heard the guilt catch in his voice and shook her head, needing to reassure him. 'Last night was wonderful,' she promised. 'If I'm tired today, I'll nap. But I'd rather be tired than…'

Her voice trailed off into nothing as she realised what she'd been about to admit.

'Than?' he prompted, standing, bringing his body close to hers, hands on her hips splayed wide so his fingers could stroke her flesh.

She stayed silent, so he moved his head forward, kissing the flesh beneath her ear, sending her pulse into over-drive.

'Than not be together?' he enquired silkily, all too aware of the power he had over her.

She made a noise low in her throat and he laughed softly, a sound that was filled with promise, and then he was lifting her as though she weighed no more than a rose.

'What are you doing?' she asked huskily, making no attempt to move from his arms.

'Let's shower.'

CHAPTER NINE

'IT'S LIKE BEING all wrapped up in Christmas magic,' she said with a smile, her hand stretching out to catch some fine snowflakes that were falling, eyes roaming across the expansive green forest. 'They're so beautiful.'

'I suppose so.'

'You *suppose* so?' She turned her face towards his, and her heart gave a funny little pang, because he was really far too handsome, and after the morning they'd had she felt a strange unreality developing around them, something she needed to fight—but wasn't sure she knew how. Here, far away from the rest of the world, in this beautiful, snowy Alpine hideaway, she felt as though she was living a fantasy. Here, it was easy to forget that life that awaited her—them—back in Hemmenway. A life of duty and order and responsibility, a life that had constrained her since birth.

'It's just a forest.'

'But filled with a thousand pines, all the richest dark green and covered in snow. They're just like enormous Christmas trees.' She sighed. 'It almost makes me want to pick one—a small one—to decorate.' A wistful smile pulled at her lips. 'I've never decorated my own tree, you know.'

'No?'

She shook her head slowly. 'The palace is decorated on the twelfth of December every year. I wake up and suddenly it's just Christmas spirit, in every direction.'

'And that's bad?'

'Of course not. I love Christmas, and the traditional decorations that fill the palace to bursting are utterly beautiful, made of the finest glass, or hand-carved timber, all so detailed you can barely believe it.'

He watched her, silently.

'But they're almost too perfect, you know? When I read books and hear them speak about ornaments that are sentimental for all sorts of reasons, I can't help but feel jealous.' She wrinkled her nose. 'Please don't repeat that to another soul. I'm very aware of how absurd it sounds, given my lifestyle.'

He hesitated a moment, his expression unreadable. 'Money isn't everything, Princess.'

She tilted her head to the side, studying him. He was as mysterious as ever, his handsome face giving nothing away. 'What was Christmas like for you, as a child?'

He put his hand around her elbow, guiding her towards the cabin. They'd been skiing that morning, but in deference to her condition, and out of an abundance of concern, he'd limited them to the baby runs, even when she'd itched to catch the lift right to the top of the craggy mountains and feel herself dropping down the side. But his worry was so touching, until she'd remembered that he was really no different to her parents or brother, that he wasn't protecting her so much as the baby she carried.

She wanted to keep their child safe too, of course, so she'd gone along with it, sliding down the soft, gentle slopes with twelve-year-olds on either side, wishing with all her heart that this man she'd married had wanted to keep her safe, as well as their baby.

'Not like yours,' he said cryptically, guiding her to-wards the doors of a quaint church that had, at some point, been converted into a restaurant. The doors were wide and the ceilings cathedral height, so, despite the fact it was busy, it didn't feel crowded.

She was aware of people glancing in their direction, but no one approached them, no one made it obvious they'd recognised her, and it was such a novel, refreshing change that her heart soared.

The waiter, however, decided they might like privacy and led them to a bay window with exquisite views and a small table, set away from the general dining area, so they had a lovely outlook, with the distant hum of conversation to remind them they were in a restaurant.

Once their menus had been delivered and drinks order taken, he leaned back with the appearance of relaxation, one arm stretched loosely along the back of her chair, so goose-pimples began to form on her skin.

She was insatiable. There was no other word to describe how she felt. Even his proximity in a crowded restaurant was enough to make her insides tighten with need.

'This is so weird,' she said after a pause, looking around them, shaking her head.

'Being married?'

'That too,' she lied, because actually it didn't feel weird, and that was terrifying. 'But I meant being here, without any security guards. I don't think I've ever been *anywhere* without security. How did you do this?'

'It's our honeymoon.' He shrugged.

'But that—it doesn't matter. I have had security with me every day of my life, even when I was away at school.'

'You went to a very exclusive school; I imagine you weren't the only one.'

'No,' she agreed, frowning. 'But I can't imagine the henchman at the palace agreeing to this.'

'The henchman?'

'Captain Muller,' she explained. 'He's Head of Palace Operations and an ongoing thorn in my side.'

'I've had the pleasure.'

She laughed because his intonation showed sarcasm. 'Not your favourite person?'

'Nor am I his, I suspect.' He held her gaze a moment. 'We came to a compromise,' he said, his lips close to hers.

'I didn't know that word was in his vocabulary. How did you do it?'

'By convincing him that your safety is my priority.'

All the breath whooshed from her lungs.

'You are carrying my baby,' he reminded her. 'There's nothing I wouldn't do to keep you safe.'

Pleasure immediately turned to something else, warmth to cold. She pulled away a fraction on the pretence of taking a sip from her drink.

'Isn't that all the more reason to have security?'

'My cabin is somewhat of a fortress,' he said.

'You don't even have a fence.'

'No, but the doors all have mag locks, there's digital monitoring on all windows, there are thermal sensors on the perimeter, as well as state-of-the art surveillance.'

'I didn't realise.'

'It's discreet. I had it installed shortly after I bought the place.'

'Is security an issue for you?'

'It's more about privacy.'

She nodded thoughtfully. 'I can't see you being a target for anyone. I mean, you're built like…'

He cocked one brow, watching her expectantly.

'Like you can handle yourself,' she finished, placing her glass down.

'Yes.' He dipped his head. 'I like to know my privacy is protected. While I'm in New York, the only person who can access the cabin is my housekeeper. There are some personal things there that I wouldn't want anyone else to see, or take.'

'Like what?'

'They're personal.' His lips curled in a smile that was derisive, probably unintentionally so, but the power to hurt was the same regardless.

She pulled back fully from him, the distance he was wedging between them with his words nothing to the physical space she now sought.

'I still can't see Muller agreeing.'

'You're perceptive. Our compromise means there are six guards stationed here in the village. I agreed to text them whenever we leave the cabin so they can keep a long-range eye on you.'

'On us,' she corrected automatically, lifting a hand to her temple. 'You're royalty too, remember?'

'I don't think I'm the one they're worried about protecting.'

'You're wrong. You're part of my family now, and that makes you valuable. You'll have to get used to an element of this when you travel.'

He leaned closer, so there was no distance between them. 'Princess, no one's going to be on my tail. I'm not interested in having a constant entourage of Hemmenwegian security.'

'But—'

He pressed a finger to her lips. 'It's non-negotiable.'

She furrowed her brow, wondering if he realised how difficult it would be for him to win that argument, but then, this was Rocco Santinova and she suspected he won every argument he entered into.

He moved his finger sideways, stroking her lower lip so her mouth opened, and his smile was one of resignation. She frowned, her heart tightening as though being strangled by a vine. How could she feel so good on one level even as her insides felt doused with ice? Her body was a contradiction and she couldn't make any sense of it.

'You were going to tell me about your Christmas traditions,' she said, clutching at straws, trying to hold on to reason and sense in the face of his body's easy assault on her nervous system.

'Was I?' He brushed his lips to hers and a thousand little arrows of heat barbed through her. She shivered, fighting her body's impulse to sway towards him.

'Yes.' But it was already becoming hard to focus on their conversation. She grabbed hold of that thought though, because it seemed important not to lose her head so easily. As soon as he touched her she fell apart and she didn't want to be so easily distracted. 'What was it like for you?'

His eyes shifted with a dark emotion she didn't understand and then it was Rocco who pulled away a little, easing back so he could see her whole face. 'Very simple.' The words were drawn from him as though against his will.

'Simple,' she encouraged, nodding as if to draw more detail from him.

He expelled a soft breath and she wondered if he was going to refuse to answer or change the subject, but after a moment he began to speak, softly, the words deep and gravelled, so despite the flatness to his tone she felt the rich emotion reverberating through them. 'We didn't have much money. My mother did what she could. A branch from a tree, some ornaments she'd bought at a discount shop, and always one gift for me that I really wanted. As a boy, I would ask for my heart's desire and she would give it to me, but once I realised her way of being able to do that involved practically starving herself for the months leading up to Christmas my wish list got a little more conservative.'

Charlotte's chest tightened. 'Your mother sounds like she was an amazing person.' She hesitated. 'How old were you when she died?'

His hand tightened on his glass. 'Seventeen.'

'Your father didn't help at all?'

Rocco's lips flattened into a line as he shook his head, once.

'Why not? Couldn't he afford…?'

'My father is a wealthy man,' he said after a beat. 'A senator, in fact.'

Her lips parted. 'Then how come—?'

'To help her would have been to acknowledge me, something he had no intention of doing.'

She gasped. 'That's cruel. Why wouldn't he—?'

'He was married,' Rocco said softly. 'And his clean, wholesome image was a part of his success. I threatened everything he had.'

'Then he shouldn't have slept around,' she muttered. 'Or taken more precautions when he did.'

'Accidents happen,' Rocco said, lifting a brow.

'But this is different,' she muttered. 'We weren't cheating.'

'No,' he agreed with a nod. 'And you weren't young and in love with a man twice your age.'

She sucked in a breath. 'Your poor mother.'

'She adored him,' Rocco said with a shake of his head. 'Even at the end, she asked me to forgive him, to look past his wrongs and be open to a relationship. *"If he only knew you, he'd be so proud."'*

Charlotte's heart splintered for Rocco's mother. 'Did you ever meet him?'

'Once.'

'And?'

He lifted his shoulders. 'What do you think? He was terrified I'd ruin his life.'

She bit back a curse. 'What an awful man,' she said indignantly. 'How could he not want to know you? How could he not be proud?'

His smile was tight. 'Because, like most people, he was driven only by self-interest.'

'How dare he do that to you?' she responded angrily.

Rocco's eyes narrowed. 'What did he do to me, *cara?'*

'Ignore you. Make you feel unwanted. He had no right.'

'I can assure you, his behaviour had no impact on me. I'm quite all right.'

She considered that a moment, then shook her head a little. 'Even neglect shapes us.'

'As you know all too well.'

She flicked her gaze away, towards the windows showing the view of a snowy mountaintop, not answering his question. Because there was no easy answer. Years of silence had made the words too difficult to form.

'This goes both ways.'

He was right. How could she expect him to bare his soul to her if she wasn't willing to do the same? Besides, it wasn't any great secret.

'You've seen my family in action. You know how they feel about me.'

'But what I don't know is why.'

'I'm the spare. It's a uniquely unimportant position.'

He watched her intently and butterflies seemed to beat their wings harder inside her belly. 'You are required for a royal heir. That makes you important.'

'Yes,' she agreed, frowning. 'But that's not really about me, is it? It's the lineage. The succession. I'm talking about who I am, what I like, what I'm good at. None of that really matters to my parents.' *Or her husband.* 'It never has.'

'You think you don't matter.'

'I don't,' she said, determined not to cry. 'Not to them, at least.' Not to anyone.

'Nicholas cannot have children, but he could still marry, adopt, couldn't he?'

'The order of succession wouldn't allow it.'

She was glad he didn't offer a sympathetic word. She couldn't have borne it. 'What would have happened if you didn't want to get married?'

'That was never my choice.'

Danger flared in Rocco's eyes, but he pushed on. 'Your brother might still marry.'

'I doubt it. He will be an excellent king, but he draws the line at having his personal life dictated by anyone.'

'A protest he gets to make but you do not?'

She lifted her shoulders.

'I went to school with people like your brother,' he said after a pause.

She didn't know exactly what he meant, so stayed quiet.

'I hated it. The whole idea of extreme wealth and power is anathema to me.'

Her brows shot upwards. 'And yet you're now a billionaire *and* a crown prince.'

'The irony hasn't escaped me.' He paused, as a waiter appeared to take their order. Having not looked at the menu, she chose something quickly, at random, then focused her gaze back on Rocco's face. 'I came from nothing. My mother had to make sacrifices for what we did have, and yet I was surrounded by obscene wealth on a daily basis. I was sickened—angered—by what my peers had, and by how little they appreciated it.'

She dropped her gaze to the table, seeing her own confessions through his eyes and hearing the privilege he must have read into her statements. 'The thing is, wealth is a blessing,' she said after a beat. 'But it's also a curse, particularly when it comes with the encumbrance of pressure and expectations.'

'Yes,' he agreed softly. 'I can see that.'

She hadn't expected the victory, and the surprise of his understanding touched something deep inside of her, so when her eyes lifted to his they were suspiciously moist. She blinked away again quickly.

'But at the time I just saw the ruins of that kind of money. Boys who had been given everything they could ever want from birth, who thought hardship was having to fly first class rather than in their private jet, who compared the size of their families' islands and boasted about whose yacht was bigger or better.'

'And you weren't like that,' she murmured.

He let out a short, sharp laugh. 'Not at all.'

'So how did you find yourself at that kind of school? Obviously not through your father's connections…'

'*Cristo,* no.' He hesitated and she held her breath, because she desperately didn't want him to go back into his shell, to stop talking to her. When he spoke, the words were almost wrenched from him. 'My mother worked as a cleaner in the boarding school. She heard about a scholarship exam that was taking place and asked me to sit it.'

'And you did well.'

He dipped his head in silent agreement. 'I was granted a full scholarship.'

'Wow. Competition for that kind of place is fierce.'

'I suppose so.'

He wasn't someone who showed false modesty, so she knew it was more that he simply didn't care about a long-ago achievement. His life had moved on. There'd been many more accolades since.

'What happened to your mother, Rocco?'

'She had a series of heart attacks.'

Sympathy tightened inside Charlotte. 'I'm so sorry.' She paused a moment. 'But I meant to ask, what happened to make you mad? When you went and…?' She couldn't finish the sentence; she didn't need to. He understood.

His features tightened as though he was bracing for a tsunami to crash down on his shoulders and she sat perfectly still, wanting him to answer her, aware that at any moment he could push her away again.

'It's disgusting.'

'I'm a big girl.'

He held her gaze for a long time and it was truly the most intimate thing Charlotte had ever felt, as though Rocco was looking deep inside her soul and seeing all the pieces that made her whole, as though he was revealing a part of himself that was buried deep, far too deep for anyone else to have glimpsed. The breath seemed to burn inside her lungs, until she could hardly bear it a moment longer.

'They delighted in tormenting her,' he said finally, the words succinct; abrupt.

'How?' She leaned closer.

His lips tightened, rimmed with whiteness, as whatever memories he was facing groaned through him.

'At first it was reasonably innocent. Unmade beds. Uniforms left on the floor.'

'I would imagine their dorm master took a dim view of that.'

'Undoubtedly. None the less, it was my mother's job to fix it.'

Charlotte shook her head. Was it any wonder Rocco thought so little of entitled children? He'd gone to school with spoiled brats. And yet it must have been worse than dirty clothes to have prompted him to do what he did.

'Then one evening my mother was white-faced when I saw her. She wouldn't tell me what had happened, but I knew it was bad. The next day at school, they were all laughing about it.'

'What?' she whispered, putting her hand on his out of an instinctive need to offer comfort.

'They had spread...defecation...throughout their dorm.' She gasped. 'Smeared it on the beds, the walls. The mirror.'

She closed her eyes on the awful humiliation of that.

'I can't believe it. Surely the school didn't tolerate their behaviour?'

'They received a two-day suspension each. Barely a slap on the wrist. My mother was still the one who had to deal with it.'

'Oh, Rocco.'

'It was to punish me,' he said with restrained anger.

'Why would they want to punish you?'

He focused his gaze on the wall beyond her shoulder, his gaze laser-like with its intensity.

'Rocco?' She wouldn't allow him not to answer now.

'Because I was smarter,' he said finally. 'And hungry.'

'For success?'

'Nothing was guaranteed for me. I didn't have a trust

fund waiting for me when I turned eighteen. That school was the best opportunity I had to make something of myself, to help my mother out of poverty, and hell, I wasn't going to waste a moment. I won every award there was. I topped every exam. I took part in debating, delighting, always, in eviscerating my opposition. Fencing. Lacrosse. Athletics. Whatever gave me college credits, I did.'

She couldn't stop the tears that moistened her eyes now. 'That's absolutely awful. You should have been celebrated for your accomplishments.'

'By a small group of friends, I was. And unfailingly by my mother.' A genuine smile lifted his lips. 'All I wanted was to graduate, and get a job, so I could finally contribute.'

'And then you lost her, before that could happen.'

His mouth tightened. 'So you see,' he said, by way of acknowledgement, 'I have hated the obscenely rich for a very long time.'

'Yet look at you now,' she said with a shake of her head. 'You are every bit as wealthy as those horrible boys.'

'But through my own efforts,' he said forcefully. 'Not because I was given any damned thing in my life.'

'How did you do it?' she asked, fascinated by how a scholarship kid could turn their fortunes around so dramatically.

'That's another story.'

'Oh, don't do that.' She couldn't help the plea that escaped her lips. 'I'm genuinely interested.'

He leaned forward, pressing a kiss to her nose. The gesture was so small, and so simple, given the intimacies they'd shared, and yet it made her feel as though she'd been lifted up high into the heavens and was basking in all the light the sky possessed. Only perhaps he felt it too—perhaps he was ignited by the heat of that light—because he pulled back as though he'd been shocked, a frown marring his face as he took a drink of water.

'I was always good with numbers. I exploited that skill.'

Her heart was cold. He had a habit of pushing her away and she hated it, but particularly when that contrasted so stunningly with the closeness they'd just felt. It was beyond bearing. 'Lots of people are good with numbers.' She brushed aside his simplistic explanation. 'They become mathematics professors or accountants, not billionaires. So? What did you do differently?'

A smile tugged at his lips, her observation amusing him. 'I got a job working at a brokerage firm.'

'Straight out of school?'

'It was an administrative position. I just wanted to look and learn.'

Her brows lifted. She couldn't imagine Rocco making photocopies.

'But the numbers…' He dragged a hand through his hair, as if searching for words. 'It is difficult to explain. They spoke to me. I could always see patterns. I studied the market obsessively. One day, the senior partner asked me to take notes in a meeting.'

She leaned closer, fascinated.

'He was wrong in his advice. Maybe a week earlier his recommendations would have held sway, but the market was moving, and he didn't realise.'

'And you pointed that out?'

'Not until after the meeting.'

She exhaled. 'How did he take it?'

'He was furious. He told me to get out of his office. I stood my ground until he agreed to let me explain it properly. An hour later, he'd emptied the office next door to his and appointed me his researcher.'

She shook her head, visibly impressed. 'That's amazing.'

'Not really. As I said, I've always been good at numbers.'

She laughed softly. 'Still…'

'My mother had died, but I was determined to prove that I deserved the faith she'd had in me, and determined to prove my father wrong. She sacrificed everything for me. My only regret is that she didn't get to see what I'd achieved. That I wasn't able to make her life easier somehow.'

Charlotte's heart turned over in her chest. She put her hand over his, drawing his attention to her face. 'I'm sorry that happened, too.'

He dipped his head in what might have been acceptance of that, but could also have been a rejection of her sympathy.

'And what about you, Charlotte Rothsburg?'

'What about me?'

'If you hadn't been born a princess, what might you have done with your life?'

Her gaze drifted into the main restaurant, her eyes landing on a couple with a young child, so her heart turned over and her hand crept protectively towards her own stomach as visions of what their child might be like danced in her head. 'I don't know,' she said, simply, catching the rest of the sentence before it could tumble from her mouth.

But I feel as though I'm right where I was meant to be.

CHAPTER TEN

REALITY FELT A long way away from that cabin high up in the Italian Alps. In the back of Charlotte's mind was the calling of her home, the requirements of her people, the duty she'd accepted as hers all her life. But here, looking out over the Aosta Valley, with Rocco half naked in the kitchen, presiding over eggs on toast, Charlotte felt as if she'd been sucked into an alternative reality, that made her somehow both ordinary and sublime at the same time.

In the three days since arriving, Charlotte had become less and less attached to her princess self. Or perhaps it was that she'd become more aware of the flesh-and-blood woman she was, and all the desires and habits she'd denied herself for a lifetime that she was now desperate to indulge.

As if he could read her thoughts, he flipped the eggs onto their plates and said, 'We have two days left here. Any thoughts on how you'd like to spend them?'

The question grated against her skin, because it was the last thing she wanted. The idea of going back to the palace sat around her shoulders like a chain. It was her destiny, but now it also felt like her prison. She shook her head, not trusting herself to speak.

'Then I have an idea.'

'Oh? What is it?'

He winked at her, slow and sensual so her tummy twisted into a billion knots. 'You'll see.'

They found the perfect tree only a few rows into the forest. Just a sapling, wild sown, it came up to Charlotte's shoulders, no taller, so it was easy for Rocco to saw through the trunk, and then to drag the tree towards the cabin. When she offered to help, he brushed the words aside with, 'Not in your condition,' so she burst out laughing.

'I think what we did this morning was far more aerobic.'

He threw her a look. 'But impossible for me to do quite so well on my own.' As if to prove his point, he hoisted the tree into his arms, ignoring the fact the branches bristled into his face.

'Okay, He-Man. If you say so.'

It took Rocco a little while to secure the tree in the rustic living room of the cabin. Using a large copper pot as a base, he added stones from the front garden to give it weight, and while he worked Charlotte made tea and coffee in the kitchen, delighting in the small act of domesticity and normality, then rifled through the pantry until she discovered the delicious shortbread biscuits he'd been supplying her with after dinner each night. Placing two on a plate—then adding another two for good measure—she carried the tray into the lounge room and gasped.

'It's so beautiful.'

He angled his face to her. 'I'm glad you think so.' Their eyes held and her heart began to run far too quickly; it was easy to believe that he really was glad. That her happiness genuinely mattered to him, rather than this being about their baby. She couldn't let herself forget that in some ways he was just like her parents—her value was in the baby growing inside of her, nothing else.

The taste of salty tears cloyed at her throat; she ignored it, needing to quash those emotions. Damned pregnancy.

'What about ornaments?'

He looked towards the tree, hands jammed in his pockets, then back to her. An emotion crossed his face she couldn't comprehend, and then he spoke slowly, voice gruff. 'I believe there are some in the attic. Hang on.'

He tried to make sense of his actions as he ascended the narrow ladder into the roof space of the cabin. Rocco wasn't in the business of making anyone's dreams come true, but when she'd spoken so wistfully about Christmas and the sterile nature of her own celebrations he'd itched to give her a slice of his mother's festive magic. Despite not having much, Allegra Santinova had made sure this time of year was filled with wonder for a young Rocco. As he'd grown older the magic had lessened, but not the feeling of love and gratitude.

It was because she was carrying his baby. That was why he was willing to crack open his past a little, to let her see something he regarded as intimate and special.

He blew the dust off the top of the box, his chest doing a strange cranking thing as he curved his hands around the cardboard and thought of his mother, and how often she'd done exactly this as a young girl.

When he stepped into the lounge room Charlotte was standing beside the tree, her fingers running over a branch, the fragrance heavy in the air. He stopped walking, something weighty in the vicinity of his heart.

The mother of his child.

Here, in this house, of all places.

But he was glad they'd started their marriage here. Glad for many reasons, but mostly because of how happy Charlotte seemed. He froze, the thought unwelcome, unfamiliar, and certainly unwanted.

'These are not what I expected,' she cooed as he opened the box to reveal the delicate heirloom pieces. 'They're really old, Rocco.'

'Yes,' because they'd been his grandmother's, as a child.

'Where did you get them?' She looked up at him, expression mystified. And he couldn't say he blamed her.

'They came with the house.' That wasn't a lie.

But she furrowed her brow, her perceptiveness telling her that there was more to it. 'I see.'

Rocco preferred to leave the past in the past. What good was there in revisiting old hurts? But with Charlotte it was so easy to speak, and he found himself elaborating, 'My mother grew up here. This was my grandparents' cabin. I bought it after they died. It was just something I'd always sworn I'd do,' he said quietly, attention focused on the tree rather than her face as he hung one of the decorations on a leafy limb.

'For your mother?'

He ground his teeth together. 'She missed her home very much.'

'Why did she move to America? For your father?'

'She never admitted as much, but I believe so. They met when he was on a trade visit. She was working at a local hotel.'

Charlotte nodded slowly, reaching for an ornament.

'After she fell pregnant, my grandparents refused to have anything to do with her. She was very young, and completely alone.'

She sucked in a sharp breath. 'That's *awful*.'

'They were very religious.' He held up one of the ornaments as proof—a Mary and Jesus with a golden glow at their backs. 'The fact she'd fallen pregnant was impossible for them to forgive.'

'Your poor mother.'

'She had it tough for a long time. She worked in town, at a hotel, when I was very young, but she never gave up hope. She'd entered the Green Card Lottery and, believe it or not, actually won her citizenship that way.'

Charlotte's brows lifted.

'I know. She was determined that America would be her fresh start, that it really would be a land of opportunity for her. What she didn't realise was that it would be just as hard to make ends meet in a foreign country, saddled with a young child and no qualifications. But she could work, and so she did, harder than anyone I've ever known.'

He couldn't contain the admiration that moved through him. Rocco was strong, strong enough to take on the world, and he credited his mother with that. She'd shown him again and again that the most important thing to do when you fell down was to get up again. To keep getting up, even when it seemed impossible.

'And each year, at Christmas, she would tell me about this place. She described it so perfectly, I could picture it in my mind's eye. She told me about the tree they would put up here,' he gestured to the large windows framing a stunning view towards the valley and the township in the distance. 'The food they would eat. The carols that are sung in the village every evening, and the ornaments in the attic. She remembered them all. As she painted pine cones for me to put on our tree in a tiny studio apartment she described this place, and I knew, even as a young boy, that her heart was here.'

Charlotte moved quickly then, coming to wrap her arms around his waist, lifting up onto the tips of her toes and kissing him. It was unexpected and—though he didn't admit it to himself—necessary. Her kiss pushed all the bitterness from the moment and memories, leaving only sweetness. Her kiss brought him back to the present, and what he had.

'I swore I'd bring her back one day, that I'd give this cabin to her. I would do whatever I could to make sure she could come here again.' He wrapped his arms loosely around Charlotte's back, holding her where she was. 'She never did.'

'No.' Just a whisper, ambivalent and tremulous. Sad. He frowned, moving his finger to her chin, tilting her face towards his. 'But we're here.' She blinked up at him, her smile shaking. 'And our baby will come here. I think…she would have liked that idea.'

He nodded slowly, because Charlotte was right. 'She would have loved that.'

His mind swam with all the stories his mother had told him, as they decorated the tree. Each ornament was just as she'd described, so from time to time he'd recount its history to Charlotte, and in doing so he felt as though a part of his mother was there with them, not looking down on them but right alongside them, happy and content that they were bringing back to life the best part of her childhood. Charlotte didn't speak unless he initiated a conversation, but her quietness wasn't concerning. She was smiling, a soft hum coming from her pink lips every now and again, her eyes sparkling with excitement as she studied the tree, working out the best place to put each decoration to perfectly balance the effect. He found himself staring at her more than the tree. Objectively speaking, she was beautiful, but it was so much more than that. It was all the little gestures and expressions that crossed her face. The curiosity in her eyes, the quickness of thought, the kindness in her smile, her ready laugh—like a bell on the breeze. These things added to her beauty, making her compelling and fascinating.

That she'd been able to remain a virgin for so long was impossible to comprehend. Men should have been throwing themselves at her feet. And perhaps they would have been, if she'd been given any true freedom of movement. Even at college, it sounded as though she faced an oppressive degree of control and management, that her time was never really her own.

With the tree almost done, her fingers curved around the base of the glass star that would go on the very top. 'How utterly delightful,' she said with a shake of her head, as though she couldn't believe anything so fine and detailed could exist, despite the fact she'd grown up in a royal palace that was bursting at the seams with precious ornaments.

'What would you change?'

She kept her gaze trained on the tree. 'I think it's perfect. The decorations are well-spaced, the colours balanced.' She sighed softly, her smile a slow lift of her lips. 'I really love it, Rocco.'

That warmed something in his chest, even as he felt a tightening there too, a constriction, a foretelling of danger that he knew he needed to heed. But their honeymoon was almost over. They'd resume separate, parallel lives within the walls of the palace until the baby was born. The thought was like being halved by lightning. Separate but parallel? What about at night? How could he be within a few dozen meters of her and not *be* with her? Struck, he moved closer, intending to help her place the star, but inhaling deeply, so the sweetness of her fragrance teased his nostrils and made his gut roll. Separate but parallel seemed impossible now.

'I meant, what would you change about your childhood?' he corrected, his voice gruff in light of his thoughts.

'Oh.' Her smile slipped and he immediately regretted having broached a subject that gave her pain. She recovered quickly enough, eyes lifting to his, face an assembly of features determined to convey the impression of unconcern.

'Our child may face the same restrictions and attitudes you did,' he said gently. 'So? What do you wish had been different?' He let the question hang in the air between them.

She turned, giving him the full force of her attention now, running her fingertip over the star's sharp edges distractedly. 'I suppose I'd try to keep things as normal as possible. But the truth is, our child will be the royal heir, unlike me. I don't want them being raised as my brother was, separate and removed. I want them to be a child first and foremost, royal second.'

'You must have grappled with these thoughts before.'

Uncertainty coloured her eyes. 'I suppose I'd never thought about it as an actual prospect. It was always some faraway notion—that I would provide the heir my brother needs. But now that our baby is inside of me, I feel it changes everything.'

He waited, his heart tight in his chest.

'It's not what any mother would want for their child,' she said with a slightly wobbling lip. 'When your child is the heir to the country, they're not really yours. You cede a part of them to the nation, and to the mechanism of the palace. The Chief of Operations was as much involved in my life as my parents were. I hated that.'

'Then we won't allow it to happen.'

A wistful look overtook her. 'It's not that easy.'

'Why not?'

'Because there's—'

'Tradition? So? Traditions can be broken.'

'Easy for you to say. Believe me, I can't just make up my own rules.'

'You think not?'

Her lips parted and curiosity brought her brows together.

'Let me tell you this, *cara*. I have no intention of allowing our son or daughter to become a part of the royal factory in Hemmenway. I too would like them to be raised with as normal an attitude as possible. If that means we bring the child here to grow up, or to New York, then so be it.'

She shook her head, dismissing the idea. 'That's a fantasy; it would never be allowed to happen.' Her teeth dug into her lower lip, her eyes scanning his as if looking for assurance, as a small ray of hope punctuated her mind. 'I don't think anyone would sign off on that.'

'And do we require them to?'

'I have no idea, honestly.' She hesitated. 'But we should find out.'

It was as though a meteorite were soaring through him. Heat and light exploded in every cell of his being, in the very fibre of his soul. That she was even considering his suggestion opened up their future in a way he hadn't known he'd needed. He'd proposed this marriage instantly, because he refused to have his own child separated from him the way he'd been separated from his father and his entire family. He believed those things mattered, but he didn't want their child to experience the same pain Charlotte had, because of her position within the Hemmenwegian royal family.

'I didn't have a family growing up,' he said after a moment, his voice emerging dark and ruminative. 'But my mother made up for it. She gave me everything I ever needed. I knew myself to be the centre of her universe. Our family won't necessarily look like every other family, but in all the ways that matter we can give this child a proper home. I will fight for that, Princess. I will fight whomever I must to ensure our baby is not seen as anyone else's responsibility. You and I are in control, understood?'

Their eyes met and the air between them cracked as if a bolt of lightning had cut between them.

'Yes,' she said finally, breathing in so her chest swelled, and her eyes glittered with determination. 'With you by my side, I truly believe that will be possible.'

She didn't know whose idea it had been to walk into the village, but here they were, bundled up in layers of clothing, protected against the icy wind and falling snow, walking close together, his arm around her shoulders, holding her to him as they meandered through charming, cobbled streets that wove amongst the ancient buildings of this lovely Alpine town. It felt as though every person who lived here, and every tourist, was on the streets tonight, so the air was humming with conversation and joy, but it was the hum of carols that drew them closer.

And then she remembered. 'Your mother told you about this.'

His eyes skimmed her face. 'It was a highlight of her childhood,' he admitted. 'She loved walking through these streets, hearing these songs.'

Magic threaded through Charlotte, and out of nowhere she was engulfed by the most delightful, pervasive sense of homecoming, as if she too belonged here, as if their baby was an anchor that tethered her to this world.

'I'm glad we're hearing them.' She couldn't meet his eyes. Too many rich emotions were flooding her body, emotions that were too complex to immediately understand. She would need to analyse them later.

They drew closer to the carollers, a group of twenty people ranging in age from teenagers to someone who looked like an octogenarian. They finished one song and the assembled crowd clapped; a moment later they began to sing 'Joy to the World'. It lifted Charlotte's spirits, and she leaned in closer to Rocco's side, snuggling into the hard planes of his body, her heart beating in her chest.

Christmas spirit was everywhere, from the wreaths on lamp posts to the lights that were strung over the cobbled paths, but that wasn't why her heart was beating faster, why her pulse was blasting through her body at a whole new frequency.

It was beautiful and it was charming, but it wouldn't have mattered where she was. Being close to Rocco like this was speaking to something deep inside of her. She tilted her face up to his right as he looked down at her, and then she understood. She was falling in love with him.

Maybe she was already knee-deep in love with him.

Maybe she always had been. Perhaps even before she'd met him? Maybe that was why the night they'd met she'd been drawn to him, unable to resist him, why she'd done something so out of character.

Standing in the middle of this sublime village, surrounded by the sort of song that had survived the march of time, anything seemed possible.

CHAPTER ELEVEN

ON THEIR LAST morning in the Aosta Valley, an oppressive weight seemed to bear down on Charlotte, so that all of the things she'd loved about this place now seemed to taunt her, to haunt her, almost to mock her for her desire to remain. For her foolishness in believing this could be real.

After all, her life was in Hemmenway, her duty to her people and land was unchanged by this marriage. For as long as she could remember, she'd been told of these expectations. She'd grown up knowing what her future would be; how could she rewrite it now?

'I'm marrying you for the sake of this baby. There is no alternative.'

His words, spoken so plainly at the time, without any intention of wounding her, cut her now as a blade might, deep to the core. They were a reminder that this wasn't real, that her feelings had to be concealed from him, that she had to remember this was all for the baby.

Where their honeymoon had felt like sunshine every day, gloom now enveloped her, so she was quiet as she dressed and placed her clothing back into the suitcase, quiet as he made their coffee and placed bread in the toaster, then spread it with the preserves they both liked.

And quiet still as they ate, Rocco reading a newspaper on his iPad, Charlotte lost in her own thoughts completely.

This honeymoon had been a terrible idea.

Perhaps on the surface there'd been sense to it. It had afforded an opportunity for them to get to know one another. Only she hadn't anticipated this unintended, unwelcome side effect of knowing Rocco: loving him.

If she were a different person she might have said something to him, told him how she was starting to feel, or at least tried to table a conversation that dealt with their relationship and its future, but Charlotte was insecure and uncertain, with no experience of men or relationships. At least, not positive ones.

Could she trust this feeling overtaking her heart? Was it really even love? Perhaps it was just desire. Or gratitude, because the marriage he'd proposed had made everything, temporarily, easier. Or maybe it was a biological compulsion, given she was carrying his baby.

But even as she analysed each option, the feeling inside of her grew stronger and more determined, so she froze, midway through placing a sweater in her suitcase, eyes lifting to the wall opposite her and fixing on a small painting.

She loved him.

There was no other way to explain the feelings exploding through her. She loved him and couldn't imagine life without him.

Which was a total disaster.

This marriage wasn't about love. He'd made it very clear that this was simply a means to an end—driven by necessity. He was Rocco Santinova, a womaniser, a bachelor, a guy who had made it abundantly clear on their very first night together that he wouldn't offer more than sex: a one-off.

He was making the best of their circumstances but that wasn't love.

Not for him.

She dropped the sweater into her suitcase and pressed a hand over her belly, pain splitting her heart in two.

'Charlotte?' His voice was deep and rumbled with concern. 'Are you okay?'

Okay? No. She wasn't okay, she wanted to scream at him, but none of this was his fault. He'd been so clear about what he wanted, and it was Charlotte's stupid problem that she'd somehow ignored all the warning signs and let her emotions get so heavily involved.

'Fine,' she lied crisply, turning away from him before the tears could mist her eyes. 'I'm going to shower. What time are we leaving?'

Silence punctuated her question but she didn't turn back to face him. A moment later a heavy breath sounded and then, 'In an hour.'

'I'll be ready.'

It was cowardly to hide in the bathroom but she did, rather than face him again. She took her time in the shower, then fixed her make-up and hair, gradually transforming herself back into Princess Charlotte of Hemmenway. Somehow, donning her usual clothes made her feel as if she was wearing a necessary coat of armour. It was important and imperative.

At the allotted time, she came into the lounge area. Rocco was waiting, reading a newspaper on his iPad, a glass of orange juice beside him, looking so utterly beautiful and perfect that something inside of her lurched completely off centre. He lifted his eyes and smiled, as though nothing in the world was wrong, as though nothing had changed for him—and, of course, it hadn't.

She turned away, gaze dropping on the Christmas tree. 'We should have put that away,' she said wistfully, her voice cracking the smallest amount.

'We might come back before Christmas.' He shrugged. 'If not, my housekeeper will take care of it.'

So matter-of-fact! No hesitation, no doubts. Everything about this was easy and simple for him. He was in control, utterly and completely.

She closed her eyes on a wave of remorse. How was she going to do this? How could she pretend their marriage was as black and white as they'd thought it would be when they'd first entered into it?

'Let's go, then.'

In the back of her mind, though, she rejected any idea of coming back here. It was too fraught, too heavy with feelings, too much a part of a world she couldn't really step into. Here she'd fallen in love with him. He'd shown her a part of himself that had made him impossible not to love. But if that love wasn't reciprocated, it would always pain her to think of this honeymoon.

More tears filled her eyes and she blinked them away quickly, before he could see. She had to find a way to act as though everything was fine: the success of their marriage depended on that.

He wasn't an idiot. Something was bothering Charlotte. She'd been walling herself off from him all morning, alternating between ignoring him and trying to secretively wipe tears from her eyes, so a strange pang of worry—an emotion he'd never felt for anyone besides his mother—formed in the pit of his stomach.

He didn't like it.

He didn't like feeling concerned for her, but of course,

it was only natural. She was carrying his baby, after all. He was genetically programmed to look out for her now.

He drove them to the airstrip in silence, but he was aware of her every movement, her hands clasped tersely in her lap, her face determinedly averted from his, so that whenever he glanced sideways he caught only a glimpse of her in profile. She was miles away from the woman he'd been spending time with, making love to.

The plane was waiting, fuelled up and ready to go, but he didn't immediately cut the engine of the car. Instead, he stayed where he was, a little way across the snowy tarmac from the plane, then turned his whole body to face Charlotte.

'Something is bothering you.'

Her sharp intake of breath was all the confirmation he needed.

'No,' she denied.

'I'm not stupid. You've been quiet all morning. What is it?'

Still she didn't look at him, and that made him angry! It seared through him, because she was off-kilter and he wanted to help her, but she wouldn't even show him her face. He didn't like being on the outside. He was a problem-solver. If she opened up to him, he could help her.

'Damn it, Princess, what's going on?'

She flinched and he immediately regretted the harsh tone of his voice, but at least she turned to face him, her lower lip wobbling a little, her eyes probing his as though she was trying to understand him. But for what purpose? Why?

'I've enjoyed myself. I…' She hesitated and he wanted to curse again, but he couldn't do that to her, so he waited, gently, hiding his impatience. 'Thank you.'

Only the words were hollow and her eyes no longer probed his; they'd fallen to the space between them.

Frustration bit through him. He reached across, lifting her chin. 'Charlotte.'

Her eyes widened, and he felt her swallow, the delicate movement of her throat bunching muscles together.

'What's happened to upset you?'

'Nothing,' she denied quickly. 'The plane's waiting.'

'And it will continue to wait until we are on board. What's the problem?'

She parted her lips, so his gut kicked with an ache to lean forward and kiss her—but that would solve nothing. Sex between them was easy. Better than easy, it was perfect. If they were going to raise a child together, they had to learn to communicate. To be partners, at least enough to be good parents. 'Talk to me,' he commanded.

'It's just life in Hemmenway,' she said after a small pause, eyes focused beyond his shoulder. 'This has been so freeing. I find it hard to imagine going back.'

He frowned. That made sense, and yet he didn't believe her. Some deep-held instinct told him she wasn't being completely honest with him.

'We can travel here as often as you would like. This isn't the end.'

Tears misted her eyes and that kicking sense of concern split his gut in two. She nodded slowly, uncertainly, then pulled away from him. 'Come on, Rocco. It's time to go home now.'

The words rang with steel; her determination was obvious, so why did he fight her? Why did he want to argue with her?

Because he didn't like being lied to, nor did he like being shut out. After all that they'd shared, she was treating him as expendable, as unwanted, just as his father had, just as his grandparents had done to his mother. She was making him unimportant, sidelining him from her life. She was pushing him away and he hated the feeling, especially from Charlotte, especially after what they'd shared. Her rejection made him feel vulnerable in a way he loathed, a way he thought he'd outgrown. It had been a long time since he'd cared what someone thought of him, a long time since he'd let someone get close to him like this.

His hand reached across, finding her knee, and he squeezed her there, so her face jerked back to his and he took advantage of the swift movement and kissed her, his lips claiming hers with fierce, angry possession. It wasn't her he was angry at, but the circumstances of their life, hers and his, and the terms of their marriage. He was angry, and he couldn't explain it.

Sex had always been a means to an end for Rocco: the first time it had been about revenge, and after that about both pleasure and triumph. The pleasure of losing himself in a woman and the triumph of knowing his body could drive hers wild. He took pride in pleasing women, in making them explode with satisfied desires, but with Charlotte something had tilted, and sex was no longer familiar, no longer a known quantity. Every time he was with her it felt as though a part of him was being gouged open, changing shape, changing tone, and this kiss was no different.

He was angry, and he was uncertain, but when she whimpered into his mouth, a familiar sound of need, he knew that sex would be about reassurance and staking a claim, of asserting their new normal.

Moving with intent, he broke the kiss only so he could push out of his door and stalk around to hers, wrenching it open and drawing her into his arms in one motion, so he thought she moved there at the same time, willingly doing whatever she could to be close to him. His heart slammed into his ribs as he carried her to the steps of his plane, pausing only briefly at the top of the steps to issue the instruction that the plane should take off without delay.

He strode past the seats, to the bedroom at the rear of his jet, and once they were inside, and only then, did he kiss her with the same intensity that had been burning him alive in the car, with a need to make her his that defied explanation.

Only this made sense. His kiss was demanding, his body strong, dominant, so when he stepped, she moved too, back towards the bed, and then tumbling onto it, her arms reaching for him, taking hold with the same desperate desire that splintered through him. Hot, hungry, sanity riven by sensuality, hands demanding as they slid over one another's limbs, tearing clothes, piece by piece until they were naked and writhing, a different sort of need compelling them this time.

This was not a teaching experience, not as their time in the Aosta Valley had been. There he'd been in control, showing her bit by bit what she'd missed out on, driving her wild with meticulous determination before allowing himself to give into the sensual heat that consumed them.

Rocco was not in control of this. Passion and desire were beasts swirling through them, angrily dominant and insatiable. He drove into her on a growl torn from deep within, and she arched her back on a frantic cry, nails dragging down his skin, scoring him with the flames of her passion so every time he moved she dug her fingers into him as though trying to hold on for life itself.

As the plane lifted off the tarmac she exploded, muscles squeezing him, so his control lurched then slipped completely and he joined her in surrender, losing himself to their pleasure, powerless in the face of their intensity, lost, for a moment, like a child in the woods.

He straightened slowly, pushing up to look at her, but Charlotte wouldn't meet his eyes. Despite what they'd just shared, she was as distant to him as before. Even as he remained inside of her, their bodies joined, she sought to shut herself off from him.

Frustration did somersaults in his gut, but he wouldn't show that to her.

He wouldn't do anything that might reveal a form of vulnerability—like caring too much. He'd learned a long time ago to rely only on himself, and he did so now, pulling away from her and standing, his expression carefully muted of feeling.

He sought for something pithy to say, something that would render the sheer power of what they'd just shared moot, that would return their interaction to a level footing, but the truth was, it wasn't a moment for glibness, so he simply gathered his clothes, turned and left.

Charlotte was becoming an expert at hiding. She stayed in the bedroom a long time, dressing slowly, then doing her hair, repairing her make-up, trying not to think about what had just happened, trying not to replay the overwhelming connection she'd felt when they'd made love, as though each of them was being burned alive.

She'd loved him before but that had been a sort of baptism by fire—for the first time since their marriage, he hadn't treated her like a student being taught how to make love. Oh, at the time she hadn't felt that, it had all seemed very genuine and intense. But what they'd just shared was a masterclass in true passion, in shared need, desperate, aching longing, and she wanted—no, she needed—so much more.

It was that thought which kept her hiding for almost the entire flight, which wasn't long, in any event. When the captain announced they were commencing the descent, she stood slowly, counting to ten beneath her breath, bracing herself to return to Rocco.

He was working when she emerged, head bent over a stack of documents; he didn't look up as she moved into the cabin, as though he wasn't even aware of her presence.

She should have been glad. It was safer that way.

But she didn't want to be ignored after what they'd just shared. She didn't want to be ignored, given what she knew about him, and how she felt for him. She loved him, utterly and completely, and, even knowing that love would be unrequited, she couldn't ignore it. She couldn't silence it.

But how could she tell him? She made a soft noise of frustration, pacing further down the aisle, staring out of the windows at the capital city of Hemmenway. Her heart gave a strange little tick.

She loved this city. This country. Both were in her blood. But she was no longer just a princess, born to serve. She wanted more.

She wanted it all.

Turning, she found Rocco's eyes on her and the breath in her lungs began to overheat, burning her oesophagus, so she reached out to grip the seat beside her.

'What is it?' There was resignation in the tone of his voice, and a hint of concern, that almost undid her.

'I need to know...' But the words died on her lips, as

she imagined saying them aloud to him. *Can you ever fall in love?*

'Yes?' He was very still, watchful, unnerving her.

She clamped her lips together.

'What's it going to be like, back in Hemmenway?'

It was a start—an important question to which she needed an answer.

'What do you mean?'

He was not going to make this easy for her.

'Before the wedding, we barely saw each other. We lived in different apartments.'

'That was your choice.'

'None of this was my choice,' she responded rashly, then closed her eyes, because they'd both walked right into this marriage, for the sake of their baby.

'You're asking how much of our lives we're going to share.' He ignored her sharp interjection. 'What living together will look like?'

Living together. A shiver ran down her spine and she almost sobbed because of how perfect that idea sounded—until she remembered that he didn't return her feelings. 'Yes.' The word was bitten out from between her lips. 'I can't imagine it.'

'What would you like it to look like?'

She made a sound of frustration and the plane dipped lower, drawing them closer to Hemmenway and the rest of their lives.

'I don't know.'

He made a curt noise of impatience, so she was forced to defend herself. 'I've never felt that I would have a say in what my life would look like. I can't just visualise a perfect future for myself and describe it to you. I'm used to being told how to live, where to live.'

'Let's start there, then. Do you seriously imagine us remaining in the palace?'

She frowned. 'It hadn't occurred to me that we would live anywhere else. Why?'

'Do you like it there?'

Her lips parted. It was another question she'd never asked herself, because the answer hadn't seemed important. Nothing would change who she was and what was needed of her.

'I…it's the only home I've ever known.'

'But if we could live somewhere else,' he insisted, 'somewhere smaller, more intimate, with more privacy, considerably less staff?'

Her heart went into overdrive, because she wanted everything he was describing. She wanted to reach out and grab that with both hands, to carve out that future for them, but then what? At least in the palace, there would be the distraction of others. Her family, the servants, the comings and goings of dignitaries and guests. Alone with Rocco, she would feel the burden of how much she loved him, and it would destroy her. There was noise in the palace, a way to conceal her feelings, and the emptiness in her heart that came from not being loved back by anyone in her life.

'I think we should walk before we run,' she said unevenly, hating herself then for being such a coward. Why didn't she fight for the future they could have? Why didn't she tell him how she felt, at least, like the throwing down of a gauntlet?

His eyes sparked with hers and she felt the argument he wasn't wagering, but he turned away with a shrug, his attention focusing back on his work. 'If that's what you want.'

'It is,' she lied, taking the seat across the aisle and

staring ahead, numb. Her fingers reached for the seat-belt, fastening it in place as the plane descended further and further, until they touched down, home again, but in no home she wanted to be a part of.

CHAPTER TWELVE

ANOTHER NIGHT, ANOTHER INSUFFERABLE outing as Crown Prince Rocco, listening to small talk and watching his wife smile and nod like some kind of automaton. In the week since returning from the honeymoon, this had been the only time in which he'd seen her, and it hadn't really been Charlotte, so much as a carefully curated version of herself that she showed to her people.

She looked untouchable, and her smile was performative at best. When they touched, she moved away from him as quickly as possible, leaving a fire burning in his veins that he refused to ignore.

She'd asked him what their life would look like back in Hemmenway and insisted this was what she wanted, but for Rocco's part he couldn't understand it. He could barely reconcile this version of his wife with the woman he'd taken to Italy. There, she'd been warm and funny, open and… He frowned, searching for the right word, his eyes roaming her freely, uncaring that they were surrounded by dignitaries and diplomats. His look was one of frank possession and open assessment, and when she happened to look in his direction and her eyes widened, panic obvious in their depths, he didn't look away.

A challenge ignited in his gaze, and he knew she felt it. Heat darkened her cheeks and then, thrown off balance, she turned back to the Queen of Al Amaan and began to speak once more, but without the same look of cool composure.

A cynical smile stretched his lips.

Good. He liked throwing her off. He liked seeing the real her.

He liked knowing she *saw* him, which it had been hard to say she had with any certainty since they'd returned from the Aosta Valley. She was ignoring him, and he was sick of it. She'd asked what form their marriage would take and he knew only one thing for certain: it would not be like this. They were not two polite strangers, and he refused to act like it. If she thought he could live in this cold, passionless marriage, she was utterly and completely mistaken.

'Charlotte.'

Oh, dear Lord, not now.

Her pulse moved into high alert as she froze, one hand on the doorknob to her apartment, salvation so close at hand.

'Yes?' She did her best to maintain the appearance of calm as she turned to face him, but the truth was, Charlotte's nerves were beyond frayed. A whole night spent in the same room as her husband, trying not to act on the storm of awareness that was besieging her, trying not to tell him that she loved him, filled her with a dull, throbbing ache and a maddening sense of fury, so she wanted to throw open the doors to her apartment, run inside and scream until there was no sound left anywhere in her body.

'We can do this out here,' he said with a nod, 'But privacy is probably better.'

She gaped. 'Do what?'

His eyes lashed hers, and the contempt she felt there curdled something in the pit of her stomach. He was angry. He was frustrated. He was…a thousand things and she couldn't understand any of them. This was dangerous. Somewhere along the way, everything had got out of hand and she could no longer keep him—them—easily boxed up as she'd decided to.

Her heart tightened, and she tried to ignore the love that was there, tried to resist how much she cared for him.

'Okay,' she whispered. 'But I'm tired, Rocco. So let's make this quick.'

For a moment she thought she saw compassion in his eyes, but it was gone again almost instantly. She stepped into her apartment and he followed; it was the first time he'd been in here and it felt as though something important shifted just with his presence. She whirled around to face him, at the same time as he came closer, so their bodies collided and all the breath escaped her. Not by physical force but from shock and raw, primal need.

'What do you want?' she ground out, groaning under the weight of trying to ignore her feelings, to control and contain them, under the pain of the futility of loving him.

'For you to act like my wife,' he responded in the same tone, and then he was kissing her, just as he had at the airstrip, in the plane, with fierce, angry, urgent need, dominance requiring submission, demanding truth and reality from her, instead of the game of pretence she'd been playing all week. And how could she fight that? How could she fight him, when this was exactly what she desperately wanted too? When they touched, when they kissed, it was as though the real world no longer mattered. No definition of what they were would hold sway, there was only the undeniable connection they'd forged, starting on that first night together.

But it wasn't enough.

She couldn't exist like this purely for sexual gratification.

Ripping her mouth away from his, forcing herself to stare at him, to catch her breath and hope for sanity to return, she lifted a hand to his chest—to push him away or hold him close, she didn't know. Her fingers curled in the fabric of his crisp shirt, and her eyes filled with stars.

'When I touch you, you ignite,' he said slowly, a warning in those words. 'And yet you spend the rest of the time acting as though I don't exist. Why?'

She didn't answer; she couldn't.

'Is this the marriage you envisaged for us?'

Her eyes swept shut: a self-protective mechanism.

'Is this how you see our future?'

The thought of that filled her with an awful sense of unreality. How could this be so?

'What do you want from me?' she whispered, no longer sure of anything in this world.

'Not this.'

Her heart stuttered. Panic filled her. 'What does that mean?'

'I'm not going to exist as an ornament, to be brought out for ceremonial events and then shelved until my next required outing. How can *you* live like this?'

Her lips parted, shock searing her. 'I warned you, you'd hate this life,' she said quietly, dropping her eyes, because she knew what would happen next. He'd leave her, and she couldn't even fault him for that.

'I'm more interested in how you *don't* hate it.'

'I was raised for it.'

'Forse!' he snapped, rubbing a hand through his hair. 'But you were *born* for so much more. You are smart and

funny and kind and beautiful, and you have so much more to give than making small talk with dignitaries.'

He was angry with her, fighting her, and yet his words wrapped around her with the force of a thousand rainbows, so even in the midst of this argument, pleasure glowed in her belly, just for a moment.

'God knows, I want more than this,' he responded, stalking to the other side of her bedroom and staring across at her, hands on hips, eyes darker than the night sky.

'What do you want?' she whispered, even when she was terrified of the answer.

'I want a way out of it.'

Her heart stammered and almost died. She could hardly breathe. He was going to leave her. And fight for custody of their child, just as he'd initially threatened? The world was spinning uncontrollably. She made a strangled noise and nodded, because even as she wanted to fight him, she understood. How could she fail to see what he was saying?

'Divorce is—'

'I'm not talking about a divorce. I mean marriage. I want to get away from all *this*.' He waved his finger around the room, indicating the palace.

'This is my life.'

'No, it's a part of your life,' he responded firmly.

'I warned you, before we married—'

'Yes,' he interrupted. 'But that was before.'

'Before what?'

'Our honeymoon. When I saw the real you. How can you bear to hide her away so often? How can you bear to be only this version of yourself?' He pointed to her now, and she felt awkward and wrong in the gown she'd worn for the state dinner. He stalked across the room, curling his hands around her arms. 'Don't you remember what it was like in Italy? Walking through those streets, listening to carollers, decorating the tree, laughing—enjoying yourself?'

'That wasn't real,' she whispered, more to herself than him. She had to believe that.

'Are you sure? Are you sure *this* isn't what's fake?'

Her pulse ran at a thousand miles an hour, gushing through her loudly and impatiently.

'What do you want me to say?' she asked, rubbing her fingers over her temples. 'Yes, Italy was wonderful. I loved being there with you. But it was—' her voice cracked '—an illusion,' she finished weakly, turning to look out of her window.

'In what way?'

Danger signs were everywhere. How could she answer that without telling him too much? But suddenly, Charlotte was sick of hiding. She was sick of sheltering her feelings, because she was scared of what he might say, of how he might react.

'Do I really need to spell it out?'

He didn't respond and something bubbled over inside her.

'What was the point of it all?' she asked wearily. 'Sleeping together, talking, laughing, everything you just listed, that was great, but seriously, why? Why bother?'

'Because we're going to be parents,' he responded without hesitation. 'Don't you think it will be easier to raise a child together if we are not strangers?'

Her heart sank, painful and withered, down to her toes.

Such a clear, sensible answer, that spoke of none of his own wishes or feelings. This was, as she'd suspected, all about their baby. Not her. None of this was personal for Rocco. She was nothing to him.

She pulled away, wrenching free of him, unable to bear being touched when that was so hollow a gesture.

'We *are* strangers though,' she whispered, closing her eyes against the fierce pain in the centre of her chest. 'Why pretend otherwise?'

He didn't speak for such a long time that eventually Charlotte angled her face, simply to see if he was still there.

'The last thing I want is for you to be unhappy. If you hate life here with me so much, then you can leave at any point. I won't hold you to our agreement, Rocco.'

'Our agreement was made for the sake of our baby. Nothing's changed. I intend to be here, to raise him or her with you. If anything, having seen your life, your family, I'm even more determined to be right here, by your side.'

More common sense that felt like arrows darting into her flesh. 'Then that's what we'll do.' She bit down on her lip, sadness washing over her at the future she wanted and how far away it felt. 'You don't have to attend formal functions. If you hate it, just…stay home.'

His features were a symmetrical mask of discontent. 'This isn't about the damned state dinners. It's about the way you are here in Hemmenway, it's about the future we could have.'

Tears sparkled on her lashes and he frowned, moving closer. 'You want that too. I know you do.'

His hands curled around her arms, sending sparks through her body.

'Admit it,' he demanded. 'Tell me what you want.'

He was goading her, pushing her, so the words she'd held as a secret for long days and nights buzzed on the tip of her tongue. 'Are you sure?'

His eyes narrowed. 'You're my wife. Tell me what you want and I will make it happen.'

His assurance was so *him*. He was a man who'd been born into poverty, who'd fought his way to the top by guile, intelligence and determination. But, for all the barriers he'd faced, he couldn't understand her world, and the strictures she felt.

'You are miserable.' A quiet plea made his voice hoarse. 'You escaped this life once, in New York, the night we met. I can help you escape more permanently, if that's what you want.'

'It isn't my royal duties that are upsetting to me.'

'Then what is it?'

'This,' she snapped, finally. 'Marriage, to you.'

His head jerked back as though she'd slapped him.

'I thought I could do it,' she mumbled, closing her eyes on a wave of grief. 'Everything you said made sense, and for our baby, for their place in the lineage…what choice did we have?'

Her eyes remained shut, so she couldn't see the pallor of his skin, the way all the colour drained from his face.

'But being married to you and pretending…'

'Pretending what?'

'Pretending I don't feel…' She opened her eyes then, looking straight into his as a wave of fear hit her. This was madness. At least if she remained quiet they could stay married, she could be near him. If she told him the truth it was impossible to predict what would happen next.

'Italy was real,' she whispered after a pause.

He squeezed the tops of her arms.

'New York was real.' The words tumbled out of her. 'But it was also a lie.'

'You're not making any sense.'

'I fell in love with you, Rocco.' She didn't dare look at him. 'I don't know when. In Italy I became conscious of how I felt. But maybe it even started in New York. I was drawn to you that night, and found myself thinking obsessively of you afterwards, even when I told myself I needed to forget, to put it all behind me.'

He said nothing, but his eyes probed hers and she felt as though he could see far too much.

'Loving you is agony,' she whispered. 'I told myself I wouldn't say anything. That I'd sit with these feelings and learn to live with them. You don't deserve to be burdened by this. But every day we're together, every time you touch me, every time you look at me, I feel it overwhelming me, and imagining the life we could have, if you loved me too, is devastating.' She swallowed a sob. 'So leaving Hemmenway won't fix it. Nothing will.'

Silence crackled around them, and with every beat of time that passed without his response hope died a little more inside her chest—a hope she hadn't realised she'd been foolish enough to hold on to.

'Charlotte, listen to me.' His voice was gruff. She angled her face to his, and her heart thumped with all the love she felt. 'This isn't love.'

Pain twisted her stomach.

'I'm the first person in your life who's been kind to you,' he added, gently. 'You're mistaking warmth and… friendship…with something else.' He leaned his head closer, brushing his lips to hers, and the contradictory feelings that swarmed through her made it hard to breathe. 'I was also your first lover. I awakened something inside of you that was new and exciting. We've explored that together, and it's natural you'd confuse those feelings with love. But it isn't. It's sex, plain and simple.'

Her lips parted on a groan and she tore herself away

from him, physically sickened by the way he was characterising their relationship. He was trying to help, and yet it was killing a part of her to hear the passionless description of their relationship.

'Not for me,' she whispered.

'Because you have no experience.'

She whirled around to face him. 'It wouldn't matter if I'd slept with every man in the world, I would still know.' She pressed her fingers to her chest, quite wild with rage and anger now. 'I would still know that what I feel in here is genuine and unmistakable. I love you.'

He shook his head slowly. 'Pregnancy hormones can make you feel—'

'Damn it, Rocco. Stop telling me how I feel. I *know* what this is.'

'How?' he pushed, but gently, kindly, in a tone that Charlotte found as patronising as anything. 'You've never been in a relationship before. You've never had a lover. Don't you think it's even remotely possible that you are misinterpreting these feelings?' She was speechless, and perhaps he took that for acceptance. 'Trust me, Charlotte. The novelty of this will fade, and you'll see that I am right.'

'You're not right,' she whispered. 'I'm sorry that your experiences have left you so jaded and cynical, and unable to see what's right in front of you, but I know how I feel, and it's love. I love you.'

He stared at her, a frown on his handsome face, and her heart splintered into a thousand pieces, broken beyond repair.

'All I ask,' she whispered, fingers shaking as she pushed her hair back from her brow, 'is that you give

me space while I work out how to live with these feelings and our marriage.'

He stared at her long and hard and she held her breath,
hoping, waiting, wanting, but it was futile. There was
no hope here.

'Space,' he repeated after a moment. 'If that's what you
want.' He nodded once, then appeared to hesitate for the
briefest moment before he turned and stalked towards the
door. He paused, turning back to face her. 'You will see
that I'm right, Princess. Give it time. You'll get over this.'

She winced at the condescending remark, and turned
her back on him, not waiting to see him leave the room.

CHAPTER THIRTEEN

HE SLAMMED THE door to his room shut, and only once he was safely inside, alone, did he give in to the maelstrom of feelings her words had stirred up.

Love.

He rejected it instantly.

It wasn't possible.

No one besides his mother had ever loved him, and that was how he wanted it. Love complicated everything. Love led to hurt. Love required trust and weakness, it required sacrifice, it required vulnerability. To love someone was to put your faith in them, to trust they wouldn't hurt you. To trust they wouldn't leave you.

In Italy he'd opened himself up to her, he'd shown her more of himself than he'd ever revealed to another person by a mile. He'd felt them grow close. He'd known it was real. He'd known there was danger here.

But when she'd pulled away from him, shutting him out, that danger had morphed into something that had terrified him, and proved his point. He'd trusted her, just a little, and she'd snapped away from him, leaving him with whiplash. Giving yourself fully to someone else, loving them, was a risk he wasn't prepared to take. Even with Charlotte, who was all that was good and kind in this world. It was needless and it was reckless. Her misery was living proof of that.

Charlotte had been hurt so often. Every single person in her life who was supposed to care for her had failed her. Every single damned one of them had let her down, and yet she actually thought herself in love with him? How did she find the capacity to hope, to trust after everything she'd been through? She was crazy.

And what about the baby? a voice in his mind pushed. One way or another, love was coming to him. Wasn't that the point of this marriage? Not just to be with his child, but to love him or her, to form a safety net for them that he'd never had? He wanted his child to have a family, a mother and father, to know love encircled them.

He was no longer a loner. He was no longer safe from the flipside of love.

But still, he could mitigate it. Still he could control how far it spread into his life. A child was one thing, a partner—a true partner—another.

Besides, he was right about Charlotte. She didn't love him, so much as she loved the idea of him, the idea of someone who was in her life, who cared for her, protected her, laughed with her, desired her. He was good for her, he realised. And she loved the way that felt. It was a different proposition to real love.

He just needed to give her space to see that, like she'd said, and then everything would return to the status quo.

He avoided any state events for the following week. But though he could avoid seeing her, he couldn't control the direction of his thoughts, nor his dreams, and in these Charlotte was ever-present.

He saw her as she'd been in Italy, content and full of wonder, he saw her as she'd been the night they'd met, mysterious and fascinating, and he saw her as she'd been the last night they'd spoken, eyes completely dulled of pleasure, face drawn, so his gut tightened and he found it almost impossible to focus.

He was worried about her. Not because she loved him, but because she was the mother of his child and she was hurting. It was the last thing he wanted.

Whenever he caught a glimpse of her she looked away, showing him that her desire for space hadn't changed. She didn't want him, she didn't want to see him.

It only hardened his resolve.

He threw himself into his work, and when that didn't succeed in pushing Charlotte from his mind he made plans to travel to New York, to put some geographical distance between them.

'What do you mean?' she asked, heart twisting.

'He left early this morning,' Iris said apologetically. 'He asked if you were awake, but when I told you weren't, he left. He asked me to give you this.' Iris held out a folded piece of paper.

Charlotte took it, stomach in knots. 'Thank you,' she murmured, and when she looked up, Iris was gone.

Charlotte,

I need to take care of something in my New York office. I'll be gone a few weeks. Please let me know if there are any problems with the baby. We'll talk when I get back. Take care of yourself,

Rocco

Tears misted her eyes and she moved to her window, staring out with a growing ache in her chest.

This was impossible. Before Rocco, she'd been, if not

exactly happy, somewhat content and at peace with her life. But now that felt almost impossible. Misery stretched through her.

She loved him. She'd told him she loved him, but he didn't feel the same way. Why was she surprised? No one loved her. Not her parents, not her brother, no one. What had she expected? That Rocco would be any different? Any why? Because he'd been kind to her, just as he'd said?

She made no effort to stem the tears that fell now, letting them roll down her cheeks and land on the carpet with soft thudding movements.

After meeting Charlotte the first time, Rocco had struggled to get back into the swing of his normal life. She'd become a fever in his blood, a fascinating enigma that had spread through him, making it impossible to see the world quite as he had before. And that had been after a brief one-night stand.

But now? After their marriage, after their honeymoon? She was more than a fever in his blood, she was a living, breathing part of him, so that when he saw the world it was partly through her eyes as well.

She was a part of him so that being here without her felt strange and wrong in every way.

It was infuriating, and for Rocco, who prided himself on being able to conquer all in his life, he knew this would simply demand more concentration and focus than anything ever had.

He worked impossibly long hours—from five in the morning until after midnight. He fell into bed when he got home, so exhausted that sleep, finally, obliterated his wife from his mind.

But a week after returning to New York, a strange

thing happened. Rocco woke thinking not of Charlotte, but of his mother, and without realising how he got there he found himself standing in front of the department store Allegra had loved so much, looking at the Christmas decorations and remembering...

His mother was crying softly...so softly he almost didn't hear her. But their home was tiny. There was nowhere, really, she could escape.

Rousing himself from his sleep, he stepped out of bed and padded down the hall, standing behind the wall, listening.

'You can't keep pretending he doesn't exist. One day he'll be a grown man. What if he looks you up? What if he decides to tell the world you're his father?'

'Then you'll only have yourself to blame. How many times do I have to tell you? That what happened between us was meaningless sex? Do you really think you mattered to me?'

'This isn't about us any longer.' His mother's voice rang with pride. 'You have a son. You cannot keep ignoring him.'

'Watch me.'

His mother gasped. 'How can you be so unfeeling?'

'I choose not to feel, Allegra. It's that simple.'

'We need to talk.' Charlotte stepped into her parents' parlour, pale but determined. Rocco had left, but he'd buried something inside of her, a confidence that, despite his rejection, seemed to grow day by day. It had started with anger at how they'd treated her, and now it had turned into something else altogether: an absolute belief in her being right. She deserved better than this. She always had.

Whatever hang-ups her parents had, and she understood how Nicholas's near-death had affected them, she had always deserved better. She had deserved to be wanted for who she was, not simply for what she could give.

If anything, her faith in herself had grown despite Rocco's rejection. It had made her even more determined to claim her space, to stand up for herself, and their child.

'Do we?'

'It's important.' She closed the door behind herself, scanning the room to be sure they were alone.

'Go on.' Her father had softened somewhat, no doubt buoyed by the favourable press coverage of Charlotte's marriage. Unbeknownst to her, some paparazzi had discovered their honeymoon location and a couple of photos taken in the village had been run in the national papers, showing Charlotte and Rocco looking completely smitten. It had hurt Charlotte to look at the photos, knowing as she did that it was all a lie, but the public had gone wild for them.

'Rocco and I are having a baby. I thought you should know. The lineage is secure.'

She turned to leave, but her mother's voice arrested her, the sound not a word so much as a garbled, shocked sound.

'What?' her father said, and when Charlotte turned, he was standing. 'You're pregnant?'

'Yes. My life's purpose is almost complete,' she added tartly, and had the satisfaction of seeing her mother wince. 'I'll have a scan in about six weeks. Naturally, I'll ask the doctor to keep you apprised of any developments.'

'Charlotte.' Her mother spoke, standing, fiddling with her hands. 'I didn't...'

Charlotte waited, arms crossed, uncaring that her mother's face was covered with tears, that she looked, in that moment, almost human. A lifetime of rejection couldn't be made up for in one afternoon, with one display of humanity.

'How do you feel?' her father asked.

How did she feel? That was a question too impossible to answer. 'Everything's fine,' she answered instead, pulling open the door. 'Thanks for your time.'

He had spent his whole life determined to be different from his father. Hell, it was the reason this proposal had flown from his mouth, before he'd given it any thought at all. His father had rejected his mother, had refused to care for her, so Rocco had known he must do the opposite. He would propose to Charlotte, acknowledge their baby, fight for their baby, love their baby. All of the things Rocco's father had failed to do.

But he'd forgotten about his father's remark. *I choose not to feel, Allegra. It's that simple.*

In this way, Rocco and his father were identical. Both men were emotionally void, determined not to let their hearts soften them, determined not to allow weakness to make fools of them.

Rocco had been so focused on that for so long, without realising that in doing so he was fulfilling his worst nightmare, and now, as he stared at the department-store window, a thousand feelings shimmered inside him, clarifying and taking shape. The past and the present mixed so he saw his mother as a child and a woman, his wife as a child, rejected by her family, turned into an item rather than a person, belittled by some trolls on the internet, always used for what she could give rather than appreciated for who she was.

Even by him.

He groaned, so a woman passing by sent him a curious glance. Rocco barely noticed.

He'd reduced her to the mother of his child so many times he couldn't believe it. He'd told her again and again they were marrying for the baby. Even his parting note had required her to notify him if anything happened to the baby, when that wasn't what he'd meant at all, only he hadn't wanted to show his hand. He hadn't wanted to tell her that he wanted to hear from her. About her.

That she was as important to him as the baby. That she had, without his knowledge, and contrary to whatever plans he'd had for his life, become the most important person in it.

'Damn it.' He slammed his palm against the wall, giving the window one last fulminating glare before he turned on his heel and ran all the way back to his penthouse.

Her hand stilled on the elaborate swirling base of the banister. Three steps from the ground, she saw him, striding into the hallway, past the enormous Christmas tree, with such purpose that she worried something was wrong.

His eyes scanned the ancient paintings that adorned the walls, moving further and further forward until they landed on her and she flinched, because it had been ten days since they'd been in the same room and her heart was ill-prepared for this.

She tried to draw breath, to regain her equilibrium, but she could barely breathe, let alone move. Rocco didn't seem to have the same problem. He changed course and began to walk towards her with long strides and a determined gait, so within seconds he was on the landing beneath her, waiting, watching, dark eyes probing hers, asking questions she couldn't answer.

'I thought you were in New York.'

Her voice emerged husky and soft, almost inaudible. She cleared her throat.

'I was. I came back.'

She nodded awkwardly. Was this what their marriage would be? So awkward, so false?

'I came to see you.'

Oh, God. Her stomach sank. In the back of her mind she'd been dreading this, ever since the other night, when he'd said he wanted a way out of this. At the time he'd flatly denied the idea of a divorce, but the look on his face was so sombre, it was impossible not to believe the worst now. Pain lashed her but she straightened her spine, putting all her energy into appearing brave and in command, even when she felt like curling up in a ball and crying.

'Okay.' She couldn't put this off. It would be better to have the conversation and be done with it. Anxiety fluttered inside her belly and she knotted her fingers together, forcing her feet to bring her down the remaining steps, being careful to give him a wide berth.

'How are you?' The question cut through her. She ignored the way her heart was racing, her pulse throbbing.

'The baby's fine,' she responded quickly. 'Everything's fine.' Just as she'd told her parents.

His eyes swept shut, his jaw clenched.

'Where can we speak privately?' he asked, short, curt, a man in charge who didn't like having to be asked where to take her.

She looked around then began to walk to one of the office suites on the ground floor. They pushed into the empty space and she did everything she could to appear calm, even when he closed the door with a click, reinforcing the fact they were completely alone. She stood there, waiting for the axe to drop, incapable of speaking.

'I went to New York,' he said unnecessarily, because they'd already discussed that.

She frowned. 'Yes.'

'And I can't explain it.' He shook his head in frustration. 'You were there.'

She blinked. 'I'm pretty sure I wasn't.'

'You were *here*.' He pointed to the side of his head. 'I couldn't stop thinking about you.'

Her heart hitched. The world stopped spinning.

'Worrying about you,' he amended, so she closed her eyes, cursing the stupid hope that had briefly flared. When would she get it through her head that he didn't care about her in that way?

'I'm fine,' she lied.

'And I was gripped with this desperate, all-consuming need to come back and fix things. I reacted badly last week. I should never have said that you don't love me. Your feelings are your own, and you understand them better than I do.'

Her mouth was bone-dry. She nodded, not capable of speech.

'So I wanted to reassure you that I won't break your heart. I will take care of you, Charlotte.'

'Because I'm the mother of our baby,' she said with a dull nod.

'Yes,' he agreed quickly, a frown on his face marring that easy agreement. 'Except, no. It's more than that.' He took a step towards her, lifting her chin with his thumb. 'It's you, too.'

Her heart stammered but her hopes had been dashed too many times. She didn't dare allow them room again.

'I haven't been able to get you out of my head. Not just

in the last week, I mean. Since New York.' He stared at her but his eyes held a faraway expression, so she knew he was in the past. 'After the night we met, I went to ground. I didn't go to bars. I couldn't date. I tried, once, and it was a disaster. All I could think of, all I wanted, was you.'

She drew in an uneven breath. 'I don't believe you.'

'Why would I lie?'

'For our baby?'

'No.' He shook his head. 'That's not it. You bewitched me, you changed me, and I have been fighting that ever since. The truth is, sex has always been about power for me. To sleep with a woman and walk away, to prove to myself that I don't need anything more than the physical. From anyone.'

'If you're trying to tell me that sex between us is so great I'm mistaking it for love, forget about it. I know the sex is great. I don't need a lexicon of experiences to prove that. I've missed you this last week and a half. You've been in my mind non-stop as well, but not your body, not the way you make me feel in bed. *You*, all of you. I'm in love.'

'I know that.'

Her eyes widened, his admission unexpected.

'I left because I hoped you'd come to your senses, and better understand your feelings, but instead I came to mine. Instead I learned what I'm feeling,' he pressed his hand to his chest, 'and why I was so determined not to let you love me.'

'Why?' she asked urgently.

'Because I'm my father's son, after all,' he muttered.

Her brows knitted together.

'I have done everything within my power to walk a different path to his. To make better choices. When you told me about your pregnancy, all I could think was that I wouldn't allow history to repeat itself. I had to show you my support, that I will care for and love our baby, and be in every way the polar opposite to him.'

She dipped her head, nodding. 'I presumed as much.'

'But my father is a cold, unfeeling son of a bitch. He once told my mother that he didn't love me because he simply chose not to love.'

The sound of Charlotte's angry intake of breath echoed in the room. 'That's a horrible thing to say.'

'Definitely not the worst I overheard, but yes. It's horrible and it's stupid and yet I was doing exactly the same thing to you. I was forcing myself to ignore how I felt about you. I've been doing it all along. After we slept together I pushed you away, because what we shared was so damned real, so damned special, I knew how loaded with risk you were. I told you I didn't sleep with virgins, I belittled you rather than looking inside myself and understanding *why* I was so rattled.'

'And why was that?'

'Because I couldn't control you,' he said with a shake of his head. 'I knew, from that moment, I wouldn't be able to walk away from you, so I pushed you, I pushed you away hard, hoping that would be enough.' His lips were grim. 'And then, when I couldn't get you out of my head, I told myself it was just sex. That you're beautiful and we connected, but that it was just a physical craving. The truth is, it's been more than that for so long.' He moved closer, hesitating a little, then lifting his hands to her face. 'Why do you think I insisted on a honeymoon? Why do you think I took you to the place that means the most to me? I wanted to sleep with you, absolutely, but mostly I just wanted us to be together. I was selfish and hungry for you, all of you.'

She closed her eyes.

'But the sex was so great,' he said with a lopsided smile, 'it was easy to keep lying to myself, to put everything down to the physical connection, or the fact you were pregnant with my baby. There was always an excuse, something to reassure myself with, to make me feel that I was still in control. And yet none of that explains why I wanted to throttle your parents the first time I met them, or why I felt like I was being burned alive when we came home from the honeymoon and you changed so much. I have loved you without letting myself acknowledge it, and if you hadn't been brave enough to tell me how *you* felt I don't know if I ever would have woken up and understood.'

She swallowed, her eyes lifting to his.

'Tell me I'm not too late.'

She bit down on her lip.

'Tell me I haven't ruined everything.'

'Do you promise you're not just saying this out of a misguided sense of obligation? Because you feel sorry for me?'

'I feel sorry for the bastards in your life who've undervalued you to the point you actually think that. I love you. The truth is, I didn't know what the emotion was, but looking back, every decision I have made since meeting you, right down to not even looking at another woman after our first night together, is because you captured my heart. I know you're going to hold it for ever. Try to be kind with it, *cara.*'

She nodded, tears of joy in her eyes. 'I'm very glad you realised how you felt, even if you did take your sweet bloody time,' she said on a small laugh.

'That makes three of us.'

And he kissed her then, with all the passion and desperate need they shared, but with love, too, because it moved between them freely now, as undeniable as air and water.

'He's asleep.' Rocco grinned as he entered the lounge room of their Italian home, the tree resplendent with the decorations that had once belonged to Allegra Santinova, including the ones he'd given her in New York, all those years ago.

Charlotte turned happily. Their three-month-old son, heir to the Hemmenwegian throne, was, she'd been reliably informed, an absolute dream. He had begun sleeping through the night at nine weeks of age, fed beautifully, and had dimples in his cheeks whenever he cooed, which was often enough to make Charlotte giddy with mother love.

'You have the Midas touch.'

'He is my son,' Rocco said with a puffed-up chest, his pride and adoration for their little bundle quite unmistakable. He came to put an arm around Charlotte, drawing her to him, and she sighed, content all the way to the tips of her toes.

'I love it here,' she said, unnecessarily, because they came to the Aosta Valley often enough, and every time she expressed her affection for the cabin on the edge of the forest, above the ancient little village.

'Especially at Christmas?'

'Oh, yes. It's the perfect way to spend our first anniversary,' she agreed.

'Do you ever think about that night?'

'In New York?' she asked, immediately understanding him, because they were so in sync with their thoughts and feelings. She nodded a little. 'Sometimes. Why?'

'I think of it often. I think about how different you

were, how captivated I was, and every now and again, when I want to torment myself, I think about how close I came to ruining all this.'

She turned in the circle of his arms, lifting a finger to his lips. 'Stop. That's in the past.'

'Thank God.'

'But you're too hard on yourself. Do you really think we would ever have left one another? Do you think there's any version of our lives that doesn't have us living together, married, raising our baby like this?'

'No,' he said simply, and they both smiled. This was inevitable, and it was perfect.

'When is the henchman expecting us back?' she asked with a crinkle of her nose that made Rocco laugh. Their life was far more liberal than Charlotte had intended, for the simple reason that Rocco refused to be told what to do. Even Charlotte's parents seemed somewhat intimidated by him. Her brother respected him and, courtesy of Rocco's insistence, Charlotte had been given more and more responsibilities.

'Next week,' Rocco said. 'For the Christmas Eve banquet.'

'Not until then?' She made a little squealing sound of pleasure. 'How on earth did you manage that?'

Rocco's nostrils flared. 'I simply told him what would suit us best.'

'My hero.' She batted her lashes at him.

'Yes, well, let's see.' And he scooped her up, cradling her to his chest. 'By my count, we have a maximum of two hours, so let's not waste them talking about the palace's chief of staff, hmm?'

'Not when we have at least two more babies to make,' she teased, earning a sizzling look from Rocco.

'You know how much I love seeing you around with my baby.'

She laughed as he carried her up the stairs and into the bedroom, ground zero for their love, the place where she'd come to understand her heart, her soul and everything she needed most in order to be happy.

Later, much later, when their baby had stirred and demanded his mummy, and the snow was swirling outside of the windows, Rocco reached into a drawer in the kitchen and removed a velvet pouch. 'I have something for you.'

'You do?' Her heart skipped a beat. 'What is it?'

He grinned, handing it to her, then taking their son from Charlotte's hands.

'Have a look and see.'

She pulled the cord on the pouch, peering in, frowning, before tipping the contents into her palm. The most beautiful little Christmas ornament fell out—dainty and handmade, out of what looked to be silver. A fine gold ribbon served as a loop from which it could hang, but it was the decoration itself that had her transfixed. Shaped like a sphere, a festive *tableau* had been carved into it.

'It's the village!' she said with a smile.

'Yes.'

'Oh, Rocco. Where on earth did you get this?'

'I had it made.'

'But where? It's so perfect. I can even see the restaurant we ate at on our honeymoon.'

'A jeweller in New York,' he said with a lift of his shoulders. 'I took a photo of the village.'

'I love it.'

'You wanted sentimental ornaments,' he pointed out.

Oh, she had. Charlotte couldn't remember saying that

in as many words, but it was proof of his love for her, his thoughtfulness, that he'd understood, and remembered.

'Thank you.' She pushed up to standing, moving to him and kissing him, before dropping a hand to their baby's head, stroking his soft, downy hair. 'I wanted sentimental ornaments,' she said throatily. 'But mostly, I wanted this.'

And it was true. Everything Charlotte had ever sought she now possessed, and every year, at Christmas, she would remember the beauty of their first Christmas together, when they'd fallen in love, and promised to live together, for as long as they both should live, husband and wife, soulmates.

* * * * *

THE TWIN SECRET
SHE MUST REVEAL

JOSS WOOD

MILLS & BOON

CHAPTER ONE

THIS WAS IT. In an hour she'd be married.

Thadie Le Roux glanced at her elaborate wedding dress on the double bed and touched the platinum-blonde micro braids threaded into her hair and twisted into an elegant knot at the back of her neck.

After numerous setbacks, insane press attention and her two brothers falling in love during the process, they were almost at the finish line. In a couple of hours, she'd be Mrs Clyde Strathern.

Was Clyde, ensconced in another suite down the hallway of this house, excited?

She wasn't. Not particularly. Then again, the last time she'd felt butterflies-in-her-stomach, gut-churning, light-headed excitement had been that night in London four years ago, when she'd, uncharacteristically, allowed a gorgeous stranger to join her in her hotel room and take her to bed.

He'd been a once-in-a-lifetime collision, and their coming together gave her the best gift of her life, her twin sons, Gus and Finn. *You can't think about Angus, Thadie, not on your wedding day.*

Tightening the belt of her short dressing gown, she sat down on the edge of the huge bed, staring at her stupidly expensive wedding dress. The doubts she'd had over the past three months rolled over her and her breathing turned shallow, her skin prickling with dread. What was she doing? Clyde didn't love her, she didn't love him...

Thadie forced herself to calm down, pushing her doubts and concerns away. *You know why you are getting married, Le Roux, it was a carefully thought-out decision, remember?*

On a practical level, Clyde had agreed to pitch in with her boys, which meant more 'me' time for her. For years she'd been glued to the twins and she, maybe, wanted to return to work, and start designing again. Part-time, of course.

And yeah, providing her boys with a dad made her feel a little less guilty about wanting to do something for herself. They needed a father, and rugby superstar and national hero Clyde, both sporty and smart, was a good choice.

They moved in the same circles, had met at an event. She couldn't even remember what for now. And, unlike her tempestuous, volatile parents, Clyde was laid-back, nothing ever ruffled him. Being around him felt as if she were sailing consistently calm waters.

It was a simple transaction: Clyde liked her high profile and wanted to be part of the famous Le Roux family. She wanted a father for her boys, to shed the loneliness and responsibility of being a single mum. She knew she'd never crave his love and, provided he kept his promise to help raise Gus and Finn, he'd never disappoint her.

Could she be blamed for wanting her boys to have a stable, old-fashioned, two-parents-who-were-involved-in-their-lives upbringing? Clyde had agreed to take on that challenge.

She winced, thinking that Clyde hadn't spent much time with the twins lately, and she suddenly wondered whether helping her raise them was something he still wanted to do. No, she was overreacting. Clyde would've said something if he had any doubts about marrying her.

Admittedly, the last few months had been horrible. She'd had her first wedding venue cancelled by an unknown person, and for a while they'd been without a venue to host what was being dubbed South Africa's Wedding of the Year. She'd had journalists publicly questioning their commitment to each other, people trolling her on social media, and she'd had to ask Clyde's stepsister, Alta, to step down as a bridesmaid due to her constant negativity. Despite a few arguments, and many tears caused by stress and frustration—hers, not Clyde's, he'd been unfazed by all the drama—they'd made it to their wedding day.

She was just stressed, being overly dramatic. It was fine, they were fine. *Everything* was *fine*.

Thadie lifted her head as her best friend, Dodi, walked into the room. As the owner of a bridal salon, Dodi had helped her choose her wedding dress. Thadie was, if she was honest, a little jealous that Dodi worked in the fashion industry when she had studied fashion design and had once had big plans to be the next Stella McCartney or Vera Wang.

Instead of making garments, she'd made babies.

'Is Liyana here?' Thadie asked her, thinking of her glamorous mother. 'She promised she would be.'

Dodi frowned and shook her head. 'She sent a message saying she'd go directly to the church.'

Despite having known Liyana would let her down, Thadie still felt disappointed, a little wounded. Her mum had never kept a promise in her life, and had never really been a mum to her in the traditional sense, so why did she expect something different on her wedding day?

It would never occur to the ex-supermodel that her wedding day was one of those iconic mother-daughter moments that was supposed to be treasured.

'Stupid of me to think that she'd put herself out,' Thadie murmured. 'Then again, if my dad was still alive, he'd probably forget he was walking me down the aisle and he'd have to be dragged off the golf course.'

Or out of one of his many mistresses' beds. Her father being a serial cheater was another disappointment. Then again, her mother hadn't been that hot on monogamy either.

Between her parents, not knowing Angus's surname and losing his unexamined business card—resulting in her not being able to contact him after their mind-blowing night together, or when she'd found out she was pregnant—she was done with being disappointed. It was far better to keep her expectations low and, above all, realistic.

'Dammit,' Dodi muttered, her attention on something happening outside the window.

Thadie stood up. 'What's going on?'

When Thadie moved to stand next to her, Dodi threw out her arm, keeping her back. 'There's a commotion at the gate. It's a fair distance away but I can see photographers, some with long-range lenses.'

No, that couldn't be right. To keep the press away, she'd arranged for a text message to be sent to their guests at the end of the church service telling them where to head for the reception.

Only a few people knew the location of the reception and she trusted most of them with her life. Thadie, still dressed in her short, silky dressing gown, crossed the room and yanked open the door to the adjacent living room. Her boys, thankfully, were with Jabu, Hadleigh House's long-term butler and the twins' honorary grandfather.

Ignoring her brothers and their fiancées and Alta, Clyde's stepsister, Thadie turned to her bodyguard—she'd opted for some personal protection due to the amount of press attention she was receiving—and asked Greg to fetch Clyde from his suite down the hallway. It was urgent.

A minute later Clyde stepped into the room but, instead of looking at her, he shoved his hands into the pockets of his tuxedo trousers and stared at the carpet. He'd clearly been expecting trouble. *Interesting.*

'We have photographers outside the gates,' Thadie stated, turning to face Clyde and Alta, ignoring her anger-induced shakes. 'I made it clear I wanted this venue to remain secret until after the church service, that I didn't want to be swarmed by the press. Yet here they are. Which one of you leaked the venue?'

The pale blonde tossed her magazine aside and rose to her feet. She picked up her flute of champagne and downed its contents. 'I did,' she admitted, without a hint of remorse.

Nobody looked surprised at that revelation. 'I figured,' Thadie said through gritted teeth. Alta had made it very clear she wasn't a fan of their union. 'Why?'

Alta exchanged a look with Clyde. He walked to the drinks trolley, poured a slug of whiskey into a crystal tumbler and tossed it back. When he turned again, his eyes connected with Alta, who nodded her encouragement.

Encouragement for what?

'I gave her permission to leak the venue,' Clyde admitted.

'Why?' Thadie whispered, shocked to her core.

Clyde looked at Alta and, being the good soldier she was, she stepped into the battle. 'Clyde and I hoped it would finally cause you to call off the wedding.'

What was happening? This was all so surreal.

Thadie saw both her brothers had stepped forward, their faces stormy, and she lifted her hand to hold them back. This was her fight, her problem to solve. 'I'm sorry to be dense, but are you saying you *don't* want to marry me, Clyde?'

Clyde pushed a frustrated hand through his hair. 'Of course I don't! We've been trying to get this wedding cancelled for weeks, but nothing we've done has succeeded in getting you to call it off!'

'Here's a novel idea—why didn't you just tell Thadie you didn't want to get married?' Micah demanded, looking furious.

Fair point.

'Why go to the hassle of having the venue cancelled, the leaks to the press about Alta being dropped as a bridesmaid, about your relationship?' Jago asked, his tone Arctic-blizzard cold.

'Clyde's brand is built on him being the good guy, the nice guy, the perfect gentleman. I didn't want his reputation tarnished,' Alta explained. 'As his publicist, that's of paramount importance. Thadie is part of the Le Roux dynasty, South African royalty,' she continued. 'She's been famous, and adored, by the public since she was tiny. You and Micah have clout and influence and are exceedingly popular as well. Clyde getting engaged to Thadie was PR gold and gave him incredible exposure. The plan was always to break up with her after six months or so.'

Right, so he'd *never* intended to marry her, to be a dad to her sons.

'I'm still not getting why you'd sabotage your wedding when a simple "I'm not interested any more" would do,' Micah stated.

'Clyde was about to break it off, but then he received an offer from a famous, family-orientated brand to be their spokesperson. It's a deal worth millions and it took months to negotiate. But he can't be associated with any scandal, he has to keep his nose clean. Breaking up with you, Thadie, the nation's princess, would've been problematic. But if *you* jilted *him*, public sympathy would be with Clyde.'

Wow. Okay, then. Thadie shook her head in disbelief.

'If you'd explained all this to me, Clyde, we could've found a solution together. But to go behind my back, to cause me, and my family, untold hours of stress is unforgivable. Micah even spent weeks out of town looking for another venue for us and Ella found this place despite all odds! Jago and Micah have paid for this wedding in advance!'

'That doesn't matter,' Micah murmured.

'It does matter!' Thadie yelled. 'And it all could've been avoided if you were honest with me, Clyde! And don't get me started on the promises you made to my boys.'

Clyde lifted one shoulder in a half-baked shrug. And the small gesture, his dismissal of her boys and their feelings, sent her revving into the red zone.

'They are spoiled brats anyway, and they don't like rugby,' Clyde said, sounding deeply bored. Who was this man? Why hadn't she seen this side of him before? Or had she ignored what she didn't like because she'd been so damn determined to snag a father for her sons?

'They are *three*!'

'Really? I thought they were older. Anyway...so Alta

is ready to face the press, she'll tell them you're calling off the wedding.'

Uh…*no*.

In a couple of sentences, he'd managed to insult her as a mother—she'd worked damn hard to make sure her kids were not spoiled!—and show her he was clueless about her kids. And he still thought she'd save his precious deal?

How had she been so blind? How had she fallen for his lies to the point where she'd agreed to marry him?

It wasn't often she lost her temper or acted irrationally, but he'd pushed all her buttons. Nobody messed with her kids and their emotions. Or played her for a fool.

She was done talking. It was time for action. She spun around, and half ran out of the room, heading for the stairs. She was dimly aware of being followed and within seconds she was at the front door of the grand Victorian mansion.

'Thads, you're in a short, very revealing dressing gown,' Dodi shouted from somewhere behind her. 'And you're not wearing any shoes! Where are you going?'

She wrenched the door front door open and stepped onto the portico, facing the press who'd gathered at the gate at the end of the long driveway. From this distance, the long-range cameras would get some good photographs of her, but that wasn't enough.

She had an ex-fiancé she needed to throw under the bus.

In his Canary Wharf penthouse office on Monday afternoon, Angus Docherty kicked up his feet and rested his size thirteens on the corner of his desk, his eyes on the screen of his tablet in his lap. He'd recently returned from

Pakistan, having completed an off-the-grid mission, and he had mountains of work to do.

The world didn't stop because he'd been unavailable for the past few weeks. Despite owning and operating an international, multibillion-pound company focusing on securing people, assets, and premises, he also carried out sensitive missions for western governments…missions that were dangerous, off the books and top secret.

Once a soldier, always a soldier.

It was still a source of amusement that owning and operating a business had never been on his radar growing up. No, like his father and grandfather, and great-grandfather, he'd been destined for military service, expected to match his father's and grandfather's illustrious achievements. His great-grandfather retired as a colonel, his grandfather died a few days after being promoted to major general.

Of all his army-serving ancestors, it was his father who'd attained the highest rank, the youngest general in fifty years. General Colm Docherty answered only to God. And, sometimes, to the Prime Minister. He was a legend in military circles, respected and revered. He had a tireless work ethic and was disciplined and focused. The General was a hard man to work for, he demanded his pound of flesh.

From his son, he demanded that pound of flesh, his spine, and his internal organs too.

If The General was difficult to deal with at work, he was ten times worse at home, pedantic and unemotional, relentlessly demanding. His only child was held to a higher standard than everyone else. Angus had to run faster, work harder, achieve more, and be better. Be the best. Acceptance by his father meant he had to be perfect. Failure was not tolerated. Ever.

Catching a bullet in his thigh, which narrowly missed his femoral artery but shattered his femur, was his biggest failure of all. Being shot not only derailed his father's plans for him to be the second general bearing the Docherty name but fundamentally changed his relationship with his parents. The pins in his thigh were enough for him to be discharged from the military, a blow he still felt today. He'd had no wish to be promoted to a desk job, but leaving his unit was a wound he'd yet to recover from…

And his leaving the military was, to The General, the worst of failures. Dochertys were soldiers, and if you no longer served under the Queen's command, you were *nothing*. Up to that point, Angus had believed his parents, on some level, loved him.

He rubbed his hand over his face, thinking he was more tired than he realised if he was walking down memory lane, thinking about his estranged parents. He yawned and stretched, pushing his hands through his thick hair, overly long from spending weeks on the road.

A rap on his door had him looking up and he waved his second in command to come in. They'd served together in the unit, and Heath was the first person Angus employed when he'd established Docherty Security.

Heath, his tablet in his hand, dropped into the visitor's chair. Angus caught the smile on Heath's normally taciturn face and wondered what was making his dour friend smile. 'What's up?' he asked.

Heath shook his head, his mouth twitching in amusement. 'I'm watching a video of a South African client. She got dumped shortly before her wedding and her impromptu press conference has gone viral.'

Angus dropped his legs and took the tablet, tapping his finger against the play button. The woman wore a silky dressing gown, edged by six inches of white lace at the cuffs at the wrists and hem, revealing most of her thighs and long, gorgeous legs. The top of her dressing gown gaped open and he, and the rest of the world, caught a glimpse of a luscious breast, covered by a strapless, lacy, pale blue bra.

He moved on to her face, and he stilled, every nerve in his body frozen. Thadie…

Angus felt his heart rate increasing—something that rarely happened—and he drummed his fingers on his thigh. He never lost his cool but one look at her lovely face and tall, sexy, curvy body had his core temperature increasing.

He'd been in firefights, had bombs explode around him, fought for his life in hand-to-hand combat, been *shot* and he never lost his cool. One look into her extraordinary eyes and he was a basket case.

Angus lifted his finger to trace her cut-glass cheekbones, her pointy chin and lush mouth. Her eyes were almond-shaped and as dark as sin, and her skin reminded him of a topaz pendant his grandmother wore, rich and a golden brown. There were freckles on her nose and dotting her cheeks and he recalled trying to kiss every one he found on her body. Not, in any way, a hardship. In the video she wore thin, long, bright blonde braids— they suited her—but he remembered her having springy coils touching her shoulders.

Angus pushed play and her rich voice rolled over him.

'I came here to tell you my fiancé, ex-fiancé,' she corrected, holding up a finger, 'has not only dumped me but has just admitted to sabotaging the plans we made for our wedding. He did that in the hope the stress of multiple wedding disasters would cause me to call it off because he didn't have the guts to do it himself.'

Her chest rose up and fury caused her cheeks to glow

with a pink undertone. She was hopping mad and, man, she was stunning. Then Thadie placed the balls of her hands into her eye sockets and pushed down. After a few seconds, she lowered her hands, but he caught no sign of tears.

'He told me he intended to blame me in the court of public opinion for the break-up so I'm out here, telling you I'd planned on getting married today, that I was *prepared* to become his wife.'

Prepared? That was an unusual turn of phrase and one that didn't imply she was wildly in love with the groom. Angus watched, fascinated, as two tall men approached her—alike enough for him to think they were twins—dressed in designer suits and, judging by the roses in their lapels, part of the wedding party. They also exuded a proprietary and protective air.

One of the men draped his jacket around her shoulders, hiding her body from the cameras. Then he wrapped his arm around her and led her back to the house. The other stood in front of the press corps, who were lapping up the drama.

'As most of you know, I'm Jago Le Roux. As stated, my sister's wedding has been cancelled,' he said, his expression grim. 'I'd ask you to respect our privacy and give her space to work through this day and drama, but I suspect that's not going to happen, is it?'

A barrage of questions punctured the air as he followed his siblings back to the house. The video cut off and Angus, still shaken but trying to hide it, lifted his eyes to look at Heath.

'Explain,' he demanded.

Heath stretched out his long legs and rested his hands on his stomach. 'We were hired to protect one of Johan-

nesburg's most recognisable faces, the heiress Thadie
Le Roux—'

Her first name, he recalled her telling him, meant
'loved one' in Zulu. It was an unusual name and one
he'd never heard before or since that night in London
four years ago. Memories of gliding his hands over her
silky, glorious skin, exploring her sexy mouth, her gasps
and her groans as he loved her, bombarded him. Those
six hours spent with her were the best sexual memories
of his life, and it took all his willpower to keep his expression impassive.

'This is a massive story in South Africa and, as a result, Docherty Security is attracting attention down there.
It's been forty-eight hours since the wedding was called
off, but the ex-fiancé is, in the hope of rehabilitating his
reputation, doing interviews. His actions are fuelling the
story and keeping it in the headlines. Now the international press corps has picked up the story and, because
her mother is a famous ex-supermodel and socialite, the
attention on her is going to double. Or triple.'

Angus listened to him, only one part of his brain focused on what he was saying. He couldn't believe he'd
found her, that he knew now who she was, her surname,
where she lived. Four years ago, on meeting each other
at an engagement party, they'd left the party separately
and met up on the pavement below the couple's penthouse
apartment. He'd invited her out for a drink but somehow,
in the taxi from the party to the bar, they'd started kissing and she'd instructed the taxi driver to take them to
her hotel suite.

All their conversation from that point on had been
done with hands and lips, with strokes and kisses. They'd
agreed, only first names, nothing more. Their attraction
and chemistry had been mind-blowing, overlaid with an

intensity he'd never experienced before. For the first time, instead of running out of the door after a sexual encounter, he had been desperate for more time with her. In a day or two, he'd reasoned, definitely by the time she was due to leave London in four days, he'd be ready to say goodbye. Because he always, always said goodbye. Back then—and now—he had sky-high emotional barriers and a gorgeous foreigner wasn't going to punch through them.

As always, he hadn't had the time, or the inclination, to make space for a woman in his life and seventy-two hours had seemed enough time to get her out of his system.

Over breakfast the next morning, he'd invited her to stay with him for the rest of her time in London, and, to his surprise, she'd accepted. Because she'd lost her phone the night before, they'd agreed she'd check out of the hotel, find a store and replace her phone. And he'd take her suitcase with him to his office. When she was done, she'd call him—he'd placed his business card on the bedside table—and he'd give her directions to his flat, and he'd meet her there, and they'd spend the rest of the day in bed.

The phone call never came and her suitcase still sat at the back of his walk-in closet. In the days following their encounter, he'd tried to find her, but soon realised it was an impossible endeavour when he only knew her first name.

But he knew more now.

It was a ten, twelve-hour flight to Johannesburg and if he flew out later, after his dinner meeting with an important client, he could be there by mid-afternoon, South African time, tomorrow.

No! Flying to South Africa was a ridiculous notion. She was a one-night stand, nothing more.

'Her family has an incredibly high profile, and she has a huge social media following. Her brothers recommended us to their younger sister when she expressed a need for a personal protection officer. I'm worried that if something happens to her, if she so much as kicks her toe, Docherty Security is going to catch flak. I think she needs more PPOs. She might not agree to pay for more bodyguards, might not want them, but this is a nightmare waiting to happen.'

Angus nodded his agreement. He understood Heath's worry about reputational damage, it was normally at the forefront of his mind too. But not today.

Yes, he'd been crazy attracted to her, and the memories of that night were seared onto his brain. But attraction wasn't driving his need to see her—his curiosity was. After four years of wondering, he might finally get answers to questions that still, occasionally, kept him awake at night. What had happened after she'd climbed into the taxi outside her hotel? Why had she changed her mind? Had she had second thoughts? If she'd decided not to see him again, why hadn't she contacted him to collect her suitcase?

How had she gone from passionately kissing him on the pavement to vanishing?

He wasn't interested in rebooting their affair, in picking up where they'd left off. He just wanted to know, *dammit*. He'd always been able to read people and situations and this ability had saved his life on more than one occasion. Where had he gone so wrong with Thadie?

He'd always been the type to dig, to understand, to gather every bit of knowledge about a situation so he had a clear, objective view of the events. She was an unsolved puzzle, an incomplete mission, an end that hadn't been securely tied. As a soldier, and a perfectionist, Angus hated unresolved questions.

He'd read her wrong and her not contacting him felt like a failure. And failure, as his father had drummed into him from the day he could understand the concept, was unacceptable.

But was he really going to fly thousands of miles and incur the running costs of his inter-continental jet just to ascertain how, and why, he'd read her wrong? Yes, he wanted to know how. And why. It wasn't wounded pride, or ego: the reality was that if he misconstrued another situation during an undercover operation or misinterpreted another person in a dangerous situation, people, including himself, could get hurt or killed. The worst failure of all.

There was also a good chance that when he got to South Africa, once he laid eyes on her, he'd wonder why he'd built her up in his mind, why he'd spent so much mental energy on one long-ago night. There was no chance she would carry the same punch she had years ago.

But he'd have the answers to his questions, and, since he was rich, he could easily afford the costs he'd incur. While he was there he'd also address the issue of Docherty Security suffering reputational damage, by arranging and swallowing the costs of additional protection officers for Thadie.

In a couple of days, he'd never have to give her another thought.

It was a plan with a solid outcome, one that had no chance of failing.

Angus liked plans. And he never failed.

CHAPTER TWO

THADIE COULDN'T BELIEVE that she had walked out of Cathcart House in her skimpy dressing gown, showing a lot of leg and, because she hadn't thought to tighten the sash, the edges of her baby-blue strapless bra. Standing up in front of all those reporters and setting out, in excruciating detail, Clyde's perfidy had been a stupid move and she was now paying the price. For the past three days, she'd had reporters standing outside her gate and dogging her every move.

As the only daughter of one of the country's richest men and a famous ex-supermodel, she was a society column regular and her engagement to a World Cup rugby superstar and national hero had been wildly reported on. Her wedding planning woes and the speculation about the health of her and Clyde's relationship had kept her in the media spotlight. She and Clyde had been keeping South Africans entertained for months.

Thadie had spent almost every moment since leaving Cathcart House examining the last nine months, trying to understand how she'd ended up unengaged in such a dramatic fashion. She'd genuinely thought Clyde would be a good father for Gus and Finn and, in their early days together, he had spent time with them, playing with them and getting to know them. Had she clung onto those memories as proof he'd be a good father and, caught up in the drama of their wedding going wrong, ignored or excused his lack of attention towards the twins? She bit her lip. Maybe.

Probably.

She'd spent her childhood and teens wishing, longing and hoping for her parents' attention so when Clyde had said he'd be the twins' dad, her eyes had filled with stars. She'd been so enamoured with giving the twins the stable family she'd never had that she'd ignored and dismissed anything that didn't fit into her fantasy of a perfect family.

She'd been so focused on netting them a father that she hadn't paid enough attention to the quality, and the qualities, of her catch. Too much fantasy, not enough reality.

Thadie sighed, feeling exhausted, wishing she were less obsessed with her need to give them a father, a role model. It was, she admitted, her issue, not theirs. But the compulsion to find them a father remained.

The memory of a rough-hewn face, attractively rugged, flashed on the big screen in her mind. The twins had his eyes, a light blue-green, a compelling contrast to their pale brown skin. Gus had his long nose, Finn Angus's mouth. Being already tall for their age, they'd also, she suspected, inherited his height. Having the boys in her life was a constant reminder of the best night of her life...

If only she hadn't lost his business card. Or had even looked at it before she lost it.

And not only because she'd wanted him to know about the twins. No, from the moment their eyes had met, she'd felt connected to him. She recalled the way raindrops glistened on his rich brown hair, the way his mouth hitched in a half-smile, and his extraordinarily wide shoulders. She recalled her heart settling and sighing. Until that moment she hadn't realised she'd been waiting for him to make an appearance in her life…

No, she was not going to add to her misery by thinking of Angus, what could've been, what had been lost. If she went down that path, she'd find herself mired in misery and she was feeling downhearted enough, thank you very much. Instead of wallowing, she needed to do something, *anything*…

The boys were with Jabu, the semi-retired butler who'd all but raised her, and she had to get out of the house. The walls were starting to close in on her. Her bodyguard Greg had tried to stop her, but Thadie overrode him, telling him that he could either accompany her or not, but she was leaving.

Greg, because it was his job, had no choice but to accompany her.

He insisted on driving, and it took him some time to manoeuvre her SUV through the throng of press at her gate. Ten minutes later, they were on the highway, heading for her best friend's bridal salon. Dodi would steer her to her office, sit her down and give her tea. Dodi wouldn't feel offended if she remained silent, or she would listen if Thadie wanted to recount every detail of the last few days. Or months. She was a truly excellent friend.

Knowing Greg would struggle to find parking near Dodi's popular salon, she told him to park a street over, not minding the walk past the art galleries, boutiques and delicatessens. She loved this area of her city. Melrose was an arty, lovely part of Johannesburg and it never bored her.

Leaving the car, she pulled her large bag over her shoulder and started walking in the direction of Love & Enchantment, Dodi's salon. Getting out of the house had been an excellent idea, she thought, as Greg fell into position behind her. She needed the exercise and maybe, if she was really lucky, she'd find a box of artisanal pastries or hand-crafted chocolates in Dodi's salon. There normally was. Dodi often calmed down overanxious, entitled or neurotic brides with sugary treats. And champagne.

She could do with a glass, or three, of champagne.

Thadie heard the beep of a text message and pulled her bag across her body, opening the zip. She pulled out her phone and pushed the sunglasses onto her head to read the message. Another publication was asking for a comment on her crazy press conference. *Was she overcome with grief? Was that why she went outside in her dressing gown?*

No, she silently replied, she had just been comprehensively, brain-shutting-down angry. Of course she'd never intended to do a press conference barefoot, dressed in an ultra-short satin-and-lace dressing gown. And if they thought she was stupid enough to give them any additional coverage by commenting on her enormous faux pas, they were the ones losing their minds.

'Thadie, I think we should go back to the car,' Greg said, from his position behind her. 'Being out in public is a bad idea.'

Thadie looked around, thinking they were just round the corner from Dodi's salon. Maybe twenty yards, thirty? 'Let's just see,' Thadie implored him. 'I'm going berserk at home, Greg, and I need to see my best friend. It will be fine,' she assured him with more confidence than she felt. 'Dodi's place is just around the corner.'

'Why do I think I am going to regret this?' Greg muttered, moving closer to her as they turned right…

And crashed straight into a mob of flashing cameras, shouted questions and smelly, less-than-fresh reporters. They must've been waiting quietly for them, having sussed they were close by. It was an ambush, Thadie realised. The press had informants everywhere and it was possible someone had followed her car and, after deducing where she was going—she and Dodi were friends long before Dodi's engagement to her brother Jago— tipped off the press.

Greg tried to keep some distance between her and the reporters, but it wasn't possible as they circled her from all sides. The questions amalgamated into an indecipherable cacophony and, being so close, the light flashes from the cameras hurt her eyes. Thadie felt as if she were in a fairground hall of mirrors where she couldn't focus on anyone's face and had no conception of distance. She started to hyperventilate and her grip on Greg's arm tightened. At least, she hoped it was Greg's arm, she couldn't be sure.

Just when she thought she couldn't take any more, a thickly muscled forearm encircled her waist, spun her around and plastered her against a very wide and very hard chest. The arm tightened and her feet lost contact with the ground. Using his other hand, and with a series of blunt and rude commands issued in a deep, don't-test-me voice, her rescuer cleared a path out of the melee.

Thadie's body stiffened. She recognised that voice, that Scottish accent...the rolled r's, stronger vowels and softer t's. No, it couldn't be, it wasn't possible. There was no way Angus was carrying her out of this mob. It had to be another six-foot-four, ripped guy who smelled like a walk through a wild forest.

Thadie placed her hand on that hard chest and looked up. A cold wave doused her, then a blowtorch seared her skin, and she couldn't decide whether she was blisteringly hot or freezing cold. Her mouth dried up and her heart rate rocketed up and, yes, she'd suddenly acquired a hundred thousand butterflies in her stomach. And they were taking flight.

She'd experienced a couple of tough days, and her eyes had to be playing tricks on her, because there was no way that Angus, her one-night—and exceedingly hot—stand was carrying her over to a massive, matte black Range Rover and tossing her inside.

What? How? Was she losing her mind?

But since he was the only person who'd ever made her feel light-headed, consumed by the urge to touch and taste, she might not be going crazy. Or not just yet.

From the passenger seat of his car, Thadie watched, flabbergasted, as Angus walked around the bonnet of the luxury vehicle, his scowl enough of a deterrent to make the reporters keep their distance. She was vaguely aware of Greg saying he'd drive her car home, but she couldn't tear her eyes off Angus—so masculine, so sexy!—sliding behind the wheel of the car.

Without a word, he started the car and slapped it into gear, his eyes on his side mirror, checking to see if he could pull into the traffic. 'What on earth are *you* doing here?' she asked, her voice cracking.

Those eyes, the mini version of which she looked into every day, collided with hers. The startling blue-green colour was infused with annoyance and a great deal of frustration.

'I'm protecting you, Thadie,' he said, transferring his gaze to the rear-view mirror. He waited for Greg to pass him and Thadie noticed his scowl. His displeasure with Greg oozed from every pore and Thadie felt the need to protect her young, albeit inexperienced bodyguard.

'It's not Greg's fault. I insisted on going to Dodi's place,' she gabbled. 'I told him that I'd go alone if he didn't accompany me.'

Angus's eyes returned to her, and she felt pinned to her seat as he silently debated whether she was telling the truth or not. While she waited, she noticed the strands of grey hair above his ears, and he now wore thick stubble instead of a beard. There were new lines next to his eyes. He looked older, warier, a hundred times sexier.

Thadie grabbed the skirt of her dress and twisted it in her clenched fists, feeling her heart pushing its way through her ribcage. She felt light-headed. Her thoughts were racing at two hundred miles a minute. How and why was the father of her sons sitting next to her, looking remote and distant and, man, even more handsome than he did four years ago?

Thadie looked out of the window and bit the inside of her lip, not knowing what to do. Or say. She'd just been dumped by her fiancé and was facing an insane amount of press attention. And now she had to deal with the arrival of her one-night lover and the father of her toddlers.

She didn't know which way was up.

'I'm sorry, I don't understand why you are here,' Thadie said, sounding utterly confused.

He didn't blame her. The last person she'd expected to see was the man she'd slept with, and forgotten about, four years later in her home city, while she was being jostled by a pack of reporters looking for a headline.

Despite seeing Hadley's car ahead of him—he and that young man would be having words later about how to say no to clients—he checked his phone's directions, pulled left and was nearly cut off by a small bus, the passenger hanging out of the window, calling to pedestrians.

'I'm driving in a strange city, and I need to concentrate,' Angus told her, his voice hard. 'Can the explanations wait?'

'I suppose they'll have to,' Thadie muttered, slumping in her seat. Angus dropped his sunglasses onto his eyes, joined another stream of traffic and rubbed the back of his neck. What he most wanted to do was find a hotel, strip her out of that sexy dress and kiss his way up and down her body before sliding inside and losing himself in her.

God, it was hot in here, he needed air. But the air conditioner was on, it was working fine. No, he was the one overheating and all because he'd, too briefly, held Thadie in his arms. Angus shoved his hand into his hair, holding back his groan of frustration. He'd thought he wanted answers, and he did, but he'd never expected this insane amount of lust, to feel so intensely, crazy attracted to her again. He was older, hopefully wiser, and he'd thought he'd outgrown his desire for her…

But…no. Not at all. If anything, it was wilder, more out of control.

Brilliant. His South African trip wasn't going to plan, and Angus felt weirdly off balance. Nothing was as he'd expected, and he felt as if he were floundering in quicksand, being battered by enormous waves. He was way out of his comfort zone, and he didn't like it.

If he'd known how seeing her again was going to affect him, he would've stayed in London. Angus didn't like feeling mentally, and emotionally shaken, or caught off guard. He'd grown up in a house where emotions were carefully regulated, if not dismissed. To achieve what he did, his father, The General, gave everything he had to the army; it was his wife and mistress, the great love affair of his life. To create his own legacy, to build an international, and respected, company, Angus needed to be as emotionally divorced as his father had been. Was.

But, unlike his father, he'd walk his road alone, he

wouldn't view his wife and kids as shiny accessories, further proof he was a success in every aspect of his life. He'd watched his parents' dysfunctional marriage, had seen his friends marry and divorce, the unhappiness relationships engendered when they fell apart. What was the point of starting something that had a snowball's chance in hell of succeeding? Not succeeding at anything was unacceptable and taking on wild-goose challenges like relationships was, simply, stupidity.

He didn't believe in love. Neither did he need it, whatever *it* was…

Besides, he didn't have the space in his life for a relationship. All his energy had to be devoted to creating a legacy of his own, to prove to himself that The General wasn't the only Docherty who could achieve extraordinary things. He had a point to prove, and nothing—not even a gorgeous woman who made his heart race—would stand in his way.

Forty minutes later, Angus closed his car door, ignored the shouts and demands from the press and followed Thadie up the stone path to her front door. She plugged in a code on the panel and the door opened on hinges placed in the middle of the door. He stepped directly into a double-volume, open-plan great room. The wall to his right was covered in hats, placed to form a sweep of colour from espresso to white. The far wall comprised double-volume glass, and, on closer inspection, he realised that the wall was a sliding door opening onto an entertainment deck and sparkling pool. Indoor plants, including a vine climbing up and across a wall, supported by hooks, added pops of colour to the room. Comfortable-looking couches squatted on expensive rugs but there were no personal items or photographs on any of the surfaces. There were also blank spaces on the wall where paintings, or artwork, had hung before.

Despite it being denuded of any personal items—was it because she had intended to redecorate with her new husband?—he liked her house. It was very different from his white and black and minimalistic flat in Knightsbridge. It was, he decided, homely, unlike the perfectly neat, emotionally cold houses he'd grown up in.

His home, like everything else in his life, had been regimented. Everything had its place, and God help you if you spilt anything or used something and didn't put it back in its proper place. He didn't know if both his parents were naturally neat freaks or if his father had trained his mother to be that way, but it had been an uncomfortable way to live. Somehow, he knew Thadie wouldn't sweat the small stuff. She was the type who encouraged people to put their feet up onto her furniture, relax, and enjoy her very pretty home.

Enjoy her. After all, they were alone in her house…

Thadie placed her hands on the island counter separating the kitchen and dining area—a wooden table with bench seats sat between the kitchen and the living area—and dropped her head between her arms. Her bright braids hung down her back, pulled together by a plain black band. Her eyes were scrunched closed and he thought she was silently cursing. They were alone and they were adults—he wasn't sure why she felt the need to keep those words silent. He'd served and worked in an industry dominated by men and could cope with a swear word or two. He had more than a few creative curses of his own.

'What are you doing here, Angus?' she asked without looking up at him.

He was a straightforward guy, someone who never

pulled his punches, but he didn't want to toss questions at her head or hear her explanations. Because if he got what he came here for—her explanation on how he'd read her wrong—he'd have no reason to stick around, to spend any more time in her company.

He wanted to hold her face between his hands, lower his mouth to hers, feel her tall body aligned with his, have his thigh between her legs and his hand on her lower back, pushing her stomach into his erection.

Angus swallowed, feeling disconcerted. His attraction had come roaring back, as ferocious as a category five hurricane, as relentless as a mega-tsunami. He was, he reluctantly admitted, in big trouble here. A huge part of him didn't care about what had happened in London, he simply wanted to take up where they'd left off.

Her in his arms, both of them on their way to getting naked.

'Angus?' Right, she'd asked him a question.

'I saw the video of your impromptu press conference,' he answered her. As long as he lived, he'd never forget Thadie, dressed in that very sexy dressing gown, taking down her waste-of-space groom and exposing his conniving, behind-the-scenes shenanigans. Good for her that she hadn't curled up in a corner and wept but instead she'd come out swinging. And looked stunning doing it.

But he was here for a reason. He'd address her need for additional protection soon—he'd been met at OR Tambo International Airport by his Johannesburg manager and briefed on the drive to Rosebank, where his offices were based. Her non-wedding and her ex's idiotic denials of her statements at the press conference were feeding the tabloid newspapers and leading to a rise in people trolling her online. There had been a couple of threats levelled against her as well.

But before they discussed business, he wanted answers to why their plans had gone so badly awry. If he could work out how he'd read the situation wrong, he could avoid repeating his mistake.

'Why didn't you contact me after London? You had my business card with every number I had written on it, all my email addresses, and my company website. What happened?'

If Thadie was thrown by the new direction of their conversation she didn't show it. She tossed her head and lifted her chin, her eyes blazing. 'Why are you so certain I wanted to contact you again? It was a one-night stand, nothing special, and I decided to move on.'

Her eyes slid to the left and Angus knew she was lying. He saw the pulse beating in her long, elegant neck, and noticed the pink flush on her skin. She was trying to be insouciant, but her body gave her away; her now hard nipples pushed against the fabric of her dress's bodice, and he knew, simply knew, that under her skirt, her thighs were parted.

She wanted him, he wanted her, and their chemistry was undeniable and extraordinary. And it wasn't something that should be left unexplored. They'd been the human equivalent of Wolf-Rayet stars, supernovas that slammed together, burned brightly and died quickly...

But, thanks to Thadie's vanishing, Angus felt as if they'd only brushed by each other instead of properly colliding. From the moment he saw her again, even before he'd hoisted her into his arms and carried her away, he'd known he was fighting a losing battle, that they'd revisit their insane attraction. It was too powerful, inevitable. It was going to happen, apparently sooner rather than later.

His questions could wait.

He crossed the room, moving quickly to stand in front

of her, looking down into her lovely face, and waited for her to push him back, or to move out of his personal space. He gave her a minute, maybe more, to put some distance between them but she stayed where she was, her eyes not leaving his.

She broke first, moving closer to him, and when her breasts brushed his chest he lifted his hands to hold her upper arms, pressing his body into hers, his chest against her breasts, his thigh between her legs. She nodded, tipped her face up in a silent plea and, giving into temptation, he lowered his mouth to cover hers, desperate to revisit the intense connection they'd shared so long ago.

He'd expected a trickle of lust, maybe a small punch of want, but nothing prepared him for the thwack of passion, the hard-hitting strike of sensation. Her lips were soft, her skin under his hands silky and her mouth was pure heaven. Kissing her was the sexual equivalent of stepping into a space both comforting and intensely exciting. She tasted of mint and coffee, smelled of apple orchards and berries, of wildness itself. Thadie whimpered and he deepened the kiss, noticing, from a place far away, that her arms were around his neck, her fingers playing with his hair. His hand was, of its own volition, holding her face, his other hand gripped her butt.

He needed more, he needed *everything*. Reality was so much better than his imagination, so he pulled up the material of her dress and stroked the back of her slim thigh, up and over the bare skin of her butt cheek, barely covered by her skimpy underwear. He slid his fingers under the edge of her high-cut panties and palmed her, pulling her closer to him so that the evidence of how much he wanted her pushed deeper into her stomach.

How could she have walked away from more of this, left him before their intense attraction burned out? He needed to know why but, more than that, he needed to kiss her. Here in her kitchen, for as long as she allowed him to. She was a wild wind sweeping across a moon-lit desert, beautiful and inconvenient, a blue-green sea teeming with wild underwater currents, a long drink of icy water after a twelve-mile hike across rocky terrain. She was... *God*...a woman a man crossed continents for.

And he wanted more, he wanted whatever she could give him. He deepened the kiss, needing to see her naked, to have her luscious body pressed up against his without the barrier of their clothing. He wanted unrestricted access to every inch of creamy skin, wanted his mouth on the back of her knee, her ankle, her hipbone, that special, lovely place between her thighs. And, judging by her breathy moans, the way she'd pulled his shirt out from his trousers, streaking her hands across his bare back, she wanted him the same way.

Her passion matched his and he thought it one of the best gifts he'd ever received.

'Love the way you kiss,' she muttered, tracing his lips with her tongue. 'The way you taste...'

He was about to reply, to cover her breast with his hand when he heard the front door open. He dropped Thadie to his feet and instinctively pushed her behind him, ready to face the threat.

Across the room, two tall guys entered the room and were advancing on them, their expressions stormy. A series of impressions bombarded him: fit, muscled and, maybe, a little trained. If this encounter ended up in a fight, he'd win but he'd take a hammering. But he'd, with the last breath he took, protect Thadie.

'What is going on here?' the blond man roared. 'Who are you and how do you know my sister?'

The haze created by passion was clearing, and it was

all coming back to him now. He'd seen them in the video Heath had showed him. These men were Thadie's brothers. Or, more accurately, half-brothers. Same father, different mother. Owners, according to the research he'd had his assistant do, of a multibillion-dollar holding company with interests in many sectors. Rich, very rich, indeed. Along with their sister, they were South African royalty.

Thadie briefly squeezed his arm as she walked past him to the closest couch. She sat down and leaned back against its thick cushions, looking exhausted. 'Angus, meet Jago and Micah Le Roux, my brothers.'

Angus nodded at them, his mouth as dry as dust. An awkward silence descended and, spotting a glass sitting upside next to the preparation sink, he grabbed it and poured himself some water. He needed a minute, or ten.

He felt like a spinning top at the end of its revolution, about to slump sideways. He wasn't a guy who overreacted—or reacted at all—when life threw him a curveball. He'd faced bullets and bombs, terrorists and predators, relying on his training to get him out of some pretty hairy situations.

Thadie pushed him way out of his comfort zone, and he didn't know how to navigate this unfamiliar, challenging scenario. He was winging it, and for someone who loved control and feared failure, it was terrifying.

Angus, his back to Thadie and her brothers, lifted the glass to his lips, his eyes falling on the covered-with-magnets fridge. Some of the magnets were from travel destinations—New York, London, Mexico, Cape Town and numerous other cities—and some held inspirational sayings. The biggest magnet, a bright, bold cartoon pineapple, kept some takeaway menus affixed to the fridge. Angus noticed the corner of a photograph peeking out from underneath a sushi menu and, keeping his back to the others, he lifted his finger and pushed aside the menus to see two young faces staring at him.

His heart slammed into his ribcage, stuttered and spluttered. Their hair was curlier, their skin darker, but other than that the two boys—the same age but non-identical—looked, in different ways, like he did when he was a kid. And, big clue, they both had his strangely coloured eyes, that hard to find blue-green with a deeper green ring encircling the lighter colour.

They couldn't be… Surely. But were they? How? Really?

Was this actually happening?

CHAPTER THREE

THIS HAD TO be a bad dream, nothing else made sense. Any moment now she'd wake up in her lovely bed, she'd yawn and stretch and long for coffee. The boys would rush in, pile on top of her and start chattering.

Three, two, one…

But…no, her life was a trainwreck. Her brothers had almost walked in on her and Angus kissing. Would've seen Angus's hand under her dress. Kissing? That was such a small word for what they'd done; they'd consumed each other. And yes, he was right, dammit, their chemistry was off the charts. Hot, crazy, inexplicable.

And, worst of all, she *still* didn't know why he was in South Africa. Their one night together wasn't reason enough for him to cross continents, she wasn't a femme fatale who lured men across oceans. And he couldn't possibly know about the twins…

The twins! Thadie resisted the urge to put her face in her hands. Angus was their *father*. And he was here.

In the months and years after the birth, she'd often cursed the fact that she'd lost his business card, the only means she had to contact him. She'd tried to find him but had had no idea where to start. All she had was his first name. She often wished she could tell him that he'd helped make the extraordinary creatures who were her sons.

What would have happened if she had? On hearing that she was pregnant, would he have offered to marry her? Even if he hadn't, she couldn't see him running, leaving her to cope on her own. She could've given up her internship in New York, stayed in London, maybe at his place, maybe at her own. He would've attended antenatal classes with her, been with her when she went for check-ups, and been in the delivery room when she tried, and failed, to push out his sons. His would've been the first face she saw when she came around after her C-section, him holding both babies, introducing her to his sons. He would've helped with nappy changes and midnight feeds, rocking to sleep.

Would he have been there for her…? And, more importantly, been there for Gus and Finn.

Unlike her parents, who'd had as little to do with her as they possibly could. She recalled so many occasions when she'd demanded their attention, and their promises to stay home more, or take her to the movies, to the beach, or simply to spend quality, family time with her. She couldn't remember one promise they'd kept, any time they'd spent with her, or them taking her on a family, kid-centric holiday.

As a result, she'd dreamed of what she'd never witnessed, a couple raising their kids, shared responsibilities, double the joy. She'd imagined a strong shoulder to rest her head on, someone to listen and to love her, to make her the centre of his world. Being the focus of someone's love and attention…

But after the twins had come along, she hadn't had the time and energy to dream any more. Her entire life was focused on her boys. She'd done everything herself, feeding and changing nappies, rocking two howling babies to sleep, one in each arm, constantly tired, increasingly overwhelmed. She'd come through it and her rose-coloured glasses had been ripped off.

She was a mum and her wants and needs weren't important, her sons came first.

And now their father, their *real* father, was back on the scene and she had no idea how Angus would respond to that bombshell. More importantly, would Angus even want to play an active part in their lives and, if he did, would he be a good father to Gus and Finn?

Hold your horses, Le Roux. You are still assuming that Angus would've wanted to play a part in the twins' lives, assuming he would've stepped up to the plate. But you don't, actually, know.

She'd made so many mistakes with Clyde, she might have made wrong assumptions about Angus too. What she wanted to believe wasn't necessarily the truth.

Angus did have the right to know about the twins, but his rights would always take second place to what was best for her sons. He'd dropped back into her life not even an hour before. She needed some time to think, gather her emotions and, most importantly, find a way to stop herself from throwing her very willing body against his.

Jago's irate voice penetrated her hurly-burly thoughts. 'Will someone tell us what on earth is going on?'

When her eyes met Angus's, his were unreadable. 'I'm not quite sure what Angus is doing here, to be honest,' Thadie told them truthfully. 'We met years ago, and earlier he rescued me from a press mob outside Dodi's salon.'

'The press knew she was going to be there. She's being followed. Or tracked,' Angus said. 'The personal protection officer who works for me—what you call a bodyguard—should never have taken her there. It was a stupid move.'

His eyes held no warmth and Thadie felt as if he'd

caught her shoplifting or joyriding. He had an air of authority that had her bossy brothers eying him with caution. Her brothers were international businessmen, and few people managed to put that hint of wariness in their eyes.

Micah's eyebrows rose. '*Your* PPO officer?'

'My name is Angus Docherty, and I own Docherty Security. Thadie is a client through my Johannesburg branch.'

Thadie watched as Angus crossed the room and held out his hand. Micah shook his hand, and then Jago did the same.

'You own the security company?' she demanded. His surname meant nothing to her. She'd never known it. When she'd been looking for a bodyguard, she'd taken her brothers' recommendation to hire someone from Docherty Security, reputed to be one of the best companies in the world, without looking into it too closely. She'd been desperate and she trusted her brothers.

In the world...

Which meant he owned and operated a huge, multinational company.

If she'd paid attention to anything other than his spectacular body and sexy face, she would've noticed the fancy watch on his wrist, his designer shoes and his expensive haircut. But no, all her focus had been on when next she could taste him. No one, before or since, made her feel so out of control.

She wasn't, she admitted, a fan of the wild emotions he whipped up. When her parents had been around, they'd fought often and with wild abandon. Volatile was too tame a word for their top-of-their-lungs fights. As a result, she did not enjoy feeling anything less than calm and in control. Especially now that she had kids. How could functional relationships be tempestuous, irrational, and loud? That was why she had felt safe with Clyde—he was the least volatile person she knew. Even when he'd been breaking things off with her, he'd been completely calm.

Sneaky and deceitful? Sure. Stormy? Never.

How could relationships be a wild wind and a tempestuous sea and still be considered healthy? No, she had danced on the banks of those rough winds, and she knew what she was talking about. Thanks to her parents, she believed love and passion involved shouting and objects being thrown. Ugly words had been followed by her parents slinking upstairs, hostility having turned to passion. Yelling and shouting had turned them on, but neither of them had given a thought to the little girl sitting at the bottom of the stairs, crying and confused. She would not do that to the twins, to herself. She would not raise them in a house where they felt bewildered and scared, unable to identify what love, like, and respect looked and sounded like. Clyde was a coward, but he was never sarcastic or ugly and he never raised his voice. She'd spent so little time with Angus and she had no idea of the person he really was. Until she figured that out, she'd keep the twins a secret from him.

Thadie remained seated as Micah made coffee—he was as at home in her kitchen as she was in the one at Hadleigh House, her childhood home they were currently renovating into two separate houses—which Angus refused. Her brothers sat down opposite her, but Angus remained standing, preferring to loom over them, his big arms crossed and biceps straining the bands of his shirt.

Thadie tried to ignore him, but it was impossible. He was too big, too unapproachable, far too sexy. Taking a deep breath, she lifted her coffee cup to her lips and took what she hoped was a reviving sip. She saw a million questions in her brothers' eyes and hoped they weren't going to ask her any—she couldn't cope with getting a third-degree interrogation.

But she did want to know why they were in her house on a Tuesday afternoon. They were exceptionally busy men.

'The press attention around you is ridiculous,' Jago said, placing his ankle on his opposite knee. 'Not only are they calling us at all hours, but they are also camping outside Hadleigh House and at work.'

Thadie placed her palm on her forehead. Her impulsive press conference was the gift that kept on giving. Nobody else should've been affected but her. Not her kids, not her brothers and not her best friends. But she had no idea how to get the reporters to back off. Another press conference would just keep their attention on her and asking for privacy was like asking for a platinum-plated moon. All she could do was apologise, which she did again.

Jago shook his head. 'We need a solution.'

Angus brushed past her legs to sit down next to her on the couch. Although there was a cushion between them, she could still feel his heat. And, strangely, being with him made her feel safe and protected. It had to be because he was so big, he made a great barrier between her and the world.

'Part of the reason I'm here is to provide additional security for Thadie,' Angus said, leaning his forearms on his thighs. 'According to my people, Thadie originally required a personal protection officer as an attention deterrent, not because she believed she was in danger.'

'I wasn't,' she agreed. Weeks ago, she'd just wanted the press and the public to keep their distance and Greg had done a good job keeping them away.

'The situation has changed,' Angus continued, looking

at her. 'I don't like what happened today. The press mob was out of control and some of the comments on social media go beyond nasty and into scary. And weird. Occasionally, stalkers decide to take their fantasies into the real world. I believe you need additional officers until the worst of this attention blows over. Of course, it doesn't help that your ex-fiancé keeps giving TV interviews and stoking the fire.'

Thadie had left both voice and text messages begging Clyde to stop giving interviews and posting on social media. But she knew he wouldn't because Alta was in damage-control mode. When Clyde reminded people to look at her unhinged video, he garnered support. And he needed public support if he was going to salvage his multimillion sponsorship deal.

'He's not going to stop,' Micah said, before she could. 'Not unless we pay him off and pay him enough to make him go away.'

'He's not getting anything from us,' Thadie insisted. 'I'll admit that doing that press conference in my nightgown was stupid, impulsive and that it was good TV. But I would rather live under house arrest for the rest of the year than give him any money.'

'That's all very well, Thadie,' Micah pointed out, 'but the rest of us can't live in our houses too. Dodi has to be able to run her business, and Jago and I would like to be able to move freely as well, without having microphones and cameras in our faces.'

Thadie rubbed her arms around her waist, feeling selfish and mortified. She would be able to handle this conversation, and her brothers, a lot better if Angus weren't sitting on the couch, listening to every word. She lifted her shoulders to her ears.

'Then I really don't know what to do,' she reluctantly admitted.

Angus picked up her coffee cup, handed it to her and told her to drink. While she wasn't in the habit of blithely obeying anybody's commands, she did as he asked.

'The best solution would be to leave,' Angus suggested. 'Treat the press as you would a stroppy toddler. Remove the object of their attention.'

Thadie sent him a quick look. His use of the word 'toddler' was surely a coincidence. He couldn't know about the twins, could he? She knew that she had to tell him, but right now wasn't that time. There were other things to figure out. Including her own feelings about her twins' father coming back into her life.

She looked for evidence of their presence but, luckily, her cleaning service had been in earlier and had returned all the boys' toys to the playroom. Ten minutes after they returned to the house, this room would look as if a bomb had hit it. Gus and Finn had her brothers' messy genes.

Looking around now, she noticed how cold the house looked, a little denuded. She and Clyde had agreed to keep her furniture but she'd taken her artwork off the walls, thinking that her new husband should have a say in what went up there. She'd wanted him to feel at home in her house.

All her photographs of the twins were being reframed into matching, stylish black and white frames, as per Clyde's request for uniformity. She must remember to cancel that order and put her mix and match frames back up.

But only when Angus was back on the other side of the world...

'Thadie should leave the city, preferably the country,' Angus said. 'Two weeks should do the trick, but a month away would be a lot better. Go to New York, to the south of France. I hear that London is nice this time of year.'

What was he insinuating? Was she reading too much into that innocuous comment?

'London with the tw—'

'I agree that leaving is a good idea,' Thadie interrupted Micah, desperate to keep the twins a secret. At least a little longer.

Micah caught her eye and she frowned at him, offering him an infinitesimal shake of her head. She only hoped he and Jago picked up on her reluctance to tell Angus about the twins. Micah returned her frown and she realised thankfully he'd received her message. She looked at Jago, who was also regarding her with a piercing stare. She'd have to deal with their questions but, for now, she was safe.

'I like Docherty's idea,' Jago said, nodding.

Thadie admitted that, on the surface, it sounded like a good plan. But Angus had no idea that taking the twins on a vacation required planning and a second set of hands. She was a hands-on mum but trying to hustle two energetic twins through airports was a nightmare. Long car journeys were even worse. She'd do it if she had to, but it wasn't fun.

Micah, always in tune with her, sent her a sympathetic smile. 'What if we all disappear for a few days? Why don't we take a family holiday? You booked Petit Frère for your honeymoon. I instructed our booking agents not to take any other bookings for the next ten days. We could fly out tomorrow and return on Sunday, and Thadie could stay longer if she needed to.

'Apart from a small staff crew, the island is empty,' Micah explained, turning to Angus. 'Petit Frère is a small, exclusive resort on an island we own in Seychelles.

The island has four villas, each separated from the other, as well as a small two-bedroom cottage. There's a central building housing the communal restaurant and bar, pool, gym and sauna.'

'Access?' Angus asked, his expression impassive.

'People can only get there by boat,' Jago replied, sounding enthusiastic. 'I think going to Petit Frère is a great idea.'

Micah flashed her a smile. 'It's simply a matter of calling our pilot, getting him to file a flight plan and getting Jabu to pack our bags. He'll insist on coming along to look after us.'

'Jabu?' Angus asked.

'Our semi-retired butler,' Jago answered him.

Thadie always felt uncomfortable calling Jabu by his official title. 'He's so much more than that,' she told Angus. 'He started at Hadleigh House when Jago and Micah were little, before I was even born. Jabu was the first person to see me walk, he taught me Zulu, because my mother wouldn't teach me the language. He's been my guide to my African ancestry.'

'He's more of a father than a butler,' Micah agreed.

'Anyway, getting back to taking an island holiday,' Thadie said, uncomfortable with the I-can-see-through-you gaze Angus was giving her. 'I think going away together, Jabu included, is a great idea and I would love it if we can make that happen.'

'When should we leave?' Micah asked. 'Tomorrow morning okay?'

Thadie nodded enthusiastically. 'Fine by me.' She turned to face Angus again. 'Since I'm going to be out of the country, I won't need additional security. But thank you for your concern,' she added, wincing at her formal tone. She needed him to leave. Needed some space to collect her thoughts and decide how she was going to tell him about Gus and Finn.

Angus stood up and put his hands on his hips. 'You're not getting rid of me that easily,' he rumbled in his water-over-gravel voice.

'I can't think of anything else we have to discuss,' she told him, lifting her nose. She hoped he didn't pick up on the fact she was lying.

'You *can't*?' said Angus, sounding intense. 'I can think of a couple of things…'

He turned to Micah and Jago, his smile cool and composed. 'If you would excuse us, Thadie and I need to talk privately. It's nothing that concerns her security.'

Or you. Thadie heard his silent subtext and did not doubt that Jago and Micah did too. Jago looked at her, his eyebrows raised. 'Do you want us to stay?'

Absolutely not!

Thadie shook her head, her braids bouncing violently. 'No, it's fine. He's right…we need to talk. I'll call you later.'

Her brothers stood up, kissed her cheek, and walked out of her front door. Thadie suppressed the urge to run after them.

She waited until she heard the slam of their car door and sighed. She turned back to Angus and straightened her shoulders. 'What did you want to discuss?'

Angus's hot look pinned her feet to the floor, and she felt like a bug under a microscope. 'I want to return to my earlier question. I want to know why you didn't contact me, given our chemistry. You said you would, and I don't think you are a woman who goes back on your word. So why didn't you call me or send me an email?'

There was something different to Angus's tone this time. Something Thadie couldn't quite put her finger on.

She started to explain but he spoke right over her. 'But, mostly, I want to know why you didn't tell me about them.'

He pulled a photograph from his back pocket and Thadie gasped, going hot and cold. She recognised the photo as one she'd pinned to the fridge months ago. Gus and Finn had put their plastic-moulded motorbikes in their bubble bath and were sitting on them, laughing like loons. The photo had always lived on the fridge, along with takeout menus and magnets and, honestly, she'd forgotten it was there.

Angus had not only noticed the photo but had managed to remove and pocketed it without her or her brothers noticing. Impressive in a slightly James Bond, scary, superspy way.

Her secret was out.

CHAPTER FOUR

'YES, THEY ARE YOURS.'

What else could she say? She'd wanted time to think, and this wasn't the way she wanted to impart the news, but she wasn't going to lie to him.

'Were you going to tell me? Or would you let me go back to London, oblivious to the fact that I am a father?' Thadie heard the anger in his voice, and she didn't blame him. She would be angry too.

Feeling as if she were holding onto a frayed rope, Thadie walked to the kitchen area of her all-in-one room and yanked open the door to the cabinet next to the fridge. She banged two glasses onto the counter and reached for a bottle of whiskey she kept behind the cookie jar. She poured them both a healthy slug, thinking that they needed it. It wasn't every day that you heard you were a father…

Or that you came face to face with the father of your twins. Thadie handed him a glass, knocked her shot back and looked longingly at the whiskey bottle. No, she had to do this sober. Not that she was in the habit of using alcohol to get through life and its many ups and downs.

Thadie told him to take a seat on one of the barstools on the opposite side of the island and, when he did, she rested her elbows on the marble countertop and tried to rub away her headache with her fingertips. 'These past few days have been the craziest of my life,' she muttered, mostly to herself.

'Still waiting,' Angus told her.

Right, here goes. She forced herself to meet his eyes. 'I'm going to explain why I didn't contact you first. Let's get that out of the way.'

He nodded and she continued her explanation. 'I lost my phone, remember? After I left the hotel, I got a new one and it was operational immediately. I was in the store when I realised that I hadn't picked up your business card when I left my hotel room. I called the hotel, frantic, but they'd already cleaned the room. I asked them to look for it in the rubbish, they said they would. I pestered them all that day, I went back to the hotel, checked and rechecked the room and talked to the head housekeeper, but they never found it.'

She didn't tell him that she cried, on and off, for days.

To her surprise, Angus closed his eyes and released a long breath. His reaction suggested that her explanation was a relief, but she didn't have the faintest idea why. She shrugged away her curiosity and continued her explanation.

'Since I only knew your first name, I couldn't track you down. I figured it was just one of those things, we had a moment, and it was over. Eight weeks later, I realised I was pregnant.'

Angus sipped his whiskey, his expression impenetrable. 'They say that condoms are ninety-nine per cent effective,' he rumbled, pushing his fingers into his hair.

She hesitated, blushing. The sex they'd shared had been hot and all-consuming, and nothing like the tepid encounters she'd experienced before, and after, Angus.

But they'd used protection, except for that one time. They said it only took once.

Judging by the way they'd almost blistered the paint on her kitchen walls earlier, that hot and all-consuming part hadn't changed.

He grimaced. 'I'm sorry.'

Shortly after meeting him, and had her brothers not walked into her house, she and Angus might be on round two. She couldn't think when he touched her, and she wouldn't be hypocritical by criticising him for his lack of control when she had none herself.

'It was a chance we both took. We knew the potential consequences. And I wouldn't change a thing. The twins are, no doubt, the best thing that ever happened to me.'

He looked past her to the fridge, as if looking for more proof of their existence. 'How old are they...exactly?'

'They turned three a couple of months ago,' she said.

'And what are their names?'

She looked down and closed one eye. 'The oldest, by five minutes, is Gus. His brother is Finn.'

He narrowed his eyes, suspicious. 'You named him after me?' he demanded. It didn't escape her attention that he didn't thank her, for creating a link between them and the father she didn't think they'd ever meet.

'I would've given Finn your second name, but I didn't know it.'

He winced and shook his head. 'It's Moncreiffe.'

'Ah, maybe not, then.'

'Look, I wanted simple English names for the boys, and I liked yours. It's not a big deal.'

His sceptical look told her he didn't believe her. 'Let's get back to the subject of my recently acquired set of sons,' he said.

He made it sound as if he'd just picked up a new car

or purchased a new watch. Or had been gifted a new pair of socks. Suddenly furious at his seeming lack of emotion, his focus on the facts, she poked his forearm with her finger. 'Let's get something straight right now—they are *my* sons. You might've provided the biological material, but my name is on the birth certificate, I have spent the last three years raising and loving them. They are *mine*, not yours!'

He couldn't possibly think that he could slide back into her life and become an insta-dad to the boys. It didn't work that way. 'You are going to go back to London, and I will stay here and raise my sons.'

He looked confused and a little shaken and she couldn't blame him.

'Look, I'm still trying to make sense of this. I never envisioned having kids. It's never been on my radar. I admit that I need time to process this but I'm not going to ignore the situation,' he told her. 'They are my responsibility. I'm not going to pretend they don't exist!'

'Why not?' she asked. 'I have enough money to provide everything they need... Medical, great schooling and, later, to pay for their university education. I don't need your money, and you live on the other side of the world. And, more importantly, I know nothing more about you than the fact that you are a good lover. I don't know you well enough to know whether you'd be a good father to them. That's all I want for them.'

But memories of that night in London rolled over her, as resolute as a rogue wave. He'd been an exceptional lover, but she also recalled him as being thoughtful and considerate. It had been cold, and he'd placed his jacket around her shoulders as they'd walked from the taxi to the hotel lobby. He'd asked her, a few times, how she was feeling, whether she was sure she wanted to make love.

And at every stage of their lovemaking, her pleasure had been at the top of his agenda. When she'd lain in his arms, sated and awash with the after-effects of sensational sex, he'd pulled a sheet up over her shoulder to make sure she wasn't chilly and the next morning he'd fetched her coffee from the tray delivered by room service at the crack of dawn. He'd been thoughtful and considerate to a woman who'd been little more than a stranger. She sensed that was simply part of his make-up.

But it was a big leap between treating a lover well and being a good father. And while she was prepared to be disappointed—her parents had disappointed her all her life—she refused to let that happen to her boys.

'You stated you wanted a good father for the twins,' Angus said, frowning. 'And you don't seem to be cut up about being dumped. Did you decide to marry Strathern because you thought he'd be good for Gus and Finn?'

Her mouth dropped open and she just managed to stop her wince. How did he manage to put those puzzle pieces together so quickly? Was he some sort of boy genius? Man genius, she corrected. There was nothing boyish about Angus.

There was no way that she was going to tell him about her lifelong desire to have a family, to recreate what she'd never had as a child.

'Well?'

'Are you always this nosy?' she asked him.

'When I'm interested. Are you going to tell me?'

'No.'

'Fair enough.' Angus placed his big hands on the marble countertop, his expression thoughtful. When he looked up again, she noticed his determined expression. 'I want to meet the twins. I want to know them. I want them to know me.'

Thadie rubbed the back of her neck, panic crawling up her throat. This was too much, too soon. The twins had been through enough…they didn't need…no! She had to be honest, at least with herself. She was the one who'd needed more for them, who'd wanted them to be raised in an old-fashioned family.

The truth was that the boys, not having seen much of Clyde lately, weren't missing his lack of input at all. Nothing much had changed in their world.

Another truth was that seeing Angus again scared her, being around him felt as if she'd been jolted with a cattle prod. He made her feel, made her yearn. And burn. She wanted his hands on her, his mouth on hers, her legs around his hips as he slid inside her…

He made her feel out of control and buzzy, as if she were sitting on the edge of a rocket and shooting through the atmosphere, burning up. Unlike Clyde, who was consistently calm and laid-back, Angus was tough, hard and direct. She didn't think he possessed a volatile personality, but he made *her* feel volatile, and that was enough for her to keep her distance.

'I am not dropping another father on them so quickly, that would confuse them.' Besides, she needed time to get used to the idea. 'The best thing would be for you to go back to London. You could start talking to them via video-call, you can get to know them that way. For the first few weeks, or months, I'll introduce you as a friend of mine and, if you manage to build a rapport with them, I'll think about the next step. I won't have them disappointed by another man who says he wants to be their father and then isn't.'

'I'm not in the habit of disappointing people, Thadie.'

People said that but they inevitably did. It was better to expect disappointment and prepare for it rather than let it sideswipe you. She'd spent her childhood and teens thinking that, waiting for her parents to see her, to spend time with her, but they could never be bothered. It was better to not want or dream than to have her hopes raised and shattered. She'd been prepared to marry Clyde because she'd known she'd never feel more for him than she should, ask or expect more than for him to be a dad.

And despite his perfidy, his underhand sneakiness, his defection didn't hurt. She was mad at him, livid, but not hurt. Her kids hadn't been disappointed by him—neither had she—and that was all that mattered.

Angus's expression turned thoughtful. 'I understand, and appreciate, your wish to ease them into the situation. But I still want to meet them.'

'I'm flying to Petit Frère tomorrow,' Thadie pointed out. 'There's no time.'

'There's tonight,' he countered.

No! She wasn't ready, not yet. She needed time to think, to plan, to work out how she was going to handle Angus's reappearance in her life. 'No, not today.'

The edges of his mouth lifted in a smile as he cocked his head. 'I don't think you have a choice,' he said. 'There's a car pulling up the driveway.'

In London, around Angus, her world had narrowed to encompass only him, and it seemed as if it had happened again. So much so that she hadn't heard Jabu's noisy Land Rover—an ancient beast he loved and adored—pull up outside. Now that she was paying attention, she heard the slam of heavy doors and the high-pitched chatter of her boys as they ran through the front door and into the great room, dumping their small rucksacks on the hall bench.

'Mum! Mum, where are you?' Gus shouted, excitement in his high-pitched voice. What had they been up to?

'Use your eyes, Gus,' Finn said, in his slow and deliberate way. Her youngest son was incredibly observant and had immediately noticed Angus. Then again, since he'd stood up on their arrival, they couldn't miss the tall, muscular stranger in their home.

Jabu stepped into the room and his eyes darted between Angus and herself, as curious as the twins. 'Jago said you were home, so I thought I'd save you a trip and deliver the monsters myself,' Jabu explained.

'Thanks, Mkulu,' Thadie replied in Zulu, as she always did. She wished she'd thought to call him and tell him she'd collect them from Hadleigh House. 'Have they been okay?'

Jabu did a mini eye-roll. 'These two are always okay. They are indestructible. Who's the guy?'

'A friend from my past. He's also the owner of the security company,' Thadie said, moving from the kitchen into the lounge. The boys hurled themselves at her and wrapped their arms around her thighs, each jostling for position. Over their heads, Thadie introduced the two men and watched them shake hands.

Then Jabu switched to English. 'So, we were at the library, and they were having a talk on nature.' He winced, just a little. 'It was aimed at eight-to-ten-year-olds, on the oddities in animals, and they insisted on staying to listen.'

That sounded like something the boys would enjoy.

'I hear we are all flying to Petit Frère tomorrow?'

Thadie blinked at Jabu's change of subject. 'Yes. It will be good for all of us to get away,' Thadie replied.

Jabu agreed, hugged the boys and told her he'd see her tomorrow. Thadie closed the door behind him, and her eyes darted from Angus's rough-hewn face to her babies. They both had his eyes, bright against their creamy, light brown skins. Finn, whose features were rougher than Gus's, looked the most like him.

Thadie took a deep breath. 'Guys, this is a friend of mine. His name is Angus Docherty.'

Their sweet faces lifted to inspect Angus, two sets of eyes alight with curiosity. 'You're tall,' Gus told him, in his let-no-thought-be-left-unspoken way.

'Your name is like Gus's,' Finn commented and Thadie stared at him, astounded. She couldn't believe he'd made the connection between Angus's name and his twin's. Finn sometimes frightened her with his big brain, and this was one of those times.

'Our names are a little alike,' he agreed. His voice sounded normal, but Thadie saw the strain in his eyes, the tension in his big shoulders. Acting normal in front of the twins had to be difficult but she appreciated him making the effort. 'And yes, I'm tall.'

'Uncle Micah says that we're going to be taller than him,' Gus boasted. 'Uncle Micah is very tall!'

'I'm sure you both will be big guys. So, I heard you went to the library. How was that?' Angus asked, surprising her by engaging with the boys. It was obvious he had no experience with kids, but he was trying.

Gus's eyes widened as he hopped from foot to foot in excitement. 'Did you know that there's a lizard that can shoot blood from its eyes?'

'I didn't,' Angus replied. 'What else did you learn?'

'Cockroaches can live for a week without their heads,' Finn replied. He looked bewildered. 'I want to know how.'

Thadie winced. The boys were at the age where anything gross fascinated them, and they were sure to recount every bit of new knowledge they'd heard.

She saw amusement in Angus's eyes. 'Maybe your mum could help you look that one up on the Internet,' he told Finn.

Great, Finn would now badger her until they did exactly that. She did not want, or need, to know anything about cockroaches!

Gus wiggled, excited. 'And moths, no…flutterbies…'

'Butterflies?' Angus suggested.

Gus nodded, his eyes wide, about to impart information of great importance. 'Flutterbies taste with their feet!'

At Angus's laughter—rich, dark and sexy enough to scatter goosebumps on her skin—the twins were off and running, demanding Angus inspect their playroom and help them build a fort from old blankets.

Well, he'd said that he wanted to get to know them…

The floor-to-ceiling doors leading onto the entertainment deck were open and Angus was grateful for the cooling breeze. Thadie was somewhere in the huge house, bathing and putting the boys to bed. He sat on the edge of her leather couch and stared down at the intricate patterns of the Persian carpet under his feet. He had survived SAS training, had been pinned under enemy fire, taking a damned bullet to his thigh…

But he had never felt this unsettled. This wasn't something he'd trained for, knew how to handle. He'd had a commanding officer instead of a father and he had no idea how to be a dad.

It was strange to think that his father could be an incredible commanding officer but a completely useless parent. His mother hadn't been great either, to be honest. But up until his mid-twenties, he'd made excuses for them, and told himself he was overreacting.

Then he'd got shot. While recovering he'd made the incredibly hard decision to leave the army, thinking that if he couldn't stay with his unit, being on the ground, then he wanted out. He'd thought his dad would understand why: if he couldn't do what he most loved, he had to leave.

Instead of providing understanding and support, The General had verbally assaulted him and disparaged his feelings and fears. He'd been mocked and dismissed. Instead of supporting him, his mum had sided with The General, telling him his father knew best.

Getting shot hurt, but the people who were supposed to love him the most had eviscerated him. Up until then, he'd been leery of love and commitment, unimpressed by the concept, but their response and lack of support had resulted in him vowing to avoid all emotional ties and bonds. It was better, safer, and less messy.

He'd lost his family over a decade ago, but he'd gained two sons today. Holy hell. Angus looked at his trembling hands and swallowed, then swallowed again. He felt disorientated, as if the world had slid off its axis and was hurtling into space.

Meeting Thadie today had been tough. She packed a massive punch he hadn't expected, and hearing he was a dad had sent him off into unknown territory. He'd never envisioned being a dad but life, or fate, had decided otherwise.

Thoughts rushed into his mind, collided and blew up. A couple hung around.

Where did they go from here? How should he handle this news? And, hardest of all, did he want to be a dad and what type of father could he even be?

As a child, he'd yearned for love, playful attention, kind words, and laughter. He'd never got anything but criticism from either of his parents. By his mid-teens, his ambivalent feelings about love solidified after his mum backed up his dad's feelings about him leaving the army. That day, he'd started creating his own legacy, and had also started constructing sky-high emotional barriers. He kept his emotional distance from people, rationalising that if he never allowed anyone to get close, he couldn't be hurt again.

The decision to avoid love, in any form, was made. Emotions were unnecessary. Discipline, focus, and hard work were what he'd need if he was to create a legacy that had no connection to The General. He refused to be distracted by relationships, by friendships, by women.

Did that extend to children he'd never known he had? Being a father wasn't something Thadie expected from him. She was very happy for him to walk straight out of her and the twins' lives.

He could do that, he admitted. He had met the boys and it was obvious they had a good life and were happy, and well looked after. He could easily put a debit order on his account and send Thadie money for maintenance. He could, as she suggested, talk to the boys via videocalls when his schedule allowed. She was making it easy for him, he just had to walk out of the door.

But he couldn't, he didn't want to. They were his *sons*, dammit, they were Dochertys, and carried clan blood in their veins. He wasn't going to force them to be soldiers or have anything to do with military life, but he did want the twins to know their family history. He might not like his father, but he was a proud Scot.

But what did he know about being a father? He'd never had one, having been raised by a general and his aide-de-camp. He'd had little contact and nothing to do with kids, hell, he'd barely been allowed to be a bairn himself, and he did not know how to raise happy and healthy—emotionally and physically—boys.

And, even if he had the daft idea to take on twin boys,

where would he find the time? Running Docherty Security took all his time, and it was hard enough trying to carve out time to take on the specialised missions he so loved. How would he fit the boys into his life? Could he be a dad who operated from the sidelines of their life? Would that be enough?

Would they, one day, question his involvement, his commitment? It was obvious that his sons were as smart as whips, especially Finn, and they'd sense if he didn't give fatherhood everything he had.

The risk of failure was high.

And Angus didn't fail. Ever.

Sometimes not failing meant weighing options, making a tactical retreat, and coming at a problem via the back or side door. Maybe he could be their 'friend' as Thadie suggested—he could still be involved in their lives.

Without the responsibility and the risk.

The problem was that he wasn't a guy who shirked responsibility and he wasn't risk averse. He was responsible for thousands of employees. But the decisions he made about them were intellectual, rational decisions. As for risk, he was the guy his government called when they needed someone to think out of the box, to take above-average chances. He could do both for his business and his country…

But neither entity involved his emotions or asked him to lay his heart on the line…

And that was what being a father was.

He didn't know if he could be what they needed, or deserved, but neither could he walk away. Rock, meet hard place.

And he hadn't even started to think of Thadie and how she'd fit into his life.

Angus sat up and leaned back, resting his head on the back of the couch. She'd disrupted his life four years ago and had done it again today. Back then, he'd thought they were going to have a four-day affair, instead she'd disappeared. He'd thought he'd come here to find out how, and why, he'd read her—and the situation—wrong, but instead he faced fatherhood and the uncomfortable knowledge that his attraction to her was ten times stronger.

Attraction? What a stupid word for the tumultuous emotions coursing through his body. He desired her, craved her, needed to see her naked again. And under the lust, curiosity bubbled.

He now understood why she hadn't contacted him—not his fault, or hers—but his initial questions were replaced by so many more...

Why did a woman, blessed with intelligence and wealth, choose to marry a man she didn't love? Yeah, she said it was to give the boys a father, but she had a close relationship with her brothers, with the older, dignified, Zulu man. There were men in the boys' lives, she didn't need to marry to give them role models.

From Docherty Security files, he'd learned her background. Shortly before they'd met in London, she'd graduated with an MA in Fashion Design, but he couldn't find any traces of her being employed. Had she gone straight from her masters into motherhood?

What else?

She had a massive social media following and was regarded to be an influencer, and she also was involved in a few charities. But neither of those were enough to fill hours in the day. She could afford to hire help to look after the twins so why hadn't she resumed her career? Fashion was, he recalled from their first conversation in London, something she loved. Look, he respected women who were stay-at-home mums, he'd heard it was one of the toughest gigs in the world, but he couldn't quite put Thadie into that box.

The truth was that he needed more time: time with her, time with the boys, time for him to get used to his new reality. Time to figure out the puzzle that was Thadie Le Roux.

And his suddenly overly complicated life.

Angus lifted his head as Thadie stepped into the room. She looked exhausted, her lovely skin tight across her cheekbones. He had been trained to adapt to new situations quickly and he was feeling the strain. After all that had happened to her over the past few days, and, as he'd heard, over the past few months, the rope holding her together was fraying. It was time to leave, to give her some space.

He stood up and walked over to the table in the hallway where he'd left his phone and car keys. He picked them up, slid his phone into the back pocket of his trousers and closed his fingers around his car fob.

'Get some sleep, Thadie,' he told her, resisting the urge to cuddle her close. She looked as if she desperately needed a hug, but, because he desperately wanted her, he couldn't trust himself not to take it further. Besides, he wasn't someone who knew how to hug. Or give comfort.

She walked past him to pull open the front door but stopped to place her forehead against the expensive wooden door. 'I wasn't going to ask you this, I promised myself I wouldn't, but I can't help myself,' she muttered, her voice so low that Angus had to step closer to hear her words.

He placed a hand on her shoulder, encouraging her to turn around. She folded her arms across her chest and stared down at the floor, her bottom lip caught between her bright white teeth.

'Ask me what, Thadie?'

She pushed the tips of the fingers of her right hand into her forehead, keeping her eyes closed. 'What you thought of the boys…'

In a blinding flash, he knew she wasn't asking whether he liked Gus and Finn—because he'd made it very clear that he did—but what he thought about her success as a mum. He cupped her cheek, using his thumb to gently lift her face, and told her to open her eyes and look at him. She looked apprehensive and insecure, and very annoyed she was looking for his approval. But he was more than happy to give it.

'They are wonderful kids, Thadie, bright and confident. It's obvious that you are a wonderful mum,' he told her. His mother had been as cold as his dad had been tough, and approval—love and affection weren't something either of his parents knew how to show—had been linked to his achievements. That wasn't the case in this house…

'Good job, sweetheart,' he added.

He saw her swallow, then she nodded, and tension seeped from her body. Then her eyes turned darker, if that was at all possible, a deep, unfathomable coal black. Unable to pull his gaze away, he stroked her full bottom lip with the pad of his thumb. The air around them crackled with electricity, and his world narrowed, filled by the beautiful woman in front of him.

Don't touch her, just walk away. It had been a long, emotional, strange day, he shouldn't complicate it further by kissing her again. Then Thadie's tongue came out to touch his thumb and he was lost, pulled into a vortex of want and desire and red-hot need. He moved so that her body was between him and the door, so close that a piece of paper couldn't slide into the space between them. He was instantly, completely hard and straining the zip of his trousers. His mouth met hers, soft, sweet, spicy, and he had to fight his instinct to strip her of her dress, her underwear, take her up against the door in the most primal and passionate way possible.

Where was all this want and need coming from?

Thadie's arms encircled his waist and her hands skated up under his shirt, cool against his fevered skin. Needing more than her mouth, to touch the bare skin of her arms, and shoulders, he pulled down the thin strap to her dress and pushed his fingers under the lace of her bra, his fingers finding her nipple. She whimpered and made that low growl in her throat that he remembered so well. It was an I-want-you growl, a take-me-now sound.

He wanted to. She had *no* idea how much.

But she was feeling overwhelmed, and he didn't sleep with drunk-with-tiredness-or-emotion women. He never took advantage of a woman just to get a temporary physical high. When they slept together again, and they *would*, he wanted her to have no regrets...

He was known for his legendary willpower, but it took everything he had to pull his mouth off hers, his fingers off her breast. He rested his forehead against hers, listening to her ragged breaths.

'I should go,' he murmured, holding her hands next to her sides.

She nodded, her tongue touching her top lip, trying to recapture his taste. He resisted the sharp, insistent urge to kiss her again and take her to bed.

'You should,' she agreed, not sounding convinced. Tugging her hands from his, she put her hand on his right pec and pushed him back, creating some much-needed space between them. Thadie opened the front door, hauled in some fresh air, and stood back so that he could pass.

'Invite me to the island with you,' he said, verbalising the thought that had been rolling around in his head.

'What?'

'Invite me on your family holiday,' he said, watching as confusion jumped into her eyes and skittered across her face.

'Like your brothers, I can work remotely. I can take some time to get to know the boys. We could figure out a way to go forward that doesn't involve video-calling. We can get to know each other, become friends, and build trust.'

Thadie didn't look convinced. 'I don't know whether my brothers would appreciate having a stranger gatecrash their holiday…' she said, and Angus knew she was looking for a reason to say no.

Luckily, he had an answer for that. 'Technically, it's *your* honeymoon and you can invite whoever you want.' He saw her waver and pushed a little more. 'A little time, Thadie, that's all I'm asking for. Time for us to wrap our heads around being back in each other's lives and for me to connect, in some way, with the sons I never knew I had.'

She stared out into the darkness beyond his car and held up her hand, asking for a moment to think. Angus pushed back his impatience. If pushed too hard, she might dig in her heels. After a few excruciatingly long seconds, she turned back to him and nodded, albeit reluctantly. 'I might come to regret this but…yes, okay.'

Angus wanted to punch the air but kept his hands in his pockets instead.

'But you can't tell anyone, not the boys or my brothers, Jabu…anyone…that you are the twins' father. As I told them, you're an old friend. I've invited you along to keep me company so that my brothers could spend some alone time with their fiancées without them all worrying, and feeling guilty, about leaving me alone.'

Whatever reason worked, as long as he was achieving his objective. 'Deal. At the end of the holiday, we'll have another conversation about the boys and how to tell them.'

'*If* I tell them,' she quickly corrected him.

He shook his head and the truth hit him, knocking him off his emotional feet. He didn't know how to be a dad, how to protect his heart, but he was not going to give up his sons, for any reason. Yes, he was terrified he'd make the same mistakes as his father, but he couldn't get anywhere if he didn't *try*. Winning the fight was impossible if you didn't step into the ring.

It was that simple. And that convoluted.

'Let's get something straight, Thadie. They are my sons, and they *will* know that I am their father. Maybe not right now, but some time soon. Start wrapping your head around that.' He bent his head to kiss her temple, inhaling her scent again. 'I'll call you in the morning, early, for details about when we depart and from where. But get some sleep, you look shattered.'

'I am,' she agreed, sounding cross. 'And your unannounced arrival didn't help.'

'We'll sort it out,' he said, not knowing whether he was trying to reassure her or himself. 'We're smart people, we can find a way to be friends, lovers and raise our kids without any drama. I don't do drama.' Not giving her a chance to reply, he stepped onto the path and walked towards his car, moving swiftly.

He was half inside his car when she twigged. 'We're not going to be lovers, Docherty!'

Oh, yes, they were. That was the only thing he was sure of. He glanced back to see her standing in the doorway, the light behind her highlighting her many curves. Gorgeous. 'Want to bet?' he asked, before sliding into his car and shutting the door.

She'd lose money if she did.

CHAPTER FIVE

THADIE TIPPED HER face up to the hot sun and released a long breath, thankful to be in the powerful speedboat on their way to the island. They'd spent the morning travelling—flying with the twins on her brothers' private plane was so much easier than flying commercial—and they would arrive at Petit Frère in five or so minutes, in time for a late afternoon swim and to watch what would be a stunning sunset.

Thadie opened her eyes to check on the boys, decked out in their small life vests, sitting between Jabu and Micah, bouncing with excitement.

Her eyes—hidden by the lenses of her very dark sunglasses—skipped over her family and fell on Angus, his nut-brown hair blowing in the wind. The wind plastered his white button-down shirt against his wide chest, reminding her of his chest and stomach muscles. Beneath his rolled-up-to-his-elbows sleeves, his forearms were tanned, the hair on his arms bleached by the sun. His easy-to-wear shorts ended above his knees and his legs were tanned too.

Could she be blamed for her insane attraction to him? The man was incredibly, deliciously hot.

Enough of that, Thadie, pull yourself together!

It had been another strange day, starting with sending her brothers a message telling them Angus would join them, explaining that he was accompanying her to Seychelles as her friend, and as extra protection in case the press followed them to the island. But, thankfully and for the first time ever, they kept their comments to themselves, shook his hand and welcomed him on board their private jet. The twins bumped the fist he held out and Finn even gave him a shy smile.

She couldn't tell her family, not yet, that Angus was the twins' father. For all she knew, they might've guessed. But she was still wrapping her head around the idea of him meeting Gus and Finn, being in her life, and wasn't ready to discuss anything with anybody. And she had no idea how to answer the questions she knew they'd ask: would he see the boys? Would they take his name? Pay maintenance? What role would he play in their lives?

She didn't know and until she did she'd keep everything under wraps. Until she was ready to explain, Angus was a friend she'd recently rediscovered.

Angus leaned forward so that his words wouldn't fly away with the wind. 'Can you orientate me?'

Thadie looked around, easily identifying verdant islands popping up from the flat blue sea. Her father had negotiated a lease from the Seychelles government the year she turned eighteen, and she'd been visiting Petit Frère for twelve years. In the beginning, there were just a couple of houses but when her brothers inherited his business, they developed the island into a super-elite, exclusive resort that guaranteed luxury.

'We're north-east of La Digue, and north-north-west of Felicite Island. The island is south-west of Petite Soeur,' Thadie explained. The speedboat did a long turn and Thadie knew they were close to Petit Frère. Two minutes later, they entered the bay and Thadie pointed to the beach. 'There's the pier.'

The boat slowed to an idle and approached the long pier. A wooden pathway started at the bottom of the pier stairs, crossed the white sand beach and zigzagged up a hill. It ended, as Thadie knew, at the entertainment area, with its huge pool, sprawling lounge, bar and open-air kitchen. Micah hopped off the boat to tie it down and the twins bounded to their feet. As her family stepped off the speedboat, Angus joined her and, without asking, helped Finn to unclip his life vest, and she bent down to help Gus. He looked at the clear water and back at the twins.

'Can they swim?' he asked, worried.

Thadie nodded, pleased he was thinking about their safety. 'Like fish,' she replied. Then she shrugged. 'But, obviously, they aren't allowed to go near water without an adult.'

The twins dumped their life vests and scrambled off the boat. After Angus picked up the vests and handed them to the skipper, who took them down below, he turned to Thadie and captured her hand, giving it a quick squeeze. 'Are you okay?'

She thought about giving him a breezy answer but shrugged instead. 'I didn't sleep much last night. It's been a stressful few days.'

In the space of four days, she'd been dumped, caused a scene in front of the press, been mobbed and been re-united with her never-forgotten lover and her son's father. It was a lot to cope with and maybe that was why she responded to Angus the way she did. Her world had been rocked, she'd felt battered and bruised and his kisses made her forget her name.

And everything else.

He pushed his hand through his hair, remorse on his

face. 'You might not believe me, but I never intended to place more stress on you. I just want to spend some time with my sons and find a way to move forward that works for all of us.'

He placed his back to the pier, creating a solid barrier between her and her family, keeping his voice low so that only she could hear his words. Unfortunately, when he lowered his voice like that, it turned deeper and sexier, like rich velvet sliding over her skin. His fresh cologne took on a hint of sea and Thadie pushed her knees together when she felt that low, warm hum between her legs.

She turned away and looked out to sea.

Pleading exhaustion on the flight to Seychelles, she'd handed the twins over to her family and disappeared into the plane's bedroom. Instead of sleeping she'd spent the five hours of flight time examining the craziness of the past few days, specifically her immediate, fire-hot reaction when Angus kissed her. Part of it was a sexual hangover from London—she'd felt young again, unencumbered. Angus was someone she found attractive, always had, and probably always would. When he kissed her, everything—the kids, her disastrous non-wedding, the responsibilities of life—disappeared and it was lovely to just *feel*.

But she knew she had to corral her attraction to him, had to get it under control because, even without his connection to the twins, it was far too soon for her to consider jumping into bed with another man. She needed to find her emotional feet again, to be on her own and to figure out exactly what she wanted. Her last attempt to create the family had backfired horrendously.

Angus wasn't the answer to her prayers, nor was he the man she needed to make her family complete. And—this was a thought that popped into her head at the beginning of the flight and wouldn't go away—maybe, just maybe, her family was perfect the way it was, with just the three of them. Her boys had Micah and Jago, and Jabu as role models and they were fine men. Yes, being a single mum was tough, but she'd survived the hardest years. She had plenty of money and her family's support…

Maybe she'd been looking for something she thought she needed but didn't. Not really. And how stupid did that make her feel?

Yes, Angus made her yearn and burn, but that was attraction, desire, a biological need for sex. She had to look at him clearly, look at their situation without rose-coloured glasses. He was the twins' dad, not a potential love interest. She wasn't ready for another relationship, not until she sorted her head out.

'I don't want to cause you more stress, Thadie,' Angus told her when she turned to face him again, his thumb stroking the inside of her wrist. 'But something is bubbling between us, we both know it.'

'And it's complicated by the fact that you are Gus and Finn's father,' Thadie agreed.

He pushed her sunglasses onto the top of his head and frowned. 'Look on the bright side—with my arrival you don't have to think about marrying to give the twins a father. I am their father so you can stop looking for another one. That's the real reason you agreed to marry your ex, right?'

'I…' she spluttered, caught off guard. She started to deny it but stopped. It was the truth.

'How did you work that out?'

Angus stuck his thumb out. 'Reason number one, when you were doing that impromptu press conference—gorgeous dressing gown, by the way—' Thadie glared at him but he ignored her '—you were angry, but you weren't hurt. Your pride has taken a beating, but your heart is intact.'

Accurate but she wasn't about to tell him that, so she remained silent.

'And, two, you would never kiss me like you did if you were still in love with another guy. I remember you checking, and double-checking, whether I was single back in London. You don't cheat, physically or emotionally. And if you still had any feelings for your ex, there's no way you would've inhaled me the way you did yesterday.'

'I think you are overstating my reaction,' Thadie told him, heat in her cheeks. He wasn't but he didn't need to know that.

He folded his arms, completely at ease in the rocking boat. 'I don't think I am. So, am I right?'

He was, but Thadie had no intention of making his head swell any bigger by confirming his suspicions. She rolled her eyes and stepped from the boat onto the pier, turning back to look at him. He looked amazing, sunlight creating gold flecks in his dark hair. He was far too sure of himself, and, worse, of her. She looked at her family, who were using the narrow wooden path to cross the hot white sand. The twins had, naturally, stepped off the deck and were running on the sand, playing tag. Her beautiful boys…

Their beautiful boys. Hers, his, theirs…

Thadie felt her vision narrow and she swayed on her feet. She was emotionally and physically exhausted and the stress and anxiety of the past few days were waiting in the wings, ready to ambush her. She felt like a wet rag that had been wrung out and left to dry. She felt the deck coming up to meet her, but a pair of strong arms held her upright and gently lowered her to sit on the deck. Angus told her to bend her legs and pushed her head between her knees, his big hand sliding under her braids to hold her neck.

'Breathe, Thadie, deeply and evenly. When last did you eat?' he demanded, his voice rough.

She thought about it and shrugged. She'd had an apple for breakfast and refused lunch. Too hyped up by Angus's unexpected arrival in her life, she hadn't eaten any supper last night.

'No food, stress, exhaustion, twin boys and a long-ish flight east will do that to you,' Angus told her, balancing on the balls of his feet next to her. She turned her head to look at him and her heart banged against her ribs at the worry she saw in his eyes. It had been a long time since a man looked at her as if he wanted to take on the world for her.

Angus's hand moved from her neck to her shoulder. 'Better?'

She nodded.

He stood up and hauled her to her feet, lifting his hand to run it over her head, his knuckles drifting down the side of her face. His eyes darkened with determination. 'Right, here's the plan. You're going to eat great food, sleep late, lie in the sun and chill. Your only job is to relax and unwind.'

That sounded like heaven. 'In case you didn't notice, I have two whirlwinds to keep lassoed,' she told him.

'I'll keep them entertained,' Angus told her. 'Give me some ground rules and I'll take over.'

She lifted her eyebrows. 'Um… I don't think that's the best idea you've ever had.'

He threw his hands up in the air, at the doubt he saw on

her face. 'I was a lieutenant in the SAS, Thadie, and I led men into battle. Don't you trust me to keep them safe?'

'I do,' Thadie quickly assured him, instinctively knowing he wouldn't let them come to any harm. But he had no idea how exhausting the twins could be, with their constant questions and their six-in-the-morning to seven-at-night energy. They simply never stopped. Angus had no idea what he was taking on.

'Then let me look after them for you,' he insisted. 'I can get to know them at the same time.'

Oh, he was going to get to know them, very well indeed. She gave him a day, maybe two. He might be a Special Forces soldier but dealing with Gus and Finn required a set of skills not taught in the military. But she wasn't sending them to another island, she'd be in shouting distance. And the best way to learn to be a father was to *be* a father. He'd be tossed into the deep end, and it would be a good way for him to learn whether he wanted to do this for the rest of his life.

She shrugged. 'Okay.'

Angus looked as if he'd won a victory. 'Really? Awesome! It'll be fun,' he stated, rubbing his hands together.

Fun? Occasionally. But it sure would be relentless.

On Friday afternoon, shortly before lunch, Thadie stepped into the entertainment area, and gratefully accepted the offer of an iced coffee from the hovering waiter. It was another hot bright afternoon, and she wore a brightly patterned sarong over a lime-green bikini.

Her non-wedding, the viral video and Johannesburg felt a long, long way away. She also felt a hundred times better than she did when she almost fainted on the pier on Wednesday afternoon. Had it been the day before yesterday? It felt like a week, maybe more.

Thadie looked down to the beach, her eyes on Angus, who sat on the sand next to where the boys were building sandcastles, his tablet resting on his knee.

She'd known many good-looking guys in her life, but Angus was the only one to ignite a flame in her belly, between her legs. His features weren't perfectly symmetrical, his nose was a little long, his chin a too strong but no one noticed because he was so intensely, utterly masculine. With his wide shoulders, his big arms and muscled legs, he exuded power. And even better, control of that power.

He was, in every way, the most alpha of alpha males. And she knew of what she spoke, her brothers were good examples of the species. But Angus seemed to have something extra, an undefinable quality that made him stand out…

Maybe it was his stillness, his complete confidence in himself. He'd been an exceptional soldier in one of the best military units in the world, and he'd fought in wars. He'd survived. Maybe that gave him the edge, that extra boost of confidence.

Whatever it was, it was as sexy as hell.

Two days had passed since her come-to-the-light thoughts on the plane. She felt rested, less stressed and a great deal more relaxed. And, hour by hour, day by day, she was far more accepting of being a single mum. Her kids were happy, and confident—had she needed to sacrifice her happiness and freedom?

Angus's arrival in her life, him being their real dad and wanting to be involved in their lives, had also removed any pressure she might feel to repeat her give-them-a-father fiasco. He was their dad…she never had to worry about that again.

Yay.

Thadie's thought was interrupted by a big hand on her back. She smiled at Micha as he joined her at the railing, and placed her temple on his shoulder, happy to lean into him, as she did when she was a little girl. And as a big girl.

Micah pointed the rim of his beer bottle in Angus's direction. 'You've got a billionaire owner of an international security company working as your au pair. You're *good*, shrimp.'

Thadie lifted her head to look at him. 'He's that rich?'

Micah nodded. 'Oh, yeah. Angus's company is as big as, maybe bigger than ours, and he's a very hands-on CEO. I don't know how he does it. Jago and I have enough to do but he does it solo. But, somehow, the man also makes time to take two or three holidays a year, and he goes off the grid and is unavailable. We want to know how he does it.'

Holidays? Why didn't that sound right to her? She couldn't imagine Angus sitting on a beach, drinking a cocktail. Or sleeping late before hitting a couple of ski slopes. That didn't gel. He seemed too busy, too focused, and too into control to leave his business for long periods and not be contactable.

Micah's information had to be faulty.

Or was she making excuses for him, or only paying attention to what she wanted to see? She'd done that with Clyde and made a mess of her life. Maybe she should learn from that lesson.

'He's an impressive guy,' Micah commented.

Yes, he was. Everything, from his gorgeous body to his masculine face, deep voice and sharp mind enthralled her about Angus. And that was why she had to be extra-careful to not let her libido override her intuition and common sense.

'He's also, currently, the most expensive childminder in the world,' Micah said, his voice filled with laughter. 'Which raises the question…why *is* he looking after the monsters? We're grateful he's keeping them occupied but one has to wonder why.'

She felt his eyes on her face and knew that if she looked at him, he'd read the truth in her eyes. She suspected they all knew Angus was the twins' dad—how could they not?—but she wasn't ready to confirm it. Or even talk about it. 'He's a friend who wanted to give me a break.'

'Yeah, right,' Micah scoffed. 'That's not why.'

Thadie was thinking of a way to answer him when a scuffle broke out between Gus and Finn, involving a spade and bucket. There was another spade and bucket, but no, they both wanted to use the blue one. Thadie watched as Angus placed his hands on his knees and stared at the sand, obviously looking for patience. Yep, she got it, she frequently felt like that herself.

'I'm actually feeling sorry for the guy,' Micah said. 'He's been with them pretty much constantly since we arrived.'

Thadie pulled a face, feeling guilty. 'I know. I think it's time for me to take them back.' She sent Micah an impish grin. 'But, damn, it's been nice.'

He smiled back, before taking a sip of beer. 'Jago and I are going to look at another island, about thirteen nautical miles from here. It's available to be leased. We want to see if it's suitable for development into a resort like this one. If we leave this afternoon, we can take the boys. We'll be back tomorrow afternoon.'

'How will you feed them? Bath them? Where will they sleep?' Thadie demanded.

Micah rolled his eyes at her. 'Jabu is coming along

too, along with a couple of staff members who'll set up the tents and cook for us.'

Thadie smiled at him. 'Ah, you're glamping…'

Micah grinned. 'Yeah. Anyway, we'll barbecue on the beach tonight, the kids will love it. It'll be an adventure.'

'Dodi and Ella?'

'They are staying here. They both want a quiet evening.'

Thadie looked over to Jago, who was reading his book, one hand resting on Dodi's baby bump. 'You're really good with the twins, Micah, but we both know Jago finds them overwhelming.'

'They *are* overwhelming but he's having a baby soon and he needs practice,' Micah told her, his voice firm. He nodded at Angus. 'And he needs a break.'

'And maybe,' Micah added, tapping his beer bottle on his thigh, 'by the time we come back you could give us the truth why Angus gatecrashed our family holiday?'

Maybe, Thadie thought as he walked away. But probably not.

CHAPTER SIX

ANGUS STEPPED ONTO the deck of the villa—the building was bookended by two huge granite rocks—and walked over to where Thadie sat by the pool, her book in her lap.

The twins had left in a flurry of excitement, and Angus watched the two powerful speedboats—one driven by Jago and containing Micah, his boys and Jabu and the other containing two Petit Frère staff members, and their food and equipment—disappear around the side of the island. Then he showered and sat at the desk in the study to pick up his emails. He'd expected to skim through his work—Heath could make most of the day-to-day decisions—but it was nearly an hour and a half before he joined Thadie on the deck, carrying a beer in one hand and the icy mojito he'd whipped up in the other.

He handed her the big glass and sat down on the lounger next to her.

'Peace,' he muttered, stretching out his long legs and closing his eyes. He opened one to look at Thadie, who still wore her brightly patterned sarong over her bright green bikini. She'd pulled her blonde braids into a high tail and, because she wore no make-up, he could count the dainty freckles on her cheeks and nose.

Despite being at Gus and Finn's command for the last forty-eight hours—he now knew SAS training wasn't as demanding as looking after those two—he'd spent a lot of his time watching her and he more than liked what he saw. Oh, she was stunning, and she heated his blood, but there was more to her than her long body and gorgeous face. She was an attentive mother, fully present. She was also a very sexy woman, someone who had no idea of the impact she made.

'Are you regretting your offer to look after the boys?' Thadie asked, amusement in her voice. He had to force himself to stop imagining how she'd taste with the mint-and-rum drink flavouring her mouth. Fantastic, he had no doubt.

He looked at her, her sexy lips wrapped around the straw of her drink. 'Regretting it? No. Just recovering…'

'There are rather full-on, aren't they?' Thadie grinned.

'I can easily cope with the physicality required, running up and down the beach, swimming, kicking a ball around,' Angus answered. 'It's the questions that threw me. Why is the sky blue? How many grains of sand are on the beach? How do birds stay up in the air? And my favourite…what does food think when we eat it? I mean, how am I supposed to answer that?'

Thadie's laugh sounded like a spring racing over baby rocks. 'My favourite is still whether God likes marshmallows.'

'Finn,' Angus stated, thinking that question could only come from his more serious son.

'Finn,' Thadie agreed. The look she sent him made him feel ten feet tall. 'How did you know that? You've spent so little time with them, but you seem to have sussed them out. Clyde knew them for nearly a year, but he still mixed up their names.'

The boys looked alike but they weren't identical. Their differences were easy to spot. And the more he heard about her ex, the more he wanted to rearrange his face. But he was out of her and the boys' life, so there was no point in discussing the waste of oxygen.

'You're good with them, Angus,' Thadie told him. 'And thank you for giving me a break. I needed it.'

'I know.'

It would be so easy to take her mouth in a hot kiss, to slide his hands over her, but he didn't want to push, didn't want to spoil this moment of connection between them. They'd get there, very soon, but for the next few minutes, he just wanted to bask in the warmth of her eyes and enjoy the softness of her smile.

Besides, the anticipation was awesome.

Angus forced his gaze off her face and looked at the ocean, thinking of his boys being on the boat with Jago and Micah. He'd personally put them into their life vests, and had watched them speed out of sight, fighting the urge to call them back.

'Will they be okay with your brothers?' he asked, despite knowing that Thadie would never let them go if she weren't fully confident that they'd be safe.

'They will be absolutely fine. Micah is even more protective of them than I am, and that's saying something,' Thadie replied, putting her glass down on the side table that separated their loungers. 'Dodi is my best friend, but Micah was who I called at three in the morning when I was at the end of my rope. He's been there for them, and me.'

Thadie half turned to face him, the nail polish on her bare toes shimmering in the sunlight. Pretty. Then again, everything about her was.

'Did you have any help apart from Micah? Did you employ a nanny? Do you have an au pair?' Angus asked, curious about her life.

Thadie shook her head and he saw her jaw tighten and her lips flatten. He'd hit a nerve and didn't know why. 'No, just me,' she answered.

He frowned, trying to make sense of her answer. 'You don't work?'

Thadie's eyes sparkled with annoyance. 'My father left me a lot of money and I chose to stay home and raise the boys. Do you have a problem with that?'

He lifted his hands, wondering at the flash of her temper. 'Of course I don't, I'm just trying to understand.'

Thadie sipped at her mojito before resting the back of her head on the lounger. She tucked her legs up under her butt and released a long sigh. 'Sorry for snapping, it's a touchy subject.'

He wondered why but knew this wasn't the right time to ask for an explanation. They'd get around to it…

Now, or later, but it would happen.

'You've done a stunning job with them, Thads, they are great kids,' Angus told her, needing her to know how much respect he had for her. 'Thank you.'

Thadie smiled at him, her irritation melting away. 'Someone once said that one's greatest achievement might not be what you did but who you raised. I hold onto that.'

Angus heard the note of longing in her voice. Did she want to do something else, something for herself, or was his imagination working overtime? If he pushed her for an answer, she might shut down and they'd be mired in awkward, tense silence. No, he most definitely didn't want that.

'I think you're raising Finn to become the president of the world.'

Thadie's smile was as powerful as an asteroid strike.

'Nope, Gus will talk his way into that role, and Finn will be the power behind the throne.'

Accurate, Angus decided.

He caught her eyes skidding off his thighs and hid his smile. He'd noticed her looking at his stomach, his arms, her dark eyes gliding over his chest. She'd been checking him out and she liked what she saw. 'So, we have a decision to make,' he said, flicking his finger against his beer bottle.

Thadie looked at her mojito, shook her head and sent him a pleading look. 'Angus, the kids have just left, it's blissfully quiet and I have a lovely drink in my hand. I know that we need to talk about the boys and your role in their life, but can we postpone it, just for a little while?'

Ah, yeah, he'd thought she'd jump to that inaccurate conclusion. He wanted something else, and he was pretty sure she did too. There was only one way to find out.

'I was only going to ask you whether I could take you to bed.'

It was a bald statement, no frills, but Angus didn't see the point in dancing around the subject. He wanted her, more than he wanted his heart to keep beating, but he now knew she wanted him too.

Thadie sent him a what-on-earth look and her drink sloshed in her glass. He removed it from her grip, placed it on the table between them and raised his head, his eyes slamming into hers.

'I want you, Thadie. Desperately.' He pushed his hand through his hair and released a laugh that was short on amusement. 'From the moment I picked you up and carried you to my car, I've thought of nothing else.'

Thadie placed her hand on her heart, half covering the breast he so desperately wanted to kiss.

Her eyes darted to his mouth, and he saw her swallow,

once and then again. 'I… Angus…' She closed her eyes, pulled in a deep breath and when she spoke, her words rushed out, like a spring tide racing to the shore. 'We've always had a crazy attraction, a hot as hell chemistry.'

That wasn't a yes. 'But?'

'But this isn't London and we're not who we were,' she insisted, looking both terrified and earnest. 'It's so much more complicated this time around. The boys…'

It shouldn't be. 'The boys and how I am going to be in their life is a separate conversation, Thadie. They have nothing to do with the fact that I look at you and my mouth goes dry and the blood drains from my head. Seeing you in your gorgeous bikinis and not being able to touch you has sent my blood pressure rocketing.

'I want you, you want me,' Angus added. 'Let's make that happen.'

She was on the verge of agreeing but something held her back, a hesitation that wouldn't let her slide into his arms. 'You make it sound so easy!'

'It is easy,' he replied, keeping his voice low and even.

She lifted her hand, her palm facing him. 'Hang on, hotshot. Let me catch my breath.'

Angus forced himself to back off and gave her some time to think. When she spoke again, she sounded a little less breathless.

Damn. Still so sexy.

'I've got to think about this, Angus. I was engaged to another guy less than a week ago.'

'He made you angry, but he didn't break your heart and you're not emotionally vulnerable,' Angus calmly reminded her. 'You're single, Thadie, and if you want to have a one-night stand or a dozen of them, that's your right. I'd like you to have one, or a couple, with me.'

'So straightforward, Docherty,' Thadie murmured. 'No hearts or flowers or fancy words.'

He'd never been and never would be the type. 'Not my thing,' he assured her.

Thadie cocked her head at him, her gaze direct. 'So, I'll be another one-night stand? Is that what you are after?'

He hesitated but before he could answer her, she was off again. 'I mean… I don't, necessarily, have a problem with that. I'm not ready for another relationship, or anything really! I'm just trying to see things as they are, not as I want them to be.'

'Can you explain that?' Angus asked.

She shrugged. 'I didn't look at my relationship with my ex closely enough. I imagined it to be better than it was. If I'd been thinking clearly, if I'd asked more questions, I might've realised that he was behind the efforts to sabotage the wedding. I thought that because he was laid-back, he wasn't ambitious. He was calm but I failed to see how sneaky he was. If I'd asked more questions, probed a bit more, was more present, I could've avoided a lot of grief and wasted money.'

'So, now you're asking questions?' he clarified.

She nodded and shrugged. 'Now I'm asking questions.'

Fair enough. He considered giving her a flip answer but that wasn't fair. The very least he could be was honest. She deserved that and giving her half-truths, as her ex had, would be insulting. And he wasn't that type of guy.

But how did he tell her that, having been rejected by his parents, and used as a pawn by his father, he was terrified of emotional engagement? He was trying with Gus and Finn and opening up to them was hard enough. Falling in love, allowing someone to take possession of his heart? He still couldn't see that happening. How could he give someone who professed to love him—someone he wanted to love and please—the power to treat his heart like a bowling ball and dictate the terms of that life?

But he had to tell her something. And it had to be the truth.

'I've never been married, engaged, nor have I had a long-term partner. I like living my life solo, having no one to answer to. I'm not good at relationships,' he told her, holding her gaze. 'I have affairs, Thadie, that's as emotionally deep as I'll go. I'd like to have one with you, for as long as that works for both of us.'

'Okay, well, that was blunt.'

He couldn't read the emotion in her eyes and that frustrated him. Was she relieved? Or disappointed? Damn, where were his reading-the-room skills when he needed them?

Did she need reassurance? And if she did, what could he tell her? That he'd change for her? That because she fascinated him, he'd allow the chains wrapping his locked-away heart to fall away and he'd take a chance on having a relationship with her? But, given his up-bringing and dismal interpersonal skills, he would fail at giving her what she needed, and he'd hurt her—and himself—in that futile quest.

He didn't fail and, since he knew he would fail at being what Thadie needed, he wouldn't even try.

But there was one thing they were spectacular at: they had a chemistry that was extraordinary and exceptional…

'I can make you feel good, Thads, better than before,' he said. 'Let me take you to bed, where I'll make you forget all the chaos of the last few months and remind you of what it is to feel sexy. Feminine, powerful. Wanted beyond all meaning.'

He saw the capitulation in her eyes, the need to be in his arms. He lifted one eyebrow. 'Yes?' he prompted.

'Yes.'

Thank God and all his angels and arch angels.

Picking up her hands, Angus tugged her to him so that her lips were an inch from his. 'Too much talking,' he murmured. 'Definitely not enough kissing.'

'I agree,' she replied, her sweet breath fluttering against his lips.

'Slide your thigh over mine,' he told her.

'Why?' Thadie asked but did as he requested.

'So that you'll be more comfortable when I do this...' Angus said before slanting his mouth over hers, tracing the seam of her lips with his tongue.

She tasted like the woman he'd met before, as an awesome memory should. But this kiss was tinged with something different, it was deeper and darker and more intense than he remembered. Thadie felt like the upgraded, full version of the woman with whom he'd spent the night in London, richer and far more interesting than he expected. She felt amazing, soft and luscious and so very feminine.

Falling into the kiss, she placed her bikini-covered core on the hardest part of him and pushed down, creating friction. His eyes rolled back in his head at the slap of pleasure as he welcomed her weight, one arm encircling her butt to hold her tight against him, letting them burn. His other hand held her jaw, his fingers tracing her sharp cheekbone as his mouth ravaged hers.

Thadie hooked her arm around his neck and pushed her breasts into his pecs, dragging her Lycra-covered nipples across his bare chest. He deepened the kiss, needing to taste her, to delve, to dip and dive, needing to explore every part of her mouth. Heat and lust ricocheted through him and, for the first time in four years, he felt his body sag, his bones melt.

Angry ninjas, machine-gun-toting Special Force soldiers and aliens could land right next to him but nothing would stop him from kissing Thadie, from exploring her satin-and-silk skin, her curves, tasting the honey between her legs, the dip of her spine.

He pulled his mouth off hers so that he could speak. 'Bed, *please*.' It was only two words but there was no way he could make complete sentences, as all his blood had left his brain.

Thadie hesitated, wrinkling her nose. She couldn't be second-guessing this, could she?

'Be with me for the rest of the time on Petit Frère,' he suggested, his voice hoarse. It was all he could give her. 'Share my bed, Thadie, let me worship your body.'

She started to speak, hesitated and bit her lip. 'Nobody can know,' she told him. 'I don't want to answer awkward questions from the twins, from my brothers and Jabu. We're lovers when we are alone, friends when we are not.'

Angus felt a momentary pang of disquiet and pushed back his urge to claim her in public. There was nothing more between them but intense chemistry and the twins. And, as he'd stated, those were two very different entities.

'This can't affect any decisions about the boys, and our way forward, it's just sex,' Thadie insisted, her fingers still dancing over his abs. 'It's just between us.'

He nodded, his hands sliding up her long thighs. Annoyed by the barrier of her sarong, he yanked it off and dropped it to the floor. It fell over her book and Angus remembered that they were outside and could be interrupted by Dodi and Ella, both of whom were still on the island. Swinging his legs off the lounger, he stood up, Thadie in his arms and carried her into the house, and into his bedroom, to lay her down on the white cotton duvet.

She looked, he thought, as if she belonged there.

It was a temporary thing, Angus told himself, a flame that needed to burn out, a rogue wave that needed to slap the shore to expend all its energy. It wouldn't last...

It couldn't.

Angus's suite was off to the side of the house and from his private, inaccessible deck, there was an endless view of the sea. But her attention wasn't on the stunning view or the way the afternoon sun danced across the mirror-like water. No, all her attention was focused on the big, intense man standing at the end of the bed, looking down at her, drinking her in. Thadie took in his tall frame, and his messy hair. His black board shorts hung low off his hips, and she licked her lips at his exposed, superhot hip muscles His skin was tanned gold from his hours in the sun. Brown scruff covered his jaw, and his bare feet were surprisingly elegant. She wanted to take big, greedy bites out of him...

Oh, she was in so much trouble, teetering on the verge of losing control.

This was about sex, about taking what she offered...a way to feel sexy again, feminine, wanted and wonderful. It had never been this good with anyone else, not even close. But she couldn't overthink this, get carried away. This wasn't anything more than unbelievably good sex. He was a gift to herself, a lovely distraction. She'd had some awful months and Angus was giving her a way to forget—great sex with no caveats—and she'd take it...

Thadie knelt on the bed and placed her hands on his rough jaw and moved to align her mouth with his. His hands tightened on her hips, and then his lips were under hers. Lust and need made the air between them shimmer, and she caught a glimpse of golden sunbeams as her tongue slipped between his open lips and into his mouth. He tasted like beer-flavoured sin. How had she lived for four years without feeling so alive? *Had* she lived?

He allowed her a minute to explore his mouth before taking control of their kiss. He wound a strong arm around her waist, pulling her up against his chest—hard with muscle. He kissed her with skill and confidence, as if he knew what she needed and how to give it to her. Overwhelmed by sensation, Thadie slumped in his arms, but Angus just tightened his grip on her.

'I've got you.' He pulled back to murmur the words against her open mouth. He hesitated, shrugged and dipped down again, and dialled up the kiss from hot to insane.

Angus painted kisses across her shoulders and Thadie inhaled his fresh sun, sea, and hot-man scent, the heat from his body engulfing her. Her nipples puckered against the triangles of her bikini and she swallowed, noticing there was no moisture left in her mouth. He was plastered against her, and being in his bedroom—a beautifully decorated space dominated by this huge bed—felt incredibly intimate. She felt as if she belonged there, that being in his arms was where she needed to be.

No, she was doing it again, reading more into a situation than there was. This was just sex and if she was going to become mushy, then she should roll away and put some distance between them until she regained a modicum of control.

His hand settled over her breast and Thadie knew she was fooling herself, she had no intention of applying the brakes to stop this runaway train. Her tongue twisted around his, and she arched her back to press her nipple into his palm. She was putty in his hands…

Thadie murmured her appreciation when his thumb brushed her nipple, her soul smiled when he pulled at the strings at the back of her neck. Her bikini fell down and, with another tug, her top gave way and Angus tossed it to the floor. He lowered his head to take her nipple between his lips, his fingers skimming over her stomach and ribcage. His tongue moved to her other nipple, sipping and sucking and rediscovering her.

Thadie's hand skated across his body, exploring the defined muscles of his back, the width of those impressive shoulders, and the strength in his big arms. He was so powerful, intensely masculine. While she liked what he was doing to her breasts, she didn't like the small space between them, needing every inch of her body to be connected to his.

Preferably naked…with him inside her.

Angus kissed her jaw, the spot beneath her ear, and raked his teeth across her collarbone, finding all those long-neglected places craving his touch. Suddenly she was a glorious combination of fire and lust and want, a kaleidoscope of energy that started and ended with him. A part of her—the teeny-tiny inch of her that wasn't desperate for an orgasm—fretted over how incredibly attuned they were to each other. Still. They knew how to touch each other, to ratchet up the pleasure.

They knew each other, even better than before. How?

Angus picked her up and laid her across the bed and bent down to suck her nipple. She sighed when his teeth scraped over her and whimpered when he moved his mouth across her breast to her sternum and licked his way down to her stomach. Angus dropped to his knees on the floor and gripped her hips, pulling her to the edge of the bed. He knelt between her thighs, his hands gripping her hips, his thumbs on her mound. Needing more, Thadie lifted her hips, silently demanding that he *do* something. Angus inserted his finger into the side seam of her bikini bottoms and traced her thin strip of hair.

'Is this what you want, sweetheart?'

She couldn't talk, only feel. When no words hit her tongue, Angus spoke again. 'Thads, do you want me? Want this?'

'Please don't stop,' she begged, half sitting up to press his hand against her and opening her legs wider to give him complete access to her. She cried with pleasure when his finger stroked her, exploring her folds and slipping inside her.

'You are so very beautiful,' Angus murmured. 'So responsive.'

'Come inside me, Angus. I need you.'

'I need a condom,' he told her, turning away to pull open a bedside drawer. She caught a glimpse of the foil packet he tossed on the bed, wanting to weep with relief.

Angus surged to his feet, his hands going to the drawstring of his board shorts. Thadie pushed his hands aside and pulled the cords apart, pulling open the Velcro fastening. Pushing her hand under the fabric, she found his hard length, thinking that, like every other part of his body, he was stunningly, ferociously masculine.

His board shorts fell to the floor and Angus stood between her falling-off-the-bed legs, his eyes glittering, his cheeks flushed. He pulled her bikini bottoms down her thighs, slid on the condom and pushed against her entrance, hard and delightful. Thadie dug her nails into his firm buttocks, pulled him forward and Angus sank in an inch. His eyes slammed closed and Thadie knew he was fighting for control, fighting the urge to plunder. To conquer. To take.

But she wanted him unhinged, out of control because she wanted him to feel the way she did. She launched her torso up, hooked her arms around his neck, and looked into his bright blue-green eyes. 'Take me, Angus, fill me. And do it *now*.'

His lips quirked up at her bossy comment and he punished her by holding back, slowing his hands down and keeping his mouth an inch from hers. Yeah, he gave the orders, he didn't like taking them.

'Think you can keep that up, soldier?' Thadie teased him.

Without giving him time to answer, Thadie lifted her hips in a fluid movement, and he slid inside her.

Angus's eyes narrowed. 'That was…unexpected,' he muttered.

She didn't want to talk, she needed action. She wanted to feel overwhelmed, swept away…completed.

'Stop talking, Docherty,' Thadie murmured, lifting her mouth to meet his. He kissed her deeply, his tongue echoing his skilled movements down below. Thadie was on the verge of shattering when Angus's mouth turned tender. He slid his hand under her butt, lifted and tilted her hips and Thadie felt him even deeper inside her.

Exquisite sensation slapped her sideways and she tumbled willingly into a bright kaleidoscope, dancing among the colours. As she tumbled through reds and greens and purples, yellow and golds, she heard Angus's shout, felt his body tense and his release, wondering if he was seeing, feeling, the colours as she was.

She hoped he was. Like him, it was too good an experience to miss.

CHAPTER SEVEN

THE SUNSET THAT evening was magnificent, a riot of pinks, purples, gold and orange, the sky tossing colours into the sky to say goodnight to the sun. Thadie watched the colours change and the sea turn an inky blue. The stars started to pierce the sky and, sitting here, she felt like a well-loved woman, and not like a harried mum. This was who she was when she took the time to be herself.

Despite her six-month engagement to Clyde, it had been four years since she'd rolled around a bed with a sexy man, feeling reckless and free. The infrequent sex she'd shared with her ex had been uninspired. But she hadn't questioned it.

She hadn't questioned much.

She'd thought that snagging a father for her boys was all that mattered.

But that wasn't true, not any more. What she wanted and needed counted too. It was hard to admit but she'd neglected herself, and her needs, over the past few years. Her parents had never put her first—she didn't think she'd even made the list of their priorities—so she had done the opposite and given everything she had, and more, to her sons. In trying to balance the scales of her past, she'd swung in the opposite extreme. And it only took being dumped an hour before her wedding, meeting her ex, forty-eight hours to recover, and two rounds of spectacular sex to come to that conclusion.

She definitely needed to be quicker on the uptake. But she was trying, and that counted too.

They'd meandered down to the beach for a swim after making love a second time, holding hands as they walked down the path, arms around each other as they crossed the sand. After swimming out to the reef, they fooled around in the shallows, exchanging long, unhurried, luxurious kisses. Standing in the sea and enjoying the warm water on their bodies, Thadie wrapped her legs around Angus's hips and leaned back into his loose grip.

She tipped her head back, looking at Rock Villa nestled into the shadows of the granite rocks, the colours of the sunset bouncing off the huge windows.

'It feels like we're the only two people on the island,' she said, her thumb brushing over his collarbone.

'It does,' Angus agreed, his eyes turning greener as the sun dipped lower. 'Are you sure no one is expecting you to join them for a drink or a meal?'

Thadie shook her head. 'Both Dodi and Ella said that they wanted an evening alone.'

'Excellent news,' Angus said, his hand covering her breast and his thumb swiping her nipple. 'I like being alone with you, sweetheart.'

Thadie saw the desire in his eyes and slowly kissed his mouth, falling into that space where nothing else existed, just him and her and a spectacular barrage of colours in the sky. Scared of the feelings rolling and rollicking inside her, she pulled away and pulled her hand across the surface of the flat sea. *Take it down a notch, Le Roux.*

'You've met everyone important in my life—tell me about your family.'

Angus looked down at Thadie, caught off guard by the change of subject. He rarely spoke about his parents, and since he'd left the army few people made the connection between him and his father. He liked it that way, liked not being compared. But Thadie wasn't just another acquaintance, and she had the right to know more than most.

'My father is a general in the British Military, some would call him a legend. Colm Docherty?'

Thadie shrugged. 'Sorry, my knowledge of military generals is lacking.'

Angus walked her into the shallows and then onto the sand. 'Let's sit,' he suggested.

Thadie sat, the waves lapping their toes, her shoulder pressing into his.

'My dad is an army guy, through and through. So were my grandfather, and great-grandfather. Each generation has climbed further up the chain of command than the one before,' Angus explained.

'You were in the army, right?'

He hesitated and he hoped it was too dark for her to notice. 'I served,' he said. 'It was expected of me. I found out that I liked it, and I went on to join the SAS.'

'They are the badasses, right?'

He smiled. Yeah, they were. 'I loved being part of the unit. I reached the rank of lieutenant but over the next few years, I refused further offers of promotion. I didn't want to sit behind a desk. I wanted to be with my guys, at the coalface. My father was not happy.'

He couldn't believe that he was opening up, that the

words were rolling out of him, a strange and unusual occurrence.

'And by not happy I take it you mean that he was furious?' Thadie asked.

'Incandescently. He wanted me to shoot up the chain of command—being constantly promoted was what Dochertys did but I wanted to stay where I was, with my team,' Angus stared out over the endless blue ocean, barely taking in the now dark island in the distance. In daylight, it shimmered with various shades of verdant green.

This was so far from everything he knew and was familiar with. His office in London, his cold flat, the missions he undertook. And without warning, instead of the perfumed island air, he could smell the dust of the village, instead of the heat of the sun, he felt the heat of a rocket exploding in a building behind him.

He hadn't had a flashback in years.

Thadie's hand on his thigh, small but strong, pulled him back to the present. 'Are you okay? You lost all colour in your face and your breathing started to hitch.'

Freaking marvellous.

'Sorry, a memory steamrolled over me,' he admitted.

Thadie's eyebrows raised. 'Of?'

He sighed and pulled up the hem of his shorts to show her the ugly scar. 'My unit was in a firefight. I caught a bullet in my thigh, and I was evacuated out.'

She stared down at his leg. 'I've always wondered how that happened. Can I touch it?'

He wanted to tell her that there wasn't a place on his body off-limits to her, but nodded instead.

'I'm so sorry,' Thadie whispered, her long finger tracing the scar. Most women recoiled from the puckered skin, white and red in places, the ridges and dents, but

Thadie touched it as if she were trying to absorb any residual pain. He watched her finger, fascinated and turned on. She lifted her eyes to meet his and he saw the warmth and empathy in hers. Thank God, because he couldn't stand sympathy or, worse, pity. He'd never told anyone what came next…

'My father came to visit me in hospital, the day after my last operation,' Angus said, capturing her hand and holding it against his thigh. 'He didn't ask me how I was, whether I'd walk again, anything to do with my injury or about the incident. He had clearance, he could've asked me anything about that skirmish, but he didn't.'

He couldn't look at her but concentrated on a crab scuttling across the sand and into the foam at the water's edge. 'All my father said was that I was up for promotion again and that if it took me nearly losing my leg to finally get me moving up the chain of command, he'd take it. Two of my best friends died in that ambush and he would've known that!'

Thadie's eyes shimmered with emotion. 'That's so awful, Angus.'

'At that moment I realised that I wasn't a son to him, but a pawn to move about as he saw fit. I told him that if I couldn't stay with my unit, and I couldn't, I was leaving the army. He told me I was staying where I was. How he thought he'd keep me there against his will, goodness only knows. We had a shouting match in the hospital ward. I resigned the next day and within a year Docherty Security was up and running. And making money.'

A small frown puckered Thadie's forehead. 'And that's important to you?'

He shrugged. 'No, not particularly. But I like the fact that it irritates and annoys my father that I can afford things he can't.'

'I suppose every man wants enough money to do the things they enjoy. To be able to provide for his family. To spoil his wife.'

Angus's low laugh held no amusement. 'Not The General. No, he had a series of mistresses and he spoiled them, as much as he could.'

Thadie winced. 'How long have you known about his extra-marital affairs?'

'My dad introduced me to the first one when I was thirteen. His dalliances weren't kept a secret, even from my mum.'

'Ouch, that's young. I was in my late teens when I realised that my parents were unfaithful,' Thadie admitted.

Angus snorted. 'My father wouldn't have tolerated my mother having an affair. She's his property, under his command.'

'Do you still have contact with him? Your mum?'

He shook his head. 'No. In my weaker moments I reached out twice, but gave up when they didn't return my calls or respond to my emails.'

Fury bounced into Thadie's eyes. 'Charming,' she muttered, and Angus knew she was holding back harsh criticism. Angus felt one or two of the icy chains encircling his heart snap. She was fully Team Angus.

He'd let her step into his inner world but now he didn't know what to do with her, where she should go. And that was more terrifying than storming a terrorist stronghold, walking straight into enemy fire. This was uncharted territory in every sense of the word.

And because she made him feel too much, threatened to snap those chains—they were industrial strength and, he thought, indestructible—and because he was floundering, he felt compelled to put some distance between them. This felt too intense, too real.

'I saw a bottle of champagne in the bar fridge. What if I run up and get it, and a couple of glasses?' he asked, jumping to his feet. He touched her bare shoulder. 'Are you cold? Do you want a towel or a T-shirt or something?'

Thadie sent him a gentle smile as if she understood why he needed to run. 'It's a lovely, still hot evening, Angus, I'm fine. But take all the time you need.'

Right, well…okay, then. He was obviously as transparent as glass.

Thadie watched Angus easily jogging up the steep path to the villa. She understood his need to be alone—she felt the same.

Like him, she needed a moment to find her bearings, to stabilise her ship, to breathe. Around Angus, she felt as if she were running out of air, her brain shut down and her body, and its needs, took over. She needed a few minutes to regroup.

To think.

She didn't regret making love to Angus. That had been inevitable. From the moment they'd met again, she'd known that being in his arms, in his bed, was just a matter of time. She might be totally addicted to the way he made her feel physically, but at least she wasn't confusing sexual chemistry with love.

Sex was sex and love was different. If they could keep the twins' relationship with Angus separate from their nuclear attraction, then she could do the same for her sexual urges and feelings.

It was just a matter of choosing her thoughts, and looking at the situation clearly.

She glanced towards the north-east, thinking of her boys on another island. Was she a bad mother for desperately wanting a few days, maybe more, to explore their chemistry and attraction? Time for them to talk, make love, be, without having a little person interrupting them, demanding something from her, whether it was a cuddle or a cookie, to be a referee or a reader.

Thadie bit her lip, feeling guilty at wanting Angus to herself, enjoying this time away from them. She'd be lying if she said she never relived their London night together, fantasised about being together like this. He was, after all, her hottest sexual encounter.

For the first time in four years, she felt free to be, wholly and authentically, herself, without reference to anyone else, including the twins.

But what would her life look like when they left the island, when Angus returned to London? Would every hour in the day be dedicated to the twins? Or could she carve out some time for herself by sending her kids to a morning-only playgroup or nursery school?

The thought immediately made her stomach clench and twist. She'd always been so hell-bent on doing everything herself. But, instead of dismissing the idea as she normally would, she decided to examine why she was beating herself up for wanting to do something for herself.

For the first few years of their lives, she was so conscious of being all the twins had and she'd been driven to do everything herself, to be a super-mum. Because if she didn't do absolutely everything herself, she would be like her parents, who'd never done anything at all.

Liyana had never changed a nappy, her father hadn't known what one was. They'd never lost sleep because she was crying, nor dealt with a childish temper tantrum. They'd simply employed nannies, then au pairs, to raise her.

Why be a parent when you could pay someone to do it for you?

Not wanting to think about her parents, she switched gears. It was, she decided, a good time for her to spread her wings. The twins were old enough to attend nursery school or a playgroup in the morning, and they would benefit from being around children their age. She could have the morning to work at…something. She could, for a few hours a day, be something other than a mum. And if she had a few hours free in the morning, maybe she could start designing fashion again.

The thought created little sparkles on her skin and her stomach rolled over in delight.

Truth was, she was jealous of those women who seemed to have it all, who effortlessly juggled the demands of a career with being a wife and a mum. They were, in her mind, superwomen. Thadie also envied Dodi and Ella. Her brothers' women supported themselves, and they did not need their fiancés'—or in her case, her father's—money. She also wanted to feel strong, capable, fulfilled…to be more than just the twins' mum.

Before she'd met Angus, before she'd seen those two lines on that pregnancy test, she'd had plans and had burned with ambition. All her life she'd watched her brothers' meteoric rise to be two of the continent's most influential businessmen, and, while she had no desire to be a captain of industry, she'd vowed to make her mark in the world of fashion.

Le Rouxs, as her father had always said, did not hide their lights under a bushel. She'd graduated top of her class and had secured an internship to work under Bryce Coin, who was now the creative force behind Quills, one of the newest and most creative fashion houses in the world. But all that had come to a screeching stop when she'd realised she was pregnant.

Maybe there was a path back to that…

But along with excitement, she felt fear, dark and harsh, swamping her tentative plans. What if she found amazing success, loved it too much and got involved in her career, in her new life, and started to neglect her sons? What if she wasn't successful at all? What if she stepped back and Angus stepped up and he became their primary caregiver, the person they turned to because she was too involved in her interests, her life?

What if she forgot that the twins were the focus of her life?

No, she'd never do that to them. She knew how much it hurt to have selfish parents. Her boys would always be her highest priority.

Thadie felt Angus kiss her shoulder before he settled behind her, legs on either side of hers. 'You're miles away, Thads. Please tell me that you don't have any regrets?'

She rested the back of her head on his collarbone as the purple colours in the sunset deepened to indigo. 'Not about what we did, no,' she told him.

He pulled back from her and changed position so that he could see her face. He bent his long legs, rested his wrists on his knees and looked at her, curiosity in his eyes. 'What do you regret, Thadie?'

She pulled a finger through the fine white sand, wondering whether he would understand her sudden second thoughts about her life, her choices to be a stay-at-home mum, her frustration at never quite feeling she measured up. Like her brothers, Angus had never let anything stand in his way. Then again, none of them had found themselves single and pregnant with twins.

'Do you ever come face to face with yourself, not sure whether you like what you see?' Thadie asked.

'I like what I see,' Angus murmured, picking up her hand and placing a hot kiss in the centre. He dropped her hand and held it against his thigh. 'What don't you like, Thads?'

And there was the sixty-million-dollar question. 'Sometimes I feel dissatisfied and unfulfilled. I've been feeling like that for a while, and I thought it was because my wedding plans were going awry because Clyde and I were drifting apart.'

'But it wasn't that,' Angus said, conviction in his voice.

She nodded. 'No, I've realised it goes deeper than that. I was, am, unsatisfied about…well, me.'

'Why? You're incredible!' His astonishment made her smile and fed oxygen to the ever-persistent flames of desire. 'You're sexy and stunning and you're such an amazing mum.'

Look, she loved hearing that she was a good mother but once, just once, she'd also like to be told she was smart and successful. 'That's the thing, Angus—people only see me as a good mum.'

'You work for charity, and you have this enormous following on social media, promoting body positivity,' Angus argued.

'I work for various charities, but that barely takes up any of my time. And, let's be honest, they like having me sit on the board, and attending their cocktail parties and balls, because I'm a Le Roux. As for the social media following, this idea that I'm a body-positive influencer is nonsense. Of course, I believe in the concept, but I was only tagged with that label because I frequently publish posts encouraging new mums to give themselves a break about their post-baby weight,' Thadie countered.

'Being a mum is hard enough without having to look as good as you did before you had kids. The last thing new mums need is to get caught up in the unless-we're-skinny-we-can't-be-happy nonsense,' Thadie added, feeling fierce.

'Being healthy is what's most important,' Angus agreed. He reached for the bottle of champagne he'd carried to the beach, along with two glasses, and pulled the tag to remove the foil. 'But we're getting distracted. Tell me why you feel dissatisfied.'

Thadie watched as he popped the cork and poured pale gold champagne into crystal flutes.

'I was a pretty good fashion designer once,' she explained. 'I was offered an internship with a famous designer.'

'What happened?' Angus asked. She simply looked at him, her eyebrows raised. He pulled a face, catching on quickly. 'You discovered you were pregnant.'

Thadie sipped at her champagne. 'Yeah. I wanted to keep working, but my brothers didn't want me in New York on my own. And then I heard that I was having twins and was expected to work twelve-to-sixteen-hour days. I knew it wasn't feasible.'

Angus rubbed the back of his neck. 'So you lost the opportunity,' he stated.

'Yep,' she agreed. 'I helped Dodi out in her bridal salon until I got too big to move, and after the twins arrived, looking after them took up all of my time.'

Angus rested the base of his glass on his knee. 'We touched on this earlier, but I'll ask again... Why didn't you hire someone to help you? I mean, you're not short of cash.'

'I had a nanny growing up—I had a *series* of nannies. My parents handed me over to whomever they could hire to look after me and I swore I would never do that to my kids. My parents didn't hear my first word, didn't see my first steps. I didn't want to miss a thing the boys did, so I knew I had to be actively involved.'

'You had to be the mum you never had,' Angus murmured. He lifted his glass to his lips, all his attention on her. When Angus listened, he really listened. Thadie knew he was taking in her every expression, listening for a change in emotion, on high alert for subtext. Like earlier, when he'd been making love to her, he paid attention.

'We both won the Horrible Parents Lottery,' Angus stated.

They had. Thadie turned her head to place a kiss on the ball of his bare shoulder.

Angus's eyes slammed into hers and her lungs stopped at the determination she saw in them. 'I don't want to be that sort of parent, Thads. I want to break that cycle and be an amazing dad. And I need you to teach me.'

She stared at him, confused.

'I need you to show me how to be interested and involved, supportive and how to communicate. You make it look so easy.'

Thadie felt tears burn her eyes. Being told that she was a wonderful mum was a wonderful compliment and a sure way to melt her heart. Best of all, she knew Angus was being totally sincere.

'Thank you. They just need to know that you are there, that you are a soft place for them to fall,' Thadie told him.

They sat in silence as the sun disappeared behind the horizon, enjoying the purple-indigo light, waves sliding up and slipping down the beach.

Thadie broke the silence. 'I'm thinking about sending them to nursery school. And I'll need to find a way to fill those hours when they are at school.

'Yes, we're a very wealthy family and my father was a terrible dad, but he had a work ethic like no one else I've ever met. My brothers have worked their tails off to get where they are, Dodi and Ella are also incredibly hard-working. We work, we don't sit at home painting and doing pottery, going to the gym.'

She waved her hands in the hair, wincing. 'That sounds judgemental. I'm not trying to insult stay-at-home mums. I've been one for three years! If that's your thing—it's been mine—and you can afford it, who am I to judge? But I'm a Le Roux and I'm not made to live off the inheritance I received. I mean, I could, but *I* don't want to!

'You should see Dodi's face when she's found the perfect dress for a bride or after she's paid out staff bonuses—she's happy and proud and she feels so fulfilled, like what she's doing *matters*. Ella feels the same way when she's pulled off an incredible event, the same way my brothers feel when they close a complicated deal,' she explained.

'The way I feel when I execute a successful mission,' Angus murmured.

Mission? That had to be Angus-speak for picking up a new client, Thadie decided. He was retired from the military, he couldn't be involved in anything dangerous any more. He was a CEO now, not a soldier. So why did she feel as if there was something he wasn't telling her, as if he was holding out on her?

Angus topped up her champagne glass and Thadie looked at it, surprised. When had she finished the first glass? She didn't know.

'So, what's the plan?'

Thadie shrugged, confused. 'For what?'

'For you to start feeling fulfilled, Thads. What do you need to do for that to happen?'

Her lower jaw dropped. She was shocked at his understanding and immediate support. 'Uh…um… I don't know, I need to think about it some more. I need to decide what's best for the boys.'

'What's best for the boys is that they go to nursery. I absolutely support you on that. Kids need social interaction. They learn more from their peers than they do at home,' Angus firmly stated. 'And, if you need more time in the day, then they can either go to an after-school programme or we can hire an au pair.'

Thadie felt instantly overwhelmed. She was just starting to work things out for herself, to plan a new life, and she didn't need him stomping in with his size thirteens and taking over. 'Whoa, hold on…*no*! No after-school programme and no au pair…that's not happening.'

Angus placed his hand on her knee and squeezed. 'Many kids grow up as children of working mothers and they are just fine. I grew up with an unhappy stay-at-home mum and, trust me, that wasn't fun. If *you* are happy, the twins will be happy. So, when I come back, I think we should visit schools, see if they can take them immediately. I can ask my PA to set up an appointment. We'll go together. Actually, that might be best because my schedule can change rapidly.'

This was all going too fast. It was too much. She hadn't thought things through with Clyde. She hadn't examined her motives or her decisions. She wasn't going to do that again, to be pliable. And weak.

She wasn't prepared to make another mistake because she was being swept away by a man who mentally, emotionally and physically rocked her world. Angus made her feel off kilter and, worse, hopeful.

Okay, she wasn't in this raising-kids-alone situation any more. She could bounce ideas off Angus and there was someone else to take responsibility. She could, maybe, lean on and rely on him...

But what if she did that and he decided, in a week, or a month, or a year, that fatherhood wasn't for him, and she was left alone, pushed aside again? She'd stood on the outside of her parents' lives growing up, and they'd disappointed her time and time again. Clyde had made her promises he'd had no intention of fulfilling and she was terrified that Angus would do the same. Scared that, one day, she'd look around and he wouldn't be there...

And because she loathed feeling scared, hated the fact that he'd given her a taste of hope—because she was sliding back into old patterns of behaviour—she lashed out.

'You've been their father for a few days, Angus, and you're presuming to tell me what to do and how to do it? Just because you're suddenly enamoured with the idea of being a father, does not give you equal rights here! They are my children, my responsibility, and I will make the decisions, not you.'

She saw her words land like missiles, detonating in his eyes. Hurt chased anger across his face before his expression turned remote and unemotional. 'I was only trying to help, Thadie,' he said, standing up and brushing the sand from his shorts.

She scrambled to her feet, the dam wall holding back her emotional floodwaters crumbling. 'Where were you when they couldn't pick up one of their heartbeats? When they were both screaming and I didn't have enough milk and I didn't know if I could do this for one more second?' she shouted, slapping her hands onto his chest. 'You weren't there. I went through that all by myself. And you don't get to swan in like a white knight now.'

Thadie felt him grip her hands, and she tugged them away to wipe the moisture off her cheeks, frustrated by her tears. She was mad, not sad. He had no *right*…and she was stupid to feel tempted to let him into her life.

Angus stepped back and held up his hands, his expression as remote as a Siberian outpost in January. He started to speak but shook his head. He bent down, picked up the glasses and tossed the remains of the champagne onto the sand. He picked up the champagne bottle and, without looking at her again, walked away.

Thadie closed her eyes, frustrated at herself and the situation. She wasn't handling this well, she really wasn't. Just when she thought she knew what she was doing, and where she was going, life threw another curveball at her. She clenched her fists, and stared at her bare, sand-covered toes, waves of embarrassment and frustration rolling over her. This was what it felt like to stand on a leaky raft in the middle of a tempest, cold and scared and not knowing where she was going or how she was going to get there.

After a few steps, Angus stopped, turned and his eyes lasered through her. 'I'm deeply sorry I wasn't there for you, that I missed the first three years of their life. But I can't change that because I didn't *know they existed*. But I'm standing here, offering to share the load. You can either make this easy on us and find a way to work with me, or we can fight about this, and make both our lives miserable. But understand this, I will be a part of their lives. I am *not* going away.'

She wished she could believe him, but a person didn't need to physically disappear to make her feel abandoned. 'At some point in my teens, I realised I felt lonelier when my parents were around than I did when they were away.

I won't let you do that to the boys,' she stated, unable to look at him.

He didn't reply and when she looked up to see if he had left, her eyes slammed into his, and even in the low light she could see his anger and frustration. 'I thought we agreed that we are going to be better than our parents. And, please, just be honest about why you are pushing me away.'

'What do you mean by that?' Thadie cried.

'You're not worried about me swanning in and out of the boys' lives, about the effect on them. You're terrified of our incredible attraction, the crazy chemistry, and you're trying to protect yourself. Just like I am. Fair enough. But blaming me for not being there? That's bloody insulting.'

With that conversational hand grenade, Angus stepped off the beach onto the wooden, slatted path and started to make his way back to the house.

Well, that hadn't been the way she'd expected this night to end. And she had no one to blame but herself.

Angus stood on the pier and watched the sleek speedboat approach from the north, Jago at the wheel. The twins, his boys, were seated on either side of Micah, life vests on. Even from a distance, he could see that they were vibrating with impatience, annoyed that they had to sit and stay.

He remembered feeling like that, needing to run and roll, to burn off all that excess energy. His parents hadn't allowed him the freedom to explore his world. His earliest memories were of his father telling him to stand up straight, arms at his sides, chin high. He had to keep his clothes and room spotless, his shoes shined, and his hair carefully combed. Spare time was to be spent studying or excelling at carefully chosen physical activity: swimming training or cross-country running, sports that would be the building blocks to his career in the armed forces. He hadn't been allowed to join the local football team, to play street cricket with the other kids. No, he was The General's son, and he'd never been allowed to *play*.

Thadie encouraged the twins to play, explore, to engage with the world. He was angry with her but she was an excellent mum, he couldn't have asked for better.

Angus jammed his hands into the pockets of his linen shorts, enjoying the cool breeze coming off the ocean. It lifted his hair and plastered his button-down shirt against his chest. He looked down at his feet, thinking that he hadn't worn shoes since he arrived at Petit Frère. Normally that would be a good indication of a great mini break...

Today he felt miserable. It was late morning, and he still hadn't seen Thadie. Late last night, unable to sleep, he'd passed by her room on the way to the kitchen to grab a late-night snack and he'd heard her crying. It had taken all his willpower not to open her door, pull her into his arms and wipe away her tears.

He couldn't help her with this, Angus reminded himself. She had to accept his presence in her life in her own way and in her own time. Her non-wedding, his sudden reappearance in her life, sex, and her realising that she needed to be more than just a stay-at-home mum were all life-changing events and her world had been flipped over and upside down.

So had his, but he had far more experience in learning to accept the things he couldn't change and in playing the cards he'd been dealt. In war, you had to adapt quickly or else you, and your men, got sent home in a coffin.

She needed time and space to wrap her head around her new realities and he was prepared to give them to her. What choice did he have, as they were going to be in each other's lives for…well, probably forever? They were bound together by the awesome creatures they'd made.

The twins waved energetically and Angus waved back, his thoughts still far away. He and Thadie were also, currently, connected by their incredible chemistry— their lovemaking last night had been off-the-charts hot. He'd had many lovers but making love to Thadie was a night-and-day experience compared to his previous encounters. He always made sure that his lovers enjoyed their time with him, but, with Thadie, her pleasure was of paramount importance. She was all that mattered…

He also felt mentally and, scarily, emotionally connected to her. Maybe it was because they had kids together, maybe it was because they'd always had this insane attraction, but sex with Thadie was different: deeper, hotter, a weird combination of emotional and mental and physical. They fell into a rhythm, as if they'd been making love for years, knowing exactly how to make each other yearn and burn.

Since meeting her again, he felt equally thrilled and terrified, energised and unnerved. She had the ability to knock his life, and his ambitions, off keel and he couldn't allow her that much power. Angus hauled in a deep breath and forced himself to be sensible.

Think, Docherty.

He liked her, appreciated that she was a wonderful mum and thought she was insanely hot. But they weren't going to be a perfect TV family when they left the island.

That wasn't going to happen…

His boys were incredible. He was grateful to have found them. They would be a huge part of his life going forward. But he had a job to do, a company to run. A company that allowed him to serve his country, to use the skills he'd worked so hard to acquire.

His covert ops aside, Docherty Security also needed more time and input than he was currently affording it. He was opening a branch in Lahore, and another in Chisinau, the capital city of Moldova. There were decisions to be made, management to hire, premises to secure. Sure, Heath could make most of the decisions, but it was his company, his legacy under construction. Why would he want anyone else to be part of its design? And if he didn't keep an eye on every detail, a crucial component could be missed. Too many mistakes and he could lose his clients and acquire a bad reputation.

It was his name on the letterhead. His company was a direct reflection of him so it couldn't be anything but exemplary. Anything less would be a failure and he never failed...

The twins complicated his working life exponentially. A week ago, he could take off at a moment's notice on a covert op, and no one would question his absence or lack of contact. Angus rubbed his hands up and down his face.

Serving his country by undertaking covert operations, doing his part to make the world a safer place, was what he was born to do—it was the legacy he'd been handed at his birth, the only thing he took from his father. But, unlike The General, he didn't need compliments or kudos. He was all about the deed, not the recognition.

If he died while on a mission, he had a cover story in place: an innocuous death in a car accident overseas. But if he wanted to build a relationship with his sons, how would he explain why he was out of communication for weeks at a time? He could bamboozle the kids—they were young enough still—but not Thadie.

He didn't like keeping secrets from her.

The boat slowed down and Angus heard footsteps on the pier, turning around to see Thadie walking towards him. She wore a white lace, off-the-shoulder crop top over a white bikini top, and her ankle-length cotton skirt split open to reveal her toned thigh with every step she took. She'd pulled her braids into two complicated plaits, and she looked fantastic. But when she drew closer, he saw her red eyes and tight mouth.

'Morning,' he said, resisting the urge to reach for her.

Thadie placed her hand on his bare forearm, just below the rolled-up sleeve of his shirt. 'I should not have said what I did. I'm deeply sorry, Angus.'

He took her hand in his big one and squeezed. It took guts to apologise, and he appreciated her doing so.

He'd accused her of being dishonest last night, but he wasn't being open either. There was no way he could tell her the truth. *'Hey, by the way, being the founder and CEO of an international security company is not all I do. Three or four times a year, me and my team...'*

Nope, he couldn't do that. Firstly, what he did was highly classified. Secondly, he didn't want to expose her to that clandestine world. She and the boys were sunshine and light, he didn't want to explain that he frequently walked through darkness.

And, not even a week after meeting her again, he was questioning what he did and how he did it. This was a classic example of her ability to upend his world.

'It's okay, Thadie,' he assured her, wanting to get back to normal, whatever that was. 'It's a new road and we're both bound to stumble.'

Thadie looked out to sea and Angus followed her gaze. The boat slowed down and then Jago cut the engine. Within seconds, they were all, including Jabu, looking over the side into the blue-green water. He wondered what had caught their attention.

'Are you enjoying the island?' Thadie asked him. 'I hope it measures up to all the other places you visit on vacation.'

He flinched at her very unexpected question and hoped she didn't notice. 'What vacations?' he casually asked.

'Micah said that you take lots of vacations. He sounded quite jealous, by the way. He wondered how you managed to run your company and make time to take so many holidays.'

He couldn't tell her that this was the first 'holiday' he'd taken in three years, the first time he'd had some downtime in forever. 'I work hard and play hard.' He shrugged.

Thadie tipped her head to the side. 'Funny, but I can't picture it.'

His eyebrows lifted. He was too well trained to let his heart rate increase, but he was conscious of it wanting to inch up. 'You can't see me taking a holiday?'

She shook her head. 'No. I picture you chained to your desk, buried in paper, juggling ten calls, emails and a video-call all at once.'

It was a fair assessment of his life as Docherty Security's CEO. 'I do, now and then, leave my office and get away.'

It wasn't a lie, he thought.

Thadie pulled him back to the present by clearing her throat. When he looked at her, he caught the excitement in her eyes. 'So, last night you asked me about my plan,' she stated, sounding hesitant.

Right, before their fight she'd been talking about how unfulfilled she felt. 'Yeah?'

'I couldn't sleep last night and, after I stopped feeling

sorry for myself—' he liked her self-deprecating manner, her ability to gently mock herself '—I started *thinking*.

'According to an Internet site tracking this stuff, I have one of the biggest social media followings in the country, around four and a half million. That's a lot of people,' she said, sounding amazed. Angus wasn't on social media, but he knew enough to be impressed. Four million people paid attention to her posts, to what she had to say.

'I then went onto some of the local fashion designers I love, and checked how many followers they had...'

Angus folded his arms across his chest, enjoying her fire. 'Not as many as you, I bet.'

Her smile widened and he felt as if he'd inserted his finger into the surface of the sun. 'Some have as little as thirty thousand followers. The top designer only had one hundred and fifty thousand. I think there might be an opportunity for me to leverage my social media following...'

Now, this was smart. 'How?' Angus asked, keeping one eye on the approaching boat.

'I promote them to my four million followers, and they take me on as an intern, as well as help me to develop my own fashion line. Obviously, I couldn't compete with them.'

'They all do the same thing, don't they?'

'Actually, they don't,' Thadie explained. 'Some do wedding dresses, some do high fashion, some easy-to-wear clothes. None of them does what I want to do.'

'And that would be?'

She nodded at the incoming boat. 'Kids' fashion. African inspired but with worldwide appeal. Strong fabrics, great colours, generous cuts.' Thadie bit down on her bottom lip. 'I think I want to launch a children's fashion line, Angus.'

It was a fantastic idea, and he had no doubt she'd do an amazing job. He couldn't stop himself—he was so damn proud of her, and thrilled by the excitement he saw in her eyes—he dropped his mouth onto hers, torturing himself with a brief taste of her mouth. He wanted to lower her to the pier, strip her out of that lovely outfit and see the sunlight on her skin.

He'd never felt like this about anyone before. Correction: he'd never felt like this before. This was territory he'd never explored, a minefield he didn't have the skills to navigate.

'Oooh, gross! Why are you kissing my mum?' Gus shouted from the boat.

Angus winced before turning around to face the twins' disgusted expressions and Micah's and Jago's amusement.

He rubbed the back of his neck, embarrassed. 'Uh...'

Thadie's hand touched the centre of his back.

'Distract and evade, Angus. Watch and learn,' she quietly murmured, before stepping around him and placing her hands on her hips.

'What did you guys see as you were coming in? Did you see a big, fat dragon? Or a mermaid with a glittery blue tail?' she asked them, sounding fascinated.

Being three, the twins rapidly forgot she and Angus had locked lips.

'No, Mum!' Gus replied, rolling his eyes as Micah lifted him from the boat to the pier.

'It was a huge whale, maybe as big as a house,' Gus babbled as Thadie helped him with his life vest. 'And, *Mum*, we slept on the beach, and I made a fire and we watched flying stars.'

Angus stepped forward to help Finn. His younger son looked up at him and Angus felt the punch of surprise to see his eyes on Finn's face. Would he ever get used to that? He didn't know.

'Hi, Angus,' Finn quietly said, as calm as his brother was wild.

'Hey, bud. Did you have a fun time?' Angus asked, dropping to his haunches to unclip his vest.

'Yes,' he replied, before releasing an annoyed sigh. 'It was a whale *shark*, which is a fish. Gus didn't make the fire, Micah did, and the stars were shooting stars! Gus never gets it *right*.'

Angus swallowed his smile as Finn turned around to hug Thadie, who was also on the balls of her feet, gathering her boys close. She shut her eyes and Angus watched them, a hard knot of something—it couldn't possibly be emotion, he didn't do emotion!—in his throat.

His family...*his*.

Dammit.

He was so caught up in the pretty picture they made— a gorgeous woman, two astonishingly good-looking boys, a flat, clear blue sea and bright sunlight—that he didn't hear Micah's comment to Jago or see their wide smiles. 'Right, well, that answers *that* question.'

CHAPTER EIGHT

THADIE TOOK ONE last look at the twins's angelic-in-sleep faces and closed the door to their bedroom.

Her twins were having the best time and an amazing holiday and that made her remember her conversation earlier with Angus about the holidays he took. What was bugging her and why did she feel as if he hadn't responded authentically?

Thadie leaned against the wall next to their bedroom, needing a moment before she rejoined Angus on the deck. There was definitely something he wasn't telling her. If asked, she couldn't explain how she knew, she just *did*.

What was he holding back?

And why hadn't she challenged him? This was where she'd gone wrong with Clyde. She'd let things slide, brushed away or ignored her concerns, her gut feelings. Why was she backsliding, revisiting old, and bad, habits?

Just hold on, Le Roux, think this through. Angus isn't Clyde and the guy has only been back in your life for a week. She and Clyde had been together for nearly a year, she'd planned on marrying the guy! Angus had been in her life for less than a week. Sure, he was Gus and Finn's dad, and they were sleeping together, but that didn't give her the right to probe.

But the urge to push, to know, wouldn't leave her.

Thadie walked through the villa and out onto the deck. Angus sat on a wide lounger, and two glasses, one half full, and a bottle of red wine rested on the wooden table next to him. She poured some wine into her glass and took a fortifying sip before blurting out her question.

'What aren't you telling me?' Thadie asked as she plopped down to sit next to him.

'Where on earth did that come from?' Angus asked her, his hand coming up to hold the back of her neck.

She gulped her wine and lifted her shoulders to her ears. 'I can't get rid of this feeling that there's something you're not telling me.'

Angus sat up straight and kissed her bare shoulder. Even though tiny flames of lust flickered over her skin, and she wanted nothing more than to kiss him, Thadie realised that her statement had hit a nerve.

Angus ran his finger over her shoulder and traced the line of her off-the-shoulder lace crop, along the cords holding the triangles of her bikini up. 'Why don't we stop thinking tonight, Thads, and just feel?'

She gripped his hand, stopping any further explorations. 'Angus, stop trying to deflect me.'

His expression hardened, just a fraction. 'Stop asking me questions I can't answer.'

'Can't or won't?'

His thumb skated along the ridge of her cheekbone. He sighed and dropped his hand, looking frustrated. 'I'm trying to work something out. Will you give me the space to do that?'

Work what out? 'Will it affect the boys?' she demanded.

'No, it's a work thing.'

Angus pushed his hand through his hair. 'Thadie, it's a beautiful night, the stars are heavy in the sky, the sea is loud, and the breeze is warm. And you are gorgeous. Talking is not what I most want to do.'

Thadie looked at him, caught between wanting to pry and, well, wanting him. The look on his face as he lifted his hand to touch her, as if she were made of indescribably rare and precious material, swayed her from the mental to the physical.

Angus's index finger gently traced the outline of her nipple and she sucked in her breath, looking down to watch his tanned hand against the white lace. So hot. The thought whispered through her as he pushed the lace away to touch her, skin on skin. Angus lifted her so that her nipple was in line with his mouth. He tongued her, pulling her into his mouth, nibbling her with his teeth. She ran her fingers through his thick hair, tracing the shell of his ear, and the strong cords of his neck.

'I want you so much, Thadie,' Angus told her, his voice growly with desire.

How could she say no? She wanted him as well, as much, possibly more.

He rested his forehead between her breasts, still holding her, and she felt his hot breath against her skin. She didn't know what the future held, how much Angus would feature in their lives, or how to navigate her suddenly complicated future, but she knew she wanted to make love to this big, hot, secretive man. To have him in her bed…

For as long as he would stay.

'Take me to my bedroom, and love all the thoughts out of me, Angus,' Thadie whispered, her fingers dancing across his lips, his jaw.

Angus simply nodded, stood up and, after scooping her up—a feat, given her height and curves, she'd never thought was possible—carried her inside. Seemingly not needing to look where he was going, he kissed her while he navigated a path through the house, avoiding furniture, sculptures and a Lego robot Gus had left in the middle of the passage. In her bedroom, Thadie held onto him as he lowered her to her enormous bed and released a contented murmur when he settled into the V-shape between her legs.

This was where he belonged…

Pushing that thought away—*too much, too soon!*—she helped Angus rid her of her lacy top and bikini bra, watching as he shed his shirt with a one-handed tug. His naked chest touched hers and she tongued his flat, masculine nipple. Yum…

Angus released an inaudible curse and pulled back to tug her skirt over her hips. His eyes moved down, taking in her breast before moving over her rounded stomach to her bikini bottoms.

'I didn't take the time to look at you last time,' he told her.

She wished he wouldn't. 'I breastfed the babies, so my boobs aren't as great as they once were, and I have stretch marks,' she explained, feeling self-conscious. Silly, but she wasn't always as confident as the world thought her to be.

'I don't care,' he bluntly told her, and she heard the sincerity in his tone. He stroked his fingers across her caesarean scar, and she visualised it in her mind, a thin slash above her pubic mound.

'I'm not ashamed of that scar. If I didn't have it, I wouldn't have my—the boys,' she told him.

Tears burned her eyes when he dropped his head and placed a series of gentle kisses from one side of the scar to the other. It was both sweet and erotic, lovely and heart-poundingly sexy.

She was on the point of begging him for more when Angus slowly peeled her bikini bottoms down her legs, before rising to shed his shorts. Scars and kids and the future forgotten, Thadie stared at him, and Angus stood there, allowing her to look. Wide, big shoulders, big, muscled arms, that broad chest. He had sexy abs, but she also adored those long hip muscles, his lean, powerful thighs, and his scar was proof of the battle for life.

Angus managed to combine his blunt good looks— he was the definition of masculinity—with the suggestion of speed. Silent, but obvious power. But under that fine package was a man who could make her feel, make her want, make her need. She enjoyed his body and was impressed by his quick, sharp mind but his effect on her emotions scared her. He could melt her mind…

But…*dammit*…she couldn't resist him. She always, as long as she breathed, would want him but she wouldn't let herself love him.

Angus leaned over her to place his hands on the cool cotton next to her head and dropped his mouth to cover hers, taking his time to explore. Last night, they'd rolled around the bed, their kisses desperate, their hands insatiable. But tonight was different. He seemed to want to take his time, to draw pleasure from the journey and not the destination. Thadie tried to touch him, but he moved his hips, nudging her hand away.

'I want to play,' he told her. 'I want to make this last, draw it out until we are both breathless with need.'

She didn't think that was a good idea. Hot and fast sex could be categorised as a biological need—they were just a pair of healthy adults enjoying themselves. But slow sex, sweet sex, profound sex was…

Making love.

She couldn't allow her feelings to get involved because

she had work to do, on herself, for herself. She needed to find out who she was, and how she was going to navigate this world without reference to anyone else. But Angus had a way of making her dream in glorious technicolour. And feel far too much...

'Angus, please,' she begged, a couple of deep breaths away from releasing a sob. They had to treat this, them together, sex, as release they both needed.

She couldn't afford to allow an emotional connection to develop and deepen.

Finally, weeks, *years* later, Angus pushed inside her and Thadie wrapped her legs around his back, pulling him closer. As he pushed her higher and higher, the physicality of the act, her yearning for release, calmed her whirring thoughts and she simply shut down. All she cared about was the crashing release he could give her. Her hands flew over his thighs, back, up and down his butt, stopping occasionally to dig her fingernails into his skin. One of her braids dropped over her eye as she thrashed her head from side to side, hovering, hovering...

She floundered on the edge of that fireball of pleasure, holding herself back from stepping in, needing another few moments of anticipation.

'I can't hold on, Thads,' Angus muttered against her mouth. Placing his hand between their bodies, he found her and stroked with just enough pressure and intent. One minute she was on the outside, the next she was burning up, in the best way possible. She became the sun, and the stars, danced with the moon and skated along the Milky Way.

Angus, breathing heavily, rested his weight on one hand and gazed down at her. He pulled her braid off her face and tucked it behind her ear. Emotions, confusion mostly, jumped in and out of his eyes and she was relieved to know that he felt equally off-balance, as un-settled.

He didn't know how to handle the situation—any of it, including their crazy chemistry—either. And, strangely, that eased a great deal of her tension, calmed her wash-ing-machine mind.

It was reassuring to know that he was also stumbling around in the dark.

While the island's staff transported their luggage for them to the boat to Felicite, and the private jet, Thadie walked down the beach with Angus, in sight but out of hearing of the twins.

Their holiday was at an end, and it was the start of a new chapter...no, the opening of a new book. Hopefully, the press attention about the wedding had died down and she could slide back into relative obscurity and life could go back to normal. Or, with Angus in their lives, a new normal.

Whatever that meant.

Thadie glanced up at him, his eyes shaded by expen-sive sunglasses. They'd been living in a bubble these past few days—him in her bed at night, making her sigh and making her scream—and they'd spent their days with the twins, swimming, snorkelling and making fifty thousand sandcastles on the beach. With good food, and unintru-sive five-star service on a stunningly lovely island, their days, and nights, had passed in a happy, hazy dream.

But they were leaving this morning and reality lurked over the horizon, rough and tough and taking no prison-ers. She and Angus needed to talk about his future rela-tionship with the twins, but should they do that now, or on the plane, or should she wait until they landed back in Johannesburg?

'Did you hear back from any of your designers?' Angus asked her.

She'd sent them a 'would you consider this?' email and all but one had replied. 'Two turned me down, four are interested. All want to see my portfolio of designs before they commit to anything,' Thadie explained. 'And they want them quickly.'

'What's the rush?' Angus asked.

She shrugged. 'One of the designers is taking maternity leave and wants to get this sorted before she has the baby, another is in the process of launching an online store and a brick-and-motor boutique in London. I guess the other two want to see if I can work under pressure.'

'You'll get it done,' Angus assured her. While Thadie appreciated his support, she wasn't as confident. She wasn't sure she would be able to produce a portfolio of designs within a few weeks. Looking after Gus and Finn was a full-time job and she could see a lot of late nights in her future.

'What's your deadline?' Angus asked.

'Two weeks for one, a month for two, two months for the other one,' Thadie told him.

He winced. 'Two weeks? That's tight.'

He had no idea.

'My favourite designer is the one going on maternity leave. I like Clara, we've met a few times and I enjoy her. I think she likes me, and we could work well together. She's my first choice.' Thadie bit her bottom lip, frowning. 'But I don't think two weeks is feasible and I might have to give her a miss.'

'You need to try, Thadie, you'll regret it if you don't,' Angus told her.

She swallowed down a spurt of annoyance. Words like that were easy to say but when they got back to Johannesburg, she would resume her normal routine. It would be impossible to look after the boys and whip up a design portfolio. And it would take time to get them into a school.

By the time she got the kids into bed, she was exhausted, and her energy levels were depleted. She'd probably fall asleep at her desk. If she got as far as her desk.

Why hadn't she given this idea more thought before reaching out to the designers? She should've waited until she got the boys into a nursery school and planned this properly. Instead of running headlong into the situation, not thinking it all the way through—just as she'd done with Clyde—she should've weighed up the pros and cons and made a more sensible decision.

But she'd remembered the approval in Angus's eyes, how impressed he'd been at her reaching out and chasing her dream and, basking in his approval—it had been a long time since she recalled someone being proud of her—she'd fired off those emails.

Such a reckless move...

Angus's arm landed on her shoulder, and his big hand cupped her arm and pulled her to his side. 'Relax, Thads, it'll be fine.'

She tried to smile, annoyed by his breezy attitude. He was so confident and had no idea how scary it was to attempt something new, putting herself out there, not sure if she could do what she'd breezily promised.

She wasn't a kid any more, a twenty-six-year-old with no responsibilities, someone who'd taken her time to get her degree. She was a Le Roux, had a dedicated social media following—a lot of them who were young mums who listened to what she said and watched what she did—and a press pack who'd dogged her every step because she was, because of her last name and ridiculously, South African royalty.

Thadie slapped her hand over her mouth, terror skittering through her. She stopped abruptly, her toes digging into the sand. 'What have I done, Angus?'

His hands skated up and down her arms. 'You're chasing your dreams, Thadie. There's nothing wrong with that.'

'You don't understand,' she gabbled, panic closing her throat as another thought hit her. 'If the press hears about this, I will be excoriated.'

'Why?' he asked, looking genuinely confused. 'You're going in a different direction. People do it all the time.'

'But if my designs aren't a success, then they'll say that I'm playing at fashion, foisting a sub-standard product on the public and thinking I can sell it because I am a Le Roux. If my designs are a success, then they'll say that it's only because I am trading on my name. That's if I get as far as launching a line. If they hear about me reaching out to designers and I don't follow through, or if none of the designers wants to work with me, then that's another story that'll dominate the headlines!'

Angus told her to take a breath and when she did, he looked down at her, shaking his head. 'Don't you think you are overreacting a touch?'

Overreacting? Seriously? She started to blast him, then remembered that he didn't live in this country and that he'd only seen the video of her press conference because she was his client. Was she still his client? Did she still need a bodyguard? She didn't know whether her and Clyde's bust-up was still dominating the headlines.

But that was, fractionally, off the point.

Angus had no idea that, as Theo and Liyana's daughter, she was often featured in society columns, and her engagement to Clyde, an ex-rugby player who was a national hero for being part of the World Cup winning squad, had set off a feeding frenzy. Her wedding woes had kept everyone entertained, there had been speculation about the health of their relationship and when she'd fired Alta as one of her bridesmaids that story had entertained the public for weeks.

Her non-wedding and viral video had been, as far as the press was concerned, an abundance of riches.

Angus, a Scot and someone who didn't overly concern himself with the shenanigans of A-List South African society, had no idea how newsworthy she was.

'I am not overreacting,' she said, through gritted teeth.

Angus linked the fingers of one hand with hers. His eyes, the same colour as the sun-speckled ocean behind him, connected with hers and she couldn't help herself, she tumbled into all that blue. 'I get that you are scared. Trying something new is always frightening. But this is your time, you need to grab this opportunity and do something for yourself.'

He didn't understand—it wasn't that easy. 'I have boys to raise. They take up a lot of time. I haven't sketched for four years. I have no idea if I even remember my training. I have wedding gifts to return—'

'You've given me lots of reasons why it won't work,' Angus agreed. 'Now give me a few reasons why it will work. Why doing this will be one of the best decisions you'll ever make.'

She had to think, and she couldn't do that when he was so close. Didn't he know that he short-circuited her brain? She walked away from him and scuffed the sand with her bare foot, scowling at the second, smaller speedboat the staff were loading. She looked at the twins, who were by the rock pool, looking into the shallow depths.

Thadie folded her arms across her chest, her heart thumping.

'Well?' Angus asked from behind her.

She wrinkled her nose, not happy that he wouldn't let this go. 'I was good,' she reluctantly admitted. 'I was told I had talent.'

'Talent doesn't just disappear so, with a little practice, I'm sure it will all come straight back to you,' he told her. Thadie felt her bands of tension loosening, a little confidence returning.

'I'm smart. I mean, I'm not as good at business as you and my brothers but I'm not an idiot. I'll know if I'm being taken for a ride or being patronised. Or used.'

'That's a valuable skill,' Angus told her, sounding sincere. 'What else?'

She released a huffy sigh. 'Isn't that enough?' she demanded.

Angus simply widened his stance and linked his hands behind his back, looking thoroughly at ease. She knew he would stand there, like the soldier he'd once been, for as long as it took her to come up with an answer that satisfied him.

'I'm willing to learn, I *want* to learn. And I can work hard, Angus. I know that I look like a trust-fund baby, who has money at her fingertips but I know the value of hard work. My father had his faults, but he wasn't shy to put his shoulder to the wheel.'

He smiled at her, and an undefinable emotion crossed his face as he looked across the sand to see the twins climbing down from the rocks. 'Thads, that I already know.' He held out his hand, and she slid hers into his.

'Feeling better?' he asked, his tone gentle. 'A bit steadier?'

She was. It helped to talk through her fears, to have

someone listen and respond, to give a masculine point of view. She wasn't brimming with confidence, but neither did she feel like a ripped-away leaf caught up in a tornado. She'd never had a conversation like this with Clyde. She hadn't been able to share her fears and doubts. It was wonderful to bounce ideas off him, and to feel supported. What would it be like to have him permanently around—?

No, don't think like that, Thadie. That way madness and disappointment lay. She couldn't start to rely on him and then, one day, look for him and he wasn't there. Just like her parents and Clyde.

'What if you stay here for another week, Thads?'

Thadie lifted her hands, confused. 'What? Why?'

'You said that the resort is empty for another five days, right?'

She nodded, not knowing where he was going with this.

'Stay here, draw, think, take a break. Recharge all those batteries so that you can hit the ground running when you get back. Take some time for yourself...'

Uh, she was a mum, she had the twins to look after, as she told him. Angus shook his head, not convinced. 'The boys will be absolutely fine without you for another few days. It's five days, Thadie, not five months or five years. Jabu will keep them occupied during the day, Micah and Elle will look after them at night and I'm sure that Jago would pitch in as well. I would stick around if I could, but I need to get back to London.'

Angus placed his big hand on her shoulder, looking serious. 'I think you need to do this, I think you should take some time on your own. You deserve it.'

The thought was both entrancing and terrifying. 'But

what would I do?' she wailed, shocked that she was considering his suggestion.

He shrugged. 'Get a massage, get lots of massages. Read, sleep, think. Sketch your designs—'

'I don't have paper or any art supplies,' Thadie told him, happy to poke a hole in his runaway-train plans.

'Make a list and I'll see that what you need comes back with the boat,' Angus told her, his eyes car-crash serious.

She bit her lip, excitement and terror mixing in her stomach. 'I don't think... I don't know, Angus.'

'I do,' he told her, his thumb stroking her cheekbone. 'Trust me on this.'

'Angus!'

He turned round, smiling. He instinctively dropped to his haunches as the boys hurtled towards him, ready to be scooped up and spun around.

Angus carried their boys across the sand, tucking them under his arm like human rugby balls, and Thadie hung back, entranced as she watched her lover interact with their sons. There went her entire world, she admitted.

Two small boys and one very big man.

She knew she shouldn't be, that it was emotionally dangerous, but right now, for the next few moments, she'd allow herself to be completely, irretrievably drunk-on-emotion crazy about all three of them.

Trust him, he suggested. She was, she reluctantly admitted, starting to.

CHAPTER NINE

ANGUS HAD BEEN travelling for fourteen hours, crossing the Indian Ocean twice, but when he stepped onto the deck of Rock Villa and saw Thadie curled up on the lounger next to the infinity pool, a half-empty glass of wine on the table next to her book, he felt as if he was in the right place, at exactly the right time.

He'd sat on the Le Roux plane, talking to various members of Thadie's family, helping to keep the boys entertained, and with every mile that had passed, the rock in his stomach had got heavier. His gut had started screaming that this wasn't where he was supposed to be, what he was supposed to be doing. He needed, for a few more days at least, to be with her. He knew it wasn't a clever move, he should be putting distance between them, emotional as well as physical, but the compulsion to return to Petit Frère was, like his compulsion to fly to Johannesburg after seeing that video, too strong.

She was the moon, and he the tide. One of these days he was going to have to learn how to break their connection because he had a company to run, a legacy to create and he didn't have time for unscheduled disruptions to his schedule.

But that was next week's problem.

His footsteps made no noise as he crossed the deck

to drop to his haunches next to her, using one finger to push a bright braid off her cheek. His heart stuttered, and he sighed as he looked at her wide, lovely mouth, the long eyelashes on her cheek. She wore a low-cut vest top without a bra, and her full breasts tempted him to touch and taste. Pulling his eyes away, he smiled at the strip of bare skin between her top and her silky sleeping shorts, printed with... He looked closer. Were those tiny, perfect sketches of positions from the Kama Sutra? He squinted and his eyebrows lifted... Right, that one needed incredible flexibility.

He smiled, entranced by the thought of seeing how many positions they could get through over the next few days. Quite a few, he reckoned.

And he'd get to that. Right now he just needed to breathe and be. He could stare at her forever, content to inhale her perfume, to trace his eyes over every luscious curve.

Her eyes fluttered open, and he smiled at her dazed look, and watched as her hand came up to touch him. 'So real,' she murmured. 'Wish you were here.'

Her eyes closed again, and she rolled over, pulling her long legs up and settling back into a deep sleep.

'Oh, no, you don't,' he said as he stood up, bent down and scooped her up and into his arms. 'I know that I said you should sleep and relax, and you will, but not for a little while yet.'

He carried her across the deck and into the house, enjoying her look of wide-eyed amazement. 'Angus?'

He dropped a kiss on her nose. 'Hi.'

'Uh...hi,' she said as he lowered her onto the mammoth double bed in the master bedroom. 'What are you doing here?'

He kissed the spot where her neck and jaw met and painted her jaw with tiny kisses. 'Right now, kissing you.'

She pushed at his shoulders. 'I don't understand. You were flying back to London!'

'I flew here instead.' He lifted his head to smile at her. Damn, he was ridiculously happy to be here, in this big bed with her, the sound of the sea hitting the shore, moonlight pouring in from the open doors. 'I thought you might be lonely.'

'It's only been a little more than half a day, Docherty,' Thadie dryly told him. That didn't, he noticed, stop her from yanking his shirt out of his trousers and trying to pull it up and over his back.

He pulled his shirt off, and reached for her vest top, bright white against her stunning, smooth brown skin. 'Well, I was lonely without you,' he told her, placing his mouth on hers. She seemed to melt a little into the bed, a little into him, and against her lips he felt her smile.

But he still needed, crazy but true, a little reassurance that she was happy he was here, that he wasn't intruding on her space. He might feel as if they'd known each other forever but it had only been a little over a week, ten days since he'd dropped back into her life.

'Is it okay that I came back?' he asked, pushing his hands inside her sleeping shorts and down her hips. Nearly naked, he thought, one of the many ways he liked her.

Thadie used her core muscles to sit up, and echoed his movements, pushing his shorts down his legs and wrapping her hand around his shaft. She ran her thumb across his tip, and everything faded, there was just him and her and the pleasure they could generate together. When she held him like this, he didn't care whether he was intruding, whether she needed time and space and quiet.

He needed her. Angus needed to feel her wrapped around him, his tongue in her mouth, her amazing legs around his hips, to hear her gasps and groans, her wet, hot heat around his length. She was the closest thing to a home he'd ever experienced.

'It's not okay that you took so long to come back,' Thadie said as he parted her legs and slid his hand over her feminine lips, testing her readiness for him. The sound she made was part sigh and part sob, and he positioned himself at her entrance, sliding his tip inside.

He intended to take it slow, to savour the moment, but Thadie had other ideas. She lifted her hips, he found himself inside her and he was lost.

And found.

Discombobulated and delighted. And very much not in control.

The island wasn't very big, and they walked it in an hour, following the wooden path that took them through the jungle-like foliage, across the huge granite rocks and over rock pools and coves. It was lovely to be alone on the island—when she'd heard she was going to be the only person on the island, Thadie had insisted that the staff take a vacation, she didn't need looking after—and even better that Angus was here with her.

She looked at his broad back as he walked the path in front of her, his board shorts riding low on his hips, the pre-dawn light accentuating the deep valleys of his spine. They'd got, maybe, a couple of hours' sleep last night, and had reached for each other time and time again, unable to get enough of each other. She was both exhausted and wired, and comprehensively thrilled to have more time alone with him.

And when Angus had suggested that they watch the

sunrise from the other side of the island, she'd sleepily pulled on a pair of shorts and a vest and followed him out of the door.

Despite knowing she had a life to figure out, a career to reinvigorate, she was in deep danger of following him anywhere.

Angus stopped, looked up at a granite rock and nodded. 'The view from up there will be amazing.'

Thadie squinted at the root-covered rock and shook her head. She had the upper body strength of a noodle and there was no way she'd managed to scramble up the side, even if the roots would hold her weight.

'The sunrise will be best from there,' Angus told her, excitement in his eyes.

'The sunrise would be great from the beach. Or even better from the deck, with a cup of coffee in my hand,' Thadie told him.

Angus simply grinned at her, backed away and ran towards the rock. At the same time his foot hit the root closest to the ground, he leapt up and grabbed a root high above his head and swung his legs onto the top of the rock, where he crouched looking down at her.

How did he do that? One moment he was on the ground, the next he was twelve feet in the air. 'That was marginally impressive, Docherty,' she told him, tongue in her cheek.

He shrugged, as if scaling a monstrous rock were nothing. He looked around and grinned. 'The rock has a flat section and an amazing view. Get your pretty butt up here, Thads.'

'Uh…*how*?'

Angus told her to stand on the lower root and reached down to grip her wrist. With a quick, sharp tug, he had her up on the rock standing next to him. Unlike her, he wasn't out of breath and Thadie realised how much pent-up power he had access to. Impressive indeed.

Dammit, everything about him was.

They settled on the flatter section on the rock, and watched ribbons of light creep over the horizon, splashes of pinks and purples and reds, and push up into the scattered clouds hovering in the distance. The sea was still and silent and it seemed to Thadie that the island was holding its breath, waiting for the light show.

They sat there in comfortable silence, happy to watch nature preen, taking delight in her many colours. When the sun was an orange ball resting on the horizon, Thadie finally turned to look at Angus, her nose wrinkling when she caught him looking at her.

'The show is out there,' she told him, sounding flustered.

'I'd much rather watch you,' Angus told her, his deep voice sliding over her skin. He stretched out his legs and placed his flat palms on the cool rock, conscious of Thadie's long, bare leg next to his.

There was no place he'd rather be than here, right now.

Thadie bit down on her bottom lip, before twisting her lips. 'Were the boys okay when you said goodbye to them? Were they upset?'

Angus wasn't going to tell her that they'd had a little cry when they'd woken up on the plane—Finn in his arms, Gus in Micah's—when they'd realised that she wasn't there, but had soon been distracted by ice cream and Ellie showing them a funny animal video on her phone.

At the airport, he'd hugged them goodbye, for long enough to make them squirm. And for Thadie's family to send him speculative looks. They knew, he thought. The members of her family were smart, smart people, they could add two and two and get four. The boys had his eyes, looked like him…you didn't need an advanced degree in genetics to work it out.

But the twins' paternity wasn't something he was going to discuss with her family. Not without Thadie's permission and certainly not when she wasn't present.

'The boys are fine, Thads, kids are far more resilient than adults give them credit for. And when we get back to the villa you can video-call and check in.'

'It was really hard to let them go.'

He'd seen the pain in her eyes and knew how much she'd struggled with the idea of handing them over, even if it was to the people she trusted with her life. 'I know.'

'It's strange being without them. I keep thinking of something I should do, looking around for them.'

'That's understandable. But having some time alone will be good for you,' he stated, then winced when he realised what he'd said. 'Except I gatecrashed your alone time.'

She leaned into him, her shoulder pressing against his. 'I'm glad you're here. I really am.'

Relief rolled over him, warm and wonderful. 'Although this place is stunning, I do need to do some work while I am here, so you'll still have plenty of time to think about the future, make a start on sketching your designs, and figuring out how to tackle your new career.'

Angus felt the vibration on his wrist and looked down at his state-of-the-art watch, on which was displayed a brief text. It was from his government contact requesting a meeting. Requests for meetings usually meant that there was a mission on the horizon…

Strangely, his heart didn't kick up with excitement, as it normally did. He lived for these texts, and silently cheered when they came through. It meant a break from his desk, from the most predictable and sometimes mind-numbing monotony running a huge company entailed. Missions meant danger, excitement and the thrill of knowing that he made a difference.

But his flight south last week had changed his life in a myriad small, and big, ways. Unscheduled flights, the twins, unbelievably amazing sex, wonderful conversation. His old excitement to undertake missions had also evaporated.

Now all he could think was…*what if*? What if something went wrong? What if he never came back?

He couldn't do it. The risk was too great. There was only one decision he could make. When he got back to the villa, he'd jump on his computer and send his contact a message, telling her he was out.

He would redeploy his team to other positions within Docherty Security, but he was out of the covert mission game. He had to put the twins' needs first. They needed a father, and he was going to be there for them. He couldn't be the father he wanted to be if he kept disappearing.

But he'd have to tell Heath the reason for his newly acquired interest in South Africa and why his jet would frequently be heading south of the equator from now on. Heath wasn't only his right-hand man, he was also his closest friend, and he couldn't wait to show him photos of Gus and Finn.

But how would he explain his relationship with Thadie…? How did he even explain her to himself? It was too easy to say they were simply connected through the boys, and would be for the rest of their lives…

No, he wouldn't allow himself off the hook so easily. She was the woman he craved. He couldn't get enough of her. He wanted to protect her, obviously, and the thought of her being hurt made his blood freeze. He loved making love to her, but he also enjoyed talking to her and appreciating her smart and unique take on life and the world around her. She didn't bore him and he felt it would take many lifetimes for that to happen.

He couldn't imagine his life without her in it. But neither could he make the mental leap to anything more solid, committed, permanent. He was becoming increasingly aware he couldn't stay away from her, but he was living in no man's land, unable to commit to her, ask her for more. And what did she want? She was also in a state of flux, needing time and space to plan her new life. For goodness' sake, she'd been about to marry someone else not even two weeks ago!

This was all happening too soon, too fast.

'What are you expecting from the next few days, Angus?' Thadie quietly asked, her eyes still on the one-hundred-and-eighty-degree view of the Indian Ocean in front of them. How did she manage to track his thoughts, home in on what he was thinking?

He thought about making a joke, saying something about good food and great sex, but swallowed that inane reaction. He honestly didn't know. When he'd left her, he hadn't thought further than getting back to her, seeing her huge smile, hearing her laugh and getting her naked. For a guy who planned everything to the max, who hated to fail, his flying to Seychelles to rejoin Thadie had been an impulsive, fly-by-the-seat-of-his-pants plan.

He liked her...

He liked her for many different reasons, but that didn't mean that he was falling for her, falling in—what an asinine expression—love. He'd outgrown the need for love in his teens. It wasn't something he wanted or needed, now or in the future. Of that he was sure.

But Thadie, as she always did—back in London,

now—turned his world inside out, made him look at life differently. She had been, still was, the only person who'd ever managed to slide under his defences and tempt him to go beyond a sexual fling. Four years ago, he'd invited her into his flat, his life—telling himself he was safe because it was a temporary arrangement—and he'd rearranged his life to reconnect with her.

She made him yearn for more, for a life he'd never allowed himself to imagine.

She terrified him.

But he wasn't prepared for her to upend his life entirely. No man's land, that middle ground between nothing and emotional capitulation, was a safe place to hang out.

He lightly touched her back and waited for those amazing eyes to meet his. 'Our boys will have a mum and dad, and sometimes I'll be with you, them, and sometimes I won't. Thanks to video-calling, I can be on the other side of a screen in a heartbeat.'

'And you and me? What happens with us?' Thadie quietly asked. 'Where do you see this going?'

He thought for a moment, not knowing how to answer her. Eventually, he spoke, and his words were the best he could do. 'Does it need to be defined? We're modern, busy, independent people, and while I wish we both weren't so busy and could take the time to get used to everything, I'm grateful for the little time I can spend with you.'

But damn, he wanted more… He shouldn't but he did.

He forced himself to smile and when her lips started to curve, he bent his head to gently nip her shoulder. 'I can give you a plan for the next few days, that's the best I can do. I'll spend some time working, you'll spend some time thinking and sketching, and in between we'll try and get through all the positions on your sexy shorts.'

It took her a few seconds to make the connection, and her laughter rolled over him, deep and dirty. She gripped his jaw in her cool hand and dropped an open-mouth kiss on his lips. 'Deal! You're strong and I'm flexible, let's give it our all.'

She was flexible? Interesting, Angus thought as he followed Thadie to her feet. Trying out all those positions might put his back out, but he was game. What red-blooded man wouldn't be?

'What time will the helicopter get here?' Thadie asked Angus as she smacked the button of the coffee machine to dispense two espressos into tiny mugs. His ringing phone had woken them up shortly before six this morning and Angus had walked onto the deck to take the call.

He'd spent the next half-hour on the phone and when he'd returned, he'd told her that he had to leave, that a privately hired helicopter was on its way from Mahé to collect him and ferry him to Seychelles International Airport where his jet was parked.

He glanced at his watch, a vintage, rare Rolex. 'Ten minutes or so.' He sipped his coffee and ran a hand through his wet-from-his-shower hair. 'I'm sorry to leave after only two days, Thadie. I wanted more. But I have a crisis at work.'

'I'm sorry you have to leave too.' The past two days had been some of the best of her life. They hadn't done much work or, in her case, much thinking or sketching, but they'd talked a lot, laughed more and loved as hard and as often as they could.

Angus ignored the cup she held out to him, choosing instead to haul her against him, wrapping his big arms around her body. With him, she felt feminine and lovely, even petite. Protected.

She stood on her toes and pushed her nose into his neck, trying to imprint his hard body and clean, masculine, soap-and-sea scent onto her psyche. She didn't want him to go. He belonged here, with her.

She'd been avoiding the thought, pushing it away but... *damn*. She was crazy about him, a heartbeat away from falling in love with him. Again. And the solid gold truth was that they belonged with him...her and the two little guys they'd made on a cold night in London.

Terrifying but still true.

'I want to tell them about you,' she murmured, her words muffled.

He pulled back and Thadie lifted her eyes to meet his, the same blue-green colour as the ocean below them. She clocked his surprise, the burst of pleasure. 'You're ready to tell the twins about us?' he asked, sounding delighted.

Thadie nodded, smiling. 'And my family. Though, to be honest, I'm pretty sure they've worked it out already.'

He kissed the tip of her nose, her cheek, the side of her mouth. 'Thank you,' he said, squeezing her tight. 'I'd hoped but...when?'

Angus released his tight grip on her and Thadie took a deep breath, feeling her lungs expand again. 'We can do it when you come back to Johannesburg,' she suggested. 'When *are* you coming back?'

'I plan on being here the weekend before you pitch your designs.'

How was she going to cope with not seeing him? Missing him was going to become her favourite thing to do. 'It's going to be a nightmare,' she whispered.

'It's going to be tough with you trying to look after the boys and get your designs done.'

Ah, that wasn't what she'd been thinking about but that too.

'I'd like you to consider hiring an au pair,' Angus suggested.

Where did *that* come from? She looked at him, horrified. 'You know how I feel about nannies and au pairs, Angus. That's not going to happen.'

'Just hear me out, sweetheart. I get your antipathy towards the idea, but you are looking at it through the eyes of a little girl who never saw her parents. You associate au pairs with being neglected and being left alone. Am I right?'

Yes, okay. She shrugged.

'I'm not asking you to hand over the boys to an au pair, but what if an au pair came to the house and watched over the twins? You would be in your study working and you could be in shouting distance if anything happened. Obviously, the point of having her there would be to allow you to work, but if Gus and Finn wanted you, you're on the other side of a doorway. You're still *there*.'

It was tempting but it still felt like a cop-out. As if she was handing over her kids to a stranger.

'Thads, I am worried that you have too much to do and not enough time to do it,' Angus told her, and her head flew up at the concern she heard in his voice. 'I want you to start designing again because I know you love it and it's something that's yours, and something you do well. But you can't do everything alone. Within a week, after running after the twins and working at night, you'll be cross-eyed with exhaustion. You can't be creative, do your best work, when you can't function because you're burning the candle at both ends.'

'You work hard,' Thadie countered. She'd listened in on some of his work conversations these past two days, with his permission, and knew that he juggled a dozen balls at any one time.

'But I have people I delegate to. You don't and your job is a hundred times harder than mine. I'm not juggling two kids and trying to get a new career off the ground,' Angus explained.

She put her hand on her heart, blown away by his words. The fact that he was trying to make her life easier, his interest and support, told her that he didn't just see her as a mum, but as a woman, and that he believed in her talent and wanted to support her.

So this was what having someone in her corner felt like. She felt a little of his confidence seep into her, and her breath evened out. She wasn't alone, not any more.

If she looked at his suggestion unemotionally, hiring an au pair made sense. An au pair looking after the twins at home, where she could keep an eye on them, seemed the perfect solution. She was not her parents and making her life harder for herself was not going to change her childhood.

She bit her lip and nodded. 'Okay, yeah, I can look into hiring an au pair,' she told Angus.

His broad smile made him look years younger. 'Excellent! That's a really good answer, Thadie.'

She caught a strange note in his voice. 'What do you mean by that, Docherty?' she asked, frowning.

'Well, because you are interviewing three au pairs next week, the day after you get back. They are from the best agency in the city and have brilliant references.'

She'd walked right into that. 'We've got to talk about your tendency to take charge, Angus,' she muttered. 'What if I said no?'

'I was banking on you being sensible,' Angus told her on a slight grimace. He looked down, then back up to her, concern flickering in his eyes. 'You've got the right to do something for yourself, Thads, to chase your dreams. I just want to make it as easy as possible for you to do that.'

Thadie kept telling herself that she couldn't fall in love with him, or not fall any deeper in love with him than she already was, but how could she stop herself when he said things like that? It was impossible. He was a great-looking guy with a body he used to make her weep and scream with pleasure, but when he dropped his guard and got real, she wanted to shove her hand into her chest, snap off her heart and hand it to him.

She was pretty sure it was already in his possession.

Angus cocked his head and a couple of seconds later Thadie heard the whomp-whomp of an approaching helicopter.

'I'll see you the weekend before your big presentation. I'll fly in on Friday evening, and I'll keep the boys occupied Saturday and Sunday if you need to work.'

Knowing he'd be around that weekend to help out with the boys was such a relief because her brothers and their fiancées were attending a wedding in Cape Town and Jabu was unavailable.

'Thank you,' she told him, dragging her mouth across his. 'I'd give you more of those if I could.'

The pitch of the helicopter's engine changed, and Angus softly cursed. 'They are landing on the helipad. I've really got to go.' He didn't move away, and his eyes darkened with desire. 'Where?' He murmured the question, his voice a couple of octaves lower. 'Where would you kiss me?'

She touched the tip of her tongue to her top lip, feeling her nipples contract and lift the material of her T-shirt. 'Everywhere…' she boldly told him.

His phone started ringing and Angus closed his eyes,

his expression irritated. 'You'd better go,' she told him. 'You're wanted.'

'No, *you're* wanted and there's not a damn thing I can do about it now,' he said, stepping away from her. 'I'll call you later.'

Thadie grabbed his arm to keep him from walking away and kissed him again, trying to delay the moment when he walked out on her. 'Thank you,' she told him, hoping he heard the gratitude in her voice and saw it in her eyes. 'For being supportive and for sorting the au pair...well, *everything*.'

He looked thoughtful. 'You can thank me with phone sex, later,' Angus told her with a naughty grin, kissed her again and strode out of the front door to Rock Villa.

Thadie wiggled her bottom and realised that she was quite looking forward to *that*.

CHAPTER TEN

HE FLEW INTO Johannesburg Saturday afternoon, delayed by a massive system dumping a ridiculous amount of snow on Gatwick's many runways and the breakdown of one of the snowploughs. And as they were waiting to be de-iced—which involved some special chemical that had to be sprayed over the jet—an emergency landing was called and they had to go to the back of the queue to be de-iced again. And then the airport was declared closed due to the snow and only opened six hours later.

His patience, by the time he made it from London to Johannesburg and then to Thadie's house, was running low. But seeing the boys hurtling out of the house to greet him with hugs before they ran back inside reminded him why he'd made the ridiculous ten-hour flight and battled Johannesburg traffic.

His boys. His woman. As always, his heart thumped with excitement, then seemed to stop, slam on the brakes. Was this how he was going to feel from now on, both elated and petrified? And if so, would he ever get used to it?

Thadie leaned against the doorframe to her house, dressed in a loose, off-the-shoulder cotton top and, low on her hips, battered denim shorts. A wide black band held her braids back from her head and he caught a glint of the diamond stud in her belly button. Angus felt a wave of lust so staggering that for a moment, he thought he might collapse on the ground.

Lust? Sure, it was there, it always was. But, more than that, he felt as if this was where he needed to be, a sense of being in the right time and place.

He'd felt something similar four years ago, but it had been a vague, nebulous, unidentifiable emotion. He had no doubt what it was now. He felt as if he'd come home.

Yeah, the boys were amazing, but wherever she was was where he was meant to be. Another scare-him-to-his-soul thought.

Thadie smiled at him, her eyebrows rising. 'Angus, you're here.'

'Finally,' he said, walking over to her. He held her face in both his hands, looked down at her and smiled before swiping his mouth across hers. She sighed, softened against him and returned his kiss, her arms wrapped around his back, pushing her lovely body into his. She needed, he realised, the connection as much as he did.

They kissed for long, lovely moments. He'd had a long two weeks and a frustrating twenty-four hours, and within Thadie's arms was where he needed to be. Until he felt a tug on his trousers and looked down at his oldest son, unimpressed by the amount of attention he was giving his mum.

'Angus, you need to come and see our Lego car!' Gus shouted, tugging some more. Angus rested his forehead against Thadie's and linked his fingers with hers.

'Sorry, I'm so late, I tried to get here sooner,' he told her.

'I'm just glad you got here at all,' Thadie told him. 'That storm was nasty.'

'Angus!' Finn shouted.

'Hold on, Finn,' he said, pulling back to look at Thadie. He'd expected red and tired eyes, for her to look stressed and harassed. But her eyes were clear, and he caught the pride and satisfaction in her eyes. 'You finished your portfolio, didn't you?'

She danced on the spot, her smile wide. 'I did! I couldn't sleep last night so I got up and worked.'

'I'm so proud of you, Thads.'

He pulled away to head back to the car to get his laptop, suit and overnight bag. Knowing he was returning to sunshine and blue skies and hot days, he'd placed an online order for clothes and opted to have them delivered to Thadie's house where, she told him, they now sat in her walk-in closet. He couldn't wait to pull on his board shorts and hit the pool.

Unfortunately, the thing he most wanted, and that was to take Thadie to bed, would have to wait. Phone sex was great but wasn't a patch on the real thing.

'Why do you have a suit bag?' Thadie asked him when he pulled it off the back seat of his Range Rover. He knew he'd need wheels if he was going to be in and out of the city, so his car was another recent, and very convenient, purchase.

'I have a meeting on Monday morning in Sandton,' he told her.

She took the suit bag from him, pulled down the zip and released a low whistle. 'Armani, black. White shirt, red tie. Power suit,' she said.

He draped the strap to his laptop over his shoulder and picked up his small suitcase. 'I thought I could meet my potential client, you can meet your designer friend and I can take you to lunch afterwards, and we can celebrate your amazing new venture.'

'You're so sure I'll get this right,' she told him, her free hand sliding into his as they walked back to the house.

That wasn't in any doubt. 'I know you will,' he told her. She was hugely talented, and she worked hard, why wouldn't she succeed?

She stopped and dropped a kiss on his bicep. 'Thanks, Angus. Thanks for believing in me.'

'Any time, sweetheart,' he replied, bending to kiss her head. He smiled down at her. 'As much as I like these gestures of affection, I'd far prefer for them to be X-rated. Can we put the kids to bed at, say, five?'

She laughed before wincing. 'Well, um, that's the other thing. Would you very much mind slipping into that suit and accompanying me to a charity fundraiser tonight?'

He'd rather pull off his toenails with pliers. 'Really, Thads? I just got in...'

She put her hand on his arm and looked up at him, her eyes beseeching. 'I know, I know... I'm sorry. I gave my apologies because I thought I would need to work but I've been feeling guilty about not going since I got the invitation.'

'Is it important to you?'

Thadie nodded. 'It's my favourite charity. They raise money to fulfil the dreams of kids who have a life-threatening condition. I thought I'd have to work so didn't think I could, but now I can. And it'll be really good publicity for the charity if my first public outing after the wedding—'

'Non-wedding,' Angus corrected. The thought that she'd come so close to marrying someone else irritated him.

'—is this function. And if I rock up looking absolutely fabulous, with an exceptionally good-looking man on my arm, well...'

He grinned. 'So, I'm just there as arm candy?'

'No, you're there because there's nobody else I'd like to take,' Thadie softly corrected him, her black eyes luminous. She wrinkled her nose in the way he loved. 'And because you're hot.'

He laughed at her, all the week's tension draining away. 'Sure, let's go to the ball, princess.' He gestured to the twins, who were sitting on the step leading into the house, their chins in their hands, looking impatient. 'Who will look after them?'

'Tumi, the au pair, is coming over at about six. They adore her. She'll feed them, bathe them and put them to bed. She'll also stay the night…'

His eyes narrowed, and deepened, at the sexy note in her voice.

'To reward you for putting on a suit and tie, and making nice with people you don't know, I booked the penthouse suite at the Edward Hotel. It has a hot tub and a very big double bed.'

All the blood drained from his head at the thought of being utterly alone with her, falling asleep with her naked and waking up to morning sex and not to two little boys jumping on his chest.

He kissed her, feeling six hundred feet high. 'I knew hiring an au pair was a great idea,' he smugly told her.

She narrowed her eyes at him, mock scowling. 'Stop smirking, Docherty, it's not a good look for arm candy.'

Angus followed her into the house, laughing.

Angus stood at the bar and watched Thadie work the room, bestowing her stunning smile on everyone she met. He sipped his red wine as she crossed the room towards him, and his weren't the only eyes following her. If she intended to show the world, and her ex, that she was just fine, she'd certainly delivered that message. Her outfit, tight satin tangerine-orange trousers and a sleeveless fitted top in fabric just a shade lighter, was one only a superbly confident woman would have the guts to wear.

Her sky-high silver heels took her height to six feet or so, and she wore statement diamonds in her ears and on her fingers and held an expensive-looking clutch bag in her free hand. She looked...well, amazing. His tongue kept wanting to fall to the floor.

But, strangely, she didn't look any better than she had earlier, dressed in a simple top and cut-off denims, or the way she'd looked on Petit Frère, a sarong covering her bikini. She was naturally lovely, inside and out. And now he was thinking in cliches...a new low.

But the fundamental truth was that she'd, in very little time at all, become a very big part of his life. She'd given him his sons, but she'd also opened herself up to him, was sharing her thoughts and feelings, dream and fears. And he'd started doing the same.

In a few short weeks, she'd become his closest confidante, the person he wanted to talk to the most. She was the first person he thought about when he woke up, the person he fantasised about at night. Over the past two weeks, his thoughts had often gone to her. He'd wondered how her day was going, whether she was happy with her work, imagined her sketching furiously, playing football with the boys on the green lawn behind the house, climbing into her large bed with a book.

Through frequent video-calling, he'd had glimpses of her day-to-day life, her world, and it fascinated him. With a little compromise, some rearranging of his schedule—he'd have to do a lot more work remotely—he could make Johannesburg his base, and her loud and noisy house his home. He'd be able to kiss Thadie's neck when he found her at the kitchen island making supper or, if she was running late, make it himself. He could easily imagine late-night, naked swims in her pool, making love to her outside on the loungers while the boys slept upstairs.

It could work, it should work. He wanted to be there for his boys, as much as he could be, and that meant relocating. The General had been present in his life but in a bad way. He wanted to be there for his boys, in all the ways his father hadn't been. He'd already missed out on three years of their lives, and he didn't want to miss any more or be a part-time dad.

And, while he was genuinely delighted Thadie had rediscovered her love of designing, thrilled that she was doing something for herself, he knew she still wanted a proper family.

Just a year ago she'd been prepared to marry someone she didn't love to provide a father for the boys. They had a much stronger connection than she and Strathern had, so Angus had no doubts about her agreeing to his moving in with her. They didn't need to get married or make huge declarations of commitment, not yet anyway. If whatever they had needed to be defined, they could do that later. They'd only reconnected a month ago, they didn't need to make promises or hard-to-take-back statements yet.

Yeah, he was edging closer to the boundary that separated No Man's Land from Commitment, but he could ease his way over. There was no need to rush.

It could work, he thought. It would work. 'What are you smiling about, my sexy Scot?' Thadie asked as she approached him.

Thanks to her heels, her eyes were nearly in line with his. 'Just that you look utterly amazing tonight, sweetheart.'

Her hand drifted over her hip. 'It's not exactly a my-heart-is-broken outfit, is it?'

He dragged his thumb across her exposed collarbone and watched as goosebumps appeared on her skin. He loved the fact that she was so responsive to him. 'We need to talk, Thads.'

She nodded. 'I know, Angus, and we need to tell the boys that you are their dad, but can we take tonight? I want us to have a night to ourselves before we talk about the boys and how we're going to co-parent and raise them when we're living a continent apart.'

He had a couple of ideas on how to get around that...

But her eyes, intensely dark, holding a million secrets and promises, begged him to push reality aside and live in the moment. He was happy to stand here and make small talk as she charmed the room, knowing that she'd be his later, naked and glorious in his arms. He would be the one who'd be settling between her legs later, sliding inside her, making her his. Listening to her crying, or sobbing, his name as he pushed her to explore the range and depth of her pleasure. And when he was done, he'd start again...

When she woke up in the morning, they'd have sleepy, morning sex and, if he was lucky, more fun in the shower later. But all that would be overshadowed if he started a serious conversation tonight.

He brushed his lips against hers, in a brief, intense, promise-filled kiss. 'Sure, we'll talk later.'

She pushed her hand inside his suit jacket, and lightly drifted her fingers down his sides, and over his ribs. Silver sparks of desire glinted in her eyes. 'As soon as the speeches are done, we're out of here,' she promised him.

He closed his eyes, took a large gulp of his wine and he instructed his body to stand down, to wait. He'd been taught self-control and patience in the army, but one touch from Thadie could decimate that hard-fought-for trait.

Late Monday morning Thadie noticed Angus's car parked under her oak tree next to her garage and smiled, happy he'd made it home before her. Instead of going to lunch at a restaurant, they'd agreed to meet back here to talk. And maybe, because they had an empty house—the au pair had taken the twins to visit Jabu and then they had mini-football—they could indulge in some sexy times before Angus had to leave for the airport and she to await the boys' return.

Thadie pulled into her garage, switched off her engine and banged her hands against her steering wheel, excitement pouring off her in waves. Clara, her designer friend, adored her designs and they'd spent the morning making plans, bouncing ideas off each other, laughing and enjoying each other.

Over the next few weeks, they'd draw up legal agreements formalising their new venture. Thadie freely admitted that she was a bit rusty, she'd forgotten some of the finer details about garment construction, but there was nothing she couldn't relearn. What was most exciting was that she and Clara clicked, instantly and profoundly. Clara loved her presence on social media and they both believed in sustainable fashion and reducing the industry's huge climate-change footprint. They both loved nature, enjoyed the same colour palettes and Clara briefly picked Thadie's brain on childbirth and raising boys, as she was expecting a little boy shortly.

They were, as the Italians said, *simpatico* and Thadie could see them not only having a wonderful business association but building a close friendship. She was thoroughly over-excited. She couldn't wait to see Angus and tell him about her morning.

Under her excitement was a small stream of irritation because life and the universe had conspired to keep them from telling the boys Angus was their dad. When they'd returned to the house yesterday, Jabu had rocked up unexpectedly and whisked them away to visit the zoo, which had turned out to be a whole-day excursion. She and Angus had spent a quiet day, alternating between dozing, swimming, and making love. The boys had returned tired and crotchety and had been too exhausted for life-changing announcements. Thadie and Angus had reluctantly agreed to delay the news until his return trip.

In the meantime, she needed to find out what it entailed to add Angus as the father on the boys' birth certificates, to tag his surname onto theirs. She and Angus wanted joint custody, but did that need to be formalised? She needed to talk to her lawyer about that. And although Angus was paying for the au pair and would pay their school fees going forward, he wanted to put them on his medical plan and pay her maintenance, a ridiculously large figure she didn't need.

They had so much to discuss, and this was a perfect time. They wouldn't be interrupted by their little men demanding attention.

Thadie left her car, slung her bag over her shoulder and walked up the path to her front door. She went inside, tossed her bag onto the coat stand and stepped out of her high heels. 'Honey, I'm home,' she trilled, shrugging out of her white linen jacket.

Angus walked through the half-open door from the entertainment deck, his sleeves rolled up and his tie pulled loose. He took one look at her face and grinned. 'You nailed it, didn't you?'

Thadie ran to him and he caught her, boosting her up so that she could wrap her legs around her hips. She kissed his mouth before pulling back, her smile ferociously wide. 'I *so* nailed it!' she crowed.

'I'm so proud of you, sweetheart,' he told her and she heard the pride in his voice. He walked her over to the kitchen area, placed her on the island and handed her an icy crystal flute, filled with pale gold champagne. 'Here's to your new venture, Thads.'

She looked at the glass, then at the bottle of champagne, one of the most expensive in the world, available only online and at specialist liquor stores. Organising the champagne would've taken quite a bit of work and she was touched. 'You didn't know that I was going to get this right, Angus.'

He touched his glass to hers. 'Of course I did,' he told her, standing between her legs. 'Now tell me all about it.'

She rattled on for twenty minutes, her mind jumping around, and she was sure she made little sense, but Angus listened patiently. Eventually, realising she was repeating herself, she sighed and shrugged. 'Sorry, I'm just fizzy with excitement.' And because she felt so alive, and because he was looking at her as if she'd hung the moon and stars—so powerful and special and clever—she threw her arms around his neck, kissed his jaw and placed her lips by his ear. They could talk later. 'Take me to bed, Angus.'

He glanced at his watch, groaned and pulled back so that she had to drop her hands from his neck. 'I'd love to, Thads, but we have just under an hour before I need to leave for the airport—'

'Perfect, we can spend it in bed.' Thadie shifted her butt to the edge of the island so that she could jump down but Angus's hands on her knees stopped her progress.

'We need to talk, Thadie. We keep getting interrupted or distracted, and this isn't a conversation I want to have over video-calling.'

She pulled a face. 'I'll talk to the lawyers about giving you joint custody, and yes, we'll add your name to their birth certificates. We'll have a meet-your-daddy party the next time you fly in and tell the boys that way. I'll take a tenth of the money you are offering me as maintenance, I do not need the monthly equivalent of a small country's gross national product. Have I forgotten anything? No? Well, then, let's go to bed.'

His hands tightened on her knees, his fingers pushing the material of her white linen trousers into her skin. 'I want us to move in together, to live together as a family,' he stated.

Maybe it was the champagne, maybe she was overloaded with excitement, but he couldn't possibly be suggesting such a massive change in their living arrangements in such an off-hand tone of voice. 'I'm sorry… *what*?'

He stepped back and rubbed the back of his neck with one hand. 'I want us to be a family, living together, raising our kids together.'

A thousand yeses, at full volume, built up in a tidal wave behind her teeth but she held them back, telling herself to calm down.

'But how would that work?' she asked, tightening her hands around the edge of the countertop and holding on as her vision tunnelled in and out. Why was she hesitating? He was offering her what she most wanted, him in her life, for her boys to have a father.

'I've thought this through. I'd essentially work from here. I'd still have to travel but Johannesburg would be my home base.' He looked around. 'I would move in here, initially, but we could find, or build, another house if we found we outgrew this one.'

'Why would we outgrow it?' she asked, confused.

He shrugged. 'Well, if we have more kids, we might need more space. And I'd need a home office—'

More children? What? How? Well, the how she knew, but why? And where was this coming from? And why did a small, low but insistent voice keep repeating, somewhere deep inside her, that something was wrong with his offer and that she needed to read the fine print?

Examine, *dissect*, the fine print.

'I'm sorry to sound stupid,' Thadie said, wincing at her ultra-polite tone, 'but I'm trying to get this straight in my head. We've known each other barely a month and you want to move continents and rearrange your business life to move in with me and the boys. *Why?*'

He looked at her as if he couldn't believe that she couldn't figure it out. 'I want to be a full-time dad. I don't want to see my kids via a video link. I want to see them every day. I want it to be the norm that I am here, the exception that I am away. I want to be *present*.'

Angus spoke before she could. 'My dad wasn't a dad, Thadie, he was my commanding officer from the day I understood what that meant. I mean to be a better parent, most definitely a different father. I want them to grow up knowing I would move mountains for them, but also knowing they can be, and do, anything they choose. And I want to raise them with you, because you are the antithesis of my cold, subservient, anal, unaffectionate mother.'

A frigid wave broke over her and shocked her back to reality. Right, it all made sense now. She had no problem believing Angus wanted to be a full-time dad; he was crazy about the boys and she could see him doing a fantastic job. She didn't have a problem with what he was saying, it was what he'd left out that was problematic.

Where did she fit in? How did he feel about her? His proposal sounded sane and sensible and clever and controlled but that wasn't what she wanted. She wanted wild and impetuous, and emotional and exciting. She wanted him to move in because of them, not because it was the most sensible option. Where was her 'I love you madly' or 'I can't live without you, and I don't want to'?

'I can see that you've given this a lot of thought. Anything else?' she asked, her voice tightening with every word. She saw the look he sent her way and knew that he'd picked up on her tension.

He slid his hands into his pockets, his big shoulders lifting in a shrug. 'We like each other, we have an amazing time in bed, we enjoy each other's company. It makes sense.'

Did it? She didn't think so. With Clyde, she'd been prepared to give up what she wanted—a husband who loved her—to give her boys what they needed—a father. But she'd never do that again. She deserved more. And if she was going to take the risk of being hurt and disappointed, take a chance on love, then she wanted her partner to be facing the same risks, prepared to put his heart on the line too.

Angus didn't want to do that. He wanted the family, but he wanted to keep her at an emotional distance. Not happening. Not again.

She deserved love, a commitment. She was more than just a mum, and she was allowed to put herself first. She wanted it all, to be a great mum, to love and be loved, to have a career. And she wasn't prepared to settle for less.

And if Angus wanted to live his life with her, then he was either all in or all out.

She swallowed, and put her hand to her throat, feeling as if it was closing.

'Do you not think it's a bit soon for such a major move?' she quietly asked him, dropping to the floor. 'Don't you think we need more between us than like and some hot sex?'

'You were prepared to marry Strathern for less,' Angus stated. 'We have more going for us than you and he did, so I don't understand why you are hesitating.

'This is the right move,' he insisted. 'The four of us, together, is what is right for all of us.'

It might be right for *three* of them…

It wasn't right for her, not like this.

'You could do everything you suggested, move here, be a part of the boys' lives, but you could buy your own house and live there,' she said, twisting her fingers together, finding it hard to believe she wasn't throwing herself into his arms and kissing his face.

Angus looked as if he couldn't believe it either and he was starting to realise that she wasn't blown away by his suggestion. Thadie caught the confusion in his eyes, tinged with a hint of what-the-hell?

'Are you saying that you don't want me to move in?' Angus demanded, confusion deepening his Scottish accent.

'I'd love you to move in, Angus—'

'Then why are we dancing around this? Why aren't we using the precious moments before I have to leave to work out the future instead of having this crazy conversation that I don't completely understand?'

She bit her lip, wishing he'd wise up.

Angus threw his hands up in the air. 'Do you or do you not want me to move in, Thadie?' he asked, making an obvious effort to keep his tone reasonable.

'I do, but not because of the reasons you stated.'

He pushed both his hands into his hair and tugged. 'I thought you *wanted* a two-parent family, a father for your boys. You were prepared to marry someone you didn't love to give them that but when I offer it to you, you are baulking.'

Yes, she was. 'I am.'

'Why?'

Okay, it was time to put her heart on the line. 'Because I didn't love Clyde, Angus. He couldn't hurt or disappoint me. He didn't touch my emotions. You...well, you touch all of them.'

'I...*what*?'

She released a laugh that held no amusement. 'I am so in love with you, Angus. I tried not to be, but I didn't succeed. And I thought I could do the part-time relationship with you, having you drop into my life, turn it upside down and then leave. But I've been fooling myself. I don't think I can. I think I'd eventually begin to resent that you couldn't spend more time with me, be with me more.'

'I'm offering to do that!'

'But you are not offering me commitment, Angus. Or love.'

'It's too early to talk love, even if I understood what it means! But I do understand friendship, sexual heat, liking each other.' He shrugged, looking bewildered. 'But if you need me to marry you, I suppose I'll have to.'

Her heart cracked, splintered in two and dropped to her toes, as heavy as a steel ingot.

'I don't want you to offer to marry me because you think it's what *I* want, Angus.'

She took two paces, stopped, and took two more, needing to work out some of the energy building up inside her.

'I've realised that I don't need to marry anyone, that I can do life on my own, if I have to,' she explained.

'I am a complete person with or without a man. I'd only marry or live with a man if I knew, with every fibre of my being, that the man in question adored me, was head-over-heels, crazy in love with me, someone who couldn't live his life without me.'

She waited for him to say something, anything, but he just stared at her, his eyes more blue than green, dejected and annoyed. He hated this emotional stuff, hated that it wasn't regimented, that there weren't rules and regs that defined it. To him it was simple, they enjoyed each other in and out of bed, and they wanted the best for their sons, which was a two-parent, present family.

But living with a man who didn't love her would make her miserable. And, even if they could go back to simply sleeping together again, she knew this conversation had changed the dynamic between them.

She wanted more, he couldn't give it…

Yes, she was hurt, gutted, but at least he'd disappointed her early, and she hadn't had the earth beneath her entirely washed away. She'd be okay…no, that was a stretch. She'd find a way to function.

She was a mum, she had no choice.

It took all her guts, but she said the words, words that would hurt her but would, ultimately, protect their friendship and the boys.

'We need to call it, Angus, to stop sleeping together, to find another way forward,' she said. 'Our boys should be our highest priority, our only priority.'

'I don't understand this, any of this,' Angus muttered, his voice growly with banked-down emotion. 'I have done everything possible to show you that I care about you. I've criss-crossed goddamn continents for you. I gave up something I loved for you! Are you saying no?'

Gave up something he loved? What did he mean by that? She could ask for an explanation, and then they'd argue some more. They could go back and forth, slicing at each other with words as sharp as rapiers, but nothing would change the fact that she loved, and he didn't.

'This has been the most surreal conversation of my life and I don't know what else to say,' Angus said, his voice vibrating with an emotion she couldn't identify. She'd hurt him, and she knew he was wondering how and why his carefully planned day had gone so awry.

'There's nothing to say,' she told him, trying to smile. She took his big hand, holding it in both of hers. 'I still intend to tell the boys that you are their father, and you can stay here, in my spare room, until you find a permanent South African base. They need you in their lives, they *do*.'

'But you don't.'

Had he not heard anything she'd said? 'Of course, I do, but I need more than you can give,' she said, her voice sad. She stood up on her toes and kissed his cheek. 'You need to get going or you're going to miss your take-off slot.'

'That's it?' Angus asked.

Thadie nodded her head. 'Take care, Angus.'

And with her eyes brimming with hot tears, she walked out of the room.

CHAPTER ELEVEN

'MUM, ANGUS WANTS to talk to you,' Gus shouted. Thadie placed a hand on his small shoulder and looked down into the screen, wondering if the butterflies in her stomach would ever go away whenever she heard his name. Angus was sitting in a wide leather seat and, judging by the inky darkness she could see in the jet's window behind him, he was in another time zone. She took in his tight lips and stiff neck, and tried to smile but couldn't. It had been two weeks since he'd walked out of her life but his frequent calls to the twins hadn't stopped. He was as much a part of their lives as before, maybe even more so.

Thadie noticed the dark smudges under his eyes and his messy hair. He'd had another long day.

Finn came rushing up to them and held his hand out for the tablet. Thadie rolled her eyes as she handed it over. Her younger son had already spent ten minutes telling Angus about his day, in excruciating detail. What more could he have to say?

Angus spoke before he could. 'Bud, I need to talk to your mum so can this wait until we chat later?' he asked.

So he was still going to call the boys later? 'I want to know why—'

'Finn, *bud*,' Angus interrupted him, keeping his voice

gentle, 'I want to talk to you but unless you're feeling sick or sad, it's going to have to wait until later, okay?'

Finn considered his words and nodded. ''Kay, bye!'

Finn shoved the tablet into Thadie's hands and ran to join his brother in the playroom. In the confines of her too-small screen, Thadie watched Angus take a slug of what looked like whiskey from a crystal tumbler, before resting the glass on his forehead.

When he looked into the camera again, he managed a rueful look. 'Just to tell you how my day is going, that conversation with my three-year-old was the most rational I've had today.'

She winced as she sat down on the wooden blanket box that she used as a coffee table. She missed him, yearned for him. She wanted his strong arms around her, for him to wake up beside her, to exchange long, lazy kisses, kisses with no beginning or no end.

She wished he loved her...

Oh, he probably did, as much as he could. But it wasn't enough.

Thadie started to ask him about his day, wanting him to tell her what had gone wrong, and then remembered that she couldn't open that door to emotional intimacy. Not when he'd made it very clear he wasn't prepared to walk through it.

'Are you okay?' he asked her.

No, she was thoroughly miserable, she felt as if she were walking around without a heart. But that was her fault—she'd handed hers to him, and he hadn't asked for it. 'I'm fine,' Thadie replied, internally wincing at her terse reply.

His eyes changed colour, turning cooler. 'I wanted to tell you that my lawyer received all the documentation regarding the boys. Thank you for allowing joint custody, for being so reasonable.'

That wasn't how she'd currently describe herself. Heartbroken, sad, joyless…they all applied. Reasonable? Not so much.

'You're a good father, Angus, I was happy to do it,' Thadie said, forcing the words out. They weren't the words she most wanted to say…

She was feeling tired and emotional, and it took all her effort not to let her always-close-to-the-surface tears roll down her face. She wanted to tell him she missed him. She wanted to ask him why he couldn't love her, why he, like her parents, couldn't give her what she most wanted. A soft place to fall, strong arms willing to catch her, a forever love to buoy and bolster her.

No, this wasn't on her and she needed to remember that. She'd done a lot of thinking and had had more than a few major revelations. Her parents were emotionally stunted and wouldn't have recognised love if it slapped them in the face. And she wasn't responsible for Angus's thoughts and decisions. She couldn't force him to love her, and she didn't want a love that was coerced. Love under those conditions would wither and die.

Thadie dug deep, sucked up another little bit of strength and forced what she knew was a brittle smile onto her face. 'Sign what you need to sign, and the lawyers can take care of the formalities,' Thadie told him. 'We'll tell them you are their dad when next you are in town.'

'Okay.' He pushed his fingers up and under his black-framed glasses—so hot!—to push his thumbs into his eyes. 'How is your new partnership shaping up?' he asked, his eyes still closed.

No, she couldn't talk to him, not yet. Not as they used

to. It hurt too much. She looked away, pretending she'd heard a commotion. 'Hey, the boys are fighting, I've got to go.'

Without giving him a chance to argue, she cut the connection, and his face faded away in an instant.

It would help a lot if her love for him would die as easily and quickly.

A couple of days later, Angus stood at his office window, watching the bustling activity on the green, grey Thames in the distance. His office afforded spectacular views of the area, but he couldn't take it in. All he could think about was Thadie's pale and drawn face, the misery in her eyes.

Sadness he'd put there, all because he couldn't tell her what she most needed to hear.

What he felt. What he'd probably always felt, from the moment he'd met her in London.

The thing about love was that it was uncontrollable, that it wasn't something he could, through sheer hard work and determination, succeed at. There were too many variables, too much that could go wrong. He knew how to be a soldier, how to run a company, and he was learning how to be a dad. How to hand his heart over, how to love? He'd never been taught or been shown that.

If he tried to love her and failed—because how could he succeed at something he'd no training for?—he'd disappoint her further.

He didn't want to hurt her...

Correction, he didn't want to hurt her more than he was already doing.

He was doing the right thing, Angus reassured himself, rubbing his chest, somewhere above his sluggish, aching heart. He was hurting them now to save them both some big hurt down the line. It was a small skirmish to avoid a major, bloody battle later.

The aching pain and awkwardness would fade, and his craving for her would, oh, in seventy or so years, dissipate. At some point, somewhere down the line, they'd be friends again.

He missed her with every bloody breath he took.

Angus heard the sound of an incoming Skype call and glanced at his watch. His US-based chief of operations was calling in ten minutes early but that was okay, anything was better than standing here, feeling as if misery were eating him alive.

He picked up a remote control, pushed a button and his computer screen projected onto the state-of-the-art screen on the wall opposite. He blinked and rubbed his hands across his eyes but instead of his dark-skinned, burly Ving Rhames lookalike VP, he saw his youngest son on the wall.

'Finn, hi,' he said, confused. He'd spoken to the twins earlier, shortly after they woke up. He normally called them after their supper. Where was Thadie, and why did Finn have her phone? And how on earth did his three-year-old know how to video-call him?

Then he remembered his youngest's big brain: he asked complex questions and Thadie suspected he could already recognise basic words when she read to them. He could do basic addition and subtraction. Finn was super-smart, and it didn't take a genius to work out how to make a phone call.

'Where's Mum and Gus, Finn?' Angus asked, resting his butt on the corner of the desk.

Finn moved the phone and Angus saw Gus sitting at the kitchen table next to his brother. His oldest looked uncharacteristically sombre. Something was up with his boys, and he was in London, a continent away. Angus pulled in a deep breath, pushing down the panic that had instantly hit him. 'Hey, bud.'

Gus's eyes filled with tears. 'We miss you,' he said.

Angus felt as though he'd been hit in the gut. 'Me too, bud. Where is your mother?'

'She's in her office, Angus,' Finn answered him, turning the camera back to him. 'She's drawing but she keeps ripping the pages off and throwing the paper balls at the wall,' Finn told him, sounding bewildered. 'And she keeps saying a lot of bad words. She looks mad but we didn't do anything, I swear.'

'And she's crying,' Gus added.

'She's always crying,' Finn corrected him.

Angus pinched the bridge of his nose, feeling as if he'd been sucker-punched. Before he could think of what to say, how to console them, he heard a stream of Zulu. He looked at the screen and saw the chagrined expression of the twins' au pair.

'Sorry, Mr Docherty, I swear I only left them to go to the bathroom. Thadie left her phone on the dining table, but I didn't think they knew how to make video-calls.'

'It's not hard,' Finn told her, sounding a little belligerent.

Angus told the boys he'd speak to them later and sent them to their playroom. When Tumi confirmed they were out of sight, and hearing, he spoke again. 'They seem a little flat. Are they okay?' he asked.

She sent an uncomfortable look towards Thadie's study. 'Maybe you should speak to Thadie, Mr Docherty.'

'Call me Angus, please,' he told her. 'Look, I appreciate your loyalty, but their well-being is all I care about. Please, talk to me.'

She hesitated before speaking. 'All I will say is that Thadie and the boys are very close, and they pick up on her emotions. They've been quieter, clingier, less loud and energetic lately.'

Angus said goodbye to Tumi and instructed his PA to cancel his call with his VP. He locked his office door and sat down on his couch, his forearms on his knees. His world felt bleak and colourless, and he couldn't go on like this. Thadie was miserable and that was unacceptable. That, in itself, was a failure.

And all his fault.

Thadie was the strongest woman and he admired and respected everything about her. She hadn't let her parents' neglect harden or break her. And when she'd found out she was pregnant with his sons, she'd given up her dreams and career to focus her attention on them. She loved them so much that she'd been prepared to marry another man to give them a father.

All she'd wanted was for someone to put her first, to love her. To be the centre of someone's world.

Despite everything she'd been through lately, she'd still had the guts to tell him she loved him, the self-knowledge, respect and awareness to know what he was offering wasn't good enough. And it hadn't been. She deserved everything he could give her. To be the centre of *his* world.

But could he love her the way she needed him to? Was there even a wrong way to love? Was love something that he could fail at? Maybe, just maybe, he failed when he *didn't* love, not when he did.

Thadie deserved him to find his courage—emotional courage was on a whole new level—and commit to her, to love her with everything he had. Proving to his father that he was worthy of being a Docherty didn't matter any more. He was over that. He'd always thought that his company would be the legacy he left behind, but raising good men, men with integrity and loyalty, would be a far bigger gift to the world.

Being with Thadie, loving her, and putting a ring on her finger, would be the gift he gave himself. And if he didn't step up, he'd lose her. And not being with her, living his life loving her, would be the ultimate failure.

And the only one that would ever matter.

The next morning, Thadie walked into her kitchen, and headed straight to her coffee machine, reaching for a coffee mug. It was early, and she'd spent another night tossing and turning, missing Angus with every breath she took. She shoved her cup under the spout and hit the button with the side of her fist.

When would her broken heart start to heal? Would it? She hoped so. She looked forward to the day when she didn't feel as if she were walking around with a knife lodged in her chest. Thadie gripped the edge of the counter as the machine dispensed coffee into her cup, extending her arms and dropping her head to look at the floor.

Dawn was breaking, and she had to find the strength to smile and laugh with the boys, to be normal. And she had to stop sneaking off to cry. One of these days they were going to catch her and ask her a bunch of questions she didn't want to answer.

What could she say to them? 'I'm crying because your dad doesn't love me. I wish he did.'

Yeah…

No.

'I want this view, for the rest of my life.'

At his deep voice, Thadie screamed, knocking her

cup out of the machine and onto the floor. She stared at the broken pieces, the brown liquid on her tiles, scared to lift her head to see if she'd really heard Angus's voice. She might just be losing her mind. And if she was, she wasn't ready to face that reality.

'Don't move.'

Thadie kept her eyes on the mess, and it was only when his arm encircled her waist, when the heat of his big body burned through the material of her short dressing gown—the same one she'd worn when she'd given her infamous press conference—that reality slapped her sideways. Angus was here.

He walked her across the kitchen, lowered her to the ground and pulled a kitchen chair out from under the table. 'Sit,' he told her.

She did, but only because her knees were feeling distinctly wobbly. Thadie watched, bemused, as he dropped to his haunches to pick up the big shards of the broken coffee mug, then mopped up the liquid. Her mouth opened and closed. She didn't know what to say.

So she went for the most obvious question. 'What are you doing here?' she asked. 'Why are you in my kitchen at—' she glanced at the oversized clock on the wall to her right '—five forty-five in the morning? How did you get into my kitchen?'

'I picked up a key from Micah ten minutes ago.'

Micah gave him a key?

Angus reached for another cup, put it under the spout and started the machine. She thought he said something about needing a slug of whiskey but wasn't sure if she'd heard him correctly. Her brain felt as if it had been slapped by a tornado. Whirly and swirly and as if she didn't know what side was up.

'You told me you could only make it back here to

see the boys at month end,' she said, her voice wobbly. 'That's in two weeks.'

'I couldn't wait that long,' Angus told her, grabbing the cup, and dumping a teaspoon of sugar into it. He took a sip, grimaced and placed it on the table next to her elbow.

Right, he had to be missing the boys. That made sense. But could he not have waited until she was dressed, her teeth brushed and with a little make-up on? Or until she was, well, awake?

'The boys will be happy to see you,' Thadie said, dully. 'They've missed you.'

Angus turned around, gripped the counter behind him and met her eyes. His eyes were red-rimmed, his sexy stubble was longer than he normally allowed, and his white cotton shirt looked creased. He looked as if he'd walked in from a hard day at the office: drained and exhausted.

'While I'm always happy to see them, they aren't the primary reason I'm here,' Angus stated.

'Is there a problem with one of your South African clients?' she asked. She couldn't think of another reason he'd fly back ahead of schedule.

Angus folded his arms, cocked his head and amusement lifted one corner of his mouth. 'You could say that. She's been a problem since I first met her.'

Thadie swallowed, realised that her mouth was bone dry and patted the table, looking for her mug. She took a sip of coffee, her eyes not leaving Angus's. He wasn't talking about work, of that she was sure.

'She not only gave me two amazing sons, but she causes my heart to stutter every time I see her. I veer between wanting to hold her, talk to her and take her to bed... That's a lie. I want to do all three at once. With her my world is colourful, without her, it's grey and un-interesting.'

Thadie placed her hand on her thumping heart, thinking it might jump out of her chest. 'Angus.'

Could he be…? Might he be…?

Emotion flooded that normally stoic face and he rubbed his jaw with the ball of his hand. 'The reason that I'm here, at the crack of dawn, is because I don't want to spend another day missing you, not feeling connected to you, not being able to talk to you. You're my best friend, Thadie.'

Oh.

Her face fell. That hadn't been what she had been expecting. For a moment there, she'd expected a smidgeon more than friendship.

Angus scrubbed his hands over his face and closed his eyes, frustrated. 'You can tell that I was brought up in a house where emotions were ignored and love was never discussed, right? I'm making a mess of this… What I'm trying to say is that you are the person who knows me best, someone I trust completely and effortlessly.'

She couldn't discount his words, they meant a lot, coming from a man like him. They just weren't what—

'I'm so in love with you, Thadie.'

Thadie stared at him, her bottom lip between her teeth. 'Say that again,' she demanded, her voice scratchy with hope and joy.

He walked across the room and dropped down to balance on the balls of his feet, his arm on his knee.

He reached up to touch her cheek, his thumb sliding over her bottom lip. 'I'm not good with love words. I was never taught them. But nobody will love you more than me, Thadie. I'll love you fiercely every moment I am with you, for as long as I live. Look, I know I'm not perfect, so very far from it, and that I don't know how to do this—love, relationships, marriage—but I promise I'll learn. You, our boys, will be at the heart of every decision I make, every action I take.'

He rested his forehead on her bouncing knee. 'Be mine, Thads. Please.'

Thadie bent down to drop a kiss on his hair. 'Angus, I've always been yours,' she murmured. He was here and she was home.

He lifted his head and she smiled at him, knowing it might be a bit wobbly. 'I love you too. I'm so very glad you saw my disastrous press conference and thought I needed sorting out.'

He stood up and pulled her into his arms, burying his nose in her neck, and anchoring her to him. 'Ah, I had this plan to flush you from my system.'

She leaned back and laughed. 'How's that working out for you, soldier?'

'Ach, very well indeed,' he replied, before lowering his head to kiss her. His mouth told her a story of passion but also the story of promise, of giving and taking. In his kiss, she was handed pictures of sexy nights and normal days, of watching their boys grow, of whispered confessions and old-age memories. Of spending a life, with all its ups and downs, perfect in its imperfection, together.

Thadie reluctantly broke away and placed both hands on his face and cocked her head to one side. 'The boys are going to come down in about ten minutes and, while there's nothing more I'd prefer to do than kiss you, I need to ask a couple of questions first.'

He nodded, lowered her hands to hold them between them and looked down at her, happiness and joy intensifying his eye colour to turquoise.

Before she got to the scary stuff, she wanted to assuage her curiosity first. 'The last time I saw you, you said you gave up something you loved for us. What did you mean by that?'

He didn't hesitate to answer her. 'I run and own Docherty Security, as you know. We provide security systems, personal protection officers, do corporate security.'

Thadie knew all this. It was on his website.

'What isn't advertised is that we do kidnap and ransom negotiations. We get those clients word of mouth. But only very few trusted people know I have—*had*—a super-specialised team that takes on sensitive, off-the-books, sometimes dangerous, intelligence-gathering missions for our government and its allies,' he explained. 'Up until a few weeks ago, I went on those missions. Those were the holidays your brothers thought I took. But Docherty Security no longer does covert missions.'

Thadie heard the note of yearning in his voice. 'You miss it,' she stated.

'I do. It was my connection to the military, the way I still served. But doing those missions meant being out of communication for up to six weeks, and they were dangerous. It's something a man who wants to spend his life loving a woman and raising his boys should do. The risks were too great.'

The fact that Angus had given up something he loved for her, for them, cemented her decision to speak her heart. 'Thank you. Thank you for doing that for us.'

He glanced at the clock and grimaced. 'Anything else? Because we're running out of time, and I want to kiss you again.'

'I want you to get me out of this dressing gown,'

Thadie boldly told him, getting sidetracked by the heat in his eyes. He pulled her to him, but she slapped her hands on his hard chest, pushing back. 'But I do have a little more to say...'

He must've heard something in her voice because his entire body stilled, his entire focus on her.

Thadie lifted her hands to hold his face, tears brimming in his eyes. 'While I have no intention of giving up my career, I want us to be a family, living together, raising our kids together,' she told him, parroting the words he used weeks ago. 'I want you to live here, or for us to buy or build another house together. Be my kids' full-time dad, be my partner and my lover and my friend.'

He looked at her, love making him look years younger. 'I could do that, but I have a couple of extra conditions.'

She tried to hold back her huge smile. 'And what might those be?'

'That you marry me in the garden of your childhood home and have the wedding you always wanted. That we limit the number of guests to fifty and go back to Petit Frère for our honeymoon. Deal?'

'Deal,' Thadie replied, not hesitating. She needed to taste that happy smile, so she stood on her tiptoes and placed her mouth on his, winding her arms around his neck, as his kiss turned hot and ferocious. She felt his hand on her butt, showing her how much he wanted her. She couldn't wait for the au pair to arrive: their love needed to be celebrated and she couldn't think of a better way than to do it in her huge bed upstairs.

Their bed.

Angus held her head, and Thadie felt loved and protected, the centre of his world, the perfect, and only, place for her to be.

'Angus! Gus, Gus… Angus is here.'

Thadie let out a groan of frustration. Why couldn't her boys sleep late? Just once?

'Angus!' Gus yelled, running into the room. 'Yay!'

Despite being unable to wrench her eyes off Angus's wonderful face—the face she'd grow old with—Thadie did realise something was amiss when neither of the twins spoke. She pulled back to glance down at them, raising her eyebrows at their folded arms and deep frowns. She sighed. 'What's the problem, guys?'

'Angus is kissing you,' Gus stated, his tone disgusted. 'Again.'

Angus's thumb skated across her cheekbone, and Thadie's knees melted at the love in his eyes. Then he dropped to his haunches, looked Gus in the eye, then Finn, and calmly spoke. 'I'm kissing your mum because I love her and that's not something that's ever going to stop.'

Gus looked a little sick at the thought. 'Ugh.'

Angus's smile was full of mischief, and they exchanged a look. In a decade, Gus would have different feelings about kissing. Angus hugged Gus, but Finn held back. Angus wrapped his arm around Gus but kept his eyes on his younger son.

'Does that mean he's going to be our dad?' Finn asked, his tone serious.

Angus looked up at her, raised his eyebrow and Thadie placed her hand on his shoulder. 'He always has been, Finn. Angus is your real dad, guys.'

Finn looked at her, then Angus, back up to her again. Finally, he nodded and stepped into Angus's free arm. Angus cuddled their sons for a minute, lifted them, and

Thadie placed her hands on their little backs, smiling at Angus, tears in her eyes.

She was so crazy happy, insanely in love with her man.

Her boys. Her man.

Her family.

EPILOGUE

THADIE WALKED DOWN the big stairs at Hadleigh House, holding the skirt of her wedding gown off the floor. She and Clara had designed the dress together and it had been made up by Clara's seamstresses. The dress was ivory, in an A-line silhouette, the bodice covered in tiny beads, causing her bodice to glitter. She loved the skirt with its deep ruffles, and she couldn't wait for Angus to see her in it.

Or, honestly, to peel it off her at the end of the night.

'Now, that's a look I should never have to see on my sister's face,' Jago grumbled from the bottom of the stairs. Thadie smiled at him, taking in his simple black suit, and his silver tie.

'You look gorgeous, Thadie,' Micah said, crossing the harlequin floor and carrying a glass of champagne. He turned to look at the twins, who wore long trousers, and silver vests over open-neck, long-sleeved shirts. 'Tuck your shirt back into your pants, Gus.'

Gus looked at Finn before sending his uncle a disparaging look. 'Why are we being punished because they want to get married? Why can't Mum and Dad just dress up and leave us alone?'

'It's a mystery,' Micah wryly replied.

'And why do we have to stay inside?' Finn demanded. 'We want to be with our dad, in the tent outside.'

Micah looked as if he was about to argue but Thadie shook her head, shrugging as she took the champagne. 'If you guys want to go and stand with Dad instead of walking up the aisle in front of me, that's fine.'

The twins grinned and ran across the hall, nearly running into Jabu as he walked into the hall, looking dapper in his black tuxedo. In the garden Angus—and his best man, Heath—stood under the fairy-tale gazebo, waiting for her to walk through the garden to him, her hand tucked into Jabu's arm.

They'd invited fifty of their closest friends, and she'd left the rest of the wedding for Ellie to organise, knowing her wedding was in safe hands. All she wanted was to marry Angus at Hadleigh House, have lots of flowers, great champagne and lively music.

All that was important were the 'I do's. Everything else was the icing on her very delicious cake.

Jabu took the champagne glass Jago held out and they all clinked glasses together in a toast.

'Here's to you, Thadie,' Jago said, his voice deeper with emotion. 'If it wasn't for you and your wedding adventures, we wouldn't have found Ellie and Dodi.'

Thadie pulled a face, thinking how close she came to making the biggest mistake of her life by marrying a man she didn't love. 'I swear, I've actually thought about hunting Alta and Clyde down and hugging them until they couldn't breathe,' she said with a huge grin. 'If they hadn't sabotaged that wedding, I wouldn't be about to marry the love of my life.'

'I hope you're talking about me.'

Thadie whirled around to see her fiancé leaning against the frame of the enormous front door, looking spectacular in a black tuxedo jacket, and wearing his clan kilt. She placed her hand on her heart, for a moment not able to believe that she was going to marry this gorgeous man.

She handed him a wide smile. 'I'm not sure, he's supposed to be waiting for me at the altar in the garden,' she teased him.

Love radiated from his eyes. 'And he will be, I promise. But he seems to have acquired two brand-new, three-foot-high groomsmen.'

Angus walked across the hall to her, clasped her face in his hands and shook his head. 'You look breathtaking. I can't wait to marry you.'

He gently kissed her lips, before stepping back and snagging the champagne glass out of her hand and lifting it in a toast. 'Here's to you, the almost Mrs Docherty.'

'Le Roux-Docherty,' Thadie pertly reminded him as he drained her glass of champagne. 'Hey! I was going to drink that.'

Angus tossed her a grin and briefly placed his big hand on her stomach.

'You can't drink alcohol, remember?' He stepped back, his hands loosely holding his silver sporran, laughing as Jabu spluttered and her brothers laughed.

'See you at the altar in—' Angus tapped his watch '—exactly five minutes.'

It took her ten. Mostly because she had to waste valuable time reassuring her overprotective brothers and Jabu that she was only baking one new Le-Roux-Docherty cupcake. They couldn't, they earnestly told her, cope with another set of male twins.

Thadie laughed, knowing that they absolutely could, that they'd love the challenge. But no, as they'd found out yesterday, she was having a girl, much to Angus's delight. He had this crazy idea that she was cooking a sweet, docile, angelic pink child but Thadie instinctively knew their princess was going to be more of a handful than her ever-mischievous older brothers combined.

Her family had no idea what they were in for.

Genuinely, she couldn't wait for the rest of her life…

* * * * *

MILLS & BOON®

Coming next month

THE COST OF CINDERELLA'S CONFESSION
Julia James

From the back of the church, footsteps – like nails striking the flagstones of the aisle.

A voice – harsh and strident, breaking the hallowed silence. Heads turning, breaths intaking across the congregation.

A voice calling out –

Announcing. Denouncing…

Luca felt his head turn. Felt his gaze fall on the figure of the woman walking down the aisle. A red suit, exposing every curve of her voluptuous body. A matching pill box hat with a black veil concealing her upper face.

A veil she threw back as she approached.

To his side he heard Tomaso give a snarl of rage, start forward.

But he himself did not move. Could not.

Could only level his eyes on her, with a fury he had not known he could possess, that should strike her to silence if there were any justice in the world – any decency.

But there was no justice, no decency. There was only her voice, ringing out like sacrilege. Freezing him to the very marrow of his bones.

"He cannot marry her!" she cried out. "I am pregnant with his child!"

Continue reading
THE COST OF CINDERELLA'S CONFESSION
Julia James

Available next month
www.millsandboon.co.uk